ADVANCE PRAISE FOR

ON TO CHICAGO

James Rogan's novel is a political classic. Not only does he deal with one of the most interesting "what ifs" in history, but also he presents a fascinating and accurate account of the tumultuous 1968 campaign of the presidency. Five stars!

— JULIE NIXON EISENHOWER AND DAVID EISENHOWER,
Bestselling authors of *Pat Nixon* and *Eisenhower at War: 1943-1945*

For me, reading *On to Chicago* brought back a very painful memory, yet in the pain I also found a healing when thinking about how it could have turned out differently. Jim Rogan brings Bobby Kennedy and the other presidential candidates from 1968 back to life, and he balances their political throat-cutting and caring sides so we can know them. Best of all, this story gave me a look into a future that was taken from us fifty years ago. I'm not much of a bookworm, but in my humble opinion this is worth the read. Thanks to Mr. Rogan for opening this door to what might have been.

—JUAN ROMERO,
The teenage Ambassador Hotel busboy wearing the white jacket in the iconic news photograph of him kneeling alongside and aiding Senator Robert Kennedy seconds after the bullets struck

There are two kinds of writers who tell the story of the 1968 Democratic presidential primary, when Gene McCarthy challenged LBJ over Vietnam, LBJ dropped out, Bobby Kennedy came in—and then was assassinated on the night of his biggest campaign victory. After that the presidential nomination devolved upon Vice President Hubert Humphrey, who was insufficiently supported against Richard Nixon, but almost beat him anyway...and afterwards it seemed as though nothing much had happened, after all.

The first and largest group of writers take the lofty view that the passion for change that briefly swept the country in '68 was an illusion or chimera, and that Nixon was the logical and destined American winner all along.

The second, smaller group, contends that the United States was on the brink of momentous change that summer, a feeling that seized upon the candidacies of McCarthy and Kennedy and was on its way to bringing about something very new—when it crashed against the rare coincidence of Bobby's assassination, Gene McCarthy's withdrawal, and the dulling re-appearance of business as usual. But there was *that moment*, when people all over the country were talking about what was right and wrong in politics on the assumption that things could change, and that we could begin to live up to our basic American values—and that created a very different mood which we have struggled ever since to recapture.

Interesting to me that Jim Rogan saw this same thing from the viewpoint of a conservative Republican, while I described it, in *Nobody Knows*, from (roughly) the Democratic Left. Since then, we've both grown a bit more skeptical. But those of us who were there cannot deny what we felt was happening.

—JEREMY LARNER

1968 Campaign speechwriter for Eugene McCarthy;

Author, *Nobody Knows: Reflections on the 1968 McCarthy Campaign*;

Screenwriter, *The Candidate*, 1972 Oscar for Best Original Screenplay

I was a teenager when my father ran for president in 1968 and vividly remember the excitement of being a first-hand, eyewitness to history. Jim Rogan has taken one of our nation's most tumultuous and interesting presidential elections and made it even more compelling. Every page makes you wonder how history might have changed with just the slightest twist of fate.

—GEORGE WALLACE, JR.

James Rogan has written a fast-moving account, part-fact, part-fiction, of political events in 1968 based on the premise that Robert Kennedy survived rather than succumbed to Sirhan Sirhan's shooting of him in June of that year. He captures and times and characters well.

—TED VAN DYK,

Senior Aide to Vice President Hubert H. Humphrey

What if Bobby Kennedy had survived the assassin's bullet? Jim Rogan's riveting, meticulously researched work imagines the answer to that question in vivid detail—while taking you on a heart-stopping ride through a fascinating-to-contemplate alternative history of the tumultuous 1968 presidential election. This stunningly provocative tour de force puts America on a completely different trajectory, leading to a radically different set of cascading events. You will be spellbound.

—MONICA CROWLEY, PHD,

Fox News Contributor

The 1968 Presidential campaign produced far more real life volatility and heart-pounding suspense than most Americans wanted. *On to Chicago* moves the excitement needle even higher—portraying Bobby Kennedy as surviving both the actual attempt on his life, and then LBJ's attempt to end his political life. Jim Rogan is a master storyteller with a perfect ear and encyclopedic knowledge of politics that captures the high level deal-making and breaking of that tense time of crisis. This book kept me up way too late for two nights, and I can't wait to see who they will cast for the major roles in the movie!

—GOVERNOR PETE WILSON,

Former Campaign Aide to Richard Nixon

ON
to
CHICAGO

WORKS BY JAMES ROGAN

MY BRUSH WITH HISTORY
(1991) (Contributor)

ROUGH EDGES
My Unlikely Road from Welfare to Washington (2004)

CATCHING OUR FLAG
Behind the Scenes of a Presidential Impeachment (2011)

'AND *THEN* I MET...'
Stories of Growing Up, Meeting Famous People, and Annoying the
Hell Out of Them (2014)

ON TO CHICAGO
Rediscovering Robert F. Kennedy and the Lost Campaign of 1968
(2018)

ON
to
CHICAGO

Rediscovering **ROBERT F. KENNEDY**
and the **LOST CAMPAIGN** *of* 1968

JAMES E. ROGAN

 WND Books

ON TO CHICAGO

Published by WND Books, Washington, D.C. WND Books is a registered trademark of WorldNetDaily.com, Inc. ("WND")

Book designed by Mark Karis

WND Books are available at special discounts for bulk purchases. WND Books also publishes books in electronic formats. For more information call (541) 474-1776, e-mail orders@wndbooks.com or visit www.wndbooks.com.

Hardcover ISBN: 978-1-944229-98-6
eBook ISBN: 978-1-944229-99-3

Library of Congress Cataloging-in-Publication Data available upon request

Printed in the United States of America
18 19 20 21 22 XXX 9 8 7 6 5 4 3 2 1

To the Titans of 1968

"The gash that Robert F. Kennedy tore in the story of 1968 aches still—aches in personal memory, but more in history itself. Of all the men who challenged for the presidency, he alone, by the assassin's bullets, was deprived of the final judgment of his Party and his people."

THEODORE H. WHITE, THE MAKING OF THE PRESIDENT 1968

CONTENTS

Author's Note .... *xiii*

Prologue .... *xviii*

PART ONE
The Democrats: Prelude to Chicago 1

PART TWO
The Republicans: Prelude to Miami 187

PART THREE
Prelude to November 319

Coda 457

APPENDIX A
Biographical Sketches of the Candidates (as of 1968) 467

APPENDIX B
Chronology 473

APPENDIX C
Background on US Military Involvement in Vietnam 483

Acknowledgements 486

Bibliography 508

Badge depicting some of the 1968 presidential hopefuls (top row, from left): Robert Kennedy, Richard Nixon, Eugene McCarthy, and Hubert H. Humphrey. (Bottom row): Nelson Rockefeller, Ronald Reagan, George Wallace, and Charles Percy (Author's collection)

AUTHOR'S NOTE

A FEW QUICK POINTS before we begin our excursion back to 1968.

First: a present-day reflection. In late summer 2015, at the initial Republican presidential debate, the Fox News hosts crammed the seventeen declared candidates onto two stages. Polls showed that fifteen of these would-be presidents registered single-digit or zero in name recognition. Of the two dozen contenders in both parties, even the hardiest of political junkies would have struggled to pick out most of them in a police lineup.

This was not always the case.

The 1968 presidential election was—and remains—spellbinding, because the contestants in that sweepstake were not pygmies: they were titans. No single-digit combatants met on that battlefield. Fifty years later, we still know them—Nixon, Reagan, Johnson, Kennedy, Rockefeller, McCarthy, Humphrey, Wallace, Romney. Most had spent decades on the national scene, and each left their imprint on the major issues of their day.

Although we recognize their names, a dwindling number of us

witnessed their epic clash. I was ten in 1968; now I am sixty, which means that most contemporary readers have no personal memory of it. To help those latecomers, you will find in the back of the book brief biographical sketches of the nine major candidates in 1968 (Appendix A), a chronology of the actual 1968 campaign history (Appendix B), and a short backgrounder on why America fought in Vietnam (Appendix C). The latter is important because, as a trio of historians noted, writing about the 1968 campaign and leaving out the Vietnam War is like explaining *Hamlet* and leaving out the murdered king.*

Second: I exercise the author's prerogative to make a few personal observations about a protagonist in this story, Senator Robert F. Kennedy. Growing up in San Francisco in the 1960s in a blue-collar, part-Irish, and all-Roman Catholic family, John and Robert Kennedy were heroes to our generation of immigrant and denominational descendants. We admired them in life and mourned them in death—deeply. I was too young to remember Jack Kennedy's 1960 race, but I was all over Bobby Kennedy's 1968 drive. Although only in the fifth grade, I followed it with the same enthusiasm that other boys my age reserved for baseball statistics. That landmark campaign infused me with such an intense interest in history and government that it led to my own eventual career in law and politics.

The excitement of Bobby Kennedy's battle, and then the horrible violence that ended it instantly, left a profound impact on me that never waned. Decades later, during my service as a Republican congressman, I still held Robert Kennedy in awe—a reverence no other conservative House colleague apparently shared. In 1998, Congressman Joseph P. Kennedy III (D-MA) and I cosponsored a bill to name the US Department of Justice building after his late father. Republicans killed the bill in committee. Thirty years after RFK's death, his memory still

---

* Lewis Chester et al., *An American Melodrama: The Presidential Campaign of 1968* (New York: Viking Press, 1969), 21 ("[N]o subject is harder to deal with briefly [than the Vietnam War]. Once it is touched upon, narrative almost irresistibly disappears in complex and important arguments[.]"

aroused so much Republican disdain that they would not have named the DOJ outhouse after him. When I tried raising the issue with Speaker Newt Gingrich directly, he cut me off. "That bill is dead—dead," he snapped irritably. Later, when my friend Lyn Nofziger, Ronald Reagan's longtime spokesman and adviser, visited my Capitol Hill office, I saw him staring at a large autographed photo of Bobby Kennedy hanging on my wall. Turning to me and looking both confused and disgusted, he asked, "What the hell is *that thing* doing here?"

This leads to my third point: fascination does not cause blindness.

Like two other supermen with whom he split the stage in 1968, Robert Kennedy shares a common fate with Lyndon Johnson and Richard Nixon: all three are the subject of countless biographies larded with pseudo-psychological interpretations of what made them tick. Here the comparison ends. With LBJ and Nixon, the pop-culture consensus is that their power-grasping temperaments sprang from sinister motives and deep-seated personal inferiorities. Bobby's biographers usually promote loftier interpretations. For example, Arthur Schlesinger softened for history Bobby's hard-edged, knee-to-the-groin political style, writing, "Because he wanted to get things done, because he was often impatient and combative, because he felt simply and cared deeply, he made his share of mistakes, and enemies. He was a romantic and an idealist."**

Romance and idealism aside, many of RFK's supporters never knew, or chose to ignore, that Bobby started his political career in the 1950s as one of the lead investigators for Senator Joseph McCarthy, whose last name became—fairly or unfairly—a liberal synonym for reckless and career-destroying witch hunts.[1] After leaving McCarthy's staff, Bobby became chief counsel to the Senate committee investigating labor union racketeering. He dragged in over 1,500 witnesses before the committee in a vendetta to "get" those he perceived as enemies, especially

---

** At the end of this poetic litany, Schlesinger conceded RFK's other side—mildly: Bobby could be "prudent, expedient, demanding and ambitious." Arthur M. Schlesinger Jr., *Robert Kennedy and His Times* (Boston: Houghton Mifflin Co., 1978), xi.

Teamster leader Jimmy Hoffa—an obsession that carried over into his tenure as JFK's US attorney general. During Bobby's stint at the Justice Department, he supported covert foreign assassinations and coups. He ordered wiretaps on enemies and friends alike, including Dr. Martin Luther King Jr.[2] Bobby knew King cavorted with communists, so he monitored King's associations and activities.[3] Incidentally, these wiretaps disclosed King's many marital infidelities, which FBI agents later used to harass and threaten King. Revisionist histories notwithstanding, Attorney General Robert Kennedy did not champion the cause of Southern civil rights marchers—he viewed them as irritants creating escalating nuisances to his brother's 1964 reelection prospects.[4] Right up to the end of his life, in private conversations, sometimes he used ethnic vulgarities when talking about blacks and Jews.[5]

Just as those of us who venerate Thomas Jefferson—the man who gave voice to freedom's greatest proclamation—must live uncomfortably with the fact that he owned slaves, one would think that the venerators of Robert Kennedy would live uncomfortably with his stark and often disturbing record.

Wrong.

Instead, RFK's biographers overwhelmingly offer a more forgiving explanation—his brother's 1963 assassination *changed* Bobby Kennedy.[6] Dallas supposedly transfigured him from vicious streetfighter into Greek tragedian: deeper, sensitive, selfless. Bobby helped in this rehabilitation by peppering his post-JFK era speeches and interviews with quotations from Camus, Emerson, and Aeschylus. He dined with poets, strikers, and migrant workers, and he walked the ghettos. Those perpetuating the RFK myth excuse his calculated backflips on Vietnam.[7] Instead, we discover he "grew" in his opposition when he saw an unjust war and its aftermath. This renovated RFK meets us in history books as one upon whom fate forced leadership, which he accepted for duty, not ambition.

The truth: Robert Kennedy, both before and after his brother's death, was a calculating politician who fought dirty, played for keeps, and (when politically expedient) took various sides of an issue to please specific and often conflicting interest groups. Strip Bobby Kennedy of the sentimental hogwash that bathes his memory, and we find that he and his brother had the same cunning ambitions and methods as their non-idealized counterparts. We forgive the Kennedys, but not the graceless LBJ or the sweat-beaded and shifty-eyed Nixon, because the Kennedys had a cultured, smooth veneer when cutting an opponent's throat.

Doubtless Dallas and its aftermath changed Robert Kennedy. All the evidence suggests that Bobby did become more soulful, patient, thoughtful, and empathetic for the underclass, but his darker political side never wandered far. Of Bobby's 1968 opponents—Lyndon Johnson, Hubert Humphrey, Richard Nixon, Nelson Rockefeller, George Wallace, Ronald Reagan, Eugene McCarthy, George Romney— if any were alive today, they would tell you that RFK understood the family business perhaps better than any other member of his clan. When Bobby fought you on the political battlefield, he fought to win, and if that meant leaving your corpse rotting in the dust, tough luck.

A final point: writing a historical novel is easy if the author just makes up the story. My goal was to twist the arc of history with *facts*. Sometimes I shuffled the timing of statements, persons, and actions to condense the narrative, but I wrote the vast bulk of this account based on actual history. Authors relegate the chapter endnotes to the back of the book because such details interest only researchers and academics. Mine are so extensive and detailed—almost the length of this volume— that the publisher had to set up a separate website for them (or else double the size of this tome). If you want to confirm how much of this "historical fiction" really happened, or if you read something that you think couldn't possibly have happened, go to **www.OnToChicago.com**. I urge you to browse the endnotes after reading the chapters, or you will miss seeing how much of this account actually mirrors reality. Many revelations may surprise even the history buffs among you.

With that, let us now journey back in time and see if we might alter what will otherwise remain a brutish crime against a man, a nation, and a cause.

—J.R.

Badge issued and worn during the mourning period for Senator Robert F. Kennedy following his assassination, June 1968 (Author's collection)

PROLOGUE

"So my thanks to all of you—and now it's on to Chicago, and let's win there."
—SENATOR ROBERT F. KENNEDY, AMBASSADOR HOTEL, 12:15 A.M., JUNE 5, 1968

THE MOST TRAGIC PART OF THE STORY is that he was not supposed to go that way. The pantry was a last-second decision. Staff had earlier prompted Bobby to turn to his right when he finished the victory speech, exit through the ballroom crowd, do a quick press conference next door, and then leave for a private celebration at a nearby discothèque.

Over the last fifty years, I have seen the film countless times. Now, whenever it airs, I no longer watch the jubilant candidate. My eyes always drift to the right corner of the footage. It is where I know there are two unobtrusive swinging doors behind the curtain and off to the side of the stage.

"And now it's on to Chicago. . . ." Bobby flashes a thumbs-up and V-for-victory sign, brushes aside a lock of hair, and then moves to his right to exit the stage as prearranged. That was the plan.

Then it happens:

"This way, Senator."

Eyeing the thick crowd through which the candidate's entourage must navigate to attend the press conference, a well-meaning aide calls to his boss, "This way, Senator." Bobby stops, pivots, and backtracks toward the voice calling to his left. Kennedy's staff has a standby plan if the throng is too dense: exit behind the stage backdrop curtain, pass through the two swinging doors, and cut through the kitchen pantry.

Every time I see that footage and hear the aide call to him, I find myself pleading silently: *press on through the crowd—don't go into the pantry.*

But he always does.

●　●　●　●　●

Shortly after midnight on June 5, 1968, Senator Robert F. Kennedy stood before 1,500 cheering supporters in the Embassy Room at the Los Angeles Ambassador Hotel. There he declared victory over Senator Eugene McCarthy in a hard-fought California primary battle for the 1968 Democratic presidential nomination. A few minutes later, Kennedy closed his speech with these words: "So my thanks to all of you—and now it's on to Chicago, and let's win there." Kennedy exited the stage, went through two swinging doors, and walked halfway across the short pantry. As he stopped to shake hands with a teenage busboy, a young drifter stepped from behind a serving table, raised his pistol and fired. His first bullet struck Kennedy behind the right ear and crashed through his brain. One of Kennedy's surgeons later said if that shot had struck a centimeter to the right, Kennedy would have recovered in a couple of weeks and resumed his campaign. Because it did not, Robert Kennedy died twenty-six hours later at age forty-two, leaving a pregnant widow, ten young children, and a gaping hole in American history.

For half a century now, many of us old enough to remember that tragic night and contemplate its impact default to the question that still haunts:

What if?

What if someone in that crowded pantry shouted a warning and Bobby flinched—even slightly? What if something—*anything*—had deviated that bullet's fatal trajectory? What if millions of voters didn't lose their hopes in a pool of blood on a concrete floor? What if Bobby survived his wound?

What if Senator Robert Francis Kennedy had gone *on to Chicago*?

PART ONE

THE DEMOCRATS: PRELUDE TO CHICAGO

Badge distributed at a Young Democrats of Wisconsin convention, summer 1967 (Author's collection)

CHAPTER 1

"DON'T CALL HIM *BOBBY*. He hates that nickname."

"What are you talking about?" asked Chris Evans. The comment caught off guard the lanky, friendly, thirty-four-year-old Southern California campaign pollster who preferred surfing the coastline to crunching the numbers.

"I'm talking about when you meet him today," replied Ted Sorensen, whose horn-rimmed glasses, conservative business suit, and serious demeanor made him appear a decade older than his thirty-nine years. Ted looked more like a CPA than one of John F. Kennedy's closest aides for a decade. He now played the same role for the slain president's younger brother, Senator Robert F. Kennedy. "I'm just telling you," Ted reiterated, "He doesn't like *Bobby*."

As the two men sat alone in a rear booth drinking coffee that late afternoon in the Plaza Hotel's elegant Oak Room, Chris' demeanor betrayed playful suspicion. "This is a joke, right? Are you hazing the new guy? That's like Truman hating *Give 'em Hell Harry*, or Eisenhower hating *Ike*."

"Yeah, I know," Ted said, smiling for the first time since they met. "He doesn't like the nickname that everybody who loves him calls him. I think Jack made it stick. President Kennedy always called him 'Bobby'— an older brother's prerogative, I guess. Bob's resigned to it, so if you call him that, he won't correct you. I'm just telling you he never liked it."

Chris gazed out the window overlooking Central Park at the stream of fast-moving people bundled against the cold. Taking another sip, he remarked, "Friends warned me about working for him. You know the rap: vengeful, icy, ruthless. Last night my wife handed me a news clipping. Some reporter who covered him for years wrote that he has all the patience of a vulture without any of the dripping sentimentality. I came up the ranks always hearing Bobby's—sorry, Bob—I've always heard he's a prick."[1]

"It depends on who you ask," said Ted. "It also depends on *when* you're talking about. I first met Bob when I went to work for JFK in 1953—Jack had just won his Senate seat. Bob was just a couple of years out of law school. Back then, I wouldn't have voted for Bob Kennedy for anything."

"Why?"

"Lots of reasons. First, he was incredibly rude and thoughtless. If you did him a favor, even a big one, he wouldn't thank you for it. Years ago I mentioned this trait to Ambassador Kennedy, and the old man told me, 'Ted, never expect *any* appreciation from my sons. These kids have had so much done for them by other people that they just assume it's coming to them.'"[2] After reaching for the creamer, Ted continued. "Back then, Bob was everything I hated in a guy: militant, aggressive, intolerant, opinionated, shallow.[3] He'd do whatever it took to win, and he didn't care who he angered or what enemies he made along the way. He almost begged people to hate him, and if you got on his wrong side, he'd hold a grudge against you forever. When he did fight you, it was bare-knuckled and savage.[4] Trust me. You *never* wanted to make Bob Kennedy's enemy list. So, yeah, I guess I know his reputation better than most."

"While we're at it," Chris added, "there's another thing. I get the whole Irish-Catholic stick-together thing, but tell me why he worked for that son-of-a-bitch Joe McCarthy? Look at all the careers McCarthy ruined with his witch hunts."

"Back then, Bob was much more like his father than his brother. One of Bob's first jobs out of law school was staffing McCarthy's committee. The old man got him that job, by the way. 'Tail-Gunner Joe' and the ambassador went way back. McCarthy hung out in Hyannis Port and Palm Beach with the Kennedy boys, and he even dated two of Bob's sisters. Most people don't know this, and keep it to yourself—when Bob's first kid was born, he had McCarthy stand as her godfather. In those early days, Bob saw himself as an anti-communist conservative crusader. He despised liberals—just like his dad. The old man once said, 'Bobby's like me. He's a hater. And when Bobby hates you, you stay hated.' The ambassador seemed proud of that trait."[5]

"If that's all true, then why are you with him?"

"Like I said, it depends on *when* you're talking about. When Jack was alive, if Bob had a job to do for his brother, he did it, and he didn't care if people liked him or not.[6] Jack's death changed him—it humbled and softened him. He became gentler, warmer. On top of that, incredible responsibilities forced him to grow—big family of his own, trying to be a surrogate father to Jack's kids while watching over Jackie, and then his own political career. Bob started out more like his father than his brother, but he ended up far more liberal than either of them. So he's changed over the years. I still find him growing and changing."[7]

Ted looked at his watch. "His meeting with Al should be over by now. Let's head over there"

"Who's Al?"

"Allard Lowenstein."

Chris nodded. "Oh, I've read about him—the 'Dump Johnson' guy. He's organized some national movement of college professors and students. He's just missing one ingredient—"

"—Yeah," Ted interrupted, "he's missing a candidate. This isn't the first time Al's tried to make Bob the horse to ride. Bob keeps telling him no, but Al's persistent." Paying the check, Ted continued, "He's not a candidate—yet. Bob's a very cautious guy. He needs to work through these things at his own pace. But I've been around long enough to know that with the Kennedys, there's *always* a campaign."

Ted and Chris left the bar and hailed a cab. The ride to their destination, a tony apartment building overlooking the East River, was only a mile away. Now, at rush hour, it was a twenty-minute crawl.

"We could have walked faster," Ted growled as the cab inched along 52nd Street.

"You never really explained, Ted. If he's not running, why do you need a pollster from California now?"

"First," Ted replied, "we hired you because you come highly recommended by people we trust. Second, the situation's fluid. He really wants to go, but he's terribly torn. I've never seen him quite so indecisive. He keeps saying no, but he wants to keep his options open. If a break came, I think he'd jump quickly. Third, if he does give the signal, California may be where the nomination is won or lost. We need to be ready with a ground game out there."

"I don't understand the hesitancy. I thought Kennedys live for this."

"You're right. He wants to be president—it's in the genes. Part of his reluctance is the family. His brother Teddy thinks Bob should wait until he has a clean shot in '72—no Dem incumbent then, but Teddy's for whatever Bob decides. I agree with Teddy. He and I are in the minority of people who want Bob to wait four years."[8]

As Ted spoke, he fished around in his jacket pocket, pulled out a small campaign button, and then handed it to Chris. "I picked up a few of these at a Wisconsin state Party convention last week. When I gave one to Bob, he looked at it, laughed, and then he told me to stop lobbying him." Chris studied the badge depicting RFK and a snow-capped peak, bearing the caption, "STOP CLIMBING MOUNTAINS BOB KENNEDY—WE NEED YOU IN '72."[9]

"Is this an extra?" Chris asked hopefully.

Ted told him to keep it, and then returned to the main topic. "Surprisingly, Ethel wants him to run.[10] You'd think with ten kids that she'd want him home. He talks about assassination sometimes—Jack's death haunts him every day, but he doesn't brood about it. Did you know he gets more crank threat letters than the president? Every psycho wants to be the guy that shoots the next Kennedy. If Bob has any worries, it's for Ethel, his kids, Jack's kids, but not for himself. There's a fatalism about him, very much like Jack."

Chris began to speak, but Ted interrupted. "I still haven't answered you—what's the holdup? Two things: one's Vietnam. Bob began as a true believer—the 'Domino Theory,' 'Can't let Southeast Asia fall to the communists'—the whole Cold War line. In the last year or so, he's become very disillusioned with the war. He feels it's a massive waste of lives and money, and with no end in sight. He thinks LBJ will continue it, and more American troops—kids really—will keep dying over there for nothing."

"So far, all I've heard are reasons why your man *should* challenge Johnson in the primaries. Kennedy wants to stop the war, Johnson won't do it, and they hate each other anyway.[11] Why the indecision?"

"Listen," Ted said brusquely, "you're already hired, so he isn't *my* man. He's *your* man, too. As for the war issue, you're right. It's the strongest reason to take on Johnson next year, but disagreeing with an incumbent president of your Party is one thing, and opposing him for re-nomination is another. Whatever their differences, Bob understands politics. If he challenges LBJ, the likelihood of beating him is slim. Johnson still controls all the levers of the national Democratic Party. The primaries next year won't choose nearly enough delegates to win the nomination. Most of them will come from the Party regulars, and they are almost all Johnson people. If Bob runs and Johnson wins the nomination, and then loses to the Republicans in November, Bob gets the blame. Even if Bob beats Johnson, it would probably divide the Party so badly that the nomination becomes worthless. That's why Bob's agonizing over this. One minute he's calling us together to plot his entry into the race, and the next minute he's telling reporters that he supports LBJ. Others in the circle disagree, but the way I see it, challenging Johnson is bad politics for the Democratic Party, and bad politics for Bob Kennedy."

"Based on what you've told me so far, I feel like I should be on the first plane back to San Clemente. There are so few of us Democrats in Orange County that when one leaves, the other six get nervous."

The taxi made its way up East 46th Street to First Avenue, and then turned onto a private driveway. It stopped in front of a gleaming twin-towered high-rise, with its bronze and glass façade sparkling against the lights of the crisp Manhattan evening. As Ted paid the driver he told Chris, "Sitting tight until 1972 is the smart and safe thing. Bob insists he's not a candidate in 1968, but I've known him for fifteen years. When Bob's sense of injustice is inflamed, things could change quickly. That's why we're both here. Just in case."

The two men exited the taxi and stepped into the plush, red-carpeted, double-height lobby of 860 United Nations Plaza. Two security men behind the desk recognized Ted, and they knew which resident he came to see. They smiled and nodded as the visitors boarded an elevator and hit the button for the fourteenth floor.

"Welcome to Ground Zero," Ted said to the pollster. "Let's go meet your new client."

1968 pennant promoting Senator Robert F. Kennedy for president (Author's collection)

CHAPTER 2

TED SORENSEN KNOCKED ON THE DOOR of apartment 14-F.[1] Fred Dutton, a longtime Robert Kennedy aide, let the two men inside the elegant, but surprisingly untidy, home.

"Is Al still here?" Ted asked.

"No, he left a couple minutes ago. I'm surprised you didn't pass him in the lobby."

"*And . . . ?*"

"It wasn't good," Fred said as he looked toward the den. "They were in there almost half an hour. By the end, I could hear them through the closed door. Bob was saying it couldn't be put together. Al started shouting, 'America's future is at stake. I don't give a damn if you don't think it can be put together. It *can* be put together, and we'll do it with or without you.'[2] Anyway, when Al barged out his face was beet red. Bob followed and pleaded for understanding as Al headed for the front door. He said he wanted to run, but the Party leaders are all with LBJ, and that Mayor Daley* told him that if he ran now he'd split the Party.

---

*   Richard J. Daley (1902-1976); mayor of Chicago 1955-1976.

That's when Al exploded. He told Bob that the people who care about this country don't give a shit what Mayor Daley thinks. Al said they'll move forward to find a candidate, and it's a shame Bob's not with them, because he could have been president. Al got choked up and left, while Bob just stood here looking pained. He's still in the den—I was on my way in when you guys arrived."[3]

The trio approached the study and pushed open the door. Seeing Robert Kennedy in-person for the first time surprised Chris. He expected to be overwhelmed, not underwhelmed. Leaning against the back of a chair, a glum-looking and silent RFK gazed out a floor-to-ceiling window at the skyline. He wore casual clothes: a button-down Oxford shirt, dark blue wool V-neck sweater, old slacks, and deck shoes. Ted introduced Chris, who was also taken aback at how small Bobby looked—thin—almost frail, a bit slouched, and much shorter than expected. In fact, his height wasn't an illusion. In flat shoes, he *was* shorter. His size-nine dress shoes carried raised arches to add a bit more heft to his slight 5'9" frame. Aside from noting the limp handshake, Chris also saw something he never saw in the magazine photos: deep wrinkles lined the suntanned face, and lots of gray in the thick mop of light brown hair.[4]

A butler wheeled in a cart carrying ice buckets filled with beer. Bobby grabbed his favorite, a Heineken, and then invited the others to join him.[5] Settling into a chair, he told Chris, "My brother Teddy swears by you, and so does my pal George McGovern. He tells me you're a great pollster and a great guy, and discreet as hell. These days, I need someone with all those qualities."

After Chris popped the cap off his beer bottle and took a drink, he asked, "Did your brother and George also tell you it will be hard as hell for me not to call you *Bobby*? You've always been Bobby to me."

Kennedy laughed, and his forlorn face lit up suddenly, making him look boyish. "Sounds like you've been exposed to Sorensen propaganda! Given what Lyndon calls me, 'Bobby' is not so bad. I've given up trying to cast it off." Then turning serious, he asked if Sorensen had filled in

Chris on the Lowenstein visits over the last few weeks.

"He told me," Chris replied, "but it isn't exactly a state secret. Everybody in the business knows he's been leaning on you as his number-one draft choice. Without you, it doesn't sound like he has a Plan B."

Taking another sip, Bobby recounted his just-concluded meeting. "Al got very emotional. He told me I had a moral obligation to challenge Johnson in the primaries, or else Johnson would win and the war would continue. I told Al I wanted a candidate to challenge Johnson, too, but I didn't see how it could be me because of my personal history with him. If I ran, people would say that I was splitting the Party out of ambition and envy. No one would believe I was doing it because of how I felt about Vietnam. I told Al that he was doing the right thing to recruit a candidate, but it would have to be someone else."[6]

"I think I saw how he took it," Fred said.

Bobby stared at the floor when he responded. "At one point I called Johnson a coward for his behavior on Vietnam.[7] Al looked directly at me and said, 'I guess *coward* is a good word to describe it.' Then he choked up, grabbed his overcoat and stormed out. When he said that, it hurt like hell."

"I know this wasn't your first meeting with him," Chris said. "I'm wondering whether it's your last."

Freckles, the family's black-and-white springer spaniel, loped into the room and over to his master. Bobby scratched the dog's head as he again looked out the window. "If I run now, I'll prove everything that everybody who has ever hated me has said over the years. They'll say it shows that I'm just a selfish, ambitious little son-of-a-bitch that can't wait to get his hands on the White House."[8] He shook his head. "Well, Al's a warrior, and he'll never quit. He'll regroup tonight, and he'll be back at it tomorrow, but—"

After taking a final swig, he finished his thought. "—when Al does get back to it, he won't be getting back to it with me."

Anti-Lyndon Johnson button, 1968 (Author's collection)

CHAPTER 3

ROBERT KENNEDY WAS CORRECT. Allard Lowenstein *was* a warrior—one who, so far, had been ineffective in combat. His previous "battle" against the Vietnam War meant visiting colleges and gathering signatures on petitions. Then, in August 1967, he adopted another strategy. Rather than simply protesting the war, he sought a Democratic challenger to the war's root cause, President Lyndon Johnson. He calculated that a nationwide movement might mobilize around a "peace" candidate. With no organization or resources beyond some old antiwar mailing lists, he launched the "Dump Johnson" drive. The task was so daunting, and the likelihood of success so remote, that the proposition seemed absurd. It was from this background that Lowenstein took up his cause. Preparing to battle a powerful establishment, and an even more powerful wartime president, he intended to make good on his promise to wage this fight—with or without Robert Kennedy.

A week after his confrontation with Bobby, Lowenstein flew to Boston and asked retired Lt. Gen. James Gavin, a World War II combat veteran who opposed US military involvement in Vietnam, to consider running. Surprisingly, Gavin expressed an interest in an antiwar presidential race, but only as a Republican. Again dispirited, he withdrew his request, asking Gavin if he seriously saw himself winning the Republican nomination running *against* the Vietnam War.[1]

Undeterred, and using a roster of the antiwar Democratic US senators, Lowenstein made the rounds on Capitol Hill. He pitched the need for an LBJ challenger to every dove on his list: Wayne Morse, Frank Church, Joseph Clark, and William Fulbright. Each laughed or chased him out of their offices when they heard the farfetched suggestion. South Dakota Senator George McGovern, another antiwar advocate, also said no—but at least he didn't laugh.

A World War II bomber pilot, history professor, and congressman before winning election to the Senate from South Dakota in 1962, McGovern was an early Vietnam War critic. Like RFK, McGovern was sympathetic to Lowenstein's efforts. Also like Kennedy, McGovern was risk averse, but for different reasons. In 1962, McGovern won his Senate seat by only 597 votes. In 1968, he faced a just-as-tough reelection campaign. Besides, South Dakota was a pro-war state. Any quixotic antiwar presidential romp might end his Senate career. Wanting to be helpful, McGovern went over with Lowenstein his list of potential contenders, and then McGovern added a couple of names to it: Senators Lee Metcalf and Eugene McCarthy.

A few days later, McGovern ran into McCarthy during lunch in the Senate Dining Room. "Hey, Gene," McGovern called to his colleague contritely, "I sent a guy over to talk to you about running against Johnson." McGovern started apologizing for the intrusion, but McCarthy interrupted.

"Yeah," he responded casually, "I talked to him." Then, as McGovern recounted later, McCarthy's next sentence left him "astounded":

"I think I may do it."[2]

Eugene Joseph McCarthy, 51, was Central Casting's version of how a senator or president looked. He was tall—well over six feet—with silver hair swept back, and he carried himself with almost regal bearing.

His manners were urbane and witty. He read—and wrote—poetry. McCarthy exuded manor-bred and Ivy League, but unlike the Kennedys, McCarthy grew up a farm boy in Watkins, Minnesota (population 760). In school he played baseball and ice hockey, and he devoured classic literature voraciously. He took his Catholicism seriously: as a young man, he briefly joined a monastery. Teaching high school after graduating from a Benedictine college, McCarthy returned to his alma mater as an economics professor. His political entry was fortuitous. Because nobody else wanted the job, he became the local Democratic Party county chairman. In 1948, McCarthy ran for and won a seat in the House of Representatives, the same year fellow Minnesotan, Minneapolis Mayor Hubert H. Humphrey, won election to the US Senate. Joining Humphrey in the Senate a decade later, McCarthy proved the ultimate anti-politician. As one observer noted, McCarthy looked down on practically everybody in his profession: he admired poets but had little use for politicians, and he disdained the ritual of politics.[*] Others observed that he thought it beneath him to engage in the glad-handing, fundraising, support-seeking, and returning calls from Party leaders. He tweaked fellow senators with biting public commentaries, and colleagues reciprocated his scorn. The Senate bored McCarthy. Despite a decade of seniority, he never sought nor won admittance to its insider "club." Instead, he mocked the Senate, calling it, "The last primitive society left on earth." Once he compared the chamber and its traditions to a savage New Guinea settlement. "Both societies are obsessed with seniority, taboos, and precedent. In that regard, the Senate is like a leper colony."[**]

If the road to New Hampshire—the first 1968 primary in the nation—appeared a discouragingly lonely one for an insurgent candidate, who better to trod it than the political world's biggest loner?[3]

---

[*]   Arthur M. Schlesinger Jr., *Robert Kennedy and His Times* (Boston: Houghton Mifflin Co., 1978), 826, 828, 894.

[**] Lewis Chester et al., *An American Melodrama: The Presidential Campaign of 1968* (New York: Viking Press, 1969), 68.

A few hours after George McGovern's unexpected encounter with Eugene McCarthy, McGovern saw Robert Kennedy on the Senate floor during a late-night procedural vote. Gripping RFK's arm, McGovern whispered, "Bob, can we talk? I've got some good news." The two walked off the Senate floor, crossed the carpeted hallway to the senators' private Marble Room, and settled into facing chairs near the crackling fireplace.

When McGovern told him the news about McCarthy, Bobby grew pale. "Goddamn it, George," he growled, "I wanted to keep that option open to myself."

Bobby's unexpected response took McGovern aback. "Bob, you can't be serious. Al Lowenstein's been *begging* you! I've urged you all year to run. McCarthy said he personally asked you to do it several times. You've said no to each of us. Now you're upset? I don't get it."

Bobby's expression tightened. "I know, George, but I wanted to keep the path clear in case things develop later."

"What 'things' need to develop? And how much later? The New Hampshire primary is ten weeks from now! We need *someone* to challenge Johnson. It's good if Gene steps to the plate. Come on, Bob, be reasonable. I don't understand your sudden problem."

"The problem," Bobby responded, "is that once he announces, McCarthy's going to get a lot of support. People like you and others will start lining up behind him. That's going to make it tough for me if I want to make a move later." Bobby banged his clenched fist down on the leather armrest of the chair, and then stood up and stared into the fireplace. "God," he muttered, "I should have done this."

When McGovern arrived home later that night, his wife Eleanor asked why he looked so dismayed. He told her about McCarthy's decision and his later encounter with Bobby. "I can't remember ever having a conversation with Bob where he looked more disturbed than when I told him McCarthy might announce for president," he told her. "I don't think Bob ever thought in his wildest imagination that Gene would do it."[4]

"I guess Bobby wants it both ways," she replied. "He doesn't want to run for president, but he doesn't want anyone else to run, either. It's like the girl who always wanted to be a bride—as long as she doesn't have to get married."

Late the next evening, the kitchen telephone rang in Arthur Schlesinger's home in Northwest Washington.[5] He recognized the caller's voice without any need for identification. "Art, are you free to come for dinner—now?"

"I ate about three hours ago, Bob, like normal people. But I'll be right over."

The historian, JFK aide, and longtime Kennedy family friend was at Bobby's disposal. He grabbed his overcoat and told his wife Marian not to wait up. Crossing the Potomac River over Key Bridge, he drove along the George Washington Parkway to Bobby's post-Civil War-era mansion, nicknamed "Hickory Hill,"[6] nestled on six acres in McLean, Virginia. Schlesinger arrived to find the sullen Bobby wasting no time airing his grievance.

"McCarthy's going to run," Bobby said. "That means he'll take up the cause against Johnson, and he'll make himself the hero and the leader of the antiwar movement. If I decide to enter the race later, I'll be called a Johnny-come-lately."

"McGovern called this afternoon and told me," Arthur said. "He said Gene urged you privately to run several times. Gene also said he told you that if you won't run, he would."

"He did," Bobby said resignedly. "We talked a few times in the last couple of months, but he was just another in a long line of guys trying to push me into the race. When he tossed out that remark about running himself, I didn't put any stock in it.[7] Can you really see McCarthy as president? He's lazy, vain, pompous, mercurial—he's totally unfit. Who the hell would ever think he'd really do it?"[8]

After eating from a bowl of clam chowder in silence for a few minutes, Bobby's mood lightened suddenly. "You know," he said optimistically, "maybe this isn't so bad after all. Maybe I should just let McCarthy run. Then he can draw all of Johnson's fire. Down the road, if I do jump in, people might view me as the less divisive candidate. I could rise above the fray and be seen as bailing out the situation."[8]

Arthur looked skeptically across the table at his friend. "Do you really believe that's likely, Bob?"

Bobby put down his spoon, rested his elbows on the dinner table, and rubbed his now-closed eyes before answering:

"Fuck no."

"McCarthy for Peace" 1968 campaign button (Author's collection)

CHAPTER 4

"IN MY TWENTY YEARS IN CONGRESS, only two colleagues ever lied to me—and both times the liars were named Kennedy."

In late November 1967, Senator Eugene McCarthy made this unexpected observation to his friend Blair Clark as both men drank coffee in the kitchen of McCarthy's small nineteenth-century brick row house at 3053 Q Street in Northwest Washington. While discussing Gene's decision to challenge President Johnson for the 1968 Democratic presidential nomination, the "liar" comment caught Blair off guard.

"Lying Kennedys?" he asked. "Bobby and Teddy?"

"No, Bobby and Jack."

Blair shook his head. "Listen, Gene, I knew Jack Kennedy since we were students at Harvard. We were friends for twenty-five years. When CBS named me vice president of news back in '61, he offered to make me ambassador to Mexico instead. Jack was a lot of things, but I never knew him to be a liar."[1]

"Then you didn't know him," Gene replied matter-of-factly. "It was in 1959, when we both were in the Senate. I wanted to offer an amendment to a union bill. It wasn't a big deal. It covered reimbursement for legal fees. Anyway, Jack was on the Labor Committee. I explained my proposed amendment to him and asked for his vote if I introduced it. After reviewing the language, he promised his support, so I presented it. Later, some opposition arose. During the debate I saw Bobby—he was a committee staffer then—I saw him walk up and whisper something to Jack. Later, Jack announced at the hearing that his committee would not accept my amendment. After it died, he walked over to my desk and said sheepishly, 'Hey, I'm sorry about that.' I told him not to worry about it."

"Well, like you said, the amendment wasn't a big deal. Come on, that kind of thing happens ten times a day in Congress—you know that."

"Maybe twenty times a day. I didn't hold a grudge against him over it, but I took note that I could never again accept Jack Kennedy's word on a legislative matter—and I never did."[2]

"So when did Bobby lie to you?"

"More than once. Earlier this year I gave an interview to Wechsler at the *New York Post*. He asked if I thought someone should challenge LBJ next year. I said I wanted Bobby to run, because he'd be the strongest antiwar candidate. All year, whenever any reporters asked me, I told them that Bobby was the one to lead an effective insurrection against Johnson. Anyway, Bobby read the *Post* interview. He came up to me on the Senate floor and said he wouldn't do it. Since then, over the last several months, I've encouraged Bobby to run repeatedly. Every time I did, he told me he wouldn't do it. He said the idea was hopeless and that Johnson can't be stopped."[3]

"So where's the lie?"

"A couple of weeks ago I called Bobby and asked to see him. We met in his office and I raised the issue again. He told me his position wouldn't change. I said someone must challenge Johnson to end this war. Bobby told me to forget about it—Johnson was unbeatable. Then I told Bobby that if he won't run, I will."

"What did Bobby say to that?"

"Bobby told me that if I challenged Johnson, he'd probably endorse

LBJ, but he gave me his word that if I got in the race, he wouldn't run against me."[4]

Blair awaited the rest of the story. There wasn't any more. Gene had made his point.

"Gene, you're the most negative guy I know. Bobby's been telling everyone he's not running. How many times does he have to say it? *Bobby's not a candidate*, period. So when did he lie to you?"

Gene winked as he put down his mug. "The day's not over yet, Blair."

The conversation drifted back to the original topic: a McCarthy presidential candidacy. "I know you're set to go," Blair asked, "but why do you need to be the sacrificial lamb on this? You have a brilliant career ahead of you in the Senate, and you could stay there forever. This race will marginalize you for good."

"Johnson's going to keep expanding the war. The last time we introduced a Senate resolution to cut off funding, we got five votes. The only way to challenge the war is to challenge Johnson. Someone has to be willing to make the case, so it looks like it will have to be me."[5]

"What are you going to say when Johnson hits you for voting for the Gulf of Tonkin Resolution? He'll claim you approved his going into Vietnam."

"That vote authorized the president to use military force to defend US troops against attacks. The resolution never authorized a four-year, full-scale declaration of war against North Vietnam. If he wins again next year, all we'll see are weekly increases in the number of kids shipped home in caskets."[6]

It was pushing midnight when Gene walked Blair to his car across the narrow street, with both men leaving footprints in the fresh snowfall that had dusted the quiet neighborhood. Standing beside Blair's car, both men shivered against the biting cold as Gene thrust his hands deep into his pockets. He had waited until the end of the evening intentionally to raise a final issue. "I reserved the Senate Caucus Room next Thursday morning for a press conference to make the announcement. I'd like you there."

"Of course I'll come, Gene."

"Well, I want something else. When I announce my candidacy, I also want to introduce you as my national campaign manager."

Blair studied Gene's face looking for the humorous reaction such a silly comment warranted. Gene had no smile. His blue eyes fixed on Blair.

"Is this a joke?"

"No."

"Are you crazy? I'm a newspaperman. I'm a reporter—ask me to be your press secretary!"

"This is going to be a non-traditional campaign with all the molds broken. I'm running because the cause needs a candidate, and you're joining me because the candidate needs a manager. Say yes, and then get in your car and turn on the heater."

"Gene," Blair pleaded, "what the hell do I know about running a campaign?"

"What the hell do I know about running for president? The press conference is 9:00 a.m. See you there."

With that, Eugene McCarthy turned, crossed the street, and walked up the short brick driveway. Stepping inside, he closed the front door and turned off the overhead porch light without once looking back at the expression of shock on the face of his new campaign manager.[7]

Badge from the 1964 Democratic National Convention promoting Minnesota Senator Eugene McCarthy as President Johnson's vice presidential running mate (Author's collection)

CHAPTER 5

"MR. BUSBY, I fear you're giving retirement a bad name!"

The short, dapper man with wavy dark hair smiled at the elderly usher's comment as the two men exited the Diplomatic Reception Room and boarded a small elevator. "Henry," the visitor replied with his slight Southern accent, "nobody who ever worked for this president gets to retire. We just stop getting paid for the privilege!"

"That's fair warning!" the usher chuckled as the doors closed and he pushed the second-floor button. "I've served every family in this house since Mr. Coolidge, but when I leave in January after forty-three years, I think I'll get an unlisted number. I don't want to end up like you!"

Horace Busby laughed at the observation. After working fifteen years as one of President Lyndon Johnson's closest aides, he quit two years earlier to start a management consulting company. However, since leaving, he put his business interests on hold countless times, and always on a moment's notice, when the White House operator tracked him down. If the president needed anything done quickly and discreetly, he called "Buzz." And when Lyndon Johnson called and wanted to see you about something, he didn't mean "at your convenience."[1]

The elevator doors opened and the two men headed down the hallway. As they approached the Family Dining Room, Buzz saw a familiar figure exit. "Good morning, stranger," called Juanita Roberts, the president's personal secretary. With a slight grimace to suggest a warning, she motioned with her head toward the nearby closed door. "He's skipping breakfast today, but there's fresh coffee in there. I'll have some rolls sent up if you'd like."

"Coffee's fine, Juanita. Skipping breakfast? Is he back on his *Metrecal* diet?"

"No, but his mood will make you think he is. He's waiting for you."

Buzz knew those moods better than most people. From that day in 1948 when the young Texan took a job in Washington working for then-Congressman Johnson, he had experienced them all over the last two decades: domineering, profane, brilliant, sensitive, brutal, gentle, crude, hilarious, loyal, treacherous—LBJ had more sides than a decagon. Buzz held a variety of jobs during Johnson's congressional, vice presidential, and presidential years: speechwriter, adviser, Cabinet secretary, special assistant, and "Texas Mafia" confidant. Although Buzz left the White House after the 1964 reelection, the paychecks, but not the tasks, stopped arriving. In the president's mind, once an LBJ staffer, *always* an LBJ staffer.

Buzz rapped on the door gently, and then he opened it without awaiting an invitation that he knew from habit would not come.

"Good morning, Mr. President."

Lyndon Johnson never looked up from the *Washington Post* spread across the dining table. His nearly six-foot-four frame hunched over the paper, and his reading glasses perched in front of that massive head.

"So, you see the *poet's* running against me?" LBJ mumbled sarcastically as he spat out his nickname for Eugene McCarthy.

"Do you think passing him over for vice president in '64 still sticks in his craw?"

"That's part of it—Hubert and Mondale both think so.* McCarthy's hard-on for me goes way back. When I became vice president, I offered to preside over the weekly Senate Democratic caucus luncheons to help coordinate our agendas. McCarthy raised a big stink and started squawking about separation of powers. Separation of powers—I had to sit and listen to his constitutional bullshit after all I did for him when I was majority leader. Besides, did that shit-for-brains think Democratic bills became laws without a Democratic president signing the goddamn things? What the hell—I just let it go—but I don't understand this betrayal of me. Since I became president we never had any major differences. He supported me on the *Great Society*** and civil rights. Until lately, he was with me on Vietnam, too."[2]

A steward entered with a fresh pot of coffee. As Buzz took a seat at the table, LBJ continued venting about his new rival's motives. "You're right—McCarthy's had a bug up his ass ever since I didn't pick him for VP. You'd think he'd be grateful that he made my final list. Look at all the national press I got him. Anyway, after I picked Humphrey, McCarthy told people I 'dangled' the VP nomination just to toy with him. Afterward, he told some people that I threatened him with a primary challenger back home if he didn't withdraw from consideration and nominate Humphrey.[3] So this is all part of some payback."

"Any worries about him getting in?"

LBJ took off his reading glasses and looked at Buzz. "McCarthy's a distraction, he's not a threat. He's a one-issue candidate—Vietnam—and he's got no public visibility.[4] Did you hear what that jackass said when a reporter asked him why he wanted to be president?" LBJ answered his own question, adopting a snooty, stentorian lilt as he mimicked McCarthy's reply to the question: "'I didn't say I *wanted* to be president. I said I'm *willing* to be president.' When another reporter asked what kind of president he'd make, he said, 'Oh, I'd be *adequate*.'"[5]

---

*   Hubert Humphrey, former US senator from Minnesota, was LBJ's vice president from 1965-1969. Minnesota Governor Karl Rolvaag appointed Walter Mondale to Humphrey's Senate seat, and he became Eugene McCarthy's junior home-state colleague.

**   The Great Society: LBJ's nickname for his domestic agenda to fight poverty and racial injustice.

Adequate? Jesus Christ! Who's running his campaign—a busload of fucking astrologers? How seriously do I need to take a guy like that? Besides, I think his entry is just a dodge. Bobby Kennedy probably put him up to it to test whether there's enough of an anti-Johnson vote out there for Bobby to grow some balls and jump in himself."

As he spoke, LBJ picked up a sheet of paper containing new polling data. "Once I got word from my spies about McCarthy, we ran a tracking poll. The overwhelming majority of Democrats still support my Vietnam policies and the job I'm doing as president. Why the hell shouldn't they? I've given 'em more houses, more doctors, more welfare, and more jobs than any other goddamn president in history."[6]

"Mr. President, you're not the only one carrying a piece of paper around," Buzz said with a grin as he tapped the left breast pocket area of his suit jacket. LBJ knew what that motion meant. Almost since Johnson won reelection in 1964, he had been off-and-on about running for a second full term in 1968, depending on his swinging moods or swinging poll numbers. A few months earlier, LBJ told Busby to draft a couple of paragraphs for a possible future speech. Although brief, the language contained the bombshell announcement that LBJ would not run again in 1968. After Buzz finished the job, LBJ told him to hang onto it "just in case I want it later."

Seeing Buzz patting his coat pocket, LBJ grabbed a thick memo from a stack of papers in front of him and slid the document across the table. Once Buzz skimmed the first couple of pages of the "President's Eyes Only" report, he needn't read any further. Written by Postmaster General Lawrence F. O'Brien, one of LBJ's top political strategists, the forty-four pages mapped out Johnson's current reelection strategy. "I've been meeting twice a week for the last few months with key people," LBJ told him. "As far as 1968 goes, we've been airborne for some time."[7]

"Mr. President, that's good news, but I'll hang onto this paper I've been carrying for you. I've been around long enough to believe Yogi Berra had you in mind when he said, 'It ain't over 'til it's over.'"

A few hundred feet away, in room 176 of the Old Executive Office Building on the White House grounds, Gene McCarthy's announcement was on the mind of another Johnson administration official—Vice President Hubert H. Humphrey.

Humphrey's relationship with McCarthy dated back to the mid-1940s when McCarthy taught college in Minnesota and Humphrey served as Minneapolis mayor. In 1948, both men went to Congress: McCarthy to the House of Representatives and Humphrey to the Senate. They campaigned for each other over the next twenty years, and they held almost identical political views until their recent split on Vietnam. At the 1952 Democratic National Convention, McCarthy nominated Humphrey as a favorite son candidate for president, and he co-chaired Humphrey's 1960 presidential race against Senator John F. Kennedy. Some traced a strained relationship between McCarthy and the Kennedys to that campaign. During the West Virginia primary, while McCarthy stumped for Humphrey, JFK asked to see McCarthy privately. During their meeting in JFK's Senate office, Kennedy got up from his desk, walked over to where McCarthy sat, stood over him, and barked, "Tell Hubert to lay off in West Virginia or we'll unload on him." McCarthy replied indignantly that he would not relay that message, telling Kennedy to get someone else to do his dirty work. Not long after this meeting, Franklin D Roosevelt, Jr. went to West Virginia on behalf of JFK and suggested to voters that Humphrey dodged the draft in World War II.[8] The devastating and false accusation hit its mark. JFK beat Humphrey there, ending HHH's 1960 White House hopes. Four years later, after LBJ selected Humphrey as his running mate, McCarthy gave the nominating speech for him. By all appearances, theirs was a longstanding alliance. However, in this case, appearances didn't tell the entire story.

The morning after Gene McCarthy announced his challenge to Johnson, Humphrey sat behind his desk in the ornate vice president's office reviewing the daily executive correspondence file when his long-time aide Ted Van Dyk joined him. "I heard from the president this morning before I heard from my alarm clock," Humphrey said with a grimace. "Of course, since Gene and I are both Minnesotans, Lyndon acts like this is somehow my fault." Then, imitating LBJ's Texas drawl, Humphrey mimicked the unwanted wake-up call received a few hours earlier. "Well, Hubert, I see *your* boy's trying to screw me. Can't you control *your* people?"

"Did the announcement surprise you?" Ted asked.

"No, I expected it. Gene came by the office recently and told me he might challenge Johnson. He spoke so casually, as he usually does, that I felt it was just a lark on his part. I asked whether he thought it through carefully, including the difficulties of unseating an incumbent president. He told me, 'Well, I don't have any feeling that I can win, but I've lost interest in the Senate, and I feel very strongly about the war. I guess the best way to show my feelings is to go out and enter the primaries.'"[9]

Humphrey stood, walked over to the conference table, and tossed some reports into his briefcase as he continued. "This is classic Gene. He hasn't changed since I first met him. He disdains whatever group he's in. When he taught college, he found most of his peers dull. When he was in the House, he grew tired of his fellow congressmen. In the Senate, he found very few things that interested him. Along the way he's created this anti-politician mask. On the outside, he has it all—handsome, witty, teacher, poet, Irish mystic, and a clever politician—he's a lot more clever for denying it and getting away with the denial. It'll be interesting to see how long it takes his fans and the press to discover he's more vain and arrogant than his admirers recognize."[10]

"I've never understood the subtle hostility I've always felt he directed toward you," Ted said. "In the three-plus years I've been here, you've always treated him as a friend and done whatever you could for him. I once heard Teddy White say that McCarthy has a festering rancor for you.[11] Your 'friendship' with him seems pretty one-sided."

Humphrey went back to his desk and grabbed the briefing book for his next meeting. "When two guys from Minnesota come to Congress together, and then spend two decades campaigning for each other, you need to let that count for something. I always considered Gene a friend. I still do, even though I know he often ridicules me privately. I just shrug it off because he does that to most people he knows." Humphrey's demeanor saddened as he continued. "A Minneapolis banker who's supported both of us once told me his theory of Gene's beneath-the-surface resentment. He said that as a rookie congressman, and then as the junior senator from Minnesota, he's had to live in my shadow since he came to Washington. He said Gene feels like every time he starts to climb the ladder, he finds my ass staring him in the face."[12]

"Any guesses about the president's temperament this morning?" Ted asked. Humphrey sighed as he snapped shut his briefcase and then slid on his suit jacket.

"Knowing him," Humphrey said, "I'm not sure whether I should bring you to the briefing, or just bring a bottle of Anacin. He's going to be unhappy—which means everyone else will end up unhappy. Lyndon's a man of intense ego who's like the second husband of a demanding wife. He's overly sensitive to every nuance, he's easily angered by real or imaginary slights, and he tries constantly to erase any memories that might lead to negative comparisons."[13] Shaking his head in resignation as he picked up his briefcase and headed out the door, Humphrey added a final thought:

"To think that in '64 I *asked* to be Lyndon's goddamn punching bag."

Eugene McCarthy for president campaign newsletter, Vol. I, No. 2, February 6, 1968 (Author's collection)

CHAPTER 6

"WELCOME TO THE LABORATORY, Dr. Frankenstein: come to inspect your creation?"

A cloud of cigarette smoke surrounded the face of Curtis Gans as he greeted his friend Allard Lowenstein, who stood in Curt's office doorway at the Concord, New Hampshire, McCarthy for President headquarters.[1] Curt, the campaign's compulsive chain-smoking and Pepsi-Cola drinking operations director, looked older than his thirty years. The small, thin, serious man with a skinny black tie drooping from his rumpled white shirt looked like he hadn't slept in days because, basically, he hadn't. Curt butted out his Tareyton into a stub-filled Styrofoam cup resting on his makeshift desk—a folding plastic banquet table covered in papers, maps, file folders, and notepads. He reached across the table to shake hands with his visitor, asking, "When did you get in town, Al?"

"Last night. I drove up from New York and stayed in Bedford. I've come to investigate the complaints for myself." As Al spoke, his eyes swept the building interior that until recently served as an abandoned electrical parts warehouse.² Randomly placed wooden boards covered gaps in the floor, and exposed plumbing pipes shared the ceiling space with bare lightbulbs hanging from duct-taped cords. Stacks of campaign brochure boxes and crisscrossing extension cords covered the cavernous area, along with more folding tables underneath telephones and piles of papers. A dozen buckets of water lining the perimeter substituted for fire extinguishers. Noticing the irregularly placed McCarthy campaign posters taped to the walls, Al asked, "Who hung those—a volunteer with strabismus?"³

"People think we aligned those posters on the wall as some sort of *op art* expression. Actually, we hung them wherever we needed to cover holes in the walls. If you think this place is a dump now, you should've seen it when we moved in last weekend. Trash piled all over the place, rats, missing floorboards, but it was cheap. Come on, I'll introduce you to the staff and volunteers."

"*Staff?* Where did you guys get money for staff?"

"Who said anything about paid staff? If someone helps during the week, they're staff. If they only show up on weekends, they're a volunteer. A guy who volunteers on Thursday is staff by Friday and a team leader by Saturday. Any questions?"⁴

Al watched the dozen scruffy college-aged kids moving about the headquarters, all with purpose, and none with any apparent direction. "No, I think that covers it."

While Al said a quick hello to the workers, Curt grabbed his overcoat, told a tall kid with a beard to keep an eye on things, and then the two men walked a half block to the Capitol Diner on South Main Street, where they settled into a corner booth.

"Would you like coffee or Sanka?" the smiling young waitress asked Curt.

"Sanka? Sweetheart, I need so much caffeine that you should just pour the pot straight down my throat." After ordering, Curt lit another cigarette and noted that day's milestone. "Happy anniversary," he told

Al. "McCarthy declared for president on November 30th. Now it's January 30th. This fiasco you created is officially two months old."

"Give me the low-down," Al said solemnly as he produced a pen and opened his notepad. "I'll need it as ammo when Blair Clark and I have it out with Gene tonight."

"Let's start with this. He's running for president, but he won't say he *wants* to be president! What's this about him only *willing* to be president?"

"Don't worry. Blair got him to knock that off. He's saying he wants the job now."

"Great—he wants the job now. But if that's true, why did he wait so long to file for the primary here? New Hampshire votes in forty-one days. We're trying to depose a sitting president and organize a revolution from scratch, and we just got the go-ahead to open a headquarters last week."

Al groaned. "Gene hesitated about New Hampshire for one reason— Bobby Kennedy. When Gene told Bobby he was going to run, Bobby advised him to stay out of the Massachusetts primary and instead challenge Johnson in New Hampshire. Bobby said that Massachusetts is a heavily Democratic state, where the Party could churn out LBJ votes. Since New Hampshire is conservative and Republican, Bobby said the Democratic infrastructure is weaker, so Gene stood a better chance here. Actually, that was great advice, but because it came from Kennedy, Gene didn't trust it. He figured Bobby wanted to talk him out of competing on his family's turf and instead get us to be the guinea pig in a GOP state."[5]

"How did you finally bring Gene around?"

"Blair Clark did it. For a guy who's not political, he did a hell of a job. Blair prepared a memo laying out all the reasons for Gene to challenge Johnson in New Hampshire. Blair argued that Gene had nothing to lose, since the guy chairing LBJ's campaign here, Senator McIntyre, keeps telling the press LBJ's going to clobber us. McIntyre's predicting Gene won't get 5,000 votes statewide. With such low expectations, Blair argued we'll claim victory with any showing above that. Also, since Gene's the underdog, if lightning did strike, New Hampshire could have national repercussions."[6]

Curt removed his cigarette long enough to take a gulp of coffee. "That's all great strategy, but have you actually campaigned with this guy? He's been running for president for two months, but he never showed up in New Hampshire until last week. When he did get here, he acted with such indifference about the campaign that it embarrassed everyone and rattled staff morale."

"What do you mean?"

"How much time do you have? For instance, on his first swing through the state, we outdid ourselves setting up appearances for him. Then he rolled in and started canceling events arbitrarily and at the last minute. No reason—he just didn't feel like doing them. We had a huge audience at a high school auditorium one night waiting to hear his advertised speech. On the way there, he changed his mind about going, so he told the driver to take him back to the hotel.[7] The next day we had a packed schedule. I called the room that morning to say the car would be there in ten minutes. He was gone—he left a message saying he wanted all events canceled—he found out there was a monastery nearby, so he decided to spend the day *meditating* there!"[8]

Curt wasn't finished: "The next day, we had a meet-and-greet scheduled with local bigwigs. Before the event, I told him not to screw around—he *had* to attend. These were important business and civic leaders interested in supporting him. Anyway, when we arrived, things looked great, and over a hundred people showed up. Gene walked in and shook a few hands. Then he turned to me: 'Okay,' he said, 'I'm bored now.' Instead of greeting people, he walked past everyone and sat at the bar until the room emptied.[9] Another time we brought in some local VIPs to see him, and Gene told a volunteer to meet with them—he wanted to talk about poetry with some local professor. A week ago, he refused to walk twenty feet to the outer office to thank a doctor who donated ten grand to the campaign. When I told him he *had* to thank the guy, he said the doc wasn't giving the money to him—he was giving it to the cause, so he shouldn't expect any personal thanks."[10]

Al started to speak, but Curt cut him off. "I'm not done. Keep writing. Last Saturday, Sy Hersh[11] booked him for *Meet the Press* the following day. After sending out press releases, Gene canceled the appearance Sunday morning because—are you ready for this?—he wasn't the lead interview! Sy and I didn't tell staff because we feared a rebellion."[12]

"You're killing me," Al said in exasperation as he rubbed his forehead.

Curt's facial muscles tightened. "Since Gene got here, I've watched him closely. His quirky style, that whole aloofness thing, it actually has a kind of bizarre appeal. It comes off as some sort of mysterious integrity. When he's on, he's articulate and elegant, but there are all these downsides. He has more moods than a menopausal woman. Whenever he feels like indulging those moods, he expects everyone else to indulge them, too. He's so indifferent about the campaign that when reporters *do* cover him, they don't take him seriously as a candidate. Since he announced, he scheduled just ten days on the ground in New Hampshire, and that was *before* all his cancellations.[13] That 'I'm only *willing* to be president' thing—we all thought it was some kind of Midwestern modesty, right? It's not. I think he means it. He's just 'willing' to be president, and if the country's not demanding his leadership, then fuck 'em."[14]

With each additional protest levied, an increasingly pained look came over Al. "Listen," Curt said in a softened voice, "I'm with you in this to the bitter end, but we're saddled with a candidate who wants to sit above the fray and observe it all with some kind of intellectual curiosity. Meanwhile, the wheels are coming off the cart up here."[15]

"This is worse than I expected," Al said as he finished scribbling. Closing his notebook, he leaned across the booth and whispered a confidence. "Once the alarm bells started ringing about Gene's performance on the campaign trail, I began some back-door discussions with Bobby Kennedy."

"I thought you two were on the outs after your blow-up a few months ago?"

"That's smoothed over. Anyway, we talk, but it's awkward because I don't want to cross any ethical lines. I'm loyal to Gene, but let's face it—we're getting killed. The other day I met Bobby at his New York apartment, and he helped me draft a series of 'conditions' for McCarthy if he wants my continued help. I'm going to confront Gene tonight and tell him that if he doesn't make substantial changes in his attitude and effort, then my allegiance to him may shift to another candidate."[16]

"Unless that other candidate is Kennedy, it won't mean anything, and at this stage it's probably too late even for him."

"Bobby doesn't think it's too late. He's had buyer's remorse since Gene got in. Now, with Gene collapsing, Bobby's worried there'll be no meaningful antiwar alternative to Johnson in Chicago. He said if he got just one more endorsement from a major Democrat, he'd jump in."

"For Christ's sake, Al, give up on Kennedy! There's always one last condition with that guy. He's like the chick in high school that keeps hinting she wants to put out, but no matter how many times you take her to the drive-in, you always go home with your dick in your hands. By the way, did you hear that some deep-pocket supporters here opened a 'Write in Robert Kennedy' headquarters down the street from us? They had donations, volunteers, precincts mapped out, direct mail, and they started running radio ads. A few days ago, Ted Sorensen flew up here and personally told them to shut down the operation."

"Where did you hear this?"

"I heard it from them! Once they closed their office, all of Bobby's people walked down the street—every single one of them—and volunteered to help us."[17]

Al checked the time. "I'd better get going," he said. "I want to sit down with Blair and go over all of this before we see Gene tonight. I'd like to have a united front when I present my conditions."

Curt nodded. "Okay, Al, You know, we've come a long way from organizing college sit-ins, but unless something changes *drastically*, Johnson's going to destroy us."

As the two young men trudged through the snow back to the

headquarters, they had no idea that in the next few weeks, things *would* change drastically—and those changes had nothing to do with overhauling the personality and energy level of Senator Eugene McCarthy.

Obverse and reverse of a campaign wooden nickel promoting President Lyndon Johnson's reelection from the March 1968 New Hampshire presidential primary (Author's collection).

CHAPTER 7

"WELL, TILLIE, when the hell are we gonna get some dinner?"

As the ending credits rolled in the darkened White House theater, Lyndon Johnson turned in his overstuffed chair and told his guests seated nearby, "That's the last scene Spencer Tracy ever filmed. He died two weeks later." LBJ wasn't much of a movie fan, but since Columbia Pictures released "Guess Who's Coming to Dinner" a couple of months earlier, it became a personal favorite—this was the third time he had screened it.[1]

Johnson and the invited members of the Texas congressional delegation retired to the library for cocktails and cigars.[2] Congressman George Mahon, who was already a congressional veteran in 1937 when the twenty-eight-year-old LBJ first won election to the House, was pleased to see his old friend relaxing after a tough few months. Eugene McCarthy's challenge last November was an irritation, but serious international problems developed later. In late January, North and South Vietnam had agreed to a ceasefire so both sides could celebrate "Tet," the Vietnamese new year. On January 31, the day of the truce, Northern communist troops launched a massive sneak attack on over 100 South Vietnamese cities, and Vietcong guerillas succeeded in blasting their way into the US Embassy compound in Saigon. Although the Tet assault took US and South Vietnamese forces by surprise, they repelled it in a few weeks with relative ease, and inflicted heavy enemy casualties in retaliation. Now, over a month since turning back the offensive, LBJ's mood was light.

"Mr. President, I assume your cheerfulness is aided by the new Gallup poll," Mahon said.

"That helped, George. I dropped twelve points after Tet—down to 35 percent approval. Now we're back to where we were before those bastards hit us."[3]

"With next week's primary, are those same high numbers holding for you in New Hampshire, too?"

LBJ's relaxed smile turned sly. "They're even better," he confided. "Governor King up there tells me that his polls show two-thirds of all New Hampshire Democrats support me—and I'm not even on the ballot. McCarthy's around 11 percent.[4] Hell, four years ago I took 64 percent of the vote up there against Goldwater. This year will be the same. I've got the governor, the Democratic senator, the big city mayors, the labor unions, and the entire state Party organization that goes with them. McCarthy's got his pot-smoking college kids and their hippie professors—and all those assholes are too busy practicing free love with each other to vote."

When the laughter settled, one of only two Republicans in the state's congressional delegation, freshman Congressman George Bush, asked the political question on everyone's mind. "Mr. President, how come you didn't file for the New Hampshire primary?"

LBJ sipped his Cutty Sark before answering.[5] "Once Bobby Kennedy refused to run, I didn't bother filing because there was no contest. After McCarthy jumped in at the last minute, I didn't want to give his challenge credibility. He's going nowhere anyway. After we squash him next week, he can go back to writing his poetry.[6] Evans and Novak said in their column the other day that McCarthy's not just facing defeat—he's facing annihilation.[7] Yesterday I got a call from John Roche—he's the president of Americans for Democratic Action. Roche said that they've started the rumor that we sent Gene there to run against me only to get his ass kicked and show how strong I am—Roche said the story's depressing Gene's troops."[8]

"Since I'm the odd man out," Bush said, "I don't pretend to understand Democratic strategy. How come you're running a write-in campaign? Why not just ignore McCarthy?"

"Well, we're not involved in the write-in effort. That's all Governor King's doing. Since I'm not on the ballot and the press is ignoring McCarthy, King didn't like all the media attention focusing on your Republican primary fight up there between Nixon and Romney. The state Party leaders wanted to generate enthusiasm for rank-and-file Democrats, so they started this write-in."[9]

Reaching into his pocket, LBJ retrieved a three-part perforated card, captioned, "N.H. Democrats are 90,000 Strong." The first part, designed for the voter to fill in and sign, was a pledge to write in Johnson's name on the March 12 primary ballot. The center section contained the same pledge and personal information to forward directly to the White House, and the third portion contained the pledge and voter data for state Party records. Showing the card to his guests, LBJ added, "Governor King is making sure every state employee gets and returns one of these.[10] The write-in headquarters in Manchester is also distributing them to every registered Democratic voter in the state. King tells me the pledges are cascading in."

Three-part card pledge card issued by the New Hampshire Democratic Party in support of President Lyndon Johnson in the state's March 12, 1968, primary (Author's collection)

As the guests examined the tripartite card, LBJ winked and added, "Besides, I have another ace in the hole. King's very motivated to collect these pledges. His term as governor ends this year, and he's let me know he'd like to finish out his career as a federal judge. That's another reason why I'm not worried about New Hampshire next week."[11]

"After you kill off McCarthy," asked Congressman Wright Patman, "do you have any worries about Kennedy jumping in at the last minute?" Usually, the mere mention of RFK's name in a private setting with friends elicited a grimace, if not a tirade, from the president. This time Johnson appeared almost blasé at the idea that the despised senator might challenge him.

"No," LBJ said confidently. "Bobby won't commit political suicide by splitting the Party. If he did, Democrats would blame him forever if a Republican wins the White House. Besides, even if he got in now, who'd support him? One day he's blasting my Vietnam policies as immoral, and then the next day he's shitting on McCarthy and telling reporters he'll support me for reelection. Bobby's managed to piss off the Party regulars who stand with me as well as his own people—the peaceniks, the libs, the Negroes, the college crowd. They feel he's betrayed them. If he runs, he's got nobody left besides his snot-nosed Harvard pals."[12]

White House ushers entered the library and stationed themselves around the room, a subtle signal to wrap up the reception. As LBJ rose from his chair, he made a final point. "We've hired our pollsters and we're organizing in the key states. The nomination is sewn up—nobody can take it away from me. McCarthy's got the college kids, but I've got the delegates."[13]

As he shook hands and said goodnight to everyone, LBJ threw his arm around George Bush's shoulder. "George," he told the young congressman, "when you see your pal Dick Nixon, tell him that in November he'll be facing the heavyweight champ, not some glass-jawed tomato can!"*

"Good night, boys," the president called as he headed out the door. "Now, get back to the Hill—and pass my goddamn housing legislation!"

---

*   *Tomato can* is a boxing idiom used to describe an unskilled opponent who is easy to defeat.

1968 anti-Lyndon Johnson campaign button promoting Eugene McCarthy's insurgent race against the incumbent president (Author's collection)

CHAPTER 8

"JESUS—THIS PLACE LOOKS LIKE FAO SCHWARZ on Christmas Eve. Last month it was a morgue. What happened?"

The crush of bodies and mad activity inside McCarthy's Concord headquarters left national campaign manager Blair Clark almost speechless. Working out of the Washington campaign office, Blair hadn't visited since mid-February, because organizing a fifty-state operation didn't leave much time for micromanaging individual segments of the effort. Now, making the rounds in New Hampshire a week before the primary, he wasn't prepared for the mob scene he witnessed.

Curtis Gans answered his boss. "What happened? Tet and a pledge card happened. Come on inside." The two men squeezed their way into Curt's office and closed the door, which muffled the outside cacophony only slightly. Sitting on folding chairs, Curt poured a cup of lukewarm coffee for Blair, and then explained the unrelated phenomena that jumpstarted their efforts. "LBJ and the generals have been telling Americans for the last year that we're on the verge of victory in Vietnam. Before Tet, most Americans believed it. After Tet, people were shocked that our 'defeated' enemy could launch such widespread attacks—even hitting our embassy.[1] After Tet, when LBJ said that he might call up 200,000 more troops on top of the 500,000 already there, this added to the psychological impact. For the first time, people feel LBJ and the Pentagon are full of shit, and they're finally listening when we say the government's been lying to them about Vietnam.[2]

"The last time you visited," Curt continued, "we were lucky to snag help from handfuls of college kids, but it was hit-and-miss.[3] Now, we're getting thousands of them hitchhiking or taking Greyhound buses here, and they're coming from almost every state—even California.[4] It's happening in the other offices, too—Manchester, Nashua—all of them. This place is so packed now that I should worry about the fire captain shutting us down, but I know he won't."

"Why not?"

"Because his wife and two daughters are outside addressing envelopes!"

Curt led Blair up a flight of stairs to another floor bustling with activity. Lined along the walls were scores of sleeping bags, pillows, and blankets. Portable typewriters and unfinished term papers shared space on tables with stacks of campaign literature and precinct kits.[5] "We've got four staffers that do no voter outreach," Curt said. "They spend all their time looking for church basements, shelters, back rooms of businesses, and spare bedrooms and couches in supporters' homes—any place our volunteers can bunk for the night. We're estimating that 10,000 kids have come to help around the state. The reporters are calling it 'The Children's Crusade.'"[6]

Blair surveyed the scene and shook his head. "They don't look like typical college students—they look like Disneyland employees. Clean cut boys—white shirts and ties, and the girls all look like Shelley Fabares. Where did you recruit these kids, BYU?"

"Come to the basement—you won't believe this." Curt led Blair down two flights of stairs into the enormous "Map Room." Precinct maps covered every wall, with each one marked in various ink configurations and with scores of colored pins sticking in them. Most of the students working the maps were long-haired and shaggy. In the corner, a line of similarly ungroomed youths waited for their turn with the volunteer barber giving free haircuts.

"*Get Clean for Gene!*" Curt said. "That's their motto. The word's already out. Guys with long hair and beards are shaving and visiting barbershops before boarding the buses for New Hampshire. The girls leave behind their miniskirts and see-through T-shirts. When our volunteers knock on doors and hand out literature, we want them looking wholesome. The voters up here love it. They invite the kids in for tea, and then they sit around the kitchen table and chat. When our kids leave the house, they leave with half a dozen or more votes—the people that live there, and the friends and family of the people living there.

"We monitor this very closely," Curt emphasized. "When any buses arrive from New York, I stick those volunteers in the Map Room for office work, haircut or no haircut. I don't want some pushy Brooklyn or Jersey kid with an obnoxious accent irritating these dignified, reserved New Englanders. The ones we send out for voter contact are polite and well-mannered.[7] Also, when they unwind here at their Saturday late-night dance parties, we ban reporters. The last thing we need are stories about our nice kids smoking pot, drinking smuggled alcohol, or screwing each other on top of a stack of McCarthy posters."[8]

As the two men returned to Curt's office, Blair asked, "You said something about another reason for all this—a punch card?"

"It's not a punch card—it's a pledge card that Johnson's people have been shoving down the throats of every state worker and registered Democrat. We've gotten hundreds of calls complaining about them. People think the cards are actually the official ballots—they're even serial numbered. Voters resent having to sign them, provide their names and addresses, and then have copies sent directly to Johnson at the White House and to the state Party, where their people can track who's not playing ball. Governor King made it worse when he explained why he's using those cards. He told the press, 'It's time for New Hampshire Democrats to stand up and be counted for President Johnson, or be counted out.' Voters took that as a heavy-handed, Big Brother-type threat.

We photographed one of those cards, and then we printed posters and ran newspaper ads depicting it with the caption, 'Whatever Happened to the Secret Ballot?'[9] We've been telling voters that Senator McCarthy respects their right to vote in secret, and they don't need to pledge anything to us. We've gotten lots of favorable publicity, and thousands of these pledge cards have arrived at our offices with Johnson's name scratched out and McCarthy's written in. Gene's jumped on the issue, too. He's been telling voters not to let Johnson treat their votes like he treats his branded Texas cattle.[10] This pledge card fiasco was another unexpected gift to our campaign—compliments of Governor King."

"I'm overwhelmed, Curt. You and your team have done a great job."

"Sometimes I think my biggest asset to the campaign is that I'm the only guy here that's old enough to have a credit card, which means I rent the cars when we need them. Besides, it's not me—it's the volunteers. This morning, when I thanked a group of them for helping Gene, one of them corrected me. He said that the first time he stood for hours in freezing snow handing out literature, he realized that this stopped being Eugene McCarthy's campaign—it became *his* campaign, too."[11]

After taking a few gulps from a warm bottle of Pepsi, Curt continued the briefing. "Your talk with McCarthy helped tremendously. Gene's a much better candidate since you and Al Lowenstein chewed him out last month. Dick Goodwin's also been a huge boost since he arrived. Dick knows how to get the press to cover events, he keeps Gene focused, and because he has gravitas, Gene listens to him. Dick helps with other problems, too. For example, before he got here, we had an issue with Gene's poet-buddy Robert Lowell showing up, staying for days, and distracting the hell out of him."

"Hey, Lowell's my friend, too! He even dedicated a book of poetry to me."[12]

"Congratulations, but he's a pain in the ass. When Lowell's around, Gene won't do interviews or call donors. Instead, Gene sits around his hotel room at the Wayfarer BS'ing with Lowell while they rewrite *Omar Khayyam* into some goddamn comedic quatrain.[13] When I complained about it to Dick, he got volunteers to set up book signings and poetry readings for Lowell on the opposite side of the state just to get him out of our hair."

"I'm glad to hear Dick's been helpful," Blair said. "We caught hell from the D.C. staff when Gene brought him on board. All of them thought Goodwin was Bobby's spy, and most of them *still* think it."

"When you get back to Washington tomorrow, tell them I said that if Dick Goodwin's a spy, I'll call Bobby Kennedy personally and ask him to send us a few more moles."

Richard "Dick" Goodwin was indeed an asset to McCarthy's New Hampshire campaign, and he was no spy for Robert Kennedy. However, he was Bobby's friend—a very close friend.

Dick, thirty-six, was a Harvard Law School graduate who clerked for US Supreme Court Justice Felix Frankfurter before becoming a speechwriter for Senator John F. Kennedy. As president, JFK appointed him as assistant special counsel and later deputy assistant secretary of state. Following Dallas, he remained at the White House as a speechwriter and special assistant to President Johnson. After voicing his opposition to LBJ's Vietnam policies, Dick left the administration in 1966 and joined the antiwar movement.

Dick was one of the few people who saw LBJ as vulnerable in 1968, and he kept urging Kennedy to challenge Johnson. After vacillating for months, in early January Bobby called together Dick and a few other close advisers. "The support just isn't there," Bobby told them. "People will think it's a personal vendetta between Johnson and me, not the war. So, I've decided I'm not going to do it."[14] Later that day, when they were alone, Dick told Bobby that if he wasn't running, Dick wanted to go to New Hampshire and help the only antiwar alternative—Eugene McCarthy.

"That would be helpful," RFK replied.

With Bobby's ambiguous blessing, Dick packed a suitcase, put a typewriter in his car trunk, drove all night to New Hampshire, and joined the Children's Crusade.[15]

One week before the New Hampshire primary, Dick Goodwin sat in his motel room late at night putting the final touches on a press release when the front desk put through a telephone call.

"Hi, stranger," Bobby Kennedy said. "How's it going?"

"Geez, I thought you were boycotting me. I haven't heard from you since I joined the campaign two months ago. How've you been?"

"I'm fine. I just wanted to let you know that I'm still considering getting into this thing, and I'd like McCarthy to know this now, so he doesn't think my decision has any relationship to whatever happens up there next week." Surprised by this revelation, Dick didn't know what to say, so he said nothing. Getting no response, Bobby continued. "I want you to pass along this message to McCarthy for me."

"I can't do that. I can't act as your messenger. I'm working for McCarthy now. I'm committed to him and he trusts me. It's not just him, either. It's all these kids—I love them, and I'm not giving them any reason to think I'm your agent. I've worked my ass off for McCarthy, and I need to keep my relationship pure." Pausing to process Kennedy's request, Dick continued, "What I will do is what any good staffer would do under similar circumstances. I'll tell Gene that you called and left a message for him, but that's it."

"That's fair," said Bobby, who then changed topics. "So, how do you think McCarthy will do next week? In D.C. the betting is no more than 10 or 15 percent, but I keep hearing stories about kids blanketing the state for him. What's your read?"

"We're not going to win, but we're going to do a hell of a lot better than 15 percent. I wouldn't be surprised if we hit as high as forty."

After a long pause Bobby asked, "What if I had run?"

"You'd have won—60 percent to Johnson's 40 percent. I've been telling you for a year that Johnson was beatable. I wish you had listened to me. Now it's too late. When the polls close next week, it's going to be McCarthy's night, not LBJ's—and not yours, either."

"It shouldn't be this way," Bobby grumbled.

"No, it shouldn't. These kids should be your kids. This army should be your army. Now you're losing them, and when they're gone they may be gone forever. You've sat as a spectator watching the battle lines form." While Dick spoke, he picked up his copy of the *Village Voice* and opened it to the editorial page. "Did you see Jules Feiffer's cartoon?"

"No."

"Feiffer caricatured 'The Bobby Twins'—Good Bobby and Bad Bobby—debating on television. Good Bobby attacks LBJ, saying we're killing innocent women and kids in Vietnam, and questions the morality of our actions there. Bad Bobby replies that he will support LBJ as the Democratic nominee, which, by the way, you're *still* saying publicly. Good Bobby ends the debate by telling Bad Bobby, 'We're going to have a difficult time explaining this to ourselves.' These kids aren't stupid, and they're sick of you telling the press that you'll probably support Johnson over McCarthy. They've started salting our rallies with protest signs, and they're not protesting Johnson, they're protesting you. The signs say things like, 'BOBBY KENNEDY: HAWK, DOVE, OR CHICKEN?' That's how they view your political schizophrenia."

Bobby turned away from the telephone and spoke to someone nearby. "Dick says I would have won. He's right." With that, Bobby hung up the phone abruptly.[16]

Later that night, Dick met with McCarthy and relayed Kennedy's entire message. When he finished, Gene said, "Why don't you tell Kennedy that I only want one term? Let him support me in '68, and after that he can have it in 1972."

"Senator, you might feel that way now, but if you win, you won't feel that way later. There's *always* much more to do after a single term, so I won't tell him that, even if you think you believe it."

"I really do feel that way. I think the presidency should be a one-term proposition. Call him and tell him what I said."

The next morning, McCarthy asked if Goodwin had passed along his "one-term" message to Kennedy.

"I called him before breakfast and told him what you said."

"What was his response?"

"It wasn't a word. He just groaned in disbelief."[17]

Six days later, Bobby called and awoke Dick to get his opinion on how things looked for tomorrow's New Hampshire vote. In his fatigue and euphoria, Dick forgot his audience temporarily and gushed about McCarthy's chances. "It's unbelievable! Forget what these pollsters are saying—tomorrow night we're going to make history and change the direction of this country!"

Bristling at Dick's unappreciated enthusiasm, Kennedy asked pointedly, "Well, what do I do now?"

The speechwriter's momentary elation crashed. "For Christ's sake, Bobby. You're putting me in a hell of a box. You're squeezing me between my loyalty to the campaign and my longstanding friendship with you. Look—you know I think you're far more qualified than Gene to be president, but that's not the point. *What should I do now?*—I don't know what you should do now, but I will tell you this. After tomorrow, you can't be neutral anymore. You could be neutral only when McCarthy wasn't a serious candidate. By tomorrow, he will be. That's going to leave you with just two choices—run or endorse him."

"What happens if I endorse McCarthy?"

"He'll win in November."

"How can I endorse a guy that I think is totally unfit to be president? That's not just my opinion. Have you read what Governor King and Senator McIntyre have been saying about McCarthy all over New Hampshire—that he's a tool of the Vietcong?"

Now it was Dick's turn to groan. "Forget King and McIntyre—they're LBJ hacks. Besides, I think the voters up here resent their attacks on McCarthy's patriotism. You have nothing to lose by endorsing McCarthy. If you're right and he really can't go the distance, his campaign will implode. If you endorse him, his supporters will rush into your arms when that happens."

A long silence hung in the air before Bobby responded. "I just can't bring myself to tell people I'd really like to see Eugene McCarthy become president of the United States." After another pause, Bobby said softly, "I think I blew it," and then he hung up the telephone—again.[18]

When Dick heard the phone click, followed by a dial tone, he shook his head sadly before speaking into the dead line:

"See ya', Bobby."

An hour later, as a dejected Dick Goodwin tossed sleeplessly in his motel bed, a historic tradition was taking place 170 miles away. The seven registered voters of Dixville Notch, New Hampshire, lined up at their precinct and, at 12:01 a.m., they became the first Americans in 1968 to cast a vote for the next president of the United States.

Campaign bumper sticker promoting President Lyndon Johnson in the March 1968 New Hampshire presidential primary (Author's collection)

CHAPTER 9

IF THE SHREWDEST POLITICAL MIND IN WASHINGTON didn't see it coming, nobody saw it coming.

And Lyndon Johnson didn't see it coming.

"Get me George Christian.* And hurry—I'm almost at the hotel."

"Yes, Mr. President."

As the motorcade racing up Seventeenth Street turned onto Connecticut Avenue, the unhappy passenger on the limousine's car phone wanted an update on the New Hampshire vote before reaching his destination. When he received the initial reports before leaving the White House at 9 p.m., Eugene McCarthy was running unexpectedly well. Knowing that the press covering tonight's speech to the Veterans of Foreign Wars convention would expect a statement, Johnson hoped those initial projections were an aberration. When the White House operator connected Christian, LBJ knew from his press secretary's tone that McCarthy's numbers were holding.

"Mr. President, with almost half the precincts in, you lead with 50 percent to McCarthy's 40."

---

*   George Christian (1927-2002) was White House press secretary to President Lyndon B. Johnson from 1966-1969.

49

"Son-of-a-bitch," the president sputtered. "Well, what are the networks saying?"

"CBS, ABC, and NBC are all treating it like David and Goliath. They're reminding everyone that Governor King and Senator McIntyre boasted just this weekend that you'd beat McCarthy three-to-one—"

Johnson interrupted angrily, "I thought we told those two jackasses last month to back off from those predictions."

"We did, sir. Before we talked to them, they were projecting you'd beat McCarthy ten-to-one."[1]

"I'm passing DuPont Circle, so I only have a few minutes before I arrive. I'm penciling into my speech a couple of comments about the primary. There's no time to get something from Hardesty's shop.** You can polish it later for the press release. Meanwhile, when I leave the hotel, I want to talk to King. Have him available in half an hour."

"Yes, sir. I'll call him now."

Ten minutes later, Johnson received a hero's welcome when he appeared before the VFW in the ballroom of the Sheraton Park Hotel. Standing at the lectern and surveying the cheering crowd, he felt an unexpected emotional surge over the great ovation given him by those who sacrificed for freedom and understood the morality of fighting evil. Why couldn't those fainthearted New Hampshire voters see what these patriots see? Waving them to silence, and then putting on a game face, LBJ tried to marginalize his pending humiliation by joking about it. "New Hampshire primaries are unique in politics. It's the only place where candidates can claim 20 percent is a landslide, and 40 percent is a mandate, and 60 percent is unanimous!"[2] The supportive audience howled with laughter, but LBJ knew that when the laughter died in that ballroom, serious political implications from New Hampshire would settle in.

**   Robert L. Hardesty (1931-2013) was an LBJ speechwriter and aide from 1965 to 1973. Emily Langer, Robert L. Hardesty, "Speechwriter for President Lyndon B. Johnson, Dies at 82" *Washington Post*, July 9, 2013, https://www.washingtonpost.com/national/robert-l-hardesty-speechwriter-for-president-lyndon-b-johnson-dies-at-82/2013/07/09/907f1834-e8b8-11e2-8f22-de4bd2a2bd39_story.html.

On the ride back to the White House, LBJ again called Christian for the final figures before speaking to King. "Mr. President, you won the primary. That's no surprise, but you took 48 percent to McCarthy's 42½ percent. Because of the state's bizarre delegate-selection process, since your name wasn't on the official ballot, even though you outpolled McCarthy, he took twenty of the twenty-four national convention delegates."[3]

"You're telling me I couldn't clear 50 percent of Democrats in one of the most pro-Vietnam War states in America?" Johnson shouted.[4]

"Yes, sir."

Then, swallowing hard, Christian added to the gloomy news. "There's one more thing you should know, because the press is talking about it already. You beat McCarthy by about 4,000 votes in the Democratic primary, but that's not counting the Republican and independent crossover votes. With those included, he came within about 200 votes of outpolling you statewide."[5]

The silence following that revelation was so long that Christian checked to see if LBJ was still on the line: "Mr. President, are you there?"

After another uncomfortable pause, LBJ murmured angrily, *"Get me King."*

A few moments later, an apologetic Governor King tried to salve the wound. "Mr. President, I'm so sorry. I just wish I could—"

Johnson cut off the governor. "John, what the hell happened up there?"

"Sir, please don't feel like the outcome was a repudiation of your policies. I think it was more of an expression of frustration over Vietnam. Our people just didn't understand why we aren't doing better over there."[6]

"I thought it was your job to *make* them understand!" Johnson shouted angrily.

"I accept responsibility for this, but this vote shouldn't cause alarm. Why not just take the position that the verdict of a handful of Democrats in a state that is over two-to-one Republican is an insignificant blip?"

"I can't treat it as insignificant when every reporter and columnist in

America will be saying tomorrow morning that it *is* significant. They're already squealing that when I had to defend my Vietnam policies for the first time at the polls, I could barely manage 48 percent—from my own fucking Party! If an unknown like McCarthy could almost beat the president of the United States under these circumstances, what does that do to my ability to lead?"[7]

"But you still won the—"

"Goddamn it, John—I didn't win by enough! Don't you fucking understand? You and McIntyre started this write-in bullshit, and then you ran around and told people I'd win ten-to-one or three-to-one or whatever-the-hell-to-one you both kept saying. If this is victory, then it's a damned empty one. Every American voter thinks I lost."[8]

"Mr. President, please try and keep this in perspective. There will be over 2,500 delegates at the Democratic Convention. With only twenty-four New Hampshire delegates going to Chicago, this vote doesn't mean anything to the overall nominating process."

"It's not the delegates, it's the psychological impact. You've handed my enemies a crowbar to beat the shit out of me."

King felt on the verge of tears. "What can I say? It was all those kids.[9] We did a solid get-out-the-vote drive—state employees, union members, registered Democrats. Nobody took McCarthy seriously because he was *never* a serious candidate."[10]

"Well, he sure as hell is serious now. And because *you* didn't take him seriously, I now have a serious problem."[11]

"McCarthy can't defeat you. This was just a—"

"I'm not worried about McCarthy," Johnson barked, again cutting off King. "This isn't about McCarthy. It's about that other little prick who'll use this as a springboard."

"Mr. President, I'm so sorry. I hope that you can—"

Click.[12]

New Hampshire Governor John W. King's term ended nine months later.

He never became a federal judge.[13]

Lyndon Johnson wasn't the only unhappy person getting news from New Hampshire. At his Virginia home, Robert Kennedy watched the election returns with a handful of advisers. With each precinct reporting McCarthy's strong showing, Bobby looked more dejected. Once NBC projected McCarthy held Johnson under 50 percent, a brooding Bobby turned to Arthur Schlesinger, saying, "This means McCarthy will never withdraw for me now. He probably feels he gave me my chance to run, I didn't, and now he's earned the right to go forward. I can't blame him. He's done a great job opening up this race against Johnson."[14]

"Bob, I hate to beat a dead horse," Arthur replied, "but I think you should endorse McCarthy tomorrow morning. If you do, you'll wind up as the nominee. Gene couldn't win the nomination in a hundred years, but he's done you a huge favor in New Hampshire. He's shown everyone that Johnson is beatable. The Party wants a winner, and they'll turn to you in the end."

Growing frustrated, Bobby replied, "Forget it, Art. It would be hypocritical for me to go out and tell people I think McCarthy should be president. I just can't do it."[15]

Bobby got up and paced the room. "Goddamn it," he said, "I was the choice of everyone wanting a challenger to Johnson, *including* McCarthy. I didn't run because I didn't want to divide the Party. Well, after tonight, the Party's divided anyway." Turning to his team, Bobby snapped, "Have any of you considered what happens if I sit this out and then an unfit guy wins? Can you see McCarthy trying to negotiate with the Soviets? Am I the only one who feels a need to stop this train wreck? I think I have an obligation to get into this thing now."[16]

Ted Sorensen offered a calm perspective. "I agree with Arthur that McCarthy can't win, and that the Party wants to nominate someone who can beat the Republicans. The problem, Bob, is that your natural constituency has always been the college campuses, and in one month, you surrendered them to McCarthy. If you jump into this race now, thousands of jubilant McCarthy kids are going to feel that you stole their Christmas presents from under the tree. They'll feel—justifiably—that you let McCarthy take the big risk when Johnson looked unbeatable, and they'll be brutally unforgiving. If you run, what happens if Johnson wins the nomination because you divided the peace vote, and then he loses in November? Who gets the blame? Not McCarthy or LBJ. It's you."[17]

"There's a way to fix all of this," Bobby interjected solemnly. Turning to his press aide Jeff Solsby, Bobby told him, "Get me a number where I can reach McCarthy."

"You mean tomorrow?" Jeff asked.

"No, now."

Up in his victory suite at the Wayfarer Inn in Bedford, Gene McCarthy loosened his necktie. Relaxing with his senior staff, the elated candidate told them, "Do you know when I first realized I might have a chance up here? When I saw that I could go into any bar in Manchester, insult Lyndon Johnson, and nobody would punch me in the nose!"[18] After another toast, they turned their attention to the black-and-white television in the corner of the suite. As Walter Cronkite and other reporters analyzed Gene's earth-shaking New Hampshire performance, CBS News aired film of him addressing over 300 cheering volunteers an hour earlier in the downstairs Bedford Room.

"It was hot as hell in there," Dick Goodwin griped when he saw the replay. "I think those screaming kids sucked up all the air conditioning."

The footage cut to Gene smiling and waving to the crowd amid chants of "We want Gene! We want Gene!"[19] He told his boisterous fans that with this momentum they could go all the way to the nomination in Chicago, and "I will run as long as anyone wants me!" Then, after suggesting that his supporters take off a couple of days before heading to Wisconsin, McCarthy closed his speech: "People have remarked that this campaign has brought young people back into the system, but it's the other way around. Young people have brought the country back into the system."[20]

"That was your best line of the night," Goodwin told Gene as they watched the broadcast. "It was so good that I must have written it for you."

While everyone laughed, Blair Clark looked ahead optimistically. "People who've been discounting us for months will now start joining. After tonight, they won't worry about being part of some symbolic 5 percent fringe movement."[21]

While the jubilant team channel-surfed and compared the other networks' news coverage, the bedroom telephone rang at 12:30 a.m. Curtis Gans answered it. Moments later, he returned to the living room. "Senator, it's Kennedy calling."

"Well, this should be interesting," Gene said, and then he walked into the bedroom to take the call. Blair Clark turned off the TV so they could hear Gene's end of the conversation through the open door.

"Hello, Bobby."

"Congratulations, Gene. You did a great job tonight."

"Thanks. It was rough. I went through more factories in New Hampshire than I've been through in twenty years of politics. Anyway, is this merely a congratulatory call?"

"No. I also wanted to let you know I just put out a statement to the press saying that I'm reconsidering my position. It has nothing to do with tonight's results. I've been considering it for some time. I was afraid that a campaign against Johnson would focus on personalities. You ran a superb issue-oriented campaign, and I think I could help you and the cause by doing the same."

"Okay—thanks for the call, Bobby. Goodnight."

"Gene, wait—this doesn't mean we have to work against each other. Why don't we coordinate our campaigns? You enter some primaries, I'll enter others, and we can endorse each other in the races where one of us is on the ballot. Together, we can collect more anti-Johnson delegates than you will get alone. I'll even start—I'll announce I'm endorsing you in the upcoming Wisconsin primary."

"You can do what you want," Gene said stiffly. "I don't need your help in Wisconsin. Tell you what—I'll run my campaign, and you go run yours. Thanks again for the call. Goodnight."[22]

When Gene returned to the living room, there was no need for him to relay RFK's message. The look on the faces of his staff said it all.

"This is like one dog stealing another dog's bone," Blair said.[23]

"I can't believe that bastard!" Curt said angrily. "I suppose Kennedy's now running to end the war? When we needed an antiwar candidate to challenge Johnson, he refused. He kept saying Johnson was unbeatable. Now that you've taken the longshot and softened up Johnson, Kennedy wants to run—and he probably expects you to step aside for him."

"He *does* expect you to step aside," a pensive Dick Goodwin chimed in. "Bobby and his people never viewed you as a serious candidate, and they never believed you'd give LBJ any significant opposition. He's always assumed you'd fold your tent if he ever decided to enter the race."[24]

After Gene relayed—and mocked—Bobby's "dual campaign" proposal, he added, "That Bobby is a piece of work. But that's the way the Kennedys are. They never offer anything real."[25]

As McCarthy's staff continued fuming and cursing, RFK's close friend Dick Goodwin listened in silence. When Curt asked what he now planned to do, Dick rose from his seat, walked across the suite, opened the door, and stepped into the hallway. Looking back, he replied to Curt, "What am I going to do? I'm packing my bags, flying to D.C., and sleeping for an entire day."

"And," Dick added, "when I wake up, I'll catch the first plane to Wisconsin and join you there."[26]

Anti-Robert Kennedy campaign button deriding his late entry into the 1968 presidential race (Author's collection)

CHAPTER 10

THE DAY AFTER THE NEW HAMPSHIRE PRIMARY, Dick Goodwin checked into a Georgetown hotel and left instructions at the desk to hold his calls. Despite this directive, a ringing telephone awakened him from a dead sleep a couple of hours later.

"Hi, Dick, it's Fred Dutton. Welcome back."

"I told the clerk to turn off my phone."

"I know. That's why I told her I was the White House operator. Listen, the team is meeting tonight at Hickory Hill to discuss the next step. He wants you there."

"Goddamn it, Fred, we've had this discussion, and it always involves him calling my hotel room and waking me up, and then him hanging up on me. The answer is no. I'm leaving tomorrow for Wisconsin. I'm not stabbing McCarthy in the back by acting as a double agent and attending a Kennedy strategy session."

"Hang on, Dick."

Fred put his hand over the mouthpiece and, after a quick muffled discussion, Bobby Kennedy came on the line: "Well, it's decided. I'm definitely going to run."

"Okay."

"What do you mean, 'Okay'? I want you on board."

"We'll have to talk about that later, Bobby. I'll call you tomorrow."

"Why can't we talk now?"

"Because I'm going back to sleep."[1]

The next morning, as promised, Dick called Bobby before leaving for the airport. When RFK came on the line, Dick wasted no time with chitchat. "I'm leaving in a few minutes for Wisconsin to help McCarthy."

"That's not going to work. I need you with me."

"Look," Dick said in exasperation, "you're not even on the Wisconsin ballot. Let me go help McCarthy there. A defeat for Johnson is just as important to you as it is to him. Please don't do this to me. I made a commitment."

Sounding angry, Bobby snapped, "Fine—if that's your decision, then—"

Dick interrupted before Bobby could finish. "That *is* my decision. Anyway, I have a plane to catch. Good luck."[2] For once, Dick Goodwin did the hanging up.

Dick flipped off the light switch and tossed his room key on the coffee table before closing the door behind him. As he lugged his suitcase down the long hallway toward the elevator, he wondered if he had just closed the door on more than a hotel room.

During the thirty-six hours after New Hampshire, Robert Kennedy continued burning up the telephone lines. Besides stalking Dick Goodwin from hotel to hotel, he did the same to Eugene McCarthy. While Gene's plane flew back to Washington from Manchester, Bobby called Gene's Senate office repeatedly and left the same message each time: Senator Kennedy wants to see Senator McCarthy as soon as he arrives in D.C.

Later that afternoon, when Gene's plane landed at Washington National Airport, reporters converged on him at the Northeast Airlines gate and asked for his reaction to Bobby's possible entry. "I don't comment on rumors," he told the press. A few minutes later, after climbing into a waiting car, an aide handed him the multiple message slips from RFK.

"I guess the rumors just gained more traction," Gene quipped.

As soon as Gene arrived at the Capitol, Bobby called again and asked to meet him privately. To avoid reporters, Gene left his quarters in Room 411 of the Old Senate Office Building, took the elevator to the first floor, entered the senators-only gymnasium, slipped out a side door, and then backtracked to the fourth floor to meet Bobby in Room 431, the office of Senator Edward Kennedy. When Gene arrived, Bobby was alone and waiting.

Twenty minutes later Gene returned to his own office to brief Blair Clark on the short visit. "How did it go?" Blair asked.

Gene grinned. "Like the walrus and the carpenter, Senator Kennedy and I talked of many things, and none of them meant anything. Other than the brisk walk I got out of it, it was a waste of time. He repeated that New Hampshire has him 'reassessing' his situation. I told him I felt it unlikely that I could wrest the nomination from Johnson, but if he ran, neither of us would win—we would just divide the peace vote. I reiterated that if things broke my way and I won the presidency, I wanted only one term. I didn't promise to support him in '72 if he stayed out, and I didn't ask for his support now."

"What did he say?"

"Nothing. He just stared past me. Finally, I broke the silence and ended the meeting by telling him that any decision he made would have no impact on my continued campaign for the nomination."

"Did he say he was running?"

"He didn't say, and I didn't ask."

"Well? What do you think?"

"He's running."[3]

During these hectic few days, RFK did more than work the phones. He remained huddled at Hickory Hill planning a two-track strategy.

The first was to prepare for a late-entry presidential campaign. The second, involving Ted Sorensen and a high-level intermediary, went in a different direction. Bobby asked Ted to meet quietly with one of Washington's most respected figures, Clark Clifford, a senior adviser to presidents dating back to Truman and a longtime Kennedy family friend. One of the Democratic Party's "wise old men," Clifford was a rare Kennedy ally who also held the complete trust of LBJ: two months earlier, Johnson appointed Clifford as his new secretary of defense.

On Thursday, March 14, Ted met Clifford at his Pentagon office, where Ted delivered Bobby's confidential proposal that he wanted Clifford to pass along to LBJ. After reading the document, Clifford looked up and smiled. "Ted, please tell me this is a joke."

"No, Clark, it's not. I told Bobby that the president would never accept it, and if he did, he would emasculate his role as commander in chief. I also said the president would probably view the offer as a personal insult, but you know the Kennedys as well as anyone. Their father taught them, 'If you don't ask, you don't get.' So he's asking."

"Can you imagine Lyndon Johnson's reaction when I tell him, '*Mr. President, Bobby Kennedy just sent you a message that says that if you set up a special war commission, and if you acknowledge publicly that your Vietnam policies are a quote-failure-unquote, then Bobby won't run against you. Oh, and by the way, did I mention that this commission shall consist of ten people: Bobby Kennedy, and these eight other names on Bobby's attached list, all of whom oppose your Vietnam policies? The good news is that Bobby has no objection to you appointing whomever you like to the tenth slot.*' Come on, Ted, Bobby was an integral part of his brother's administration—he knows that no president could ever agree to such an idea."

"We all know what will be the president's likely response. I think this is an exercise in self-justification for Bob. I guess he wants to feel satisfied psychologically that he offered LBJ a chance to avoid a showdown."

Shaking his head, Clifford muttered, "I hate to contemplate being in the same room with Lyndon Johnson when he reads this."

"Bobby didn't say he expects the president to accept it. He just said that he hoped you'd deliver it. Will you?"

Two hours later, an aide escorted Secretary Clifford into the Oval Office. After Clifford explained his mission to the president, he handed LBJ the two-page proposal. Johnson sat at his desk and read its contents. His response was Texas raw and unambiguous. "Tell that little asshole to go fuck himself."

"Thank you, Mr. President."

Clifford left the Oval Office without further comment. Walking down the corridor to an unoccupied desk, he picked up the telephone and called the home of the proposal's author. "Bobby, I've just met with the president. Regrettably, he cannot accept your proposition. The president believes that no matter how we handled such arrangements, it would appear to the press and public to be a political deal. Further, he believes that setting such a precedent would be unwise. No commander in chief can surrender foreign policy authority to an outside commission. However, the president appreciates your input."

"Thanks, Clark, for carrying the water on this. I won't forget it." Chuckling, Bobby added, "I bet the president will keep 'appreciating my input' all night long—until Lady Bird washes out his mouth with soap!"*4

Bobby Kennedy was wrong. When LBJ retired that night to the family quarters, RFK was not the center of his focus. The president now concentrated his full attention on the senator representing Minnesota, not New York.

"Mr. Vice President, it's all hands on deck."

Postmaster General Larry O'Brien, handling President Johnson's reelection effort, was calling every senior Johnson administration member and relaying the president's personal marching orders: deploy to Wisconsin and crush Eugene McCarthy. At the top of his call list was an old friend, Vice President Hubert Humphrey.

---

*   "Lady Bird" Johnson (1912-2007), the wife of President Lyndon B. Johnson, was First Lady from 1963-1969.

"Hubert, we need to end this New Hampshire earthquake before it turns into a tsunami. If Kennedy jumps in, we don't want to fight a two-front war in the later primaries. After what happened in New Hampshire, we need to contest Wisconsin seriously and put McCarthy to bed for keeps. We've already dispatched experienced field organizers to every county in the state, and the DNC** is coordinating local and state Party operations. The president wants everyone on the ground there, and he said you're a key player in this."

"This is awful, Larry," HHH replied. "Gene and I have our differences, but we're friends and fellow Minnesotans. We came to Washington together. I've known him for over twenty years. What Lyndon's asking me to do is going to be hard as hell."

"The president said this is now war, and it's not one he started. He wants McCarthy finished after Wisconsin. The operations people will be in touch with your staff within the hour to work out the logistics. The president said he wants you to clear your schedule and to keep Air Force Two's gas tanks full. I'm sorry, Hubert. You know I'm just the messenger here."[5]

As the two men talked, Humphrey's office television broadcast a news bulletin. "Hang on, Larry," HHH said as he put aside the phone to listen. One minute later, he returned to the call. "Larry, the tsunami may have arrived."

"What do you mean?"

"NBC News is reporting that Bob Kennedy just called a press conference to announce he's running for president."[6]

**   *DNC*: the Democratic National Committee.

Campaign button promoting Senator Eugene McCarthy in the April 1968 Wisconsin presidential primary
(Author's collection)

CHAPTER 11

"MR. PRESIDENT, I have the final draft of your speech for tomorrow night."

George Christian entered the Cabinet Room carrying the document in a dark leather speech box emblazoned with a gold presidential seal. Lyndon Johnson, sitting alone, looked up from a stack of aerial photographs taken of the North Vietnamese province of Quang Ngai that lay scattered across the coffin-shaped table.[1]

"Are the networks lined up?" the president asked.

"Yes, sir, you go live tomorrow night at 9:00 p.m. Eastern from the Oval Office. We've clocked it at thirty-seven minutes."

"Did they gripe over the timing?"

"NBC and CBS complained about the speech airing on the eve of the Wisconsin primary. I told their VPs for programming that you're announcing major developments in Vietnam, and military priorities don't suspend for the political calendar. I did tease them that the news was big, and that—"

LBJ interrupted, snapping at his press secretary, "You didn't leak that I'm ordering a bombing halt, did you?"

"No, sir, just that you have a significant announcement relating to Vietnam and the peace process. Anyway, after they grumbled, they reserved the time for us. By the way, White House Communications has asked that we get them any last-minute revisions by three o'clock tomorrow, so they can include them on the teleprompter scroll."

LBJ took the folder from George, removed the document, scanned the text briefly, and then tossed it aside. "I'll go over this tonight and give you any changes in the morning," he said.

Curious over the president's political assessment, George asked, "Sir, do you think the speech *will* be helpful for Tuesday?"

LBJ removed his glasses and rubbed his eyes. "We'll see. There's a strong antiwar movement in Wisconsin, so I hope the speech will help. We've dumped tons of money there in the last two weeks—I'll bet we've outspent McCarthy ten-to-one. Since Bobby didn't announce in time to get on the ballot, his Wisconsin supporters will probably vote for McCarthy to embarrass me. We can't afford any more screw-ups, so I sent Larry O'Brien to Wisconsin a few days ago to oversee our effort."

"Have you heard from him?"

"He's flying back tonight and coming here directly." Standing up and stretching, LBJ continued with his prognosis. "You know, we made a mistake ignoring New Hampshire, but that's not happening in Wisconsin. We have every senior administration official with a pulse campaigning there, along with a dozen or more senators and congressmen. The *New York Times* poll had some good news for us this week, so I'm hopeful."[2]

"How do you see Kennedy's entry in all of this?"

"It's hard to say, but it's not nearly as troublesome as if he had jumped in months ago and consolidated the peace vote. Now he's divided it, and on top of that, Party regulars despise him for betraying me.[3] Yesterday Harry Truman called him a goddamn smart aleck, and even old Ike blasted him as untrustworthy and indecisive. *Indecisive*— coming from the general that led the D-Day invasion, that's probably the worst thing Ike can say about a man."[4]

Taking a sip of coffee, the president continued. "All of that's mild compared to what McCarthy's people say about him now. They think he's an immoral, selfish bastard trying to steal McCarthy's lunch money. Kennedy was too chicken to run himself, so he let McCarthy do the rock plowing. After McCarthy got lucky in New Hampshire, that self-entitled little shit pops up and wants McCarthy to step aside for him. Even those editorial writers in the Kennedys' hip pockets for years have brought out the long knives. Kempton's a perfect example—he's a longtime Kennedy pal, but in his new column he compared Bobby to the wartime coward who hides in the hills during the battle, and then comes down when the fighting's over to shoot the wounded."[5]

"Do you think it ever dawned on McCarthy or Kennedy what it's going to mean having Mayor Daley controlling every detail of the national convention in Chicago?"

"*Every* detail—from security to who gets hotel rooms, gallery tickets, and floor passes. Within minutes of Bobby announcing, Dick Daley went on TV and declared he was solid for me.[6] When I called Dick to thank him, he assured me he'd handle everything, so when Bobby and his mob of fawning ass-cracks limp into Chicago—if his campaign makes it that far—they may find themselves standing in the park while our people take care of business inside the hall. Bobby'll need Papa Joe's checkbook to pay people if he wants to hear anybody clap for him at the convention. In the meantime, we'll play the hand we're dealt—let Bobby and McCarthy fight each other for the hippie vote, while mainstream Democrats stand with me.[7] If McCarthy doesn't knock out Kennedy earlier, I'll settle his hash once and for all in Chicago."[8]

Two hours later, President Johnson sat alone in his second-floor study making his final edits for tomorrow night's Vietnam speech. A gentle knock on the door broke LBJ's concentration, and he looked up to see an usher escorting into the room a grim-faced Larry O'Brien.

"Welcome home, Larry—how does it look?"

"Mr. President," replied LBJ's campaign manager, "I'll give it to you with the bark off. We've done private tracking polls all week in key

Wisconsin precincts and counties. McCarthy's built a substantial lead. I've traveled up and down the state and back again for the last five days. Every Party leader I've met—all old friends of yours and mine—tell me it's hopeless. They think the primary's over, and that we can't stop McCarthy.[9] On Tuesday, he could hit as high as 60 percent."[10]

A stunned LBJ's stared gape-mouthed at his postmaster general before finding his voice. "Larry, I don't—how the hell can this be?"

"It's multiple problems. First, Wisconsin allows crossover voting. Since there's no real Republican contest there, we could see 200,000 GOP voters crossing over and voting for McCarthy just to embarrass and weaken you. Second, the state has about 100,000 draft-age college students, so they have a great motivation to support McCarthy.[11] Third, the peace movement is very strong there, so McCarthy's message resonates. It also helps McCarthy that he's represented a neighboring state for twenty years. In the end, we're up against the same army of kids that descended on New Hampshire. Now they've blanketed Wisconsin, and we can't come close to matching them in manpower, not to mention enthusiasm. I've never seen anything like it. They campaign with a religious fervor, and their religion is peace in Vietnam."

LBJ paced the floor while listening to this unexpected field report. When Larry finished, LBJ exploded in a rage. "Peace my ass! If those bastards in Congress—including that fucking McCarthy and Kennedy— wanted to end this war, they could end it *today*. Just defund all military operations and stop passing appropriation bills! Do you know why those cocksuckers won't? Because all they really want to do is attack me, but they also don't want anyone to say they turned their backs on our fighting boys."[12] Picking up his draft speech, LBJ passed it to Larry. "Have you read this? Won't it help?"

Larry looked down at the carpet while responding. "Mr. President, three days ago George couriered to me an early draft. We tested its theme in our final poll. It barely moved the needle. I hope I'm wrong, but I think the announcement tomorrow won't do much for Tuesday's vote."

LBJ banged his fist on the table in frustration. "None of these sonsabitches care that I'm ordering a bombing halt!" he fumed. "Why? Because they don't want peace. They just want to destroy me politically."

"Anything can happen in an election, sir. Maybe your speech won't *win* you votes, but it might suppress McCarthy voters' enthusiasm. Even if it doesn't, it's just one primary. You weren't on the ballot in New Hampshire, and we only moved into Wisconsin a couple of weeks ago to contest it. A loss there isn't fatal. We can explain it away, and in the end, it's our friends—not theirs—who will pick the convention delegates. We can weather any storm out of Wisconsin."

After a silent pause, a dejected LBJ shook his head sadly. "First it's McCarthy in New Hampshire, and now it's McCarthy in Wisconsin. And then, after Tuesday, I have Bobby Kennedy lying in wait for me. If McCarthy wins on Tuesday, those Kennedy people will be dancing in the streets, because they'll know their turn is coming."

Sinking back into his chair and staring ahead blankly, LBJ continued, "You know, I feel like I'm being chased on all sides by a giant stampede of out-of-control threats: Vietnam, inflation, rioting Negroes, demonstrating students, radical professors, and hysterical reporters. And behind it all is Bobby Kennedy invoking the sacred memory of his martyred brother to reclaim the throne—the same brother who selected *me* as his successor and whose policies I remained faithful to. I tell you, Larry, the situation is almost unbearable. After thirty-seven years of public service, I deserve better than being dumped alone in the middle of the plain to be trampled like this."[13]

"No matter what happens Tuesday, you'll still win the nomination, and you can lead our nation to peace and prosperity."

"Well, maybe I can, but if a president has to spend ten million dollars to win the re-nomination of his own goddamn Party, then it might be time for him and his Party to go their own ways. Maybe I *can't* get peace in Vietnam and be president, too."[14]

Larry couldn't believe the president's physical transformation. In five short minutes, he morphed from confident and strong leader to a haggard, exhausted old man.[15] Trying to buck up his friend, Larry walked over and rested a hand on his shoulder, but LBJ registered no reaction.

"Mr. President, let's assess this after we see the public's response to your speech tomorrow night. We all might be surprised."

"All right, Larry. We'll talk more then."

After Larry left, LBJ walked over and stood at the window looking out toward the now-desolate park. A few minutes later he picked up the telephone and told a White House operator, "Call Horace Busby. I want to see him at the White House tomorrow morning at nine. Tell him I said to come directly to the family quarters and that I don't want him stopping to visit with anyone on the way."

"Yes, sir."

"One more thing," LBJ added. "Tell Buzz I said to bring his suit jacket. He'll understand."

"Mr. Vice President, shall we retire to the library for President Johnson's speech?"

Hubert Humphrey had spent the evening trying to focus on the reception and dinner given in his honor by President Gustavo Diaz Ordaz at the home of Mexico's ambassador to the United States, but through it all he kept one eye on the clock.[16] Twelve hours earlier, he and his wife Muriel were packing for Mexico City—LBJ had asked Hubert to represent the United States at a treaty-signing ceremony. A sudden commotion outside their co-operative apartment on Washington's Southwest Waterfront caught their attention. When they looked out the window they saw a fourteen-car motorcade parked on their street.[17] Coming down the pathway toward the building entrance was the tall, lumbering figure of President Lyndon Johnson. Muriel turned to her husband and asked nervously, "Why on earth is the president *here?*"

"He probably just wants to wish us good luck on the trip," Hubert replied.

"In all your trips abroad as vice president, how many times has he come to our home to wish you luck before leaving?"

"None."

"Then there's trouble."

The Humphreys rushed to open the door before their visitor rang the bell. LBJ entered, kissed Muriel on the cheek, and then asked to meet privately with Hubert. While Muriel went to the kitchen to start the coffee pot, both men huddled in the bedroom.

"I'm giving my speech tonight at nine announcing the unilateral bombing halt in North Vietnam," LBJ told him. "I know you've seen a working draft, but I wanted to show you some final text before you leave for Mexico."

"Mr. President, you sure chose a dramatic way to deliver a mimeographed press release!" the vice president joked.

LBJ didn't smile. "What I'm showing you won't be in the embargoed pre-speech press release," he said seriously, and then he handed Hubert two sheets of paper. "These represent alternate endings."

Hubert grabbed a pair of reading glasses off his nightstand and then read the first page silently. It was two brief paragraphs containing LBJ's formal announcement that he would seek reelection in 1968. "No surprise there," Hubert thought as he slid the first page aside to review the next page.

The second alternate ending left him speechless.

"Hubert, I haven't decided which way to go," LBJ said when he saw his vice president's reaction. "You'll have to listen to the speech tonight to learn the answer. Don't tell anyone about what I've just showed you, not even Muriel. Have a nice trip." With that, LBJ strode out of the apartment and walked back to his waiting motorcade.[18]

During their drive to Andrews Air Force Base, and later on the Air Force Two flight to Mexico City, Muriel tried vainly to learn the purpose behind LBJ's visit. Hubert told her the president planned to announce major developments in Vietnam, but that was all he could say until Johnson delivered the speech. She concluded that the mystery visit didn't mean much, because Hubert seemed calm and unexcited over any secret existing between them.

Actually, there was reason for Hubert's increasing nonchalance over the astounding potential announcement. Having dealt with Lyndon Johnson for twenty years on an almost daily basis, Hubert *knew* that even if LBJ felt tempted to retire, Bobby Kennedy's entry foreclosed that possibility. "This is more of Lyndon's theatrical streak," Hubert told himself, and then he stretched out in his private cabin for a nap. He slept easily, confident in the belief that LBJ would never surrender the White House to a man he detested.[19]

Later that evening, in Mexico City, as the time for LBJ's speech approached, the US delegation and their hosts assembled with refreshments in the ambassador's opulent library. At a few minutes to eight Mexico City time, and with everyone seated, the ambassador tuned in to a San Diego radio station to hear the local announcer declare, "We interrupt our regularly scheduled programming to take you live to the White House. The next voice you hear will be the president of the United States."

While the Humphreys listened to the broadcast in Mexico, two thousand miles away, Eugene McCarthy addressed a college audience in Milwaukee. Midway through his remarks he noticed a distraction in the rear of the auditorium. Reporters covering his speech huddled suddenly, and then they ran down the aisles to the foot of the stage.

"Johnson just announced he's not running!" one of them shouted at the candidate. "He won't be a candidate!"

After asking a reporter to repeat the unexpected news to ensure he had not mistaken the message, Gene relayed the information to the crowd. Not surprisingly, the pro-McCarthy audience responded with unrestrained elation. Ignoring the remainder of his prepared text, Gene spoke cautiously, saying only that the revelation came as a surprise. Ending his remarks quickly, his staff threw a body block around the candidate, rushed him outside to his car, and they sped back to the Sheraton. Once settled in his suite, Gene and his staff celebrated the news while ruminating until 3:00 a.m. about how this affected their campaign. An elated Gene saw LBJ's sudden exit as beneficial. He grinned broadly and told everyone, "Well, if we do get to the White House, we'll have lots of fun."[20]

That same night, an American Airlines commercial flight from Phoenix taxied to the gate at John F. Kennedy Airport in New York. No sooner had the hatch opened than Clint Bolick, Robert Kennedy's administrative assistant, pushed his way into the cabin and elbowed past the deplaning passengers as he rushed to the first class section looking for his boss. Robert Kennedy and his wife, Ethel, seated in the third row, noticed the commotion Clint caused as he barreled toward them.

"Is everything all right?" Bobby asked.

"There's a crowd of reporters and TV cameras waiting for you at the gate—they want your comment on Johnson's speech," he reported breathlessly.

"Fred and I discussed it already," Bobby said as he motioned to campaign manager Fred Dutton seated behind him. "We obtained an advance copy from a friendly in the White House press office before we left Arizona. I'll commend Johnson for the bombing halt but also add that no permanent peace will be established until—"

"Don't you know?" Clint interrupted.

"Know what?"

"He's not running! Johnson announced it at the end of his speech. The press doesn't care what you think about the bombing halt—they want your reaction to being the new front-runner for the nomination!"

Shocked by the revelation, RFK turned to his manager for guidance.

"Say nothing until we can digest this," Fred cautioned.

At Fred's request, an airline supervisor arrived and escorted the Kennedy party down the aft mobile steps, allowing them to avoid the terminal gate where reporters congregated. Making their way across the tarmac quickly, they entered a car and drove immediately to Kennedy's Manhattan apartment. Although he bypassed the press successfully at the airport, his luck ran out at home. The pack converged on him, thrusting microphones from every direction and shouting variations of the same question—what was Bobby's response to the news? Following Dutton's advice, Bobby said he would reserve any statement until tomorrow morning. With that, he and his group hustled to the elevator that whisked them to the fourteenth floor.

Once upstairs, Bobby's family and staff broke out in joyous celebration—everyone except the candidate. Bobby sat in a chair looking morose and detached. "Come on, Bob!" Fred Dutton said merrily. "Your main obstacle to the White House just cleared out of your way!"

Bobby shook his head. "Your joy is premature," he said gloomily.[21]

With the initial shock of Johnson's announcement, neither McCarthy, his staff, nor Kennedy's team recognized what the wily Bobby saw. In one speech, Lyndon Johnson wrenched away from McCarthy and Kennedy both of their two reasons for running—ending the bombing in Vietnam to pursue negotiations, and dislodging LBJ from the White House. In a forty-five second passage, Lyndon Johnson turned his two Democratic opponents into candidates without causes. Come tomorrow, rather than battling a beleaguered and unpopular president, the peace candidates would have to train their cannons on each other.

Bobby also foresaw another, and bigger, problem down the road. Johnson's withdrawal made likely a third entrant into the nomination battle—one whose grip on the Party faithful promised to be almost as tight as LBJ's, and who dragged far less political baggage around than the departing president.

1968 Hubert Humphrey for president campaign button (Author's collection)

CHAPTER 12

With America's sons in the fields far away, with America's future under challenge right here at home, with our hopes and the world's hopes for peace in the balance every day, I do not believe that I should devote an hour or a day of my time to any personal partisan causes or to any duties other than the awesome duties of this office—the presidency of your country. Accordingly, I shall not seek, and I will not accept, the nomination of my Party for another term as your president.

—PRESIDENT LYNDON B. JOHNSON
ADDRESS TO THE NATION, 9:38 P.M., MARCH 31, 1968

BACK IN MEXICO CITY, the wheel that Robert Kennedy foresaw had already begun turning.

Sitting with her husband listening to the speech, Muriel Humphrey excused herself from the library when she heard President Johnson's jarring announcement. Going upstairs, she closeted herself in a bathroom and wept. After a few minutes, Hubert entered and closed the door behind him.

"I'm sorry for not telling you in advance. He swore me to secrecy, and he said only that he *might* do it. I had no idea this was a possibility until he came by the apartment this morning, and I never believed he'd go through with it."

"I'm sorry for the waterworks. I just wasn't prepared for what this means for our family."

"We've been down this road before."

"Yes, but when you ran in 1960, we had two years to prepare. Now we have about two minutes. Here it is April, the convention's in a few months, and the election's a couple months after that. You have nothing ready, but now you'll be expected to carry his banner."

"Well, if I run, I'll carry my own banner, but you're right. To be honest, I'm in shock, too. This morning Johnson's reelection team met in the White House basement to finalize their Wisconsin plan—I reviewed the agenda and executive summary on the plane coming over this morning. Now I hardly know where to begin, and the primary season's already under way. There'll be filing deadlines coming up, and filing deadlines already missed. It may be too late to enter any primaries. Even if most of the convention delegates won't come from them, they'll want to nominate a proven winner. If Bobby or Gene sweep the primaries, it won't matter that I was too late to compete—I might be finished before I get started."

"He could have given you a warning. This is so unfair—and very selfish of him. I resent deeply the position he's put you in."

"I'm sure he did what he felt he needed to do. He's been under tremendous pressure, what with the war, inflation, McCarthy, and now Kennedy. If it had been—"

"—This is just like you," she interrupted. "You're too forgiving of the people who take advantage of you."

A gentle knock on the bathroom door interrupted their conversation. Ted Van Dyk, standing outside, called to his boss. "Sir, the Washington office is on the line. It's urgent. You can take it in the bedroom at the end of the hall. I'll tell them you're on your way."

Hubert kissed his wife's forehead. "Come downstairs when you're ready, Mother." He walked to the bedroom and reached it in time to see Ted replacing the telephone handset in the cradle.

"Why did you hang up?" he asked.

Ted relayed that Hubert's longtime executive assistant Bill Connell had called. "He told me he couldn't waste any more time waiting for you to come to the phone. He wanted you to know that he and other senior staffers are phoning key Party and labor union leaders around the country to urge support for your candidacy. They're also asking everyone to keep their powder dry. Bill told me to tell you he wasn't asking your permission to do this, because he'll do it with or without your okay."[1]

A few minutes later, the Humphreys returned downstairs to find the embassy library a scene of near-bedlam. Within moments of LBJ's announcement, scores of reporters seeking comment overloaded the embassy's switchboard, while in the outside lobby, the press pool covering the trip pounded on the library door shouting questions to the official party on the other side: was Hubert Humphrey now a candidate for president?[2]

By the time HHH reached Bill Connell on the phone later that night, Bill and his crew already had contacted almost a hundred leaders. He relayed to the vice president the recurring concerns he heard expressed: Humphrey was too late to compete in the primaries, and some bigwigs felt that gave Kennedy a grip on the nomination. "I've explained to everyone where most of the delegates will come from, and how that will favor us greatly," Bill reported. "I think the bulk of our people will hold in place to see what the president wants them to do, at least for now."

"I hope that helps keep them in check," Hubert said. "If I run, we'll probably have to bypass most or all of the remaining primaries and round up our delegates by other means. As long as the president helps us, or at least doesn't screw us, we stand a good chance of putting this together. Be sure you warn our friends not to fall for the inevitable news stories that will surface in the next few days claiming that Kennedy has it locked up. When this shakes out, I think everyone will see that Bobby has far less organizational support than most people think—and Gene McCarthy had even less than that."[3]

"I agree, but with Johnson's surprise withdrawal,[4] we can't pretend we have what we don't. We have no money, no organization, and no ground game in key states. Hell, we have no ground game in *any* state."

"That's true, but that was true for Bobby when he announced two weeks ago, and it's been true for Gene since he got in. We're all starting from scratch."

"You'll have another disadvantage, sir. Your longtime liberal base has pretty much disowned you for supporting the president on Vietnam."

"That's also true, but we have other things in our favor. Beside incumbency, our old constituencies remain loyal to us—civil rights leaders, pro-war Democrats, and organized labor. Most of the unions support the administration on Vietnam, and they'll support me over Bobby or Gene. Besides, as long as Johnson doesn't blackball us, we'll have the operational and organizational support of the national Democratic Party and all that entails. So let's focus on what we do have, at least for now."[5]

After the call ended, Bill relayed the conversation's substance to another longtime Humphrey aide, Max Kampelman, who reminded Bill that Humphrey had an additional intangible plus: Johnson, Kennedy, and McCarthy all have two things on common. First, they all hate each other. Second, none of them hates Hubert Humphrey—he's perhaps the most likeable man in politics, and he's helped all of them over the years. That distinction may come in handy later."

"In fact," Max added thoughtfully, "it might prove decisive."

The day before Lyndon Johnson's blockbuster speech, he felt depressed and abandoned. The morning after, he strode into the Oval Office with the step of an invigorated man, having relieved himself of the likely brutal rejections that lay ahead on the electoral calendar. Staff members commented on how, almost overnight, the president's physical appearance improved noticeably.

LBJ's sense of relief turned to bliss when his chief of staff, Marvin Watson, arrived and showed him the results of an overnight poll. In one evening, Johnson's approval rating shot up an unprecedented thirteen points—from 36 percent to 49 percent. After his speech, Americans in droves jettisoned nearly four years of the anger they directed at LBJ, and now viewed him as a statesman.[6]

"Not to ruin your moment, Mr. President," Marvin added hesitatingly, "but you received a telegram from Senator Kennedy this morning. He's asking for an appointment to meet as soon as possible to talk with you about his campaign."

Johnson guffawed at the news. "I'll say this for Bobby—he's got brass balls. Did you see him stroking my ego on TV this morning? Now that he's worried about me pig-stickin' him, he's telling the press I'm a devoted leader who sacrifices for his country! Two days ago he gave a speech and called me an evil man who appeals to America's darkest side. Well, I won't bother answering that grandstanding little runt."[7]

Plopping into his large, high-backed, green leather Gunlocke chair positioned behind his old US Senate desk, LBJ appeared to enjoy the ironic turn of events as he reminisced about his relationship with RFK through the years. "You know," he said, "Jack Kennedy never would have won the presidency without me on the ticket. He couldn't win Texas or any other Southern state, and without Texas, he'd have lost to Nixon in 1960.[8] Do you think any of that ever mattered to Bobby? When Jack was president, Bobby ridiculed me every chance he got. Behind my back, he called Lady Bird and me 'Little Porkchop and Colonel Cornpone.'[9] That hurt Lady Bird terribly. The only thing that dear woman ever did to Bobby was show him unending kindness.

"After Jack died, I put aside all the memories of him treating me like a shit-pile. I reached out and tried my best to get along with him. I did all I could to show him friendship and affection, but he rejected me at every turn.[10] He and his circle of Harvards resented that someone from Southwest Texas Teachers College was in the White House—and they weren't. They saw me as a usurper of the job that belonged to them—like I was some illegitimate pretender to the throne. From my first day as president, he and his Eastern intellectual crowd tried to knock me down before I could even stand up.[11]

"I'll never forget a few years ago—Bobby told people I was a pathological liar, a bitter and vicious animal, and he said I'm not even a human being.[12] And while he was calling me all those things behind my back, the double-dealer was angling and begging to be my running mate in 1964.[13] After I picked Humphrey, he packs up for New York and runs for senator—even though he never once lived in the state—against Ken Keating—a good man, by the way. Keating was a liberal Republican, very popular, and he supported our programs in Congress more than many Democrats.

"Anyway, at first, Bobby jumped out with a huge lead, but by October he started wearing thin on New Yorkers with that grating, high-pitched voice of his. Keating came back in the polls. By the end of the campaign, I was beating Goldwater in New York two-to-one, but Bobby was six points behind and dropping every day. The New York Republican Party put out thousands of 'Johnson-Keating' campaign buttons, and they urged their voters to split their ticket: vote for me for president and Keating for senator. Meanwhile, everyone bashed Bobby as a carpetbagger. I remember seeing the signs and badges all over the state, 'Keep Keating—*New York's Own!*' and 'If Johnson did not need him, New York certainly does not!' Bobby was getting his ass kicked, so, at the last minute, he begged me to interrupt my own race and campaign for him. Despite the years of insults and hostility, I went to New York and crisscrossed the state with him—twice. I personally ordered the Democratic National Committee to blanket the state with 'Johnson-Humphrey-Kennedy' posters, badges, and anything else we could use to put his picture and name next to mine. Just before the election, I spoke for him at a Madison Square Garden rally. On Election Day, instead of losing, he won by 700,000 votes—*two million votes less than I got in New York on the same day*, by the way. Without my personal help, Keating would have humiliated Bobby, and his political career would be dead. So, at his victory party that night, what did he do?

Bobby got up and thanked everyone—everyone but me. The goddamn ingrate never mentioned my name—not one word![14] It was as if I didn't matter to his win. Now he wants to meet and ask for my help again, or ask me to remain neutral and not campaign against him? He's gotta be pullin' my pecker."

Pro and anti-Robert F. Kennedy campaign buttons from RFK's 1964 US Senate race (Author's collection)

"The press already knows he's asked to see you."

"He's a two-faced, ungrateful little bastard."

"What do you want George to tell the reporters?"

"What the hell do you think?"

Then, breaking into a broad grin and lacing his fingers together behind his head as he reclined in his chair, LBJ answered his own question. "Have George tell the press I'm looking forward to meeting with Senator Kennedy at his earliest convenience."

Two days later, on April 3, Robert Kennedy arrived at the White House for his "summit" with President Johnson. Accompanied by Ted Sorensen, Bobby asked the usher where the president planned to hold the meeting. When told he would see them in the Oval Office, Ted leaned over and whispered to Bobby, "Perhaps the Indian Treaty Room would be more appropriate!"

Their wait was not long. LBJ bounded into the room carrying an infant boy, calling to his guest, "Bobby, take a look at this little fellow—he can walk at eight months old!" With that, LBJ showed off his grandson Patrick's early developmental skills before a nanny whisked away the child. LBJ settled into his Carolina rocker, a near-replica of the one President Kennedy favored when he occupied the White House. Bobby and Ted sat on the sofa across from him and near the fireplace.

For an hour, LBJ offered a monologue on Vietnam and the progress of the peace efforts. While the principals talked, Ted was pleased with their tone, especially when the meeting became conciliatory. At one point, both men acknowledged the unfortunate hostility that had marked their relationship for so long.

"Mr. President," Bobby said humbly, "I regret very much that our association deteriorated. A lot of it was my fault."

"Bobby, listen," LBJ replied warmly, "for years people tried to divide us, and because of it, we both suffered, and so did our relationship. Let's put all of that behind us and move forward."

Seeing his opening, Bobby raised the point that led him to request the meeting—determining the president's intended role in the upcoming battle for the Democratic presidential nomination. "Mr. President, may I ask where I stand with you in the campaign? Are you opposed to my effort, and will you marshal forces against me?"

In an almost-fatherly tone, LBJ replied, "I want to keep the presidency out of this campaign. Of course, I feel toward Hubert the way Ted here feels toward you, but I want you to know something, and it comes from my heart. I do not hate or dislike you, and I still regard myself as carrying out the Kennedy-Johnson partnership. After your brother died, any thought I had for wanting this job died with him. I tried to find a way to avoid running in 1964, but I felt I had an obligation to Jack to carry through on his programs. I like to think that Jack, looking down on us, would agree I've done that."

Pressing the issue, Bobby asked, "Will you get involved in the race for or against any candidate?"

"I'm not helping or hurting anyone on our side. If I thought I could be involved in this campaign and hold the country together, I would have run myself. Now I'm out of it, and I told the American people that I will put my entire focus on peace in Vietnam and bringing our boys home. If I jumped out there tomorrow and started campaigning for or against someone, it would defeat everything I'm trying to do. If I change my mind, which I don't plan to do, I'll tell you in advance. As for now, I'm neutral, and I plan to stay that way."

"Mr. President, I couldn't ask for anything more."

As the three men stood, Bobby tried to speak, but the words caught in his throat and came out as a whisper, as if he had gulped too much air before talking.

LBJ looked at Bobby and grinned. Leaning his towering figure and massive face closer, LBJ said, "I'm sorry, Bobby, I couldn't hear you. Would you mind repeating that?"

Bobby cleared his throat and again spoke the words that Ted Sorensen never dreamed he would hear come from the lips of Robert Francis Kennedy:

"President Johnson, you are a brave and dedicated man."

Throwing his arm around the uncomfortable looking senator, and pulling him into a half-bear hug, LBJ replied with an emotional catch in his own voice. "Thank you, Bobby. I mean that—thank you—from my heart. Now, you go give my love to Ethel and all those kids."[15]

RFK and Ted Sorensen exited the Oval Office. As they negotiated the familiar corridors on the way out of the White House, Bobby said enthusiastically, "You know, I thought the meeting went exception-ally well. The president really was magnanimous—more than I'd have been if I were in his shoes. Maybe this *will* be the beginning of a new relationship between us."

Ted Sorensen agreed. "I think I just witnessed a miracle on the scale of turning water into wine!"

Moments after RFK and Ted left, Marvin Watson returned to the Oval

Office and asked the president how the meeting went.

"It went great. I think Bobby and I started a new chapter today."

"What's your position on his campaign?"

Unbeknownst to Marvin (and everyone else at the time), LBJ secretly tape-recorded all of his Oval Office conversations, so instead of answering Marvin audibly, LBJ offered a nonverbal response to his feelings regarding Robert Kennedy's presidential ambitions:

Lyndon Johnson smiled, took his index finger, and made a slow, slashing motion across the front of his throat.[16]

NBC News reporter's identification badge worn while covering the 1968 presidential primary campaigns
(Author's collection)

CHAPTER 13

"HOW DO *YOU* THINK his meeting with Johnson will go today?"

Ted Van Dyk and freshman Senator Fred Harris (D-OK), the co-chair of Vice President Hubert Humphrey's still-unannounced presidential campaign, met for lunch in the nautical-themed, US Navy-run White House Mess. The basement restaurant, reserved for the exclusive use of senior staff, provided sufficient privacy for their conversation about a sensitive subject: would the president endorse his vice president against the two men who challenged Johnson in the primaries?

"He should endorse," Fred said. "Hubert's been a loyal VP, but I get the feeling that you think what Johnson *should* do and what he *will* do are different things."

"Senator, if the past is prologue, then I expect Johnson to keep the boss on a tight leash and hold any endorsement just out of reach to keep him in line on Vietnam. The vice president has had reservations about the war since the Gulf of Tonkin, and he's paid a tremendous price for expressing them. If he runs, he'll want to chart his own course, but Johnson will squash him if he asserts himself."

Ted then shared with the young senator how Humphrey learned the price of dissent in the Johnson administration. "Right after the 1965 inauguration, Johnson called a Cabinet meeting and asked 'advice' on whether he should expand military operations in Vietnam to counter random guerilla attacks on our troops. When his turn came, the vice president urged caution and argued against massive retaliatory strikes.

"Apparently," Ted continued, "Johnson didn't want advice—he wanted validation. A few days later, Johnson started 'Operation Rolling Thunder,' and that kicked off the Vietnam War. Because the vice president didn't anticipate what Johnson wanted him to say, Johnson cut him out of the policy loop. Since that day three years ago, Johnson has banned him from all Pentagon strategy sessions and National Security Council meetings. When the agencies do send us intelligence reports, they're abridged or heavily edited. Then, to twist the knife, Johnson ordered that he have no access to any Executive Branch resources, from motor pool cars to Air Force Two, unless the vice president begs permission from Johnson's chief of staff.[1] Asking to use the car is a nuisance, but withholding critical intelligence creates national security concerns. Johnson knows better than anyone that a vice president must be prepared to step into the commander-in-chief role in an instant. I've often wondered what the press would say if they knew Johnson forces his vice president to keep up with administration policy by scouring newspapers, begging information from White House friends, or having our staff cull through diplomatic cable traffic."

"I don't understand," Fred replied. "Hubert's been such a consistent Johnson defender on Vietnam that his old liberal cronies have disowned him."

"Vietnam leaves the vice president deeply torn personally. He didn't want the war escalated, but he feels he owes Johnson loyalty.[2] After

Johnson shut him out, the boss spent the last three years traveling the country promoting Johnson's agenda to prove his loyalty. Finally, after three years in purgatory, Johnson recently returned the boss to his partial good graces. Just after the Tet offensive last January, Johnson invited him to attend his first Cabinet meeting since the '65 inaugural. When it ended, the VP met with Johnson privately, and he again expressed his reservations about the latest plan to bomb the North.[3] For raising that issue, Johnson reinstituted the freeze. Today is the first time the vice president has seen the president alone since January, and Johnson's meeting with him now only because he's also met with Kennedy and McCarthy.[4] We're caught in a vice, and Johnson's back to excluding him from all policy discussions and decisions. Because he remains loyal to the war publicly, the antiwar activists with whom he personally sympathizes hate him as much as they do Johnson.[5] And, since Johnson avoids almost all public speeches to avoid the demonstrators, he sends out the vice president to absorb their brutal heckling. Everywhere we go, he's taunted and jeered by protesters chanting 'Dump the Hump,' or much worse. The wrath pouring from these crowds is hard to comprehend, and it wounds the boss down to his soul."

"Of all the people in the world to hate, you'd think Hubert would be at the bottom of everyone's list," Fred observed. "I've never known a kinder man with such a genuine love for people. Hubert loves people like an alcoholic loves booze. It's real—it's not affected. That level of rejection must hurt him deeply."[6]

Changing the subject, Ted asked how the campaign staff saw Humphrey's path to the nomination. "Once Hubert declares," Fred suggested, "he'll likely be a 'submarine' candidate. Since we'll be too late to file for any primaries, the reporters will cover the McCarthy-Kennedy battle, while we focus on the non-primary states where there's no press but plenty of delegates. While Kennedy and McCarthy slug it out publicly, we'll travel the country and scoop up votes quietly at state Party conventions, caucuses, and from Party leaders directly."[7]

A few minutes later, Vice President Humphrey arrived at the mess.

After table-hopping and greeting each diner, he joined Ted and Senator Harris in their private corner.

"How did it go?" Ted asked.

HHH shook his head. "Let's not talk here—he has spies everywhere. I'll brief you on the walk back to the office."

As the three men exited the White House and strolled across the pathway to the annex, Humphrey told them that Johnson was noncommittal. "The president said he's remaining neutral for now. He said he probably won't endorse publicly, but behind the scenes, he'd line up Party leaders to support me—*eventually*. What that means in LBJ-speak is that he will control all the cards at the convention, and he'll use that leverage to make sure I stick by him on Vietnam to the bitter end."

Then, with a rare grimace from the normally ebullient politician, Humphrey added a final observation. "Knowing him as I do, it means one more thing. Despite what he told America on March 31st, he still hasn't relinquished control of the Party, and if he has his way, he won't."

"What do you mean?" Ted asked.

"I mean that until the Democratic National Convention formally— and irrevocably—selects its candidate, I don't put it past Lyndon Johnson to try and be the man standing before the cheering delegates accepting the nomination in Chicago."

With attention diverted to the Democratic primary fight between the two "peace" candidates, Humphrey's formal entry into the race on April 27 received only passing notice, and he preferred the media's indifference. While RFK and McCarthy ramped up their mutual attacks on each other in their quest for the small pockets of delegates in primary play, a few days after Humphrey announced, his private survey showed that without entering a single contest, he already had 900 pledges from the 1,312 delegates he needed to win the nomination.[8]

Antiwar campaign button promoting a 1968 Eugene McCarthy-Robert F. Kennedy ticket (Author's collection)

Even with Kennedy's late entry into the race in mid-March, it would be almost two months before he and McCarthy met head-to-head in a state primary. Meanwhile, two days after Johnson's withdrawal, on April 2, Wisconsin voters went to the polls. With neither Kennedy nor Humphrey on the ballot, McCarthy scored his anticipated big win.[9] In the next two primaries—Pennsylvania and Massachusetts—McCarthy again had the field to himself and won both easily.

Indiana's primary on May 7 was the site of the first direct faceoff between Kennedy and McCarthy, yet between McCarthy's Wisconsin victory and the Indiana showdown, the political campaigns of every presidential candidate screeched to an unexpected two-week halt. At 6:00 p.m. on April 4, inside room 306 of the Lorraine Motel in Memphis, Reverend Ralph Abernathy walked over to the television set and turned on the NBC News *Huntley-Brinkley Report*. Abernathy's roommate, Dr. Martin Luther King Jr., stood outside on the second-floor balcony. At the same moment, James Earl Ray occupied a boarding house bathroom opposite the motel parking lot. At 6:01, from his window perch, Ray lined up the civil rights leader in his rifle scope and pulled the trigger.

Badge worn by supporters of Dr. Martin Luther King Jr. during the early days of the 1968 presidential campaign. This badge predates his assassination on April 4, 1968 (Author's collection)

For the next two weeks, with public presidential campaigning suspended in King's memory, rioting erupted in over one hundred cities, leaving thirty-nine people dead, over 2,500 injured, and more than 75,000 state and federal troops patrolling the streets to restore order.[10] The bloody ghetto rampages consumed network news coverage each night, which added to the nation's unease. Although the post-King assassination carnage did not affect the Democratic nomination contest, the aftermath of three years of urban unrest (beginning with the 1965 Watts riots) would figure prominently in the 1968 general election drama.

During the campaign suspensions following King's assassination, Gene McCarthy spent much of the time resting at his Washington home. His manager, Blair Clark, joined him for lunch one afternoon to discuss strategy for the upcoming series of primaries against Robert Kennedy.

"You know," Gene sighed discontentedly, "When I announced, I said I'd enter a few primaries to challenge the administration on Vietnam. With the way things have gone, now I feel more like a relay runner than a candidate—after every lap I have to face a different competitor. It started with New Hampshire and Wisconsin, when I ran against Johnson, first as a write-in, and then under his own name.

Now, in the next eight weeks, I have to run against Kennedy in states like Indiana, Nebraska, Oregon, and California. If I make it past those hurdles, I'll have to run against Humphrey all the way to Chicago."[11]

"So far it's worked in your favor," Blair said. "New Hampshire and Wisconsin turned you into a national candidate. I think Kennedy in the race gives you new opportunities to cement your antiwar credentials against him. Bobby talks a good game on Vietnam today, but look who's running his campaign. Larry O'Brien left Johnson for him. He's got Pierre Salinger, Ted Sorensen, and Robert MacNamara—all the same JFK Cold Warriors that got us into Vietnam."[12]

"You're right, and now, with Johnson out, Bobby faces a hell of a dilemma. People have forgotten that Vietnam was a Johnson-inherited, but President Kennedy-created, mistake. Ever since Dallas, Bobby's gotten unending mileage playing the stand-in for Jack Kennedy's ghost. Now, instead of letting him continue *being* Jack, I'm going to make him run *against* Jack."[13]

As Gene sipped a martini,[14] he continued his analysis of the political chessboard. "When Bobby announced, he expected our supporters would defect to him in droves. Instead, once the dust settled, our support increased. The crowd enthusiasm at our rallies is greater now than before he entered."

"In fact," Blair added, "within a week of Kennedy announcing, both the number of our new volunteers and unsolicited contributions increased tremendously."[15]

Gene nodded at the update, and then added an unexpected twist to his hypothesis. "The great irony is that if Bobby hadn't entered the primaries against me, he probably would have ended up winning the nomination."

Gene's observation surprised Blair. "What makes you say that?"

"I would have beaten Johnson in a few early primaries and made him look weak, but the boss-driven Democratic Party machine would never nominate me, even if I routed Johnson in every contest. Bobby would have become the unifying force—the compromise candidate who didn't challenge the incumbent.[16] Now, with he and I splitting the peace vote, Humphrey will win the nomination instead.[17] That's the byproduct of Bobby's ego and selfishness. I guess my doomed campaign does have two important functions, though. It keeps the focus on Vietnam, and it keeps a spoiled, unintelligent demagogue from seizing the White House.[18] I only regret that as we continue along on the campaign trail, we'll have to keep listening to Bobby misquoting philosophers and poets in his unending and comical exercises in intellectual self-improvement."[19]

Abigail McCarthy entered the dining room and interrupted her husband. "Dick Goodwin's on the phone for you."

"I was just leaving for the airport anyway," Blair said as he stood and shook hands with the candidate. "See you Thursday in Indiana." Gene said goodbye to his manager, and then took the call in the hallway alcove. Dick, who had proved so helpful to the New Hampshire and Wisconsin efforts, asked Gene if he could come over and talk about something important. Dick's tone suggested to Gene the purpose underlying the request.

Dick arrived an hour later and found Gene sitting in his backyard enjoying the rare spring sunshine on his face. "Sit down, Dick. Would you like something to drink?"

"No thanks, senator," he said haltingly. "I need to talk with you, and there is no easy way to say this. If I stay with your campaign, I might be able to help you beat Bobby Kennedy. I think he is beatable, but I just can't be a part of taking him down."

"Does that mean you'll remain neutral?"

Dick looked down and shook his head. "With the Kennedys, there is no neutral. You're for them or against them. There's no middle ground. I'm sorry, senator, more than you know, but I just can't be part of a campaign whose purpose is to end the political career of one of my best friends."

"Well, that's the kind of a race it has to be, but it's not by my choice. Since your best friend set up shop in Indiana, he's been campaigning against me the same way he did against Ken Keating in New York in '64—by twisting and distorting my voting record. He's taking dishonest and cheap shots, but I think you already know that."[20]

Both men sat in uncomfortable silence as Gene looked off at the cluster of trees flanking his yard. Finally, bringing the stillness to a merciful end, he said quietly to his visitor, "Maybe we'll meet again."

Dick nodded without replying, rose from his seat and left. Returning to his car parked on the street, he climbed inside, started the engine, and drove to McLean.[21]

As Dick Goodwin said his awkward goodbye to Eugene McCarthy, across the Potomac River, Robert Kennedy and his team took advantage of the campaign lull by holding yet another strategy session at his Hickory Hill estate. While they discussed the primary calendar dominating the next two months, a maid told Ted Sorensen he had a phone call. Excusing himself from the room, Ted took it in the kitchen.

"Bob's been running for over two weeks already," the voice on the other end said. "When do I start earning my paycheck?"

Chris Evans, the California pollster Bobby Kennedy hired four months earlier, exaggerated his idleness. Long before Bobby jumped into the race in mid-March, Chris and supportive state Democratic Party leaders began laying the RFK groundwork for a potential June 4 California showdown near the end of the primary season.

"Don't worry about earning a paycheck—we're so disorganized that we don't even have paychecks printed yet!" Ted Sorensen laughed at his own comment, but not because it was a joke. For all the endless planning sessions Bobby held since last year about a possible presidential race, when he finally made the move, he entered with no organization beyond a handful of friends, advisers, and family members.

"Winging it doesn't sound very Kennedyesque," Chris noted.

"This is nothing like Jack's race in 1960. Back then, we had an entire operation perfected. He had almost four years of careful planning behind his launch. What we are doing now is managing chaos. We have no staff or organization, and almost no endorsements."[22]

"But you have what the other teams lack—a rock star. Those crowds I'm seeing on the news each night almost look scary. It's like watching one of the Beatles run for president."

"Even the Beatles have a schedule, which is more than I can say for us. We're trying to get ground troops organized in the key primary states where we can still get on the ballot and compete for delegates—Indiana, Nebraska, Oregon, California, South Dakota, and New York. While that's been going on behind the scenes, we've been shoving Bob on airplanes, flying him to cities with college campuses and getting him out to rally our base back to us. If there's a nearby ghetto, we stick Bob in the back seat of a convertible and drive him through the neighborhood. You're right—the ghetto crowds are immense, and they treat him like he's Moses, but none of those people yanking off his cufflinks and shoes for souvenirs will be delegates in Chicago, and images of it on the news each night won't impress the Party chieftains. They're only interested in who can beat the Republican in November. To win in Chicago, Bobby will need more than a hodge-podge of minorities and students screaming for him. He needs to show he has significant support with middle-class white voters."[23]

"That's not as easy as it sounds."

"It's not. Southern Democrats are prowar, and they despise Bob. Old-line liberals never forgave him for working for Joe McCarthy. With those ancient rumors of Bob authorizing J. Edgar Hoover's wiretapping of Martin Luther King now hitting the mainstream press, it cements a negative image.[24] Then we have many in the antiwar crowd who resent his late entry as ruthless opportunism, and they're hanging tight with McCarthy."

"So how do you cobble victory from those impediments?"

"Bob tailors his message to the communities that we need. When he campaigns in ghettos, he speaks passionately about equality and civil rights. It comes from the heart, and it resonates there. When he's in white suburban areas, he skips all that and instead sounds like Ronald

Reagan—he's for law and order, against forced school busing to integrate schools, denounces wasteful welfare, and favors local control.[25] Of course, when Bob's in minority neighborhoods, he steers clear of all that, since Negroes associate those topics with Nixon, Wallace, and the others that they think are racists."[26]

"Not that this is any surprise in the world of politics, but are you guys bothered by the inconsistency—some might say hypocrisy—of that approach?"

"I'll be honest—the civil rights activists and the students are driving us to the left, and because Bob feels those emotions that run before those groups, he has no problem speaking to their issues. But let's face it. Bob's not just running to better the world, he's also running to advance the Kennedy banner. Indiana is a perfect example. Bob's trying to maintain a balance there. The TV news footage of Bob reaching into crowds of ecstatic Negroes grabbing at him frantically is very off-putting to many white voters, and we know it. With so many blue-collar voters in Indiana, we're cutting back his appearances in the Negro communities there. The other night, while we were on the plane, he complained to me that the blacks in Indiana seem to want to view him as a member of their race, and he said he can't win if he lets that happen.[27] That's the bottom line. Bob wants to win so he can do good, but he's also a power animal. He's not running to be a hero. He's running to be president."[28]

"How will you play this off McCarthy and Humphrey?"

"Our first goal is to blitz McCarthy in the primaries and knock him out early, but avoid attacking him to the point that we alienate permanently all those kids lined up behind him. When Gene folds, we want his thousands of precinct walkers to join us.[29] Beyond that, we need to stop the Party regulars from delivering the nomination to Humphrey. By sweeping the primaries we can show them that Bob is the overwhelming choice of rank-and-file Democrats, and that he's the Party's biggest vote getter. Johnson will try and steer the delegates to Humphrey, but if we can convince the Party bosses that Bob can beat any Republican nominee and Humphrey can't, then we'll own the

Chicago convention—despite Johnson."[30]

While Ted continued speaking to Chris, Bobby entered the kitchen and grabbed a Coke from the refrigerator. Hearing a knock on the front door, he walked down the hall and saw a servant admit Dick Goodwin, who stood in the foyer with an overnight bag in his hand.

"Well," Bobby said to Dick unappreciatively, "it's about time."

Irritated by this ungrateful and cold greeting, Dick raised his voice in frustrated reply: "Listen, Bobby, it's not my fault you chickened out at the beginning and didn't run. We all begged and pleaded with you to get in, and you wouldn't do it because you didn't want to lose to Johnson. Now I've had to shit on McCarthy and all the friends I made over there because of you. You're the one who put me in this position."

While Dick vented angrily, he noticed RFK's assembled strategists seated in the nearby living room glowering at him disapprovingly. Adding them to his tirade, Dick continued, "And as for the rest of you bastards, none of you had the courage to do the right thing. I did, and I'll be damned if I'm going to let any of you make me pay for it—so screw all of you, too."

Dick walked into the living room, tossed his satchel on an unoccupied corner of a sofa, and plopped himself into a chair.

"Now that we all understand each other," he growled at his once-again colleagues, "let's get busy and elect a goddamn president."[31]

Campaign buttons promoting both Eugene McCarthy and Robert F. Kennedy as the anti-Vietnam War "peace" candidates in the 1968 Democratic presidential primaries (Author's collection)

CHAPTER 14

"PETER, GO GET MY FUCKING SHOES. They're in my room. And don't wake up Ethel, for Christ's sake."

Robert Kennedy, agitated and clad in a T-shirt and boxer briefs, had thrown open the bedroom door of the suite used by his national and California campaign staff. After trying to nap unsuccessfully there, Bobby began dressing while his senior team, all holed up in San Francisco's Fairmont Hotel, worked in the outer conference room putting together some last-minute updates to RFK's debate preparation notes.[1] Ethel Kennedy, the candidate's wife, rested in Bobby's private suite down the hallway.

This go-fetch order interrupted the concentration of Peter Edelman, RFK's thirty-year old legislative director, as he typed suggested responses to anticipated McCarthy attacks in tonight's only debate between them. As Peter got up to run the demeaning errand, Bobby spied two young campaign aides drinking beer and chuckling over an unrelated joke. Angered over their light moment, he charged toward them. "What's so goddamn funny? All you people do around here is goof off and play the guitar." A look of horror overcame the young aides, especially when he castigated them for strumming folk songs during downtime aboard the campaign airplane. As they began apologizing, Bobby continued his harangue. "If you jackasses have nothing better to do, then go out and ring some doorbells." With that, he stepped inside the bedroom and slammed the door in their faces.[2]

"If he's that stressed over debate prep, I'd hate to be around him in the White House when the hotline rings," Chris Evans told Pierre Salinger, who registered no surprise at RFK's eruption.

Salinger was a nationally recognized political figure in his own right. He once worked as a reporter before serving as JFK's and, briefly, LBJ's White House press secretary—and that was before his four-month stint in 1964 as an appointed US senator. Now one of Bobby's top campaign lieutenants, Pierre knew the candidate perhaps as well as anyone inside the "bubble." When Bobby decided to run, he asked Pierre to join the campaign. "I will if you'll work on softening your hard-ass image and your nasty tone," he told RFK. "Selling you to the public will be like selling tuna cans after a botulism scare. Everyone likes tuna—but before they buy it, they want to feel confident it won't hurt them."[3] Now, sitting with Chris and poring over Northern California polling data, the gruff, chunky, round-faced campaign veteran puffed on his ever-present cigar and asked Chris, "Have you spent much time with him?"

"Not until the last couple of weeks," Chris replied. "I didn't know him at all until six months ago. Before Oregon, I met with him now and then. My focus has been on the West Coast—especially California, and the Kennedy show just rolled into town full-time for that last Wednesday. Since then, we've spent so much time huddled together that if we were any closer, we'd be dancing."

Pierre took a long draw on his stogie. The ash behind the glowing red ember looked dangerously close to toppling onto the polished mahogany table. Ignoring the threat, Pierre shared his interpretation of Bobby's outburst. "What you just watched is about a lot of things, and tonight's debate is only part of it. McCarthy's been demanding a debate since Bobby got in. As long as we kept beating McCarthy in the primaries, Bobby could ignore the challenge and claim McCarthy wasn't a serious contender—why dignify him as a candidate of equal stature?[4] Personally, I think Bobby refused because he's not a very good debater. Gene's smart, smooth, and condescending with people he views as his intellectual inferiors, which is exactly what he thinks of Bobby. McCarthy's always thought himself more qualified for the presidency than Bobby—or Jack, for that matter. Gene thinks the Kennedys are a product of public relations, not substance.[5] In Gene's mind, he's worked harder, studied harder, is a better economist, and knows more about philosophy, poetry, and theology—the elements of an educated man—than any Kennedy.[6] Even though Bobby will never admit it, I think Gene intimidates the shit out of him. Did you hear about what happened at the zoo?"

"What zoo?"

"A couple of weeks ago they ended up at the Portland Zoo at the same time. It was a scheduling coincidence. When McCarthy learned we were there, he and his large press contingent came charging down the hill to confront us over Bobby refusing to debate. When Bobby saw the pack coming, he jumped into his car and told the driver to get us out of there. As we're speeding away, with every TV camera recording our escape, McCarthy's people stood along the route shouting 'Coward!' The local news stations replayed endlessly the footage of Bobby fleeing while McCarthy's crowd mocked him. It looked terrible.[7] Anyway, after McCarthy beat us in Oregon, Bobby couldn't dismiss his candidacy anymore.[8] So yeah, he's nervous about tonight. It's their only scheduled debate, and with your latest data showing McCarthy closing on us here, he's worried a bad showing will cost us the whole enchilada."

While laying aside an updated tracking poll that showed Kennedy still ahead of McCarthy in California, but with continuing slippage, Chris asked Pierre a question—the answer to which he feared he knew in advance: "If Bobby loses California, what happens?"

Finally flicking his cigar ash into a nearby dish, Pierre answered unemotionally. "If McCarthy wins on Tuesday, I'll accept the offer I have to join a big investment firm back east, and you'll be out of a job—at least with us. Bobby told me on the plane this morning that if we lose California after losing Oregon, he'll withdraw from the race."[9]

"Why withdraw? So far he's won two out of three against McCarthy?"

"The whole basis of Bobby's convention strategy was to swamp McCarthy in the primaries and drive him out of the race early, so we could consolidate the peace vote and take the battle to Humphrey directly. Bobby beat McCarthy in Indiana, but he did it winning a measly 42 percent—hardly a mandate—and that was after McCarthy pulled out of the state completely. The same thing happened in Nebraska two weeks ago. Bobby poured in huge amounts of time and money; McCarthy spent one lousy day there, and Bobby barely cleared 50 percent. We needed a knockout punch in Oregon, and instead McCarthy beat us—badly. Besides delivering a political setback, Oregon made him the first Kennedy ever to lose an election. Believe me, that *really* sticks in his craw. If we lose California right after losing Oregon, we're done. Bobby will get out so the antiwar forces can unite."[10]

"I can give you my demographic data on Oregon, but what's your political take on why the magic failed there?"

"Everything fell flat. Wherever we went, he got no traction. Those screaming, frenzied mobs greeting him in other states weren't there. He traveled around giving his usual stump speech about civil rights, the poor, the blacks, and the ghettos. The problem for us was that in Oregon there are no poor, no blacks, and no ghettos. One night on the plane, after another long, shitty day, he said, 'You know, these Oregonians just ain't my people, and unless we move some ghettos up here, we can't win.'[11] The topper was when we orchestrated a photo op of him strolling along the beach for reporters. In front of all the cameras, he decided to show some youthful energy—he stripped down to his shorts and dove into the surf. Instead of looking brave and vigorous, Oregonians thought he looked like a show-off—or a fool. In Oregon, I guess people swim in the Pacific Ocean in August, not May.[12] Add to that Ethel being three months pregnant with kid number eleven, he's gotten about four hours of interrupted sleep a night for the last three months, he's feverish, he's living off milkshakes and heavy daily doses of vitamin shots, and he knows that if he doesn't stop McCarthy's surge in the debate tonight, it's over on Tuesday. Given all that, I guess I can excuse him showing an occasional flash of temper."

"Under the circumstances," Chris said, "I guess playing shoe flunky is a small price to pay to help a guy carrying that load, but those two other kids with the guitars may need therapy after that ass-chewing he gave them."

"Listen, that 'go get my shoes' demand is the one thing that's probably not from stress. That's how Bobby is. I've been around Kennedys for years—ever since Jack started sniffing around the presidency. Bobby's just like his brother. He thinks his staffers are supposed to double as his personal valets.[13] If those kids with the guitars stick around long enough, they'll learn to roll with it, or they'll go find other jobs."

Ted Sorensen checked the time, and then he knocked on the bedroom door. "Bob, we need to head to the studio." A few moments later, RFK emerged dressed in a dark pinstripe suit. "Ethel's already downstairs in the car," Ted told him as they headed out.

"Hey Bobby," Pierre yelled to the departing candidate. "That New York investment firm will pay me half a million to join them next week, so if you fuck this up tonight, I don't want you to worry about my future." As the staffers laughed at Pierre's tension-breaking comment, a wide grin spread across Bobby's face.

"Thanks, Pierre. I'll do my best tonight to keep your children living in abject squalor a while longer."

As Eugene McCarthy and his team prepared to leave the Mark Hopkins Hotel for tonight's debate, Blair Clark chastised him: "I wish you had spent less time today hanging out with your poetry buddies and more time studying your briefing book."[14]

"If I need prep time to debate Bobby Kennedy, then I don't deserve to be president."

"He's tough—he may surprise you."

Gene scoffed. "Bobby's tough? He plays touch football, I play football. He plays softball, I play baseball. He skates at Rockefeller Center, I play hockey.[15] Come on, let's go."

As they were leaving, a campaign staffer in the lobby called the suite to issue a warning: "There are TV cameras and about forty Kennedy supporters standing outside the main entrance near the senator's car waiting to heckle him."

"Okay, thanks," Blair said. "We'll handle it." Hanging up the phone, Blair turned to Jon Fish, the McCarthy team's odd-man-out. While on spring break from Orange County's Whittier Law School in 1967, Jon recognized McCarthy at a financial services reception in a D.C. Irish bar. After introducing himself, the brash young student told McCarthy jokingly that any conservative Republican Protestant from Spokane like him could drink under the table the heartiest liberal Irish-Catholic Minnesotan. Jon's abrasive charm amused McCarthy, and after Jon proceeded to prove his point, the two became unlikely friends. Even though Jon favored Governor Ronald Reagan for the Republican GOP nomination in 1968, he took a semester leave of absence from law school to help do advance and informal security for McCarthy's primary campaign.

"Hey Jon," Blair said, "we have a bunch of TV cameras and Kennedy troublemakers out front wanting to rattle Gene when he leaves the hotel."

"Give me four minutes," Jon replied, "and then bring the senator through the front door to the car." Jon rushed down the hallway and took the elevator to the ground floor. As he dashed through the lobby, he mussed his hair, loosened his necktie, and then reached into his pocket and pulled out a jumbo-sized Kennedy campaign button. After pinning it to his jacket lapel, he ran outside and stood in front of the crowd of Kennedy partisans.

"Hey everyone," Jon shouted at them, "I just learned they're sneaking McCarthy out the side door to avoid us. Come on! Follow me!" With that, Jon bolted around the main entrance of the Mark Hopkins and ran down Mason Street. Like lemmings, every Kennedy supporter and television camera followed. A minute later, Gene McCarthy strolled undisturbed from the main entrance to his waiting automobile.[16]

Outside KGO, the San Francisco local ABC network affiliate on Golden Gate Avenue, a large gathering of pro-McCarthy supporters stood waving signs and cheering when their candidate arrived. Surprisingly, no Kennedyites were there to hiss as McCarthy's car pulled up. Gene acknowledged his cheering fans, and then entered the secure lobby and took the elevator to the fifth-floor studio.[17] A mile away, as Bobby's car traveled down Turk Street, his driver received word over their two-way radio that a hostile crowd awaited his arrival. Instead of stopping in front of KGO, the Kennedy caravan bypassed the pro-McCarthyites gathered outside the main doors and turned into the nearby alley, where Bobby entered the studio unnoticed through a side door.[18]

After sitting for makeup, the candidates stepped onto the small set a few minutes before the 6:30 p.m. airtime. McCarthy looked relaxed, while Kennedy appeared nervous and edgy. They took their seats around the small round table with three reporters. The producer threw a cue to the moderator, and the one-hour debate began.[19]

For all the buildup, the confrontation showed few differences between the two liberal Democrats. On issue after issue, the candidates generally agreed (or disagreed only at the margins).[20] At one point, McCarthy tried to draw blood when he asked Kennedy directly whether, as attorney general, he wiretapped Martin Luther King, Jr. Kennedy balked at the question, called King a great American, but declined to answer. When McCarthy didn't press the point, Jon Fish, a budding deputy district attorney, grew irritable watching the failed cross-examination. "Goddamn it, Gene, don't let him off the hook! Make him answer!" he shouted angrily at the monitor in McCarthy's dressing room.

"Relax, kid," Blair told him. "Gene made his point. He wants to call out Bobby but doesn't want to alienate his supporters."

Later, when the moderator raised the issue of civil rights, Gene complained that America's ghettos had created an "apartheid" situation for blacks in the United States, and he called for programs to help move black families out of these slums. That set the scene for one of the lowest blows thrown in modern American politics. Bobby spun in his seat, faced Gene, and countered with this claim: "You want to take ten thousand black people out of the ghettos and move them into Orange County."[21]

Blair Clark, watching the exchange, almost had a stroke when Gene failed to respond to Bobby's cheap shot. Now Blair did the shouting at the monitor. "Did you hear that? He just told every suburban white voter in the state that Gene's going to move the slum Negroes into *their* neighborhoods. What in hell are you doing, Gene? Jam it down his fucking throat! Why aren't these goddamn reporters challenging Kennedy on this racist remark?"

Jon Fish patted Blair on the shoulder. "Relax, kid," he parroted back. "Gene made his point. He wants to call out Bobby but doesn't want to alienate his supporters."

After the debate, Gene and his team left the studio and returned to their Nob Hill hotel. Unwinding in the candidate's suite over cocktails, Jon complained about Gene letting Kennedy get away with that racial kidney punch.

"That comment was nothing new," Gene replied. "Kennedy campaigns in Watts preaching black and white reconciliation, and then he drives down the freeway into your heavily conservative Orange County and tells the white voters I want to dump Watts into their bedroom communities. He's been saying it for weeks and the press ignores it—that and his other hypocrisies. For example, he tells veteran groups that I'd negotiate with communists in Vietnam, yet he and his brother negotiated with communists from Russia to China to Cuba. When he speaks to non-Jewish groups, he says I'll threaten Middle East peace by providing jets to Israel. When he addresses Jewish groups, he pledges to provide Israel those same jets.[22] His campaign has put out a barrage of paid ads lying about my record on everything from civil rights to the war.[23] No matter how many times I challenge him on it, the press gives him a pass. He's running the same kind of smear campaign against me that he ran in New York to win his Senate seat.[24] He's a cheap, petty campaigner. He's like the rich Victorian father whose daughter fell in love with the chimney sweep—he'll spare no effort to destroy me."[25]

"Well, you had the chance to bypass his press coddling tonight and smack him directly in front of millions of people. If you had, you might beat him for sure next Tuesday."

Grinning, Gene gave Jon an almost fatherly look. "What makes you think I want to *beat* Bobby on Tuesday?"

The reply dumbfounded Jon. "I don't understand—if you don't want to win, then what's this all about?"

"Oh, I want to win, I just don't necessarily want to win *on Tuesday*. I do want to come in at least a close second."

"But—"

Gene put down his drink. "Look, Jon, if Kennedy loses California, he'll leave the race, and then he'll endorse Humphrey, or else he'll quietly urge his supporters to shift to Humphrey. He'll never endorse me. However, if he wins California, but not by much, he'll stay in the race and the press attention will remain on our campaign for the nomination. It's ironic. I believe losing California strengthens my position."[26]

"Senator, you're either suicidal, a maniac, or a genius."

Gene laughed. "When will you let me know what you decide?"

"Wednesday morning."

Gene added a final thought before bidding his team goodnight. "You know, after tonight's debate, I've come to a firm conclusion—Robert Kennedy is utterly unfit to be president of the United States."

Jon's VO and water went up his nose when he laughed mid-swallow at the observation. "Hell, I could have told you that," he guffawed, "and saved you lots of time and trouble campaigning!"

"It's more than that, my young Republican friend. I came to a second conclusion as well—

"—I've concluded that if Robert Kennedy wins the Democratic presidential nomination, I will *never* support him for the presidency."[27]

Poster promoting RFK's motorcade through Oakland, California (June 1, 1968), and a primary day election handbill (June 4, 1968) (Author's collection)

CHAPTER 15

EARLY SUNDAY MORNING, as soon as Bobby Kennedy boarded his American L-188 Electra campaign jet at San Francisco International Airport, he joined his war council in the aft section as the plane lifted off for the final two-day push before Tuesday's make-or-break California primary.

After bumming a cigar from Pierre Salinger, Bobby asked pollster Chris Evans how his debate performance against Eugene McCarthy played last night. "We did some overnight tracking in key media markets," Chris said. "Most Democrats viewed it as a draw, which I think translates into a slight edge for you. McCarthy has been slicing into your lead out here all week, so a draw will probably slow or stop the bleeding."

"How does it look in today's clips?" Bobby asked deputy press secretary Jeff Solsby.

"About the same. Most of the reporters and columnists are calling it a tie. The *New York Times* said there were so few policy differences between you and McCarthy that it was like watching an electronic tennis match, with both contenders playing on the same side of the net."*

"I wish the national preference polls showed a draw," Chris said unenthusiastically. "We're still hurting there." Chris handed Bobby the latest Gallup poll, showing Bobby running third in the three-man nomination race. Among Democrats nationally, 32 percent favor McCarthy, Humphrey gets 29 percent, and only 25 percent want Bobby.[1]

"Goddamn it," Bobby griped as he reviewed the results. "This poll shows 60 percent of Democrats nationally reject the Johnson-Humphrey policies, but I can't break through and go after Hubert until we get rid of McCarthy."

"Here's some good news," Fred Dutton volunteered. "In the last few days we've been getting resumes from some of McCarthy's mid-level staffers. They're hoping to line up jobs with us because they think their man will lose badly on Tuesday and end his campaign."[2]

"McCarthy's holding his own in Southern California outside of Los Angeles," Chris said. "Your greatest opportunity is in the San Francisco Bay Area."

Bobby asked Pierre Salinger what the campaign was doing to turn out the black voters there. "Our people are working with Willie Brown and Jess Unruh in San Francisco," Pierre replied. "They're buying up as many pastors in the black churches as they can, and they're spreading the 'walkin' around money' pretty heavily to get their people out to vote."[3]

Bobby grinned. "When Jack was accused of having my father buying votes for him, he joked in a speech later that Dad had just sent him a telegram reading, 'Dear Jack, Don't buy a single vote more than necessary. I'll be damned if I'll pay for a landslide!'"**

"I still think you ought to spend less time in the minority neighborhoods these next two days and more time in the suburbs," Chris

---

*   Jack Gould, *New York Times*, June 3, 1968.

**   Paul Burka, "Presidential Hopefuls Juggle Appealing to the Common Man While Benefiting from Their Sizable Bank Accounts" *Los Angeles Times*, July 25, 2004. See http://articles.baltimoresun.com/2004-07-25/topic/0407240265_1_wealth-kingdom-of-god-john-f.

cautioned. "Your schedulers keep putting you out in the Mexican and black neighborhoods. You're going to get those votes anyway. The footage on the news each night of you surrounded by frenzied mobs of minorities grabbing at you registers as a violent picture, and white voters frightened by Negro riots for the last three years don't like these images. By concentrating on those communities, you may be surrendering large pockets of the suburban vote to McCarthy."[4]

Bobby concurred in the advice but balked at ordering any late schedule changes. "Our entire strategy for Tuesday is based on a large percentage of minority voters turning out. We need to finish McCarthy off with a big win so we can concentrate on Hubert." Then, with a final puff on Pierre's loaner cigar, he closed the session as the plane prepared to land in Los Angeles. "We have forty-eight hours, and everybody knows what to do—

"—Let's go kick some ass."

Hotel room key to the Royal Suite, Room 516, the Ambassador Hotel, Los Angeles, used by the Kennedy party June 2-5, 1968 (Author's collection)

For the next two days, Bobby barnstormed up and down California in his final push, taking only a few hours off that Sunday to fulfill a longstanding promise to his children by taking them to Disneyland, where they rode the new "Pirates of the Caribbean" ride.[5] Later that afternoon, while his family checked into room 516, the Royal Suite of the Ambassador Hotel (their home until after Tuesday night's primary), he returned to the campaign trail and pounded McCarthy relentlessly in the minority communities of San Francisco, the Central Valley, and Los Angeles. In each sector, he pleaded for the heavy turnout he needed to offset McCarthy's blue-collar and middle-class strength.[6]

On Monday, June 3, the last full day of campaigning, Bobby blanketed the state with a grueling schedule. He crisscrossed California so many times that by late afternoon he had no idea where he was heading. Late that night, when he reached his final event, a speech and rally at San Diego's El Cortez Hotel, he suffered from horrible nausea and fatigue. Still, with over 3,000 fans crammed into the ballroom, he took the stage gamely as the crowd cheered itself hoarse. Halfway through this last speech, his senior staff watching from the wings saw him appear to grow dizzy. Suddenly, he stopped speaking, stepped away from the lectern, sat on the edge of the stage, and put his head in his hands. He could no longer hide his exhaustion.

An eerie hush fell over the ballroom as Chris Evans and Fred Dutton rushed forward and half-carried the candidate behind the curtains and out of view. Meanwhile, Jeff Solsby grabbed the microphone and pleaded: "Everyone, if you'll just remain in your seats, Senator Kennedy will be right back. He's been burning the candle at both ends, as you know. He just needs some water. Give us a few minutes for an intermission."

As the audience waited, Chris led Bobby to the backstage men's room. Bobby fumbled into the nearest stall, knelt on the tile floor and threw up. Then, while Bobby splashed cold water on his face, Chris grabbed a paper towel and cleaned splashed vomit off the candidate's pants and shoe. Looking up as he finished the job, Chris grinned and said mischievously, "I guess it's true—everyone on your staff does end up as your goddamn valet!"

"I'll make it up to you," Bobby said as he dried his face. "Tell you what—when we win I'll make you ambassador to France."

A minute later, Bobby strode back onstage amid thunderous applause and finished the last speech of his California primary campaign.[7]

It was almost midnight on Election Day, Tuesday June 4, when Bobby's plane landed in Los Angeles. While his older children slept at the Ambassador Hotel, he and Ethel drove to Malibu, where they spent the night at the secluded beachfront home of movie director John Frankenheimer.

That night, Bobby slept an uninterrupted twelve hours—his first solid night's sleep since early March.

Tuesday afternoon—California primary day—Vice President Hubert Humphrey arrived in Denver, where he planned to spend the night at the United States Air Force Academy before delivering a speech to the cadets Wednesday morning. Riding in the limousine from the airport to his Colorado Springs destination with aide Ted Van Dyke, they listened on the car radio to early bulletins on turnout projections from California. Ted said that he assumed Humphrey preferred to see McCarthy, his fellow Minnesotan, defeat Kennedy tonight, since Kennedy promised to be a far more difficult rival at the Chicago convention.

Humphrey's answer surprised Ted: "I want Bobby Kennedy to win as decisively as possible. I want it to be so one-sided that McCarthy will be driven from the race entirely."

"Mr. Vice President, putting aside the fact that Kennedy is your biggest threat, didn't you once tell me he smeared you terribly in 1960?"

"Yes, that's true." Humphrey looked out the window at the passing scenery as he recounted his experiences with Bobby during HHH's failed campaign against John F. Kennedy for the 1960 Democratic nomination. "Bobby didn't just fight hard. He also fought dirty. When I challenged Jack in the Wisconsin primary, Bobby pedaled the story that Jimmy Hoffa and mobsters bankrolled my race.[8] You'd think the claim might be laughable, given that we ran our campaign on a shoestring, and we bumped down the backroads of Wisconsin and West Virginia in a beat-up rented bus. While our driver fixed flat tires and called for tow trucks, the Kennedys covered both states in their luxurious Convair jet. You should have seen that thing—it had an office, a full kitchen, a bedroom, a masseuse, and a chef.[9]

"The worst of it came in West Virginia, when Bobby pressured

Franklin Roosevelt Jr. to go there and tell voters that I dodged the draft in World War II.[10] That horrible smear finished me off. I guess I've never quite forgiven Bobby for his terrible behavior during that race."[11]

"With that history, and with the cheap shots he's thrown at you in this race,[12] why would you want to see him win big tonight?"

Hubert turned to face his aide. "I'll tell you why. It's because Bobby Kennedy and I understand each other. We've talked privately on a couple of occasions that you don't know about. If I win the nomination, he'll campaign for me without reservation.[13] If he wins, I'll campaign for him. In spite of everything, he's a Party regular, but if he loses California, he'll get out of the race. Then I'll be stuck with Gene as my opponent, and he'll plague me all the way to the convention—and beyond.[14] I know Gene, and I have affection for him, but he's a spoiler. He won't endorse either Bobby or me, so I want him gone after tonight."[15]

"Aren't you worried that if Kennedy wins California and McCarthy gets out, it'll give him momentum heading into the convention?"

"No. There are too many Party leaders opposed to Bobby for him to have any real chance of winning the nomination. Once Johnson dropped out and started moving toward peace, and then after McCarthy's strong showings in Wisconsin and Oregon, and Bobby's anemic wins in the other states, any chance Bobby had to close the deal was gone.[16] Besides, every time I've faced his forces in state convention fights—Pennsylvania, Vermont, Idaho, Iowa, and others—I've won."[17]

"You're pretty forgiving to a guy that won dirty against you in 1960 and is hitting you below the belt now."

"Ted, this morning, before we left D.C., Fred Harris called. He said that as of now we have enough delegate pledges to win the nomination on the first ballot." Then, with a wink, Hubert finished his thought:

"Under those circumstances, I can afford to be forgiving."[18]

By the time Bobby awoke in Malibu and came downstairs, it was past lunchtime. After a quick meal, he played on the beach with some of his children. Later, returning to the house in his swim trunks, he poured a large glass of orange juice and joined Ethel, John Frankenheimer, and a few senior aides and friends around the pool. As they stretched out on beach chairs under the warm sunshine, Chris brought up an issue that was always on everyone's mind, yet few ever raised directly—and Chris did it without varnish. "You know, don't you, that somebody's going to try to kill you eventually?"

Unfazed, Bobby replied, "I know. That's the chance I have to take."

"Besides Bill, Rafer, and Rosie, do you take any special precautions?"****

Bobby shrugged. "There's really no way to protect a presidential candidate stumping the country. You have to give yourself to the crowd, and beyond that, you're at the mercy of that old bitch, luck. You have to have luck on your side to win the presidency anyway. Either it's with you or it isn't." Taking another gulp of orange juice, he continued unemotionally, "I expect someone will try eventually. If it happens, it probably won't even be for political reasons—it will be someone who is just a nut. There are plenty of them around. Do you know how many times Charles De Gaulle survived assassination attempts?"

"I don't know—six or seven?"

"Thirty-one. De Gaulle had luck. Like I said, you can't make it without that old bitch, luck."[19]

As the group continued soaking up the warm afternoon sun, Bobby shared an impulsive idea with press aide Jeff Solsby. "I'd like to skip the hotel speech tonight. Why don't we just stay here at John's and watch the returns on TV? We can invite the press over, and they can interview me here. I'm too tired to have to deal with all those crowds tonight."

"Let me see what I can do, senator." Jeff left the pool to place the phone calls to the networks.

By mid-afternoon, everyone wandered inside the house and watched

---

**** In an era before Secret Service agents protected presidential candidates routinely, RFK's "security detail" was very informal. During the California primary, it consisted of friends: former FBI agent Bill Barry, former Los Angeles Rams defensive tackle Roosevelt Grier, and 1960 Olympics decathlete Rafer Johnson.

intermittent news bulletins. By three o'clock, Bobby heard CBS News project that based on early voting patterns, he would win the California primary with 49 percent.

"That's not good enough," Bobby grumped to Dick Goodwin. "What the hell happened? Last night they projected I'd win 52-39.[20] We need to make sure the final vote pushes me over 50 percent."

"What's the practical difference between beating McCarthy with 49 percent and beating him with 50 percent? A win is a win."

Bobby handed Dick a sheet of paper that Chris Evans gave him a few minutes earlier. It contained the latest Gallup estimates of the delegate breakdowns. "Without entering any primaries, Humphrey's got over 1,000 delegates already. After tonight, we should have 500 or so. McCarthy will have around 200. There'll be another 900 delegates up for grabs, and they won't be grabbed in the primaries—they'll get picked in state caucuses and conventions, or in the back rooms. If we don't knock out McCarthy tonight, we'll have to spend the rest of June fighting him in the New York primary. I can't lose my own state to him, so we'll have to spend the next three weeks standing on every street corner begging New Yorkers to vote for me—all while Hubert's running around the country reeling in the remaining uncommitted delegates. We need to chase Hubert's ass after tonight. I need to spend every minute of the next ten weeks traveling to other states and meeting those delegates before it's too late."[21]

Putting an additional damper on the moment, Ted Sorensen walked in the room and said that the situation was worse than Gallup projected. "I just got a call from our people in Ohio and New Jersey. It looks like both delegations will go all-out for Humphrey next week."[22]

"Damn—see what I mean?" Bobby said. "I've got to take out McCarthy tonight. We need to drive those numbers over 50 percent between now and eight o'clock. You guys figure out how to do it—I'm going to take a nap."

"Ethel, it's five o'clock. Shall we wake up Bob?" Ted Sorensen asked.

Ethel Kennedy looked up from her magazine. "Give him a few more minutes. If we win tonight, it may be a long time before he gets any rest."

An hour later, Ethel opened the bedroom door and saw her husband still sleeping soundly. Shaking him gently, she whispered, "Come on, Bob. We need to leave for the hotel soon." Bobby put on a borrowed bathrobe and walked into the living room. "Hey, Jeff," he called to his press flak, "did you work it out with the networks to skip the hotel speech tonight?"

"Sorry, senator. I called around. The networks and affiliates won't haul all their equipment out here to Malibu. They're already setting up at the Ambassador—about eleven TV cameras alone, not counting klieg lights, still photographers, and print media. We'll need to go."[23]

Bobby grimaced. "Shit," he muttered, and then went back into the bedroom. After showering and dressing, he was ready. At 6:45, he and John Frankenheimer climbed into John's Rolls Royce Silver Cloud III for the drive to the hotel.

"What will you do if you lose tonight?" John asked as he started the engine.

"I'll go home and raise the next generation of Kennedys."[24]

While John raced down the Santa Monica freeway during the thirty-minute drive to the mid-town hotel, Bobby chastised him jokingly about his speeding. "Take it easy, John. Slow down—life is too short!"[25]

At 7:15 p.m., with Hollywood's iconic Brown Derby restaurant in sight, John's car turned off Wilshire Boulevard and into the long driveway passing the Coconut Grove. He pulled around to the loading dock at the back of the Ambassador Hotel. The assistant maître d', Karl Uecker, greeted the Kennedy party, escorted them through a maze of corridors into a service elevator, and then delivered them to their suite.

After the polls closed at 8:00 p.m., and as the next few hours ticked away, the secure fifth floor hallway became claustrophobically crowded with friends, family, staff, photographers, and sympathetic reporters. Tables of bland deli snacks sat near the hosted bar in the corner of one room. Throughout the slow vote count, Kennedy smiled and joked often, but his demeanor grew serious each time he scoured Chris Evans' updated returns showing McCarthy dominating the northern part of the state unexpectedly. Bobby counted on winning Southern California, but now he worried whether he would get a large enough margin there to offset McCarthy's unexpected strength in the Bay Area.

It wasn't until 11:00 p.m. that Bobby started pulling ahead of his rival. By 11:30, he knew he had won, but the results disappointed him. His desire to hit 50 percent fell far short—he won a narrow 45-42 win over McCarthy.[26]

Bobby huddled with senior staffers Ted Sorensen, Larry O'Brien, Chris Evans, and Dick Goodwin in the only private place they could find on the fifth floor—an empty bathroom in the Royal Suite. "This is disappointing, but not surprising," Larry said as he interpreted Chris' updated delegate count. "While all those mobs were fawning over you in the small primary states, Hubert's quietly lining up overwhelming delegate numbers in the big states like New Jersey, Pennsylvania, and Ohio. Unless we can find a way to shake loose those commitments, he'll win the nomination no matter what your margin looks like tonight."

"McCarthy hates me so much that he'll never step aside now," Bobby lamented. "What if we throw him a Hail Mary pass?"

"What do you mean?" Larry asked.

Turning to Dick Goodwin, Bobby said, "Dick, you're the logical go-between on this. What if you call McCarthy right now and float a deal. Tell him to leave the race tonight and endorse me, and if I win, I'll appoint him secretary of state."[27]

"Why don't you just promise to appoint him to the papacy?" Dick replied sarcastically. "You'll have just as much chance to get him out of the race with *that* promise. Forget it. Gene will never quit and endorse you now. Besides, you're right—he hates you."[28]

Jeff Solsby knocked on the bathroom door to let everyone know McCarthy was on television conceding defeat. The six men squeezed their way to a nearby set and watched their opponent congratulate Kennedy, and then vow to continue the fight to Chicago. At one point in his remarks, Gene told his cheering but dejected volunteers that winning wasn't the most important thing in life. When Bobby heard that, he nudged Chris Evans in the ribs with his elbow playfully. "That's not what my father taught me," he whispered with a grin.[29]

"Okay—let's go downstairs," Bobby said after McCarthy finished, and most of the crowd on the fifth floor rushed toward the hallway elevators. Maitre d' Karl Uecker told Bobby he would escort him and his staff down to the rear of the ballroom through the kitchen. "You'd never get through that thick crowd tonight," he told the candidate. "We removed all of the ballroom's divider panels, and we still have hundreds of people that we can't fit inside."

"Couldn't we just squeeze them in?" Bobby asked.

"No. An L.A. fire captain is keeping a careful watch on the ballroom capacity, and he's a Republican."

As the Kennedys followed Karl out of the suite, with senior staff in tow, Bobby looked back and saw Dick Goodwin talking on the telephone. "Hey, are you coming down with us?" he asked.

Dick covered the mouthpiece with his hand. "You guys go ahead. I've been trying to reach this big McCarthy donor for days, and he just called. I'll watch on TV and then meet up with you at the party later." Once Bobby gave his ballroom speech, and then did a quick press conference in the adjacent Colonial Room, his family and friends planned a private victory celebration for him at The Factory, one of Los Angeles' newest discotheques co-owned by Pierre Salinger and several Hollywood luminaries.[30]

"Okay," Bobby told him, "I'll go do this now. We'll compare notes at the party." Dick, who was already back on the phone talking with the prospective supporter, nodded but didn't answer verbally as he watched Bobby and the entourage leave.[31]

Karl brought the Kennedy party down a service elevator to the second floor, where the nearby Embassy Room blared with music, election return updates, and loud applause. They cut through the hotel kitchen and nearby pantry. It was a slow process, since Bobby stopped every few feet to shake hands with the cooks, maids, waiters, and bus-boys. One ecstatic fan encountered his hero by chance and scored a coveted autograph on a rolled-up Kennedy campaign poster.

After exiting the pantry's swinging service doors, Bobby's staffers filed through the curtains that led onto the Embassy Room stage, while Bobby and Ethel remained out of sight awaiting his introduction. Roger Mahan, one of the campaign's advance men, briefed him. "Senator, we have a huge crowd and they're fired up. When you finish your remarks, we'll move you offstage to your right. The press is waiting in the Colonial Room about 100 feet away. We'll form a wedge around you and Mrs. Kennedy as we move through the mob. Just keep moving stage right with us. We promised the press ten minutes max, and then Karl will get us down to the garage and on our way to the party."

"Never mind me, Roger, form your wedge around Ethel. With her pregnancy, I don't want her delivering prematurely on the way to the press conference. And tell Pierre if the beers aren't cold when we get to his club, he can go join his investment firm tomorrow!"

Bobby was still talking when the emcee introduced him, so he missed hearing his cue. "Come on, Bob," Ethel said as she took his hand and led him up the seven stairs to the curtain opening. Bobby paused just before they stepped onto the stage and told her, "When we're done out there stay right next to me. It's a thick crowd, and the staff will huddle around to get us out."

Bedlam erupted among 1,500 ecstatic supporters when Bobby and Ethel appeared. Looking tanned and rested, he stepped to the rostrum and pulled from his breast pocket an envelope on which he had jotted some notes. Giving a brief speech intentionally so he could wrap up the evening and get to the party, he congratulated McCarthy, called for Party unity, and expressed hope that his campaign might end the divisions in America.

Standing at the edge of the stage, Roger and fellow advance man Dan Swanson surveyed the thick crush of people blocking the right side of the stage all the way to the Colonial Room entrance. "We'll never get him out that way," Roger said. Turning to Karl Uecker, he asked, "Can we move him to the press conference another way?"

"We can backtrack the way we came—through the pantry and kitchen. It's not a direct route, but it will avoid the mob."

"Okay, let's do that." Roger relayed the message to Dan as Bobby slid his speech notes back into his jacket pocket, which signaled to his staff that he was wrapping up. Bobby finished his remarks extemporaneously: "We are a great country, an unselfish country, and a compassionate country. And I intend to make that my basis for running." Pausing until the cheers died down, he added,

"So my thanks to all of you, and now it's on to Chicago—and let's win there."

With a wave and a thumb's up sign, Bobby started moving to his right as planned originally. KRKD radio reporter Andrew West delayed him onstage by thrusting a microphone forward and asking a question about Humphrey's current delegate strength. Because he stopped briefly to reply, that eight-second delay gave Roger time to catch up and reorient Bobby to the change in plans.

"This way, senator," Roger said as he gripped Bobby's forearm. "We're going this way."

Bobby stopped, pivoted, and backtracked as he followed Roger and Karl Uecker offstage through the slit in the drapes as they retraced their earlier steps. Because of the last-moment redirection, Bobby and Karl ended up leading the crush of bodies pressing forward rather than finding themselves inside any protective wedge.

With Karl at his elbow, Bobby entered the pantry through the two swinging doors and saw the kitchen help lined up along the wall applauding for him. He moved slowly down the line shaking hands with each. Near the ice machine and steam tables, a seventeen-year old busboy, Juan Romero, was thrilled to congratulate his hero on this historic night. As Bobby grabbed Juan's hand, he heard a woman's voice call out, "Where's Ethel?"

That random question concerned him—he assumed Ethel was right behind him. Had the surging crowd separated her from the protective huddle? Now worried that the exuberant mob pushing forward might jostle or injure his pregnant wife, Bobby spun his head quickly to look back while calling to her simultaneously:

"Ethe—"

Memorabilia from the Ambassador Hotel, Los Angeles, 1940s-1960s (Author's collection)

CHAPTER 16

IT WAS AFTER MIDNIGHT ON JUNE 5 when Robert Kennedy made his victory speech. As soon as he finished, the network news coverage began signing off for the night. Vice President Hubert Humphrey stayed up watching the returns in his VIP cabin at the US Air Force Academy lodge. Satisfied that Bobby would remain in the race, but disappointed that his margin failed to drive out McCarthy, he switched off the television. Five minutes later, his phone rang just as he began nodding off. Ted Van Dyk was on the line asking, "Mr. Vice President, I assume you know?"

"I just shut it off a few minutes ago. At least Bobby's still in the race—that'll help. I only wish his margin—"

"Sir, you'd better turn the TV back on. Senator Kennedy was just shot, and it sounds like it might be serious."

"Oh, no—"

Hubert jumped out of bed, switched on the set, and watched as CBS cameras broadcast live images showing pandemonium and confusion in the Embassy Room. A man on stage stood at the microphone where Bobby spoke just a few minutes ago and asked if there was a doctor in the crowd. Hubert recognized him—Steve Smith, Bobby's brother-in-law and one of his campaign chiefs.[1] A few minutes later, along with several senior Air Force generals who arrived, Ted joined the vice president in his room. The men watched the developing nightmare in silence.

After making a brief concession speech, Gene McCarthy returned to his seventh floor suite at the Beverly Hilton with campaign manager Blair Clark, Jon Fish, Curtis Gans, and a few other aides.[2] As they gathered around a table to discuss scheduling before flying to New York tomorrow for the next push in the final primary state, a room service waiter rolled in a cart with two large coffee urns. When Jon saw his limited beverage option, he walked over to the dresser, grabbed a mini-bottle of bourbon, and dumped it into his coffee cup. "I can see that a white trash Lutheran needs to show all you Jesuit stiffs how to drink coffee properly," he said.

Jon heard a television set playing in one of the bedrooms, so he walked in to turn it off. There he saw the initial panicked reports beaming from the Ambassador Hotel. After absorbing the startling news, he rushed to the other room and interrupted the staff meeting: "Kennedy was just shot!" After the law student flicked on the nearby television, he noticed that Gene appeared blasé while everyone else at the conference table looked shell-shocked. When Gene did respond, the man reporter Theodore H. White once called the most religious person in American politics[3] said something very unreligious:

"That Bobby—demagoguing to the last."

"Holy shit, Gene," Blair Clark said angrily. "How can you say that now?"

Gene sipped his coffee dismissively. "Why not? He brought this on himself."[4]

"Uh, okay," Jon mumbled, and quickly poured another mini-bottle into his coffee cup.

As the drama unfolded on television, Gene never budged from his callous reaction until he saw images of Ethel Kennedy, distraught and looking lost, entering the hospital. Suddenly, his iciness melted. Crossing himself, he said quietly, "Jon, please get me the number for the hospital. I need to call her." Over the next hour, Gene called Good Samaritan Hospital several times asking to speak to her. Each time Dick Goodwin intercepted the call; each time Ethel refused to come on the line.

"We need to go there," Gene said. With no formal security detail yet attached to them, Jon doubled as bodyguard and chauffer. He led Gene and Blair down to the garage. Taking the wheel of their rented sedan, he drove to Good Samaritan, a ten-mile straight shot eastbound on Wilshire Boulevard. When they neared their destination, he parked illegally on Shatto Place. "Senator, I'll stay here with the car and keep it from being towed. You guys get going."

Gene and Blair walked past the scores of cameras and reporters congregating outside, refusing comment as he entered the hospital lobby. Pierre Salinger and Dick Goodwin met him near the rear elevator bank.

"Senator," Pierre said, "Ethel's not seeing anyone. The doctors are worried about her pregnancy. We need to speak to you, though."

"Of course."

Pierre and Dick led Gene into a private room off the lobby and then closed the door behind them.

"We have a request for you. It isn't easy to ask, and it won't be easy for you to do it," Pierre said.

"What is it?"

Pierre and Dick looked at each other briefly before Pierre proceeded.

"Gene, we'd like you to fly to Washington immediately, meet with President Johnson, and ask him to announce he will be a candidate for reelection. We don't know how badly Bobby's injured—we just know it's a head wound."

While Gene listened to the unexpected plea, Pierre continued. "Respectfully, you can't win the nomination, and Humphrey can't win the general election. For the sake of the Democratic Party, you need to urge Johnson to run again."

At first, Gene said nothing. Then, without making any promise, he replied, "I can see logic in what you are saying. I'll think about it."[5]

Pierre left the room to take a call, leaving Dick and Gene alone for the first time since Dick quit McCarthy's campaign two months ago.

"Do they know who did this?" Gene asked.

"They have him in custody. He's twenty-four. A part-time jockey. Some Palestinian misfit named Sirhan Sirhan."

"Sirhan Sirhan," Gene lamented. "It's just like in Camus' *The Stranger*—the protagonist's first and last names are the same."[6]

Pierre stuck his head back in the room. "Excuse me—Dick, the Washington office needs to speak to you."

"Senator, I'll be right back." Dick Goodwin left for five minutes. When he returned, he found an empty room. Gene McCarthy was gone.

In Chicago, at the Green Duck Metal Stamping Company on West Montana Street, Jeremy Burks worked the graveyard shift at one of America's oldest campaign button manufacturers. Not long after midnight, the telephone rang unexpectedly. Jeremy answered a call from the plant supervisor, Dean Allevato.

"Hey, Jeremy, did we process that order for 10,000 new Kennedy badges yet?"

"We printed the flat metal sheets already, but we haven't run them through the blanking press to punch out the badges. I was going to do that tonight so the girls could pin and finish them in the morning. They should be ready to ship by late afternoon."

"Don't blank them," Dean instructed. "Kennedy was just shot—I think he's dead—and his campaign hasn't paid for the order yet. It looks like we'll have to eat those charges for the work already done."

While Jeremy expressed shock over the developing story, Dean came up with another idea. "Hey, have you run those George Wallace three-and-a-half inchers yet?"

"We've printed the face plate, but we haven't assembled them. That's scheduled to run on Thursday."

"Tell you what—take those Kennedy badge sheets and use them as the back plate for the Wallace badges. We can cut our losses that way."

Jeremy hesitated for a moment before raising an issue with his boss. "Isn't taking Bobby Kennedy campaign buttons and turning them into George Wallace campaign buttons, under the circumstances, sort of, well—sacrilegious?"

"Sacrilegious?" Dean scoffed. "Hey, I'm a Wallace man myself. If I can take some lib's badges and turn them into Wallace badges, that's not a sacrilege—that's patriotism.

"Run the order."

Actual 1968 George Wallace campaign button manufactured by Green Duck Co., Chicago, with the back pried off showing uncut Kennedy buttons the manufacturer used for the Wallace campaign button back plates (Author's collection)

Ted Van Dyke noticed the time on the nightstand clock—almost 1:00 a.m.—when he answered the ringing telephone in Vice President Humphrey's cabin. A moment later, he passed the handset. "Mr. Vice President, it's Pierre Salinger. He's calling from the hospital."

Hubert took the call. "Pierre, my God—is he all right? What the hell happened?"

"Mr. Vice President, we don't know much. He was unconscious when they got him in the ambulance. Ethel said blood was pouring from his head. He may also have a chest wound, too. The ambulance rushed him to the closest hospital about a mile from the hotel. Once the ER doctors saw a head wound, they ordered him transferred to Good Samaritan, where they have neurosurgeons on standby. They wheeled Bobby in about five minutes ago. I don't know if he's in surgery yet."

"Where's Ethel? Is she okay?"

"She's very shaken but unhurt. She was with him when it happened. Ted Sorensen's sitting with her in a private room down the hall. Ted Kennedy's flying in from San Francisco—he should be here within the hour."

"Pierre, please, tell Ethel if there is anything—"

Fighting back tears, Pierre interrupted, "Hubert, we *do* need your help—desperately. It's a head wound and we don't know the extent of the damage. We're told one of the premiere brain neurosurgeons in the world is on vacation in Boston, Dr. Alex Dourbetas. We need you to intercede and arrange immediate military transportation for him. Please, Hubert—we need help *now*, and we don't have time to screw around."

"It's done, Pierre. Here, give Ted the details." Hubert handed the phone back to Ted Van Dyk while he gave the order for the special plane to the commandant of the Air Force Academy, General Robin Olds, who had joined other officers in the vice president's room earlier.

"Right away, sir," General Olds replied, and left to execute the command. A few minutes later, the base operations officer arrived to speak with Humphrey. "Sir, before I can release any plane, regulations require I ask by what authority you are ordering it."

"Goddamn it, young man," Hubert barked, "I am ordering that plane under my authority as vice commander in chief of the United States Armed Forces!"[7]

"Yes sir!" the young officer answered as he saluted and ran from the room.

Ted leaned over and whispered to his boss, "*Vice* commander in chief? I didn't know such a position existed in the Constitution."

"It worked, didn't it?"[8] Picking up the phone, Hubert called Pierre Salinger back at the hospital and told him the plane would be ready for takeoff at Hanscom Air Force Base in Bedford upon Dr. Dourbetas' arrival.

"Hubert, you have no idea how—how very grateful—" Pierre choked up. He couldn't finish his sentence.

"I'm here, Pierre, for whatever you and the family need."

"Thank you. I'll check back later with an update once we get it."

After hanging up, Hubert and Ted sat before their television awaiting any new bulletins while watching hundreds of people gathering outside the hospital carrying candles and wearing hastily printed "Pray for Bobby" stickers across their backs. Fifteen minutes later, the cabin telephone rang again. "Ted, grab that," Hubert said as he studied the unfolding events on his screen. Ted walked over and picked up the phone, listened for a moment, and then hung up. He looked stricken as he asked to speak to the boss alone. Hubert followed Ted into the small kitchenette.

"Oh, God," Hubert said hesitatingly. "He's gone, isn't he?"

"No, sir. That call wasn't from the hospital. It was from the Pentagon. I don't know how to say this—the president countermanded your order. The Air Force will not be allowed to fly the surgeon."[9]

"I just—I just can't believe he'd do this."

"Sir, shall I call Pierre for you?"

"No. No, I'll do it." Hubert picked up the phone, dialed the hospital, and then told Pierre the humiliating news.

"I understand," said Pierre unemotionally. "I understand completely.

We'll take care of it. And Hubert—thank you for trying. I mean it. That's from Ethel, too."

After hanging up, Hubert told Ted, "The Kennedys will arrange private transportation. I'll call you if there are any new developments. I'd like everyone to leave now."

When Ted and the Air Force brass left the room, Hubert sat on the edge of the bed, lowered his head, and wept.

A few hours later, at Good Samaritan Hospital, Dr. Thomas Barker held a cup of coffee as he knocked on the door of the private fifth floor room where Ethel Kennedy, brother-in-law Steve Smith, Senator Teddy Kennedy, Pierre Salinger, Ted Sorensen, and other family and senior staffers congregated. Everyone looked tense as Dr. Barker introduced himself as Bobby's neurosurgeon, and then offered Ethel the warm cup. "Mrs. Kennedy, we've just finished operating on your husband. We're cautiously optimistic, but with wounds like this, we'll need to wait and see."

"How bad was he hit, doctor?" Teddy Kennedy asked.

"Under the circumstances he was very lucky. A detective told me that witnesses saw the gunman fire his pistol point blank at the senator's head—from only a couple of inches away. The sooting and stripling pattern from the discharge confirms this. The bullet struck Senator Kennedy at the mastoid process, which is the bony area behind the right ear, and it shattered on impact. Instead of penetrating the skull directly, the main projectile struck at an angle and burrowed under the scalp. It then ran like it was on a railroad track wedged between the scalp and the skull. It traversed from the mastoid around the circumference of his posterior skull, and then it exited the scalp behind the left ear. I've seen a few other head wounds like this. Once a bullet strikes bone there's no predicting how it will travel. My guess is that if that bullet had struck the senator one centimeter to the left, I would be telling you right now how very sorry I am for your loss."[10]

"So he has no brain injury?" Teddy asked hopefully.

"Well, that's the complication. We're not sure. As I said, the main projectile didn't penetrate the skull, which is a miracle in itself. The bullet shattered when it struck, and several fragments burrowed into the skull without penetrating the inner cavity and intruding into the brain. We were able to retrieve those fragments from the outer skull area without difficulty. However, the x-ray shows that three small fragments did penetrate and are lodged several centimeters in the outer region of the cerebellum, which is the back of the brain."

"So what does that mean?" Ethel said, growing increasingly frantic. "Is there brain damage? Does he need brain surgery?"

"Mrs. Kennedy, we will know much more when he comes out of the anesthesia. We need to check many things, such as sensory responsiveness, cognition, reflexes, and other neurological indicators. I'd like to remove those fragments and clean the wounds, but the dangers of brain surgery are so significant that the cure might be far worse than the injury. If those fragments cause limited or no impairment, we may need to leave them."

"If you leave them, is there any risk that they'll travel around in the brain and kill or cripple him later?"

"Not usually. Think of embedding a small piece of fruit—like a grape—in a Jello mold. On its own the grape won't travel through the mold. Of course, a future head trauma could jar it into another position, but generally, I would expect the fragment to remain stationary. As long as the fragments cause no severe neurological impairment, he's much safer leaving them alone than if we have to remove sections of his skull and then dig into the brain to retrieve them. Right now, I'm more concerned about infection than I am about retrieval. When any foreign body like a bullet causes a wound, it can carry other debris with it, like bone chips, hair, and pieces of clothing. There's also the concern of germs on the projectile itself. We'll need to watch Senator Kennedy carefully over the next few days for any signs of infection inside the skull. If that occurs, all of our preferences won't matter—we'll need to go in, remove the fragments, and try to repair any damage."

After taking a sip of the coffee Ethel declined, Dr. Barker continued.

"The head wound caused us the most concern, but it's not his only wound. He also suffered a moderate shoulder wound. A bullet entered his right armpit, passed through soft tissue, and lodged just inside the area between the rear shoulder and the base of the neck."

"How could a bullet enter his armpit?" Teddy asked.

"My guess is that the initial head trauma caused the reflexive action of raising the hand to the head, which would leave the axilla—the armpit area—exposed. Again, he was very lucky. The bullet just missed striking the subclavian artery by an inch. If the bullet had severed that artery, he might have bled to death before reaching the hospital. We retrieved that bullet and repaired the tissue damage. He won't be shaking any hands with his right arm for a few weeks, and he'll probably need some physical therapy before his arm and shoulder are 100 percent. A third bullet ripped through the sleeve of his suit jacket, but it did not strike him."

"When can we see him, doctor?"

"We moved him from the ninth floor surgical suite into the intensive care room just down the hall. He'll be sleeping off the anesthesia for several hours, but you can sit with him if you like."

Dr. Barker led Ethel and Teddy down the hallway to a room where three uniformed LAPD officers stood outside. Opening the door, they entered a forty-foot long, green-tiled recovery suite. Six empty hospital beds formed a line; a semicircular drape obscured the seventh one at the far end of the room. Dr. Barker pulled back the curtain. There lay Bobby Kennedy, unconscious and eyes closed. A white wrap-around bandage covered his upper head, IVs protruded from his left hand and arm, and his right arm rested in a sling. A blackened right eye looked like someone gave him a shiner.[11]

Teddy bent over and kissed his brother's forehead, and then knelt by his bedside, removed rosary beads from his jacket pocket, and prayed quietly. Ethel climbed onto the bed and lay alongside her unconscious husband. She put her arm around him and whispered in his ear as she wept softly:

"Bob, please—please come home."

Headline from the Dallas Times-Herald carrying the optimistic United Press International story of RFK's shooting and his anticipated recovery after successful surgery, June 5, 1968 (Author's collection)

CHAPTER 17

"I THOUGHT SOMEBODY HAD SWUNG A BASEBALL BAT into the side of my head. My legs crumpled out from under me, like they were kicked. I was conscious, but I couldn't see. Everything was blurry. I could hear noises—screaming, maybe crying. My body started shaking. I remembered having seen TV cables on the floor when we walked through the pantry earlier—I thought they were now electrocuting me.[1] I tried telling someone to move me, but I don't know whether I really was talking, or just imagined I was talking. Then I heard Ethel. I asked her if everyone was all right, but she didn't answer. I tried to focus my eyes, but I could only see shadowy images and lights flashing. Then—blackness. I don't remember anything after that."

Detective Walt Lewis, assigned to LAPD's robbery-homicide division, took notes while interviewing Bobby. Still bandaged and in an arm sling, Bobby sat up in bed as he recounted vague details from three days ago.

"Did you ever see the assailant?" Detective Lewis asked.

"No. I was shaking hands with a kid—a busboy. He works at the Ambassador. I recognized him—he brought me room service a couple days earlier. He was smiling and wishing me luck. Then I heard a woman say something to me."

"What did she say?"

"She asked, 'Where's Ethel?' That concerned me. There was a last-minute change leaving the stage. I thought she was right behind me. She's pregnant—when I heard that, I worried that she got separated. I remember turning to look back for her. I think I was still holding the kid's hand. Then someone hit me—at least that's what I thought. I never heard a gunshot."

"When that lady asked about your wife, she probably saved your life. The busboy told us he saw a gun emerge out of nowhere and pointed right at your temple, and your head spun just as it fired. He thought you saw the gun and flinched. You should find that lady and send her flowers—forever."

"Do you know why he did this?"

"Who knows? He's some young Palestinian kook. We're finding all kinds of nutty writings in his place. We'll piece it together eventually."

Dr. Barker interrupted, "Detective, that's probably enough for now."

"That's fine, doc. Senator, thank you. I'm glad you're doing better. We'll follow up later."

"Detective, wait," Bobby said. "I've heard that others were injured that night, but nobody's given me any details. Was anyone hurt seriously?"

Lewis looked around seeking silent guidance from the other people in the room. "We haven't said anything yet," Ted Sorensen told him, "Go ahead."

"The gunman fired an eight-shot .22 revolver loaded with Mini Mag hollow point lead bullets, which are designed to flatten, or mushroom, on impact. He hit you twice.[2] He wounded five other people. Four will recover. There was one fatality."

"Who?" RFK asked resignedly.

"Bob," Ted told him softly, "it was Chris Evans."

At the news, Bobby sighed heavily, closed his eyes, and dropped his head. Detective Lewis filled in the details. "Ballistics showed that when the bullet fired at your head shattered, the main projectile hit the victim straight in the pump—sorry, in the heart. It severed his aorta. He was quite a bit taller, which accounts for a head wound to you and a chest wound to him. He probably never knew what hit him—he bled out very quickly. I'm told he was on your staff. I'm sorry."

"You know," Bobby said ruefully, "we talked about it that day."

"Talked about what?"

"Assassination. Death. That old bitch, luck. I can't believe he's gone. The last two weeks he traveled with me. I got to know him. He had a great sense of humor, and he did things to crack me up intentionally. Last week we were at a fundraiser in Beverly Hills. Some bore had me cornered, and I couldn't shake him. I saw Chris across the room, so I signaled for him to get me away from the guy. Chris walked over, tossed me his cigarette lighter, and then said, 'Hey Bobby, I'm out of fluid. Be a good guy—go fill this for me.' Chris then started shaking the guy's hand while telling him that the only reason the Swedes beat the Czechs in canoeing at the '48 Olympics was because of Postum rationing in Eastern Europe. The guy stared at Chris—he thought he was a lunatic—and then the guy asked him, 'Who are you?'

"As I walked away, I heard Chris tell him, '*Who am I*? I'm the guy that gets Bobby Kennedy to fill his fucking cigarette lighter!' I almost fell over laughing when I heard it. I told Chris later that win or lose I'd fill his lighter anytime. He saved me from a big embarrassment last week. One of our local press guys set up a photo op—I was supposed to stand on a beach wearing a wetsuit and holding a surfboard. Chris saw that on the schedule and killed it. He told me surfers always know a poser when they see one, and they'd make me a laughingstock with reporters. He said if I wanted to learn how to surf for real he'd take me to his secret spot after the primaries—Cotton's Point in San Clemente— and teach me how to 'regular and goofy foot' surf, whatever the hell that means. He was also going to…." Tears welled in Bobby's eyes; he stopped recounting their plans while composing himself. When he did, and while looking down, Bobby said quietly, "I'm so goddamn sorry."

"The suspect will be charged with Mr. Evans' murder, attempted murder on you, and ADW—assault with a deadly weapon—on the other four people. If convicted, he'll get the gas chamber. If we do our job—and we will—that's where we'll put him."

Shaking his head, Bobby said, "Executing a crazy kid—what the hell good will that do?"

"Let's give the patient some rest now," Dr. Barker instructed. As everyone else filed out of the room, Ted Sorensen lagged behind, telling the doctor he needed a minute alone with Bobby. When only he and RFK remained in the room, Bobby said mournfully, "Chris is dead because I'm alive. He took my bullet. That's going to be a hell of a thing to carry around."

Ted picked up a manila envelope resting on a nearby chair. "Last night I visited Chris' wife," he said. "She and their two kids are holding up okay. She asked me to give you this when you were up to it."

Bobby opened the envelope and retrieved its contents—a note and a new gold cigarette lighter.

"What's that?" Ted asked.

Bobby cupped the trinket in his hand. "Tuesday night at the Ambassador, before we all went downstairs, I pulled Chris aside and gave him a little present. It was this lighter and a can of Zippo fluid." Bobby handed the lighter to Ted, who examined the engraved message on the side: *To Chris Evans, who will need a new excuse. From his friend RFK 6-4-1968.*

Bobby opened the note and read it aloud.

Dear Senator Kennedy,

Just before Chris went downstairs with you on Tuesday night, he called me from your suite and told me the story behind this gift. He was thrilled when you gave it to him, and he said it would one day be our family's proudest heirloom. It was in his pocket when he died. I think Chris would approve my returning it to you. Knowing you are carrying it will make me feel like Chris is still part of your team. He gave his life helping to make you president. When you are better, please get back out there and finish the job you both started.

God bless you,

Nikki Boncè Evans

Seeing his boss struggling to fight back tears, Ted told him softly, "It's okay to let go, Bob. You've been through hell this week."

"No. It's not okay. My dad—he drilled into us from childhood—'Kennedys don't cry.'"

"Get some sleep. I'll see you tomorrow." Ted dimmed the lights and closed the door as he left.

Bobby stood the lighter upright on the hospital's aluminum overbed tray. In the stillness of his empty room, he studied the sleek trinket in silence for a few moments, and then did something he hadn't done since November 1963:

He sobbed.

CHAPTER 18

"HEY! THAT HURTS WORSE THAN GETTING SHOT!" Bobby complained.

Trudy Kruse, R.N., was in no mood for a complaining patient, and she didn't care if his name was Kennedy. "Listen, senator, the stitches have to come out. So sit still, be a good boy, and when I'm done, you can have a candy. For goodness sake, I have four small kids, and you're a bigger baby than any of them."

Bobby laughed through his repeated grimaces. "Wouldn't you know they'd have a McCarthy precinct walker removing my stitches!" he told Ethel.

When Nurse Trudy clipped and removed the last stitch, Bobby asked how the wounds looked. "Well, the side of your head looks like someone took a lawnmower to it. In the back, if I didn't know better, I'd swear a midget in a dune buggy spun a couple of donuts on your skull. Be glad you're alive, and don't worry about your hairdo."

Ted Sorensen stepped into the room. "Bob, we have the barber outside. He came over from the Century Plaza hotel. I thought we should do something before we go downstairs and talk to the press."

"Hey, Florence Nightingale," Bobby jested with his nurse, "will you get me a mirror?"

"You don't need a mirror. You look beautiful—for a guy who got shot in the head three weeks ago." Nurse Trudy retrieved two hand-held mirrors from the nearby nurses' station. Bobby scowled as he studied the side of his head where the surgical team shaved a broad swath through his thick mop from his right temple backward. In the rear, he had two irregular shaved circles around the places where doctors removed fragments.

"I'll bet you cut your sons' hair like this."

"Oh, I'm so sorry you don't like your trim, senator. As luck would have it, when they wheeled you in that night, our ER hair stylist was on her break. We had to call in her backup—and wouldn't you know it—she was wearing a Nixon button."

Bobby grinned at his staff while pointing to Trudy with his thumb. "If I win, I want her as our lead Soviet negotiator."

When the Century Plaza's Harry the Barber entered the hospital room and unpacked his clippers, Bobby joked, "Please tell me you're a Democrat."

"Senator, I've been cutting Ronnie Reagan's hair for thirty years, but all my haircuts are nonpartisan." Studying the patient's uneven coif, Harry said, "Something tells me you won't be very particular about what I do today." When Harry finished shaving with the clippers, Bobby studied his new look in the mirror. "The last time I had a crewcut like this," he grumped, "my Dad was putting me over his knee for misbehaving."

"Knowing the ambassador," Ted cracked, "that remains a continuing possibility."

Dr. Barker entered to find Bobby tying his own necktie. "Look, doctor," he boasted, "I'm able to raise my right arm almost even with my shoulder."

"That's fine, Bob, but if I were you, I'd keep that arm in a sling for a couple more weeks—if for no other reason than to discourage people from yanking it to shake hands." Then, checking Bobby's eyes with an ophthalmoscope, he asked, "Any headache today?"

"They come and go—not as bad these last few days. The vision in my left eye is still blurred. The new glasses help—I can read with them, but my eyes get tired after a while."

"Will these symptoms clear over time?" Ethel asked.

"The back of the eye looks good. I see no distress in the optic nerve, the blood vessels, or the macula. My guess is that one of those fragments lodged in the right hemisphere might be pressing on a vessel or nerve. Fortunately, there is no sign of brain infection or edema. Hopefully, these will clear over time, but it may be that occasional headaches and partial blurred vision in one eye are the price you pay to be alive."

Jeff Solsby entered the room. "They're ready downstairs," he advised. "All three networks are covering it live and they're linked up."

"What's the setup, Jeff?" Ted Sorensen asked.

"When we exit the front door there'll be a bank of microphones on a lectern. The press and cameras are on a riser directly in the front. The Secret Service has set up rope lines to the right—"

"Secret Service," Bobby interjected. "That'll take some getting used to."

"You won't have to get used to them for long if you lose," Ted joked. "After that night Johnson ordered Secret Service detailed to all the major candidates, so you aren't the only one."

"Anyway," Jeff continued, "behind the rope line to the right are hospital staff and supporters—it's a pretty big crowd out there to greet you. The cars are to the left. I've already told the press we're not taking questions—just a quick statement before we depart."

As Ethel straightened Bobby's tie, he thanked Dr. Barker and the hospital staff now gathered to say goodbye. "Trudy," he said with a smile to his head nurse, "I'll miss you the most."

"I don't want you to forget me, senator, so I brought you something." Reaching into the pocket of her smock, she handed him a See's Candy lollipop. "I give these to all my patients who behave." She hugged and kissed him on the cheek, and then she told him, "Well, that's a first for me."

"You mean it's the first time you ever kissed a presidential candidate?"

"No—it's the first time I ever kissed a Democrat. And senator—it's also the last."

An attendant pushed a wheelchair into Bobby's room, calling out cheerfully, "Good morning, everybody. Are we ready?"

Jeff eyed the wheelchair suspiciously. "What's that for?" he asked.

"Regulations—every patient at discharge has to exit in a wheelchair."

"That's not happening," Jeff snapped, insisting he didn't want images of the candidate looking like an invalid in tomorrow's newspapers. As a compromise, they agreed to the attendant wheeling Bobby to the elevator, down to the main floor, and through the hospital—only until they neared the main entrance. When Bobby left the hospital, he would walk out under his own power for the cameras.

As the Kennedy party reached the ground floor, an aide at the nurse's station called to him, "Senator, you have a call from Vice President Humphrey." The attendant wheeled him over and handed him the phone.

"Good morning, Lazarus!" Hubert greeted his friend and rival.

"Hubert, I was going to call you when I got back to New York tonight. I wanted you to know how grateful I am for all you've done. And suspending your campaigning while I've been in here is about as classy as it gets."

Hubert laughed. "Well, Bob, don't thank me *too* hard. Just because I wasn't out campaigning doesn't mean I haven't been on the phone."

"I know—because I was calling the same people from my hospital room."

"*And I know you know*—because I started calling delegates once I heard you were calling them from your bed. That gave you an unfair advantage, so I was thinking of admitting myself to Walter Reed for the gout just to even things up!"

Growing serious, Bobby told his competitor, "Listen, Ted and Pierre told me about the Air Force plane you ordered for me—"

"Bob," Hubert interrupted, "please don't think ill of the president. I'm sure it was a misunderstanding or a mix-up in communications."

"I'm not worried about Lyndon Johnson or his motives right now— I'm worried about your delegate count. Am I still in the hunt against you?"

"Well, you're always in the hunt, no matter what the numbers. My count showed I went over the top the day of the California primary. With all the drama you've generated we started seeing some initial movement to you, but the White House and the Party elders put the kibosh on that—quickly. It looks like some of McCarthy's people are sliding your way, but I'm still planning on having you campaigning for me in the fall instead of the other way around."

"Starting tomorrow I'm back in the fight, so you'd better suit up because I'm going to pound the hell out of you between now and August. But if you win, Hubert, and you probably will, you won't have a more enthusiastic campaigner. I'll never forget what you did for me."

"God bless you, Bob. Give my love to Ethel, and I'll see you in Chicago."

Bobby handed back the telephone, climbed out of the wheelchair, and told his staff, "Okay—time to get back to work."

When Bobby, Ethel, and his entourage stepped out of Good Sam into the bright sunshine, a roar came from the right that swept over the entrance area. So many camera shutters clicked from the front that it sounded like a locust plague. Reporters noticed his baggy suit hanging on his already thin frame—he lost weight in the hospital. His usually suntanned face looked pale under the brilliant glare off the asphalt. Despite his new buzz haircut and a thin red stripe visible along the side and back of his head, there stood Bobby Kennedy smiling broadly and waving with his left hand. It took almost five minutes for the candidate to quiet the cheers. Even the reporters broke character and applauded.

"You know," he said in his first public comment since the shooting, "at almost every campaign rally we held, someone in the crowd always shouted at me, 'Get a haircut!' To those people I want to say that I finally did—the hard way!"

Bobby thanked everyone for coming to welcome him back into the race. He expressed appreciation for his surgeons and nurses, the hospital staff, and the other candidates who declared a moratorium on campaigning while he recuperated. "Today we fly to New York," he said. "It's a necessity—I haven't been home to get fresh socks in almost a month!" When the laughter ended, he added, "Tomorrow we begin our final push for the nomination. I will fight for every vote, for every delegate, and for the cause to which we have dedicated ourselves, and for which one dear friend gave his life."

Then, turning upbeat, Bobby closed his remarks. "I pledge to carry this fight and this crusade for peace all the way to the convention. So, as I said over three weeks ago—before I was so rudely interrupted—" Once again, laughter and applause rose from the crowd. Bobby smiled and waited for quiet before finishing his sentence:

"My thanks to all of you—and now it's on to Chicago, and let's win there!"

1968 presidential primary campaign buttons for Eugene McCarthy, Robert F. Kennedy, and Hubert H. Humphrey (Author's collection)

CHAPTER 19

ROBERT KENNEDY REENTERED THE CAMPAIGN against Hubert Humphrey and Eugene McCarthy in an environment far different from the one in which a gunman sidelined him almost a month earlier. The raucous primary season that mobilized tens of thousands of young volunteers had ended in late June. Now, in the two-month interim before the August convention, suddenly there were no precincts to walk, no envelopes to lick, no brochures to distribute, no rope lines to navigate, no get-out-the-vote drives to organize. The candidates' decommissioned soldiers drifted, carpooled, bused, or hitchhiked back to their college campuses, youth hostels, and parents' homes. Meanwhile, the principals waged a publicly symbolic, but mostly behind-the-scenes, battle for the remaining unpledged delegates.

The contenders approached the goal line using different playbooks. Eugene McCarthy, iconoclast to the end, impulsively suspended his delegate hunt during those critical weeks, trading it for a prolonged vacation on the French Riviera despite the furious objections of his campaign staff and donors.[1] When he resumed his speaking schedule a couple of weeks before the convention's start, it was too late for any meaningful further effort. Still, McCarthy remained a powerful draw at colleges and rallies. On one night in August, over 45,000 people turned out to hear him at Fenway Park,[2] but when it came to the meetings that mattered—with convention delegates and Party leaders—he showed indifference to the task. "I won three million votes in the primaries," he told his increasingly frustrated campaign manager Blair Clark. "Bobby won two million, and Johnson and Humphrey combined won half a million. I'm the proven vote getter. The delegates know it, and they know my record. I shouldn't have to go begging for their support. They can take me or leave me."[3]

Many chose to leave him.

McCarthy aided in the slippage when, in what he thought was an off-the-record interview with the Knight Newspaper syndicate, he admitted he had "zero" chance of beating Humphrey for the nomination. The next morning, a *Chicago Daily News* headline blared McCARTHY CONCEDES HE'S A LOSER.[4] After reading this candid assessment, many McCarthy delegates traded their MAKE THE SCENE WITH GENE campaign buttons for ones that read RFK FOR THE USA, seeing Kennedy as the only antiwar candidate still challenging Humphrey seriously.

Unlike his apathetic archrival, Kennedy sought delegates the old-fashioned way, hitting the campaign trail and pleading for support. Since his hospital release, Kennedy's enthusiastic crowds grew by the tens of thousands, and he outpolled Humphrey in many states. Now, for the first time, he even showed strength with independents and center-left Republicans.[5] Still, Kennedy and his team understood that it would take more than crowd enthusiasm to pry loose from Lyndon Johnson's iron grip the pro-administration delegates.

Kennedy tried desperately to convince Party leaders that he, not Humphrey, offered Democrats their best chance to beat the Republican nominee in the fall,[6] but the effort proved futile. Although many antiwar (and previously anti-Kennedy) rank-and-file Democrats viewed him more favorably after his harrowing escape, Johnson loyalists extended no clemency. Most remained in LBJ's camp—firmly—and neither Camelot nostalgia nor emotional sympathy changed that. This reality allowed Hubert Humphrey, the establishment candidate, to follow his original blueprint to the nomination—showing slavish loyalty to the Johnson administration.

It worked.

As the convention approached, and despite RFK's aggressive efforts, the *New York Times* reported that Humphrey had over 1,600 delegates, well beyond the 1,312 he needed to win the nomination.[7] The math meant Humphrey had no reason to fear the increasingly popular, but delegate deficient, Bobby Kennedy—and both men knew it.

Poster welcoming delegates to Chicago for the 1968 Democratic National Convention (Author's collection)

On Saturday morning, August 24, two days before the start of the Democratic National Convention, Hubert Humphrey called a meeting of his senior campaign advisers. Seated around the conference table in the vice president's ceremonial Washington office, Humphrey opened with a surprise revelation. "Last night I called Gene McCarthy and Bobby Kennedy. I told them what they knew already—the delegate battle is over, and now it's time to unite the Party. Johnson's ego has created problems for the ultimate nominee. He chose the late August date for the convention when he was a candidate because he wanted it to coincide with his birthday. For an incumbent president, a late start is fine. For a non-incumbent, late is awful—especially after a lengthy primary. The nominee needs time to heal wounds, rebuild the Party organization, raise money, and put together the fall campaign. By the time the delegates declare me the winner next Wednesday night, I'll have lost the entire month of August, and the general election campaign starts on Labor Day.[8] We no longer have the luxury of wasting any more time, so I offered Bobby and Gene an olive branch. I told them I'm ready to propose to the convention's Platform Committee new compromise language on Vietnam so we can leave Chicago united."

Bill Connell, Humphrey's designated convention manager, smirked. "I'm sure the suggestion of 'unity' with Gene McCarthy went over great—like a turd in a punchbowl."

"Actually, he was positive. He told me he should just endorse me now because I was the only one who can beat the Republicans.[9] He also said that if I accepted a peace plank, he might endorse me at the convention, or later if his supporters needed time to cool off.[10] I'm not sure if he's softening toward me because of his enmity toward Bobby, but either way, he said it, I need it, and I'll take it any way I can get it."

"What did Kennedy say?" asked Ted Van Dyk.

"Bobby's on board. I knew he would be. He knows he can't win the nomination. He told me he tried to crack our pledges and had almost no success, since half of all the delegates are either from the Southern states that despise him, or from labor—the same unions he investigated in the '50s and tried to jail their leaders in the '60s when he was attorney general."[11] Chuckling as he recounted their conversation, he related, "Bobby told me that if these unions had any longer memories, or if their desire to get even with people who screwed them was any stronger, they'd all be Kennedys! He said he called everyone—mayors, governors, state Party officers. They all told him that I worked with them over the years, done them favors, raised them money, and I've earned just too many chits."[12]

Hubert continued, "Bobby said that if we adopt a platform that moves toward peace, he'll release his delegates before the roll call. God bless him—I always knew he was a Party man. No matter how hard he hit me, I knew I could count on him in the end."

"Do you think he's jockeying for the VP slot?" Bill asked.

"No. In fact, I told him that I already asked Ed Muskie* last May to be my running mate.[13] He likes Ed and called him a great senator, although he reminded me jokingly that New York has a lot more electoral votes than Maine."

"He's right, of course. Have you considered that?"

"Forget it—Muskie's my pick. If Lyndon Johnson thought Bobby was on my short list, even if I just put him on it as a courtesy, he'd walk precincts for Nixon personally."

Humphrey tasked his campaign co-chairmen, Senators Walter Mondale and Fred Harris, along with Connell and Van Dyk, to meet with the McCarthy and Kennedy representatives immediately. "We need to hammer this out now, and then get Johnson's approval. Do what you can to let the antiwar Democrats know that I'll end American involvement in Vietnam, but don't accept any language that undercuts our Paris negotiators. Keep the State Department, the White House, and our ambassadors informed. When I bring it to Johnson for his blessing, I want all our bases covered."

"Does Johnson know about this?" Bill asked.

"I called him last night and told him. All he said was, 'Keep in touch with Dean Rusk.'** *Keep in touch with him*—hell, I'll marry him if necessary! Okay boys—

"—let's get this done."[14]

---

*   Edmund S. Muskie (1914-1996), governor of Maine (1955-1959), US senator (1959-1980), US secretary of state (1980-1981).

**   Dean Rusk (1909-1994), US secretary of state from 1961 to 1969.

It took a day.

After twenty-four hours of round-the-clock negotiations, the Johnson-Humphrey-Kennedy-McCarthy representatives found their compromise. Bill Connell called the boss Sunday morning, shortly before Humphrey left for Chicago, and gave him the good news. Remembering Lyndon Johnson's mandate, Humphrey called Secretary of State Dean Rusk and read him the proposed Vietnam plank. After making a couple of minor suggestions, Rusk said, "We can live with this, Hubert. It isn't all we'd like, but under the circumstances, it's a sensible plank." Wanting to foreclose any possible White House objections, Humphrey next called LBJ's National Security Advisor, Walt Rostow, and read it to him. Rostow said the language sounded fine, and he wanted no changes.[15] Ambassador Harriman, in Paris for the peace negotiations with North Vietnam, also had no objections.

Five hours later, Air Force Two landed at Chicago's O'Hare Airport, where a small crowd welcomed the presumptive nominee.[16] Humphrey spoke optimistically about the history they would make at the International Amphitheatre over the next few days. For the first time since he entered the race, he brimmed with hope that the badly fractured Democratic Party might now unite around his candidacy. At the end of the airport rally, Humphrey's motorcade rushed him across town, where his Secret Service detail escorted him to Suite 2525A of the Conrad Hilton Hotel on Michigan Avenue.

That afternoon and evening, Humphrey and his convention staff holed up in his suite and presented the compromise plank to a parade of Party leaders. Louisiana Congressman Hale Boggs, Johnson's personally selected chairman of the Platform Committee, arrived to review the text, and he accepted it.[17] Next came the Southern governors—including John Connally of Texas, a former LBJ congressional staffer and long-time Johnson crony. Later Humphrey met with AFL-CIO President George Meany, each member of the Platform Committee individually, and key governors and congressional leaders. Every stakeholder accepted the compromise language. It was past midnight when the last visitor departed, and an elated Humphrey instructed Bill Connell, "That nails it down—go file the plank with the committee."

Word of the compromise leaked quickly. By Monday—the opening day of the 1968 Democratic National Convention—thousands of young protesters from across America assembled in Grant Park. Originally they came to demonstrate or disrupt; the rumors of a peace plank turned their protest into a massive celebration. Handmade signs and banners denouncing Humphrey, Johnson, and the war disappeared from the scene. Instead, peace banners and American flags unfurled. They swapped their chants and taunts for folk songs and enthusiasm. For the first time in four years, the national Democratic Party stood on the verge of a lovefest.

Humphrey arose early that morning, bleary-eyed but ebullient over their negotiation triumph. Standing in a bathrobe and slippers and sipping coffee, he gazed out toward Grant Park from his twenty-fifth floor suite. Meanwhile, Connell filed the Vietnam plank with the Platform Committee for debate and vote at the next session—Tuesday—the convention's second day.

Humphrey could barely contain his glee as he spent most of Monday making the obligatory visits to various state delegation caucuses, interspersed with dozens of television, radio, and newspaper interviews. It was almost dinnertime when Humphrey returned to his suite for a rubdown and shower before a private dinner with Midwestern governors when an unexpected request arrived.

Newly appointed Postmaster General Marvin Watson, until recently Lyndon Johnson's White House chief of staff, called and asked Humphrey to come to his Hilton room. Johnson had assigned Watson to oversee White House interests at the convention, which meant he was LBJ's muscle inside and outside the hall. Even though Humphrey stood on the verge of winning his Party's presidential nomination, Watson made Humphrey's son-in-law stand in line each morning at the convention's ticket office to get passes for the Humphrey family to attend each session.[18] Fed up with such petty tyranny, Humphrey almost wanted to win the presidency for the sole purpose of excommunicating Watson from any government position for the next eight years.

Accompanied by three Secret Service agents, Humphrey took the elevator down to Watson's room. When he arrived, his voice dripped with sarcasm, "Hello, Marv—did you call me down here to pick up gallery tickets for my family?"

Watson didn't respond to the remark and came to the point. "The president doesn't like your Vietnam plank. He wants you to drop it and go with the original language."

Humphrey stammered at the news. "You—you can't be serious. It's cleared—I cleared it with Rusk and Rostow personally. I did what the president asked. Everyone's on board with—"

"—Everyone's on board except the one person who matters," Watson interrupted. "It doesn't meet with the president's approval. He wants the convention to adopt the original language. That's all there is to it."[19]

Suppressing his rising fury, Humphrey demanded, "Where's the president now?"

"He's at the ranch, but calling him won't change anything."

Humphrey stormed out, returned to his own suite, and then recounted the news to his stunned camp. Picking up a Secret Service-installed secure line, Humphrey asked the White House operator to route him through to the LBJ Ranch in Stonewall, Texas. Lyndon Johnson awaited the expected call.

"Mr. President, I just met with Marv Watson. He told me you find unacceptable the Vietnam plank we negotiated. That just can't be. We cleared that language with State, NSA, and our negotiators in Paris. Kennedy and McCarthy are both on board. The governors and Party leaders signed on, as well as the entire Platform Committee. This Party needs to come together—right now. You just can't allow the election of a Republican president as your legacy to the Democratic Party."

"Now let me tell you something," LBJ fired back. "I don't give a shit about any of them, and I especially don't give a shit about what Kennedy and McCarthy like." His voice rising as he shouted into the receiver, Johnson laced into his vice president. "Your so-called 'peace plan' will destroy our negotiating position in Paris—those talks going on might already be dead thanks to you buckling to your liberal friends. You're blocking our efforts, and you're doing it to appease the Kennedys— and all those fucking hippies camped out in the park across the street. You're endangering the lives of American boys—including my own son-in-law fighting there right now. You'll cost American lives with your recklessness, and you'll have their blood on your hands. Drop it now, or I'll denounce you publicly for playing politics with peace, and I'll destroy you politically. My Party's not going to do this to me, and my vice president sure as hell isn't going to do this to me, especially since you've been a part of this policy from the start."

"Mr. President, please—please don't do this. Rusk, Rostow, Harriman in Paris, they all found the language fine. If we don't unite—"

"Fuck them, too!" Johnson screamed into the phone. "That plank is dead! Drop it!" Johnson slammed down the telephone in Humphrey's ear.[20]

Humphrey was so livid when he hung up that his hands shook. It took several moments before he could recount for his assembled team what they already knew from the boss' end of the conversation. As he spoke, his anger boiled to the surface. "You know," he told the men around the table, "I've eaten so much of Johnson's shit in this job over the last four years that I've grown to like the taste of it, but no more. This is our nomination, this is our time, and we're going to heal this Party. We're going to move forward with the compromise plank, and Lyndon Johnson can shove his gripe straight up his ass."[21]

Applause erupted among most of Humphrey's staff, but they had no chance to discuss this bold strategy. A Secret Service agent interrupted and said that Congressman Boggs was outside and needed to see the vice president immediately. When the convention's Platform Committee chairman entered, he gasped for air as if he had run up several stair flights. "Hubert," he said apologetically, "the president called and ordered me to drop the language. I know how you feel, but it's my duty as chairman. I will instruct every member of the committee that President Johnson wants the original language adopted, and that's what we're going to adopt. I'm sorry."[22]

There was nothing left to say. Boggs turned and walked out.

Humphrey sat at the head of the table looking despondent. "Son of a bitch," he whispered.

"Sir, we have other options," said Ted Van Dyk. "In forty-eight hours, you'll be the nominee. Then you can go your own way. You can break with Johnson on Vietnam and unite the Party—to hell with the Platform Committee. You can set your own vision once you wrap this up Wednesday night."

"If you want to make a really bold move," Max Kampelman suggested, "why not announce you are resigning the vice presidency. Then Johnson's grip is broken for good."[23]

Bill Connell led the dissent among Humphrey's few advisers opposed to the "Screw LBJ" consensus: "You've already got the nomination sewn up. Why do anything to inflame Johnson and let slip away the two thousand delegates loyal to him? He'll turn on you at the first chance if he thinks you aren't playing ball. Also, what about our recent intelligence reports indicating that North Vietnam might be preparing for a major new offensive against our troops? What happens if you call for a bombing halt and then they attack us the next day? Johnson will cram it down your throat. Besides, if you start calling for a bombing halt *now*, then why should North Vietnam negotiate with our ambassadors in Paris for a halt when you're saying you'll give it to them free?"[24]

Ted countered, "What good is winning the nomination if you lead the Party to defeat in November? Sir, your national poll numbers are in the toilet, we have unenthusiastic crowds, and we beg each day for campaign contributions. That won't change unless we change. The Party needs you to lead it, and the place to lead it is away from Lyndon Johnson's Vietnam nightmare. You can unite us."[25]

Bill grew irritated. "Look, nothing will bring the peaceniks back to us unless you take a piss on Johnson's picture in the middle of Times Square while television cameras film it—and then they'll demand to know why you didn't do it earlier.[26] If you reject Johnson and move toward the doves, you'll risk a Southern delegate revolt and a walkout— just like what happened to Truman in '48."

"But we can make up the loss with the liberals now pledged to other candidates," Ted argued.

"That's true, but you can't make up with the month of November. If we break with the South now, the break may become permanent, and that will wreck the coalition that FDR created and has allowed Democrats to dominate the White House for most of the last four decades."

Hubert heard enough. "For sticking by Johnson so long," he lamented, "all my old friends in countless progressive battles have turned on me with a hateful vengeance.[27] If I follow Johnson and turn my back on the peace delegates, their voters will stay home in November, and that'll put a Republican in the White House. If I follow my heart and support a peace plank, I can unify the liberal factions of the Party, but then we'll end a century of Democratic domination in the Southern states. Either way, they win. I'm trapped, and I don't know how to break free."

Terry Green, a former Minnesota prosecutor and retired superior court judge, was a friend of Humphrey's from their boyhood. Now a senior adviser to the vice president, he joined the meeting to relay some news. "I just spoke to a friend of mine who works for UPI. He said the Illinois delegation just finished caucusing over at the Sherman House. Mayor Daley was supposed to announce that Illinois was declaring for us today, right? Well, he just told a press conference that Illinois will remain uncommitted until Wednesday's balloting. When a reporter asked why he's stalling your endorsement, Daley only said his delegation wants to wait and see 'if something develops.' It looks like Johnson is putting a gun to your head—again."[28]

"This is bad," Bill groaned. "If Johnson next orders the Southern states to pull their 527 delegates and Illinois does the same, while the peace forces stick with McCarthy and Kennedy, we're through. Sir, you need to make a call on this—now—before the White House bleeds us to death."

Hubert got up from the table and stood in the center of the room, still shaking his head in disbelief. "None of you understands Johnson like I do," he said sadly. "When he is enraged like this, he's unbeatable. He'll cause so much trouble for us that we will *never* recover."

"But if we stand our ground—" Ted never got the chance to finish his thought.

"How do I fight this fight?" Hubert asked rhetorically. "A vice president has a very small pistol in a battle against presidential artillery. Johnson will shoot me down before I can take off. He's spent the last four years scrutinizing every word I've uttered looking for the slightest variation from his policies, and then he's turned on me angrily and publicly—too many times to count. If Johnson instructs Party leaders to block my nomination, then it's blocked. Even if every Kennedy and McCarthy delegate ran to me, we couldn't come close to winning this fight. We can't even begin to fight."[29]

While Hubert lamented, an out-of-the-loop campaign aide entered the room jauntily to report the news that HHH just picked up 110 more delegates from Kentucky, Utah, and West Virginia. "Sir, this brings your total up to 1,642, and that still doesn't include Texas and Illinois. Are you ready to break out the champagne yet?"

Hubert stared at the floor. "Kentucky, Utah, West Virginia—all *solid* LBJ states. Great."[30]

HHH walked to the bedroom and then stood in the doorway with his back to everyone at the table. "Bill," he said to Connell, "call the McCarthy and Kennedy people. Explain the situation. Tell them I'm sorry."[31] Hubert entered the room and closed the door behind him.

As the staff meeting took on a funereal air, Terry asked, "Where's Johnson right now?"

"He's still noncommittal," Bill replied.

"No—I mean *where* is he—as in *physically?*"

"He's in Texas at the ranch. He told reporters he's staying away from the convention and watching it on TV."

"Hmmm, that's interesting."

"What's so interesting about it?"

"My UPI friend also said that he saw a couple dozen Daley people moving thousands of signs into the arena. They were stacking them in locked storage areas underneath the bleachers around the amphitheater."

"So what? Every convention has thousands of signs for the candidate."

"Yeah, I know—but these aren't Humphrey signs."

"What are they?"

"They say HAPPY BIRTHDAY LBJ and WELCOME TO CHICAGO MR. PRESIDENT—*they're Johnson signs.*"[32]

Bill looked around the room at his colleagues and saw the same expression on their faces that he knew his own face portrayed. "Oh, shit," he said, and strode into the vice president's bedroom without knocking.

When Bill apprised Hubert of this revelation, the boss registered no surprise, which in turn surprised Bill. "Just before Johnson left for Texas and I left for Chicago," Hubert said forlornly, "I went to see him at the White House. Instead of wishing me luck, he lectured me. He said I was inadequate to the challenges of the presidency, and he accused me of being too soft on the people dividing the Party and damaging American foreign policy. Although he didn't say he was reconsidering his decision not to run, I suspected he might try to manipulate himself as a last-minute possibility, so I'm not surprised about this. He's been trashing me for months to his staff and to mutual friends.[33] He tells them that I lack what it takes to be a strong president—that I'm a weakling who'll give in to the peaceniks, the college professors, the Kennedys."

Pouring a stiff drink, Hubert continued, "I just hung up from Fritz Mondale. He said that Johnson's people placed under the hotel room door of the arriving convention delegates a new poll that shows me losing every key Border State in November to the Republicans. Fritz said his sources told him that the White House ordered and paid for the poll.[34] I didn't need to know that to see the screw job coming. Once I learned tonight that Daley didn't endorse me and that he's holding out to see what develops, I knew what that meant."[35]

"How do we address this?"

"We don't. We'll play ball with Johnson and act as if nothing happened. But we'll need to be careful, because now we've got a much bigger problem than just getting some goddamn platform plank adopted."

Campaign button urging President Johnson to reconsider his decision not to seek reelection in 1968
(Author's collection)

CHAPTER 20

THERE WERE MANY REASONS WHY President Lyndon Johnson changed his mind, but three drove the decision.[1]

The first was power. His March 31 speech announcing that he would not seek reelection was something he came to regret almost from the moment the words fell from his lips. Leaving the White House meant leaving power, and if ever a president understood, relished, and exercised the command of the presidency, it was LBJ. He exploited it both deftly and crudely to accomplish his ends. He also mastered knowing the strengths and weaknesses of men whose cooperation he needed, and once having taken their measure, he used flattery or threats—or both, as the situation required—to bend others to his wishes.[2]

The second reason was the immediate renaissance of Johnson's public standing following his withdrawal speech. Since stepping away from an anticipated reelection campaign, and after having absorbed over three years of bruising public opinion and bitter protests targeting him, he enjoyed a renewed admiration unseen since the day he swamped Republican Barry Goldwater in the 1964 election. In fact, his initial popularity surge after quitting the race magnified a few days later when North Vietnam finally joined the peace negotiations. Suddenly, the long-despised president became the symbol of a selfless leader sacrificing ambition for peace. Before that March speech, and with his poll numbers in the cellar, LBJ remained bunkered in the White House, avoiding public exposure to any but the most controlled and friendly audiences. After the speech his approval rating shot to 57 percent, and an even higher percentage of Americans believed his Vietnam policies were "morally justified."[3] Speaking invitations and acceptances abounded, even from the Ivy League colleges that for three years burned him in effigy during their now-routine antiwar marches and demonstrations.[4]

As enticing as those first two justifications might be, there was a third—and decisive—reason for Johnson to reconsider his exit from the stage. He concluded that Hubert Humphrey was weak, ineffective, and destined to lead Democrats to a stunning defeat. To prevent this calamity, Johnson resolved that he must be the nominee again, but he recognized that engineering this coup required delicate subtlety. If he simply jumped back into the race, he might appear grasping and opportunistic, wiping away the patina of statesmanship he now enjoyed. Instead, the convention delegates must *demand* his candidacy. With a real convention draft, America would see him answering duty's call. Tossing Humphrey over the side for the nation's good was mere collateral damage.

On Monday, August 26, the opening day of the Democratic Convention in Chicago, Johnson met privately with his closest advisers and aides in his study at the LBJ Ranch in Stonewall, Texas, overlooking the Pedernales River. Everyone there knew of the president's change of heart and had been urging this path on him for months. Now that Johnson had decided to run, they met to execute the plan.

"I love Hubert like a brother," Johnson began. "Hell, I picked him to be my successor, but whenever the shit hits the fan he turns into a crybaby.[5] He's weak and unreliable when it comes to Vietnam.[6] One day he's the war's biggest supporter, and the next day he's pissing his pants because his old liberal friends are mad at him. Jesus, even Nixon supports me on Vietnam, while my own vice president keeps trying to undercut me.[7] Every few weeks he runs over here with some new idea just so the hippies will stop heckling him. And every time Kennedy or McCarthy kicks him in the head he looks for ways to make them happy when he should look for ways to stick a boot up their asses."[8]

Pacing the room while sipping from a can of root beer, LBJ continued, "It's not just Humphrey. My negotiators in Paris are telling me that those Hanoi pricks are dragging their feet on peace talks. They want to wait and see if they can get a better deal from the next president. If they think I'm it, they'll stop messing around and get down to business."[9]

Horace Busby opened the staff discussion. "Mr. President, everything you said is true, and that's why almost all of our Party leaders nationwide are terrified of Humphrey at the top of the ticket. Both the Gallup and Harris polls show the Republicans creaming Hubert—this morning's Gallup has Nixon beating him by sixteen points! The same poll has you running nine points ahead of Tricky Dick—that's a twenty-four point swing between you and Hubert.[10] In every poll, the only man who beats the GOP ticket consistently is you. Lou Harris will release a new poll on Tuesday—the last one before our convention picks the nominee. He's keeping the results under wraps until then, but I expect it will show the same result—the Republicans squash Humphrey in November."

"That's because everybody knows that if Humphrey gets elected, he'll start caving to Bobby Fucking Kennedy within two minutes," Johnson snarled. "You'll have Bobby as the real president—he'll be sitting in the Oval Office holding Hubert on his knee like some goddamn Charlie McCarthy dummy. If Hubert's the nominee, the Republicans will mop the floor with him in November. Humphrey couldn't get elected mayor of Baghdad if he ran against Izzy Goldstein."[11]

Jack Valenti, president of the Motion Picture Association and a former LBJ aide, concurred. "Every day we're getting calls and telegrams from the Southern governors pleading with you to announce you're available for a draft. They're furious with Hubert—he promised to support their unit rule* at the convention, and now he's about to screw them and support abolishing it."[12]

"Mr. President," Buzz interrupted, "have you spoken with Mayor Daley yet about withholding the Illinois votes from Humphrey?"

"Yeah, we spoke a few hours ago—he announced the pullback after the Illinois delegation caucused. That'll slow down Hubert's train. Daley agrees that he'd be a disaster as our nominee—and you should have heard him squawk when I told him that Hubert asked me, at the last minute, to move the convention from Chicago to Miami. Daley was so mad that he didn't know whether to shit or go blind.[13] I've also sent word to the Southern and Northeastern governors to continue as 'favorite son' presidential candidates** in their home states to hold back their delegations from endorsing Humphrey."

"Humphrey's a loser, your poll numbers are through the roof, and the Party leaders want you back in," aide Jim Rowe said. "Why not just announce you've changed your mind?"

"No—I don't want to be the Nelson Rockefeller of the Democratic Party—I'll look either power-hungry or indecisive. Rocky embarrassed himself running for president this year—*I'm in! I'm out! I'm in again!*[14] Instead, I want the convention to come to me, and I know how to get them to do it."

LBJ continued pacing as he lay out his plan. "Since the Vietnam War started in '65 until I announced I wouldn't run, the only time my popularity spiked was when we hosted the Soviets at a summit conference

---

* The Southern Democratic Convention delegations favored the "unit rule," which required the entire state delegation to vote for the candidate supported by the majority of delegates in the state. With the unit rule intact, blocs of smaller states, especially in the South, could flex muscle through their collective strength.

** "Favorite son": A political figure nominated for the presidency by his or her state's delegation to the Party's national convention. By running as a "favorite son," the delegation pays an honorary tribute to its home-state "candidate," while the real purpose is to delay a formal commitment to deliver the state's votes to a serious contender. See *The American Heritage New Dictionary of Cultural Literacy, Third Edition* (Boston: Houghton Mifflin Company, 2005). http://www.dictionary.com/cite.html?qh=favorite-son&ia=ahcl.

in Glassboro last year. Premier Kosygin offered to reciprocate and host a US-Soviet summit in Russia.[15] Two weeks ago, I directed the State Department to advise the Soviet Union privately that I'm accepting their invitation to go to Moscow and discuss arms control and a possible Vietnam settlement. A few days ago I received a confidential cable from them inviting me for an October summit. This will be earthshaking and historic. I'll be the first American president to visit the Soviet Union.[16] I plan to make a surprise appearance before the convention tomorrow night—the night before the balloting for the presidential nominee—and announce it. I'll stand before the cheering convention as a peacemaker, and then Dick Daley, John Connally, and our other friends will make sure that the galleries and delegates erupt in a 'Draft Johnson' frenzy. Nobody will be able to stop it."[17]

"How will you be able to keep the summit news from leaking?" Jack asked. "Won't your sudden departure for Chicago tip off everyone that something big is brewing?"

"No. Daley's handling the smokescreen. In about an hour he'll announce that tomorrow night, after the convention adjourns for the evening, Chicago will hold a party in honor of my sixtieth birthday at the Stockyards Inn, and all the delegates are invited. If it leaks out that I'm going to Chicago, people will think it's for that. Then, tomorrow night at the convention, and before the birthday party, the delegates will see a special film we made on my administration's accomplishments. After the film plays, I'll step out and make a surprise appearance at the hall to announce the Moscow summit, and then our boys will go to work. By Wednesday night, the convention might well nominate me by acclamation. Hell, they might just suspend the rules tomorrow night and nominate me on the spot."[18]

Badges produced for delegates to the 1968 Democratic National Convention in Chicago supporting the renomination of President Lyndon Johnson (Author's collection)

The next day, Rufus Youngblood, the Secret Service agent who threw himself on top of LBJ when shots rang out during President Kennedy's Dallas motorcade, entered the master bedroom suite. "Excuse me, Mr. President. Colonel Thornhill is ready anytime you and Mrs. Johnson are."****

"I'm waiting for Valenti to bring me the new poll before we leave," Johnson said. "He should be here anytime. Tell Bird**** to be ready in ten minutes so we can get going. Are we taking the Boeing or the JetStar out of Bergstrom?"

"The JetStar, sir. It's already on the strip.[19] Last night we transported your limo to Chicago, so it's at O'Hare for your arrival."[20]

"Have the local authorities been notified?"

"No, sir, not yet. As of now, I'm told that besides Mayor Daley, no Chicago officials know you're coming. He kept the news from his own police chief to avoid leaks. Since the entire convention area looks like an armed camp because of the thousands of protesters there, security

***   Lt. Col. Paul Thornhill, LBJ's Air Force One pilot (May 1968 to January 1969).

**** "Bird" was President Johnson's nickname for his wife, Lady Bird Johnson.

isn't a problem, and we decided it was safer for you to make a surprise visit than to give the agitators advance notice."

Jack Valenti entered the bedroom as Agent Youngblood left to assemble the ranch detail for departure.

"Jack, did you bring me the poll?"

"No, Mr. President. Lou Harris is being stubborn. He says he can't release the results until tomorrow. He says he won't release it—even to the White House."

"Bullshit—if this is the last poll, then I want those results out before tomorrow's balloting. He probably wants to hold it back because it'll show—again—the Republicans stomping Hubert, and me stomping the Republicans. That poll needs to be in the hands of every delegate *tonight*, and no goddamn pollster is telling me otherwise.

"*Juanita!*"

After LBJ shouted for his personal secretary, Juanita Roberts entered the room hurriedly. He told her, "Get Lou Harris on the phone—I want to talk to him."

"Yes, Mr. President. Also, Mayor Daley called a few minutes ago. He asked me to inform you that the convention's Platform Committee adopted all of the Vietnam language you wanted. Did you need to speak with him?"

"I do. Put him through when you reach him."

"Yes, sir."

While LBJ continued venting to Jack about Harris refusing to release the poll results early, the direct line connecting the ranch to the White House rang. Jack answered, listened for a moment, and then said, "Sir, it's Secretary of State Rusk on the line. He's calling from the Situation Room."

LBJ took the phone. "Dean, I'm glad you caught me. We're leaving in a few minutes for Chicago. Do you have the summit details locked down?"

Secretary Rusk cleared his throat, and then said gravely, "Mr. President, I have some very disturbing news. Last night, at 2:40 Washington time, Soviet and Warsaw Pact armies invaded Czechoslovakia to crush the democratic reform movement of Secretary Dubcek and President Svoboda. Tanks and ground forces have overrun Prague. We don't know the whereabouts of Dubcek and Svoboda. They might be under arrest or executed. I just spoke with Soviet Ambassador Dobrynin. He would only say that they invaded because they feared Dubcek's liberalization policies might spread to the other Warsaw Pact nations. He asked me to assure you, on behalf of Premier Kosygin, that the Soviet Union has no intention of advancing beyond the Czech border."

Jack saw the president's face turn ashen. When Rusk finished his report, Johnson responded angrily, "Tell Clark Clifford I want all forces on full alert. If the Soviets continue moving toward Berlin, World War III could be upon us very quickly. Set up a conference call immediately with the National Security Council. I want everyone on the call—the Joint Chiefs, CIA, Defense, everybody. Also, contact our allies and ask them to join us in requesting an immediate meeting of the U.N. Security Council. Have the White House issue a strong statement denouncing this brutal act of Soviet aggression."

"Mr. President, do you want the call patched through to Air Force One? What time are you wheels up for Chicago?"

After a long pause, Johnson replied, "I'll be here at the ranch. I want that call ready within the hour."

"What about the summit announcement?"

Another pause before Johnson replied sadly, "I think you already know the answer to that question."

"I'm sorry, Mr. President."

"I am, too, Dean—damn sorry," LBJ said as he hung up.

The last time Jack Valenti remembered seeing this look etched in that massive face was almost five years ago, when he and LBJ stood together in a green-tiled room at Parkland Hospital in Dallas receiving the news that President Kennedy just died.

"Mr. President—I—I just wish…." Jack's eyes teared.

LBJ put his arm around Jack's shoulder. "I need you and Jim Rowe to fly the JetStar to Chicago—*leave right now*—there's no time to pack anything. I'll let Marv Watson know you both are coming to oversee Humphrey's acceptance speech."

"Yes sir. We'll do our best."

Jack left the room and walked by Juanita's desk on the way out of the main house. "Oh, hang on, sir," she said to someone on the telephone, and then put the caller on hold. "Jack, I've got Lou Harris on the phone. Do you want to talk to him? The president's back on the secure line to the White House at the moment."

"I'll take it, Juanita." Jack grabbed the phone and got to the point directly.

"Lou, this is Jack Valenti. I'm here with the president at the ranch. He wants the results of your final convention poll now instead of tomorrow."

"Come on, Jack, it's a commissioned poll. I'm not supposed to turn this over."

"Listen, Lou, the president wants it *now*, and you know damned well if I put him on the line, he'll get it. Please just make it easy on all of us."[21]

Knowing from previous experience how futile it was to resist the "full Johnson treatment" once unleashed, Lou caved quickly. "Okay Jack, but he isn't going to like it. He's taken a huge dip. He's now tied with Kennedy, Humphrey, even McCarthy—and each of them is running six points behind the GOP candidate. He's no stronger a candidate against the Republicans than any of the others. Sorry to break the news, but that's what I'll be reporting tomorrow."[22]

Jack rubbed his forehead, and then made an emotional plea. "Lou, we've known each other for years, and I've never asked for anything. Now I'm asking, and in exchange, I'm taking you into my confidence. I'm leaving for Chicago this minute to order the leadership not to place the president's name in nomination. He's out, Lou, and it's irrevocable. I can't tell you why just yet, but there are national security implications. I don't want your poll to be his swan song. When you release it, I want you to drop his name from the survey. It doesn't impact your data, since he won't be a candidate. Please, Lou—he's up to his ass in alligators.

Don't kick him in the balls with this news. I *need* this favor from you."

After a pause he replied, "Okay, Jack, your word has always been good. He's out of the survey."

"Thanks Lou—I mean it."

A few minutes later, and now alone in his room, LBJ heard the JetStar engines revving in the distance as it taxied down the nearby airstrip carrying Valenti and Rowe on their political mission. LBJ opened a nightstand drawer and fished around in the back for his hidden package of Winstons.[23] After lighting one and taking a couple of deep drags, Juanita buzzed him and said that Mayor Daley was on the line. He took another drag and picked up the phone.

"Dick, is the platform issue fixed?"

"Yes, Mr. President. We had the committee stacked two-to-one in your favor, so the result was never in doubt."[24]

"Any blowback from the Kennedy or McCarthy people?"

"McCarthy just did a press conference and blasted you and Hubert.[25] He's ginning up those assholes across the street in the park, but my police will handle them."

"Are you satisfied Hubert will stand firm on the platform vote tomorrow?"

"He's solid, Mr. President. In fact, he had Ed Muskie present the administration's Vietnam language before the Committee. Muskie did a great job."

"He's a solid guy—unlike Hubert."

"On another note, sir, we're set for your birthday party. There's lots of excitement over it. What time will you arrive tonight?"

"Dick, I need you to cancel the birthday party. I'm not coming to Chicago. Tell everyone I said it's time to line up behind Hubert."

LBJ's sudden about-face shocked Daley. "Mr. President—I—I don't understand. What about the summit announcement? I thought that—"

"You've done a great job for me, Dick, but now I need you to do as I ask. Tell Carl Albert I want him to announce to the convention that my name will not be placed in nomination. I'll explain later."[26]

Butting out his smoldering cigarette into a Time magazine cover on the table, LBJ had a final word for the Chicago mayor:

"Tell Hubert I'll be staying at the ranch and watching his acceptance speech on TV. Tell him I said that when he's finished, if he backtracks on Vietnam to get Bobby or McCarthy rushing onto the stage to hug him, I'll fuck him so bad that by Election Day he'll wish he was still filling gall bladder prescriptions at Walgreens."[27]

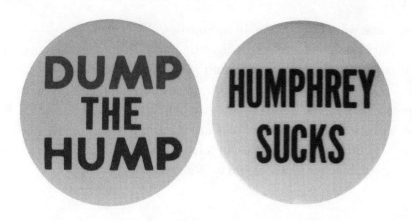

Anti-Hubert Humphrey badges worn by protesters at the 1968 Democratic National Convention (Author's collection)

CHAPTER 21

WEDNESDAY, AUGUST 28, 1968, should have been the proudest day of Vice President Hubert Humphrey's professional life. Later that evening, he expected to become the presidential nominee of his beloved Democratic Party, but the cost he paid for that honor, in both dignity and independence, tarnished the prize immeasurably. To carry his Party's banner, Lyndon Johnson made him curtsy before policies against which millions of Democrats—himself included—chafed bitterly. For Humphrey, things couldn't get any worse.

And then they did.

With Humphrey's convention victory apparent for weeks, antiwar organizers viewing him as Johnson's proxy targeted the convention for protests. These demonstrators fell into two independent groups. The first were idealistic students coming to oppose the war peacefully. The second, however, didn't assemble in Chicago to hold candles aloft or sing folk songs—they came to sabotage the convention with violent confrontations. Knowing in advance that these agitators targeted the city, Mayor Daley ordered his police department to preserve order at any cost. When the convention opened, peaceful protesters mingled with organized rioters in Grant Park, with the latter group awaiting their chance to erupt.

Their moment came on Wednesday, the third day of the convention, after the Johnson-stacked Platform Committee rejected the Kennedy-McCarthy peace plank.[1] When the delegates adopted formally the pro-Vietnam War platform that LBJ demanded and to which Humphrey capitulated, rocks and bottles started flying at the police surrounding the park. Dressed in full riot gear, they responded by firing tear gas canisters and wading into the crowd swinging their billy clubs indiscriminately. Police arrested hundreds of people, with scores of police and protesters injured—mostly innocent students trapped in the melee. News footage of young kids with blood running from their cracked skulls shocked delegates inside the hall and millions of Americans watching the bedlam on live television.

After the Vietnam platform vote, amid anarchy erupting outside the hall, weary delegates adjourned for a dinner break at 5:00 p.m. They agreed to reconvene ninety minutes later to select their presidential nominee.

"I think I'm going to be sick."

Standing at his Conrad Hilton hotel window and watching the violent confrontation in the park across the street, Vice President Hubert Humphrey felt a wave of nausea. It came from inhaling the tear gas now wafting up to his room, but also from watching the brutal treatment of so many kids directly below and from the unending hate-filled chants spewing from them:

DUMP THE HUMP! DUMP THE HUMP!

HUMPHREY IS A FASCIST PIG!

HUBERT HUMPHREY - SIEG HEIL! HUBERT HUMPHREY - SIEG HEIL![2]

A few feet from where Humphrey watched, and seated at a large conference table, his senior aides labored furiously on a draft acceptance speech for tomorrow night's final session. The task was made more complicated by Johnson's on-site censors. They shredded every passage that Humphrey's staff crafted to bridge the divide between the Party's Vietnam factions.

Humphrey remained at the window, strangely disengaged from the speechwriting struggle. The appalling violence twenty-five floors below held him in a near-hypnotic clutch. "Thousands of these young kids came here to protest peacefully," he mourned aloud. "They aren't the problem—it's the revolutionaries and anarchists out there. They've done everything they can to start these violent confrontations with the police."

"Nobody watching this on TV sees any difference between the two groups," Max Kampelman said. "All they're seeing are Gestapo-like tactics from Daley's cops beating down college kids who came here to march for peace."

"The press is reporting it that way, even though it isn't completely true," Humphrey replied. "That park is filled with professional rioters—people who hate our government and who came here to use these students as bait. They'll do whatever it takes to destroy the process and to destroy me."[3]

"Do you think some of these cops are overreacting intentionally, hoping to embarrass you?" Max asked.

"Why would you ask that?"

"I'll tell you why—because every day that I've walked in and out of this hotel, I've seen dozens of cops out there wearing Wallace-for-president campaign buttons pinned right on their uniforms."[4]

"Good Lord. Well, I shouldn't be surprised. Mayor Daley's never really been for me."[5]

Ted Van Dyk noticed HHH rubbing his irritated eyes while looking out the window. "You should step away from there, sir. The tear gas is getting worse."

Ignoring the advice, Humphrey continued watching and lamenting. "I'm going to win the nomination tonight, but I don't feel like a winner. I feel like a victim. This should be the greatest moment of my life. Instead, it's one of the worst. Under normal conditions, I could beat the Republicans any day of the week, but now I'll have to take them on while fighting a guerilla war in my own Party at the same time."[6]

Judge Terry Green returned from Marvin Watson's suite carrying the latest speech draft vetoed by the White House. "Look at this shit," Terry fumed as he tossed it on the table. Large ink "X's" marked through page after page of the manuscript. "This is my fifth waste-of-time trip downstairs to meet with those Johnson assholes. Between Watson, Moyers, and Wirtz, they won't approve anything *they* haven't written.[7] Every time we propose language that has a softer or more flexible approach on Vietnam, they tell me, 'Oh, no—Johnson won't like that.' Hubert, how in hell can you go down to that amphitheater tomorrow night and make a speech that you don't believe in? You can't win this election if you don't unite the Party."

"The judge is right," Ted urged. "Besides, even if you stand by Johnson on the war, you still can't count on carrying the Deep South— you're running *third* behind both Nixon and Wallace there."

"We've been through this before," Bill Connell said. "We'll be in deep trouble if we spurn Johnson on Vietnam. He'll yank our Southern support away, and then he'll go on a revenge rampage against us."

"Even if Johnson pulls back the South," Terry countered, "you can't tell me that a Democratic-majority Congress will hand the White House over to the Republicans if nobody gets a majority in the Electoral College."

Turning away from the window for the first time in half an hour, Humphrey looked exhausted as he addressed his team: "No matter how hard I try, I can't forget what Johnson told me when I became his running mate in '64. He said, 'Hubert, we're old friends, but you have to understand that this is a marriage with no chance of divorce. I need complete and unswerving loyalty. That's what I want in a vice president, Hubert. Do you think you're that man?' To my deep regret I told Johnson I was that man. I accepted the vice presidency under the conditions he demanded, and I promised to perform under his contractual terms. I told him he could trust me. Little did I know the cost of that promise."[8]

"Excuse me, Mr. Vice President," interrupted aide Ursula Culver as she entered the conference room. "The nomination speeches are over, and the convention secretary has started calling the roll of state delegations. Don't you want to watch?"

"I'll be there in a few minutes. Do we have press in the room?"

"Yes, sir. There are a few still photographers, and the networks have a pool TV camera set up in the living room. They want footage of you when the vote total puts you over the top."

"Okay. Come get me when it starts getting close. Thanks, Ursula."

Terry Green had heard enough. Exhausted and angry, he jumped out of his chair and confronted his friend. "Live footage when you go over the top? Over the top for what? To be Johnson's whore—even as the nominee of your Party?" Pointing at his fellow aides, Terry unleashed. "Some of you worry about what Johnson is going to say if we call for a bombing halt. Some of you are worried about what Bobby or Gene will say, and the rest of you are worrying about what the Republicans will say. Let's worry about what Hubert's going to say for a change! Goddamn it, Hubert, I'm not going to let you do this to yourself. You've worked your whole life for this moment. There's only one thing that matters, and you have to decide *right now*—before you go out in that room and sit in front of that TV camera. You need to decide to bite the nail and be your own man. You've got to break with Johnson on Vietnam. Unless you become your own man—right now—you're going to lose this election. And if you lose it for this reason, then, by God, you don't deserve to be president anyway." Terry stormed out of the room and then stopped abruptly, turned, and shouted back at Bill Connell, "And don't ask me to go down and meet with those fucking Johnson people again!"[9]

Terry's angry departure left Hubert grimacing. "I've known Terry Green for forty years. This is the first time he's ever talked to me like that." After a minute of uncomfortable silence, Humphrey said, "Boys, let's take a break and go watch the roll call. I don't want to miss my moment in history." As everyone stood to leave, Humphrey asked Ted to call Senator Ed Muskie's room and tell his vice presidential pick to come directly to his suite as soon as he went over the top and secured the nomination.

"The press has the entire hotel staked out. If they see Muskie coming to your room right after you're proclaimed the nominee, they'll know he's your pick, and within a minute or two, so will everyone in America," Ted cautioned.

"I know. That's okay. Tell him to be here as soon as I secure the nomination."

Humphrey and his aides walked into the living room. Cameras clicked as he greeted everyone assembled, and then he sat in an over-stuffed chair positioned in front of a large color television set to witness his victory. After watching a few camera "pan shots" across the convention floor, Humphrey leaned in and whispered to Ted, "How come the delegates all have Humphrey signs, and there are almost no McCarthy or Kennedy signs down there?"

"Mayor Daley called about an hour ago. During the dinner break, he said the Chicago police 'accidentally' tear-gassed the storage rooms where they stockpiled all the McCarthy and Kennedy posters. The tear gas made their signs unusable."[10]

Humphrey shook his head. "I'm glad Daley's on our side *now*—at least I think I'm glad of it."

At 11:47 p.m. Chicago time, the convention secretary calling the roll reached the Pennsylvania delegation. State Party Chairman Jon H. Jacobs stood and intoned solemnly, "Mr. Chairman and Madam Secretary, the great state of Pennsylvania—the state where our Founding Fathers convened the First Continental Congress—the state where they wrote and signed the Declaration of Independence—the state that gave birth to the Constitution of the United States—the state that is America's cradle of liberty—is proud to cast 103¾ votes and make a majority for the next president of the United States—the Honorable Hubert H. Humphrey!" The convention floor erupted in a burst of loud cheers, but booing from both the floor and the galleries was evident. The applause was more audible because the Johnson convention organizers situated their favored states closest to the front, which also made them closest to the convention microphones. The White House dispersed all the Kennedy and McCarthy states and seated them in the back of the hall.[11]

By prearrangement, Chairman Albert then recognized Mayor Daley in the Illinois delegation, who moved to proclaim Humphrey the nominee by acclamation. Albert pretended only to hear the "aye" votes, and ignored the thunderous "no" votes scattered through the arena. Banging his gavel, he declared Hubert H. Humphrey of Minnesota the Democratic Party's presidential nominee for 1968.[12]

"That's it," Humphrey said as he bolted from the chair. Seeing a shot of his wife Muriel celebrating on the convention floor, he bounded toward the television and kissed the screen for the photographers, and then led his aides back into the conference room. Turning to Ted Van Dyk, he instructed, "Call Carl Albert at the podium. Tell him to let the delegates know that I'm coming to the hall."

"You're going now?" Ted asked in surprise.

"Right now. And tell Carl that I'm bringing Ed Muskie with me. Have Ursula let the Secret Service know I want to leave as soon as Ed arrives."

"This breaks all tradition—the candidate never appears until the next night to accept the nomination."

"I know, but if we want to have a chance of winning, we need to run a nontraditional campaign. So let's start right now."

Ursula stuck her head into the room to say that Senator Muskie just arrived. "Great," he said. "I want Ed to ride alone with me. The rest of you guys ride in the chase cars. Okay, let's go."

As Hubert greeted Ed Muskie in the living room, Ursula told him that Senator Kennedy was on the phone calling to congratulate him. "Apologize to Bobby and tell him I've left for the arena with Ed—I'll call him from the holding room. Tell him I need to talk to him, so ask him to please stand by." By the time Eugene McCarthy called to congratulate his fellow Minnesotan, Humphrey had already departed for the International Amphitheatre.[13]

Edmund Muskie was a safe choice for the vice presidency. As a senator he showed allegiance to LBJ's war efforts. When Humphrey's staff vetted him a few months earlier, Muskie received high marks. Of particular importance was that the Southern governors and congressmen who hadn't already jumped ship for George Wallace or Richard Nixon gave him positive reviews. All that remained was for Humphrey, now the nominee, to make him the official offer.

As Humphrey and Muskie exited the hotel and walked to the waiting motorcade, klieg lights and flashbulbs almost blinded them. Friendly Democratic partisans stood behind the barricades chanting, "HUM-PHREY MUS-KIE! HUM-PHREY MUS-KIE!" to drown out the jeers and epithets heard in the nearby park.

Once inside the limousine, the motorcade raced to the amphitheater, where volunteers already began passing out "Humphrey-Muskie" floor signs, minted hastily in the arena's basement print shop.

"I'm a bit surprised we're going there right now, Hubert. Do you plan on speaking?"

"Yes, Ed, I want to address the delegates informally. I'll save the official acceptance speech for tomorrow. But this convention, the riots—in fact, this whole damned campaign—has been one bitter shock after another to our Party. I need to address it, and I don't think I can afford to wait one more day to do so."

"What are you going to say?"

Humphrey smiled for the first time today. Patting Ed's shoulder, he replied, "Ed, if I told you now, you wouldn't listen when I'm talking. I can't have you standing next to me on the platform looking bored!"

Peering out the car window as his limousine sped on Interstate 94 heading toward the arena on South Halstead Street, Humphrey said to his intended running mate, "Ed, we have about ten minutes before we arrive. Let's have a final conversation about the vice presidency."

At his ranch, while watching the convention coverage on CBS, Lyndon Johnson spoke on the telephone with Marvin Watson in Chicago.

"Muskie's a good pick," LBJ assured his former chief of staff. "He did a fine job for us at the platform hearings. He's been loyal to me in the Senate, and he'll be loyal to Hubert. Hell, he'll be more loyal to Hubert than Hubert was to me. You did a great job out there, Marv. I'll see you back in Washington on Monday."

Hanging up the phone, Johnson watched Humphrey's and Muskie's arrival at the convention hall. He said to Mrs. Johnson, who sat alongside him on the sofa in their living room, "Muskie will add a lot of heft to the '68 Democratic ticket."

The First Lady patted her husband's leg, "Lyndon dear," she said with a smile, "that's exactly what I thought about the VP pick at the 1960 Democratic convention."[14]

The original "Jefferson Gavel" used by Congressman (Later Speaker of the House) Carl Albert to chair the 1968 Democratic National Convention, Chicago. The oversized gavel was carved from a 1770 white oak beam from President Thomas Jefferson's home, Monticello, and trimmed with an alloy of metal made from the original structure (Author's collection)

CHAPTER 22

BANG!

"The convention will come to order! The delegates and alternates will take their seats!"

Bang!

In the forty minutes since Pennsylvania's vote secured a majority for Vice President Humphrey's nomination, word spread through the arena that he and his new running mate were making a surprise appearance. Many of the dejected Kennedy and McCarthy delegates had already left in protest and anger, but the White House team made sure television viewers would not notice their absence: for every peace delegate that left, Mayor Daley's credential spotters let three loyalists onto the floor to take their place. By the time Humphrey arrived at the amphitheater, it was standing-room-only for thousands of partisans waving "Humphrey-Muskie" signs.

Bang!

Oklahoma Congressman Carl Albert, the convention's chairman, slammed down the heavy gavel once more, calling the convention back to order: "Delegates, alternates, honored guests of this great convention, and my fellow Americans, I now have the high privilege of presenting to you the Democratic nominee and the next president of the United States, Hubert H. Humphrey!"

Accompanied by Senator Muskie, the vice president stepped from behind the curtains and strode confidently across the stage to the large blue lectern, where a round, three-dimensional vice presidential seal already hung in place thanks to a detail-oriented junior aide. Both men smiled and waved, and then struck an old-fashioned boxer's victory pose for the photographers. The band played "Happy Days Are Here Again" while 10,000 Democrats from all fifty states cheered for their new ticket.[1]

This rare Humphrey-Muskie campaign button was printed hurriedly in the basement of the convention center and distributed to dignitaries on the speaker's platform moments before Hubert Humphrey arrived to deliver his acceptance speech before the 1968 Democratic National Convention (Author's collection)

It took several minutes before the demonstration subsided. With order returned, and with Ed Muskie standing at his side, Humphrey addressed the delegates, who interrupted almost every sentence with applause:

"In coming before you now, I am breaking a longstanding custom. By tradition the nominee appears on the last night of the convention to deliver a formal acceptance speech. By your vote, you have rendered to me that invitation, and when I return tomorrow I think you already know what my answer will be.

"As your nominee, in my formal acceptance speech tomorrow night, I will set forth my vision for America and for the Humphrey administration. I can sum it up in a few sentences. If I am permitted to be president, I intend to be president. I've noticed most presidents are like that. They don't take orders from vice presidents or anyone else. Hubert Humphrey as vice president is a member of a team. Hubert Humphrey as president is captain of a team. There's a lot of difference."

Humphrey had to let yet another lengthy ovation die before continuing. "If I am to captain this team, then you need to know—on my first day as president of the United States—on my first day as commander in chief of the United States Armed Forces—I will order a halt to the bombing of North Vietnam as an acceptable risk for peace. I believe this action would be in the best interest of our country."

Many delegates never heard the end of that last sentence. At the announcement of a proposed bombing halt, an ear-splitting ovation echoed through the hall, which competed with the angry epithets shouted from various Southern and other prowar delegations. "Draft dodger!" "Traitor!" "Appeaser!" and worse arose from the LBJ loyalists seated under the podium, but much of it was lost in a roar of approval. It took five minutes before Humphrey could proceed.

"I will do this because it will show our willingness to negotiate a peaceful solution in Vietnam, to shorten this war, and to bring our boys home. However, in ordering a bombing halt, I will also demand that the communists negotiate in good faith. If we take this bold step for peace, and if the government of North Vietnam shows bad faith, then

I would reserve the right to resume the bombing."[2]

From the stage, Humphrey saw men and women vacating entire blocs of seats in the Southern delegations and head for the exits. The scene struck a familiar chord. Twenty years earlier, Minneapolis Mayor Hubert Humphrey's speech leading the charge for a civil rights platform at the 1948 Democratic National Convention caused a walkout on Harry Truman. That year, the Southern delegates quit the Democrats and formed a new third party. For the second time in his political career, Hubert Humphrey precipitated a convention walkout. Now, as he watched that scene repeating at his own nominating convention, he hoped that, like Truman, he would survive it.

Carl Albert stepped forward and again banged the gavel repeatedly to restore order. Humphrey then continued:

"I call on Chairman Hale Boggs to convene a special meeting of the Platform Committee immediately upon adjournment of tonight's proceedings. I ask that the committee adopt the compromise peace plank offered and rejected yesterday that reflects this position I have just outlined. I ask that the delegates meet tomorrow morning in special session to adopt that plank. If you do, I will return tomorrow night and have the honor of accepting your nomination for the presidency of the United States."

Another lengthy round of enthusiastic cheering and angry boos had to burn itself out before Humphrey could conclude his remarks. "If I do have that honor, then tomorrow night you will also meet and hear from the leader and statesman who now stands by my side, a dear friend, the senator from the great state of Maine, Edmund Muskie, who will—"

At the mention of Muskie's name, a new demonstration erupted. Muskie stepped forward and waved; Maine's delegation chairman hoisted the state standard resting atop a long pole and paraded it around the front of the hall, while the spectators in the galleries chanted, "Hum-phrey-Mus-kie! Hum-phrey-Mus-kie!" Humphrey smiled and waited, allowing Muskie his moment of recognition before finishing the sentence interrupted by the spontaneous demonstration:

"—Tomorrow night you will hear from Ed Muskie, who will place in nomination the name of the man I want by my side in this battle—the next vice president of the United States—

"—Senator Robert F. Kennedy!"

Down below, front and center in the Illinois delegation, Mayor Richard Daley jumped to his feet. His was the first voice in the entire arena to respond to the unexpected bombshell:

"No!"

Daley's throaty objection never had time to register. Like a mighty wave crashing over the hall, the applause turned into a roar, and then a crescendo that shook the walls of the old arena. Delegates cheered, stomped their feet, chanted, blew horns, and threw their already-obsolete Humphrey-Muskie signs into the air. Humphrey and Muskie shook hands, gave the crowd a final wave, and then both men crossed the stage and disappeared behind the curtains.

It took ten minutes before Chairman Albert regained order, and then he recognized Iowa Governor Harold Hughes, who earlier that night placed in nomination Eugene McCarthy's name, for the pre-arranged adjournment motion. Instead, Hughes surprised Albert: "Mr. Chairman, I ask unanimous consent that the convention suspend its rules, that we amend the Party platform by deleting the previously adopted Vietnam plank and inserting the substitute as suggested by our nominee. If Hubert Humphrey will run on that platform, then so should we!"

As the people on the floor and in the galleries began a new wild demonstration, Albert looked down at Mayor Daley, who had climbed onto his chair screaming to him, "Adjourn! Adjourn!" Daley wanted to stop this runaway train; he needed time to regroup LBJ's forces and give the White House time to reinforce Party discipline. An adjournment motion would buy him that delay.

Carl Albert surveyed the tempestuous hall, uncertain whether this motion would, for his Party, create magic, or cause suicide. Below him, Mayor Daley continued shouting for an adjournment and making frantic, chopping motions with his hand. Taking a deep breath, Albert made the call, knowing his decision either way would change history:

"There is a motion before the convention to suspend the rules and adopt by acclamation the vice president's Vietnam plank. All in favor say aye—

"—All opposed say no—"

Albert ignored the votes that registered in opposition to his preference. Raising his gavel aloft, he announced the result:

"The ayes have it—unanimously. The platform is deemed amended, and this convention stands adjourned until six o'clock tomorrow night."

Bang!

"So what do you think, senator? Now that the Vietnam issue is settled, will you go to the hall tomorrow night for the big kumbaya hug?"

Eugene McCarthy, sitting with staff and friends in room 2320 of the Conrad Hilton hotel—his suite was only two floors beneath Humphrey's—answered Jon Fish after watching Humphrey's surprise dual announcements. "I won't be going there to join him and Bobby on the stage tomorrow night, if that's what you mean."

"Why not?"

"Hubert can talk peace all he wants. His Vietnam maneuver doesn't impress me. In the end, he'll give you nothing more than Lyndon's Johnson's war policies wrapped inside peace rhetoric. Hubert bends like a reed in the wind. Besides, how can I appear with both of them? I can't betray the trust of so many of my supporters, especially with Hubert putting an irresponsible and unqualified man a heartbeat away from the presidency merely to curry political favor."[3]

"Don't you think you owe it to your Party to rally behind them?"

"No. At no time during Bobby's campaign against me did he ever say he would support me for president if I won the nomination.[4] Oh, well, it's no use being bitter about Hubert picking him—Hubert's too dumb to understand bitterness."[5]

"If you don't endorse, many of your supporters might sit out the campaign as well."

"That's their decision to make."[6]

Looking around the suite at the senior staff, Jon grinned. "Well, I don't know about the rest of these guys, but as the only Republican here, that 'divide and conquer' strategy works for me!" Then, after raising his glass in a faux toast to nobody in particular, Jon asked Gene, "I'm curious, since you've known him for over twenty years. What kind of a president do you think Humphrey would make?"

"Oh, I think he'd make a good president."

Jon looked puzzled. "You won't endorse him, but you think he'd make a good president?"

Gene smiled. "Of course. You can be a good president and still have bad policies. If you understand that principle, then you understand Hubert Humphrey."[7]

Back at the arena, and after Humphrey and Muskie took their final bow, the Secret Service hustled them into the VIP holding room just behind the stage. Once closeted inside the secure area, Humphrey told Ted Van Dyk to get Bobby Kennedy on the phone—ASAP.

"Sounds like an emergency," said Ted jokingly.

"It is," Humphrey replied with a smile. "I haven't asked him yet."

Ted stared wide-eyed at his boss "Sir, I'm sorry—you haven't asked him what?"

"I haven't asked him to be my running mate."

"Christ!" Ted exclaimed excitedly as he grabbed for the nearest telephone and dialed the convention's communications operator. "This is Van Dyk with Vice President Humphrey's staff. Connect me to Senator Kennedy's suite at the Sheraton Blackstone. Hurry, please, it's very important."

While Ted undertook this stunning mission, Humphrey shook hands with Muskie and thanked him again for helping in tonight's subterfuge, and especially for accepting Humphrey's last-minute running mate switch. "Ed, I'll never forget this. I owe you."

"You don't owe me anything, Hubert. The vice presidential

nomination is a Party resource. It doesn't belong to any one person. Your winning is what counts. And Bobby was right—New York does have a hell of a lot more electoral votes than Maine."

"You'll make a great secretary of state, my friend. Give my love to Jane and the kids, and we'll all get together when this madness is over after November."[8]

As Muskie left, Bill Connell whispered to his boss, "Secretary of state? How many more Cabinet slots have you bartered away?"

Before Humphrey could answer, Ted thrust forward the telephone. "Mr. Vice President, Senator Kennedy's on the line."

Steadying his nerves, Humphrey took the handset from Ted. "Oh, hiya, Bob!" he said nonchalantly, as if checking casually on an acquaintance. "Just thought I'd call and see how your day's going."

Robert Kennedy's voice displayed no hint of amusement: "Hubert, are you fucking crazy?"

"It's the sanest thing I've ever done. Besides, I need a running mate who is certifiably bulletproof, because now that we've adopted your peace plank, Lyndon's going to start shooting."

"What in the world makes you think I'd do this, especially without even being asked?"

"Two words: Richard Nixon—and don't forget, you still owe me for being such a bastard in 1960."[9]

"This is insane—I'll bet you haven't even talked to Johnson."

"I've been talking to Lyndon Johnson for twenty years. Now he can talk to me. Besides, with Lyndon it's easier to ask forgiveness than ask permission." Adopting a serious tone, Humphrey spoke from the heart. "Bob, look—as of tonight, I'm trailing Nixon by twenty-two points in the polls.[10] I'm probably going to lose this election, and if you run with me, then that means you'll lose, too. Not much I've done this entire year seems to have come out right. But win or lose, I've decided that I'm going to speak my mind and I'm going to fight my fight. I'm not going to let Lyndon Johnson or anyone else keep me from saying what I need to say. You're the guy I want—*I need*—at my side in this battle. Just say yes."[11]

When Bobby replied, his tone had changed, too. "Mr. Vice President, I'm very sorry—"

Hubert's chin sank to his chest as he closed his eyes tightly. Ted saw his boss' countenance turn from hopeful to hopelessness in that moment.

"—I just can't consider running—unless you meet my conditions."

When Bobby spoke about "conditions," Hubert's mind flashed back to those horrible 1960 primaries. *"Here I go again,"* he thought. *"He's about to stick the knife in me up to the hilt. He's got me, and he knows it. Why did I ever do this?"*

Steadying himself, Hubert asked, "What conditions, Bob?"

"It's this—when your son stands in line tomorrow for gallery passes, have him grab two extras—one for Ethel and one for me—

"—We'll need them to get into the hall tomorrow so I can give my acceptance speech!"[12]

Hubert's head snapped upward. Beaming broadly, he gave his anxious staff a hearty "thumbs-up" signal before exhaling in relief. "Bob, if we were in the movies, I know exactly what I'd say to you."

Laughing, Bobby asked, "Okay, Hubert, tell me—what would you say?"

"I'd say, 'Louie, this is the beginning of a beautiful friendship.'"[13]

Campaign button manufactured in the spring of 1968 supporting Hubert Humphrey for president and Robert Kennedy for vice president (Author's collection)

At his ranch, Lyndon Johnson glowered at the television as he and Lady Bird watched in silence as Chairman Albert adjourned the convention for the evening. Juanita Roberts entered to tell him Marv Watson was calling.

"Let me take this in private," LBJ said grimly. After both ladies left, Johnson closed the door and picked up the phone. "Marv, I assume this was all news to you."

Watson sounded apoplectic. "Mr. President, this is an outrage. Until ten minutes ago, our crew was in Humphrey's suite working with his staff on his acceptance speech. When he left for the hall, we all assumed he was going there to introduce Muskie as his running mate. His people at the Hilton—and Muskie's—are just as shocked as we are. They can't be faking. Nobody's that good of an actor. Humphrey planned this well in advance—he had to. I can't—"

"Humphrey didn't plan it," Johnson interrupted. "He just did it. A few weeks ago, once Humphrey started back-pedaling on Vietnam, I called Hoover* and ordered FBI wiretaps on all of his phones.[14] When the vice president wants to undermine his country's war policies, then he's a security risk. Edgar's been sending me daily confidential reports on all of Humphrey's incoming and outgoing calls. There was no indication he planned to betray our troops in Vietnam and no indication that his VP pick was anyone other than Muskie. I guarantee you this wasn't a Humphrey drill. It has Kennedy fingerprints all over it. Bobby's just using that stupid-ass Hubert as his mouthpiece—again."

"Sir, excuse me, but I just got a message from Hale Boggs. He said that tomorrow he and Dick Daley will raise parliamentary objections to the way the platform vote was handled. With our people back on the floor—they stalked off in protest tonight once Humphrey started screwing us—Boggs says they can reverse—"

"Tell Boggs and Daley I said no. Give the peaceniks the platform—it's theirs, not mine. If Hubert wants to play stooge for the Kennedys,

---

* J. Edgar Hoover, FBI director.

then let's see how far that gets him. Tell our boys to clear out."

"Mr. President, please—Boggs and Daley say they can fix this. Our people were off the floor, and we can handle that little drunken bastard Carl Albert."

"Forget it," LBJ snapped. "That village idiot Humphrey can make all the speeches he wants, but his platform won't mean a damn thing. I'm the president. The Democratic Party's policies are what I say they are. They won't be decided by a bunch of emotion-swept retards in a goddamn Chicago stockyard."

LBJ lit another cigarette, took a puff, and then added this thought: "I'll tell you this—if Bobby Kennedy thinks dividing the Party and crossing me will land him in the White House, then he doesn't know which end of the bucket the bear shits." After hanging up, Lyndon then buzzed Juanita on the intercom. "When do we get back to Washington?" he asked.

"You're scheduled to return to the White House Sunday afternoon."

"Call Hoover at the FBI. I want to see him in the Oval Office first thing Monday. Tell Edgar I said to come alone—I have a project for him, and I want to discuss it privately."

"Yes, sir."

Switching off the intercom, LBJ rose from the sofa and turned off the television. "Oh, I have a project for old Edgar, all right," he mumbled to himself as he watched the cigarette smoke swirl around his face, "and when I'm done those two traitorous bastards aren't going to like it—

"—not one goddamn bit."

PART TWO

THE REPUBLICANS: PRELUDE TO MIAMI

REPUBLICAN PREFERENCE BALLOT

My choice for the 1968 Republican Presidential Nominee is (check one):

☐ Richard Nixon   ☐ Charles Percy   ☐ Ronald Reagan

☐ Nelson Rockefeller   ☐ George Romney   ☐ John Tower

☐ Other _____

Results of this URA sponsored poll will be released to the national press.

1968 Republican presidential nomination preference ballot sent to members of United Republicans of America (Author's collection)

CHAPTER 23

JASON ROE HAD HEARD ENOUGH.

Thirty minutes into the high-level strategy meeting held at 812 Fifth Avenue, he rose from his chair in the opulent den of one of New York City's most exclusive pieces of real estate and headed for the exit, saying nothing. "Hey," the property owner called to his thirty-eight-year-old political director, "where are you going?"

The handsome man with a perpetual tan, wavy black hair, and a level of cockiness incommensurate with his slight stature never looked back as he turned the doorknob. "You've turned this into a fucking coffee klatch," Jason replied indifferently. "I have work to do." Then, after breezing past the gathering of assorted governors, United States senators, former chairmen of the Republican National Committee, and the current mayor of New York City, he walked out.

Senator Thruston Morton,* the dignified Kentuckian, broke the uncomfortable silence hanging in the room as the door closed. Appalled by the disrespectful exit, Morton looked at the unfazed target of Jason's rudeness and asked, "Didn't you hear what he said? Why would you tolerate such insolence from an employee?"

The meeting's host smiled. "Being an asshole is part of Jason's charm. Besides, how many people do you think I have working for me who'll speak that bluntly to my face?"

How many indeed when your name is Nelson Aldrich Rockefeller, the three-term governor of New York, grandson of John D. Rockefeller, and heir to the greatest concentration of wealth in human history. Writer Norman Mailer once described Rocky (a nickname so universally identified with him that he used it when signing autographs) as having an almost perfect president's face—as if Spencer Tracy's younger brother went into politics.[1]

Holding court in his Lenox Hill apartment overlooking Central Park, the middle-aged, sturdily-built governor was meeting with leaders of the Republican Party's "Eastern Establishment"—the liberal and moderate major domos—over whether, in 1968, he should make a third try for the presidency of the United States. The delegation pleaded—again—with their de facto leader to challenge the more conservative Richard Nixon, an unannounced but certain contender for the GOP nomination. Rocky had sat patiently through several such meetings throughout most of 1967. Today's meeting, held in the late fall of that year, brought the same result.

The answer was no.

---

*   Thruston B. Morton (1907-1982), US senator from Kentucky (1957-1968).

190

His continued refusals came not from timidity. He *wanted* to be president, but he understood, even if these high-level supporters didn't, that the aftertaste of his last White House bid likely dashed such overt ambition, at least for now. After considering a challenge to Nixon for the 1960 nomination, Rocky made a vigorous play for it four years later promoting his brand of liberal Republicanism—free enterprise *and* massive government spending. One writer noted that of all the big-spending governors, "Nelson Rockefeller was the biggest spender of them all—in his decade [as New York's governor] spending in the state budget had almost quadrupled.... Rockefeller's dreams dazzled large scale planners—but the costs shocked ordinary Republicans."** Rocky loved government and the programs that bureaucracies and tax revenues created.

If Rocky's freewheeling outlays shocked ordinary Republicans, they positively enraged the Party's conservative base, who registered their disapproval by supporting Barry Goldwater over him for the 1964 presidential nomination. Goldwater was the anti-Rockefeller, opposing virtually every federal income redistribution program from Social Security to Medicare to welfare. During their primary campaign, Rocky attacked Goldwater as a tightfisted, trigger-happy, anti-civil rights oddball. For Goldwater's part, along with attacking Rocky's extreme profligacy, they hit the New Yorker for his moral deficiencies, citing his recent divorce and marriage to his mistress.[2] The fratricidal campaign left the Republican Party divided bitterly. After Goldwater bested him for the nomination at the Cow Palace in San Francisco, Rocky refused to endorse Goldwater and drove home that message by declining to accept or wear an offered Goldwater campaign button.[3] When Rocky tried to address the convention, conservative delegates booed him for sixteen uninterrupted minutes.[4] After Election Day, with Lyndon Johnson's utter destruction of Goldwater and many down-ticket Republicans, conservatives blamed Rocky for the catastrophic Party losses. For decades thereafter, center-right Republicans meant an insult

---

**   Theodore H. White, *The Making of the President 1968* (Atheneum Publishers, 1969), 226.

when calling someone a "Rockefeller Republican."

"Jason's exit was abrupt," Rocky conceded, "but he has a point. We've covered this terrain before. I'd like to run, but as I've told you previously, I can't. The nut-job wing of the Party would vote for the Boston Strangler for president before they'd vote for me. They'll never forgive me for Goldwater. All my candidacy would do is tear the scab off that old wound."[5]

"That may have been true three years ago," Senator Charles Percy[***] countered, "but circumstances have changed. All year long, polls show you running ahead of Johnson consistently, and Nixon running behind him. Conservatives might not like you, but they hate Johnson, and they hate him much more than they dislike you. Republicans of all stripes want a winner in 1968, and right now that's you."

"Chuck, I've been slapped down twice before, and I'm not doing it again. They know my record. If they want me, then let them come to me."[6]

"You know politics as well as any man in this room," Percy replied. "If a candidate isn't willing to seek, the delegates won't be willing to find."[7]

Senator Jacob Javits,[****] Rocky's fellow liberal New York Republican, tried to plead the case anew, but Rocky's raised hand silenced his friend. "Jack, I'm out of it. If we don't stick together on this, we'll just deliver the nomination to Nixon. So that's it. We go with George—

"—And that means we *all* go with George."[8]

"Who's George?"

Gabriela "Gabby" Cervantes, Rocky's personal assistant, blanked at the name Jason shared when he stopped by her desk near the den. Her inquiry diverted Jason from his impromptu agenda, so he brushed it aside. "George Washington—he's our candidate. So, what about tonight? I'll take you to The Palm."

***   Charles H. Percy (1919-2011), US senator from Illinois (1967-1985).

****   Jacob K. Javits (1904-1986), US senator from New York (1957-1981).

Gabby threw back her head and laughed at his persistence. "That would be no—again. First, you can't afford The Palm, and—"

"Oh, I can afford it. I've got the campaign charge card in my wallet."

"*You* can't afford it. Second, I'm Mexican, you're white. I like Latin men."

"I'm darker than you."

"If your sunlamp ever broke you'd be as pink as the rest of them. Besides, I bet most of your tan washes off in the shower."

"Well, we could test that theory—your shower or mine? Anyway, I asked you to dinner, I didn't ask you to marry me. But if it helps to close the deal, will you marry me? That'll save the campaign money if we skip going to The Palm."

"I told you before—I don't like pink men."

"They don't get much pinker than the guy you're working for."

"The Blue Cross card and the clothing allowance he gives me makes him look like Fernando Lamas. Besides, I'm old enough to be your mother."

"Call me Oedipus."

Jason's comeback amused Gabby, but she didn't budge. Though in her fifties, Gabby was an exotic dark-haired beauty with more curves than a winding road, and she still turned the heads of men half her age—often. When it came to men her age or older, they risked snapping vertebrae when they took their inevitable second, longer look. Her stiletto heels made her appear much taller than her petite frame betrayed, noticeable only when someone caught her at the end of a long day walking through the office barefooted. A longtime superior court clerk from Southern California, after Gabby's divorce she moved to New York City when a friend landed her a job in the office of State Comptroller Arthur Levitt. Six months after she relocated east, Governor Rockefeller visited Levitt for a budget review meeting. Catching the eye of the affable governor, she soon found herself with a much better paying job—and a clothing allowance—as Rocky's executive assistant.[9]

"So who's George?" she asked again, bringing the conversation back to business.

"George Romney—governor of Michigan. That's the horse the boss wants everyone to back next year."

"Can he win?"

"Who knows? He has a good record and a rags-to-riches story. Personally, I think he's a stiff, but with Rocky and the establishment backing him, and if Nixon fumbles—which he always does—it's possible. Why? Are you looking to leave me for the White House and break my heart?"

Gabby slid on her stylish reading glasses, turned toward her desk, and resumed typing on her IBM Selectric as she answered her would-be suitor without looking up from the keys. "Gee, I don't know, Jason—

"—I'll have to compare clothing allowances."[10]

"Hey, Gabby," boomed Rocky's voice over her desk intercom, "is Prince Charming around?"

"I haven't seen him since he left your meeting a couple of hours ago, governor. I'll track him down for you." After confirming with the household staff that Jason had left the residence, she called the bar manager at the Knickerbocker Club across the street and left an all-points-bulletin for him. Not long after, Jason reappeared at Rocky's apartment.

"I'm still trying to figure out how you're able to get into the Knick," Gabby puzzled. "That place is so exclusive that even the governor's not a member."

"Pick your evening, and then learn my secrets."

"Good night, Jason—and he's waiting for you."

Jason entered Rocky's den and found the governor sitting on the sofa, coat off, necktie askew, holding a glass of wine and going over sketches and plans for yet another Bedford-Stuyvesant park project. Rocky looked up and winked. "It's amazing how everyone now loves me."

Unmoved by the self-laudatory comment, Jason lit a cigarette. "They only love you because you're not running. Don't let the polls seduce you. The minute you become a candidate, people will remember why they hated you before."

"Funny how some of the same pricks wanting to drum me out of the Party four years ago now are begging me to run."

"That's because Republicans want to kick the shit out of Johnson. After Goldwater destroyed the Republican brand, the Party wants to nominate a winner."

"If I stay out, what are the real chances of a convention draft? A million-to-one?"

"Maybe ten-to-one. It's a longshot, but if polls show LBJ still beating Nixon and Romney by the convention, and your numbers show you beating Johnson, the people that wanted your scalp in '64 will be your best friends in '68. The GOP regulars like Nixon personally, and most of the state and local leaders owe him for thousands of past favors. They'd *like* to be for him next year, but he's a two-time loser. After eight years of Democrats, war, and welfare, they want a winner, and Nixon hasn't won an election in his own right since 1950. Shaking off his loser image won't be easy, especially since the press hates him. Your non-candidacy has put you at the top of public esteem—even with many of the haters who swore vengeance after Goldwater."

"You still think the smart play is get behind Romney?"

"No, it's not the smart play, but it's the only sensible play, at least for you. First, when it looked like you might lose your reelect last year, you promised New Yorkers if they returned you to Albany you wouldn't run for president, so you need to keep your word.[11] Second, putting all your muscle behind Romney lets him work over Nixon while the press works over both of them. They'll draw the scrutiny, and you'll be above the fray. If Nixon snuffs Romney in the primaries, and then Nixon is still behind Johnson in the polls by convention time, those delegates are going to give you a very serious second look. If Romney actually wins—which I doubt, since I don't think he's big league—then you're the kingmaker."[12]

Rocky sipped his Dubonnet red wine and munched from a bag of Oreo cookies while listening to Jason's analysis.[13] When his aide finished, Rocky asked rhetorically, "Who'd have dreamed we'd be in this position after the Cow Palace?"

"I did, but it was just a dream. And the dream will end quickly if you listen to all those ass-kissing idiots trying to get you to jump into this thing. The minute you start running, the long knives come out and Nixon benefits. Keep to the playbook for now. Push Romney, stay off television, stick to print media, and don't spout off on Vietnam, welfare programs, and rioting Negroes. Avoid the hot topics and then there's no reason for anyone to attack you. Keep showing your only interest is in being a good governor."

Butting out his cigarette, Jason added a final thought:

"With a little luck, the nomination—from a *united* Republican Party—might still come your way."[14]

RETURN TO THE MAINSTREAM—George Romney for president 1968 campaign button (Author's collection)

CHAPTER 24

"CUANDO CALIENTA EL SOL, aquí en la playa—oh oh oh!"

"Oh, oh, brother," Gabby said, dismayed at the flat rendition of her favorite Spanish folk song now assaulting her through the telephone headset she wore.

Wayne Paugh had many talents, but singing wasn't among them. Tall, blond, and athletic, the forty-year-old looked like he grew up surfing on Southern California beaches (in fact, he was a hiker, not a surfer). An engineer-cum-attorney who found both professions boring, Wayne bounced around Washington in a series of political jobs during the early and mid-1960s: Patent Office examiner, legislative director for a congressman, staffer for a House of Representatives subcommittee, and then to California as legal counsel for the state Republican Party. During the Goldwater campaign, Wayne became close friends with the then-political director of the San Diego County GOP, Jason Roe. In 1966, former Vice President Richard Nixon recruited Wayne to join Nixon, Mudge, Rose, Guthrie & Alexander. However, it wasn't Wayne's legal acumen drawing Nixon's primary interest. The Manhattan law firm, housed on the twenty-fourth floor of the slate-gray office building at 20 Broad Street, was the command center of Nixon's embryonic 1968 presidential campaign.[1]

Coincidentally, as the battle lines formed for that race, Wayne and Jason found themselves not only in New York working for nomination rivals, but operating frequently out of the same building—Nelson Rockefeller and Nixon both lived at 812 Fifth Avenue, with Nixon on the fifth floor and Rocky on the thirteenth.[2] Their principals' competition had no impact on the two California friends, who treated their private discussions regarding adversarial campaign strategy like the Mafia treated the ancient omertà code of silence.

"Welcome back, Wayne," Gabby responded to the deficient vocalist. "How was Europe? I heard you were over there cavorting with the enemy."

Wayne laughed at the warfare reference. "To paraphrase Commodore Perry, I have seen the enemy—and he lives eight floors above us!* Are you asking how my trip went officially or unofficially?"

"Both."

"Officially, none of your business. I can't share classified intel with spies. Unofficially, it was great. RN knows everyone, and watching him work the world leaders is like watching a master painter work his canvas. Anyway, enough about my peripatetic life—I hear the Little General is back in town."

"He flew in last night with Governor Romney. They're both meeting with Governor Rockefeller right now, but he wants to catch up with you. He should be free by noon. Shall I send him to your hangout about 12:30?"

"Tell the world's highest-paid babysitter I'll see him there."

"I wouldn't repeat the 'babysitter' line to him. He hates this Romney assignment, and he hasn't stopped griping about it since it began—as

---

* During the War of 1812, after defeating the British fleet at the Battle of Lake Eerie, Commodore Oliver Perry sent a message to General William Henry Harrison: "We have met the enemy, and they are ours[.]"

you'll find out. Anyway, welcome home."

"Thanks, beautiful—hey, since I can't come up to your palace without drawing suspicion here at the mother ship, why don't you dangle out the window and wave to me?"

"Goodbye, Wayne."

Growing impatient, Wayne waited at a rear corner table at the Carnegie Deli on Seventh Avenue and Fifty-Fifth Street until Jason Roe arrived—forty-five minutes late. "Hey, pal, I'm on the clock here," Wayne greeted him sarcastically. "Nixon bills me out at fifty an hour. Rocky now owes Nixon forty bucks."

"Fuck off. And buy me a beer."

After placing their lunch orders with a waitress old enough to be an original Ziegfeld Follies girl, Jason unloaded on the source of his irritation. "Can you believe JFK feared this guy? What a joke."

"JFK feared Romney?"

"Yeah. Before he died, Kennedy told an aide—who told me—the only Republican that worried him about his 1964 reelection was Romney.[3] After his 1966 reelection Romney topped every poll as LBJ's toughest opponent for 1968.[4] Then he started opening his mouth and it all fell apart.

"How did you end up managing this turkey?"

"This is a Nelson Rockefeller production, not mine. Rocky's conscripted all of us—he's moved his entire political and policy operation behind Romney, and he's dumped about four hundred grand of his personal money into it.[5] Rocky's running the campaign from behind the scenes—he's clearing all of Romney's speeches and press releases.[6] He even sent guys like Henry Kissinger** to teach Romney about foreign affairs, but it wasn't enough—and all poor Kissinger got out of it was a big horse fart in his face."

** Dr. Henry Kissinger (born 1923), a Harvard professor in the 1950s and 1960s, served as Governor Nelson Rockefeller's foreign policy adviser in the 1960s. He later served as US secretary of state (1973-1977).

"He got a what?" Wayne asked, puzzled.

"A horse farted in his face—I'm serious! We were up at Romney's home on Mackinac Island—no cars allowed on the island, so it's all horses and buggies. Henry arrived for a weekend policy briefing, and when he walked behind the horse to climb into the buggy, the horse ripped a big, wet fart right in his face!"

"How did he handle that?"

"He gave a little cough, and then said in his thick German accent, 'I can see vee have lots of ground to cover.'[7] Anyway, briefings didn't help. When Romney slides in front of a microphone or camera, he unravels."

"Is he a dummy?"

Jason took a big chomp out of a mountainous corned beef sandwich. "I'm tempted to answer 'yes' in frustration, but he's not. I mean, the guy grew up dirt poor—his father went bust trying to farm potatoes during the Depression. He's worked every low-paying job imaginable. He never finished college, and he basically rose from the mailroom to chairman of the board at American Motors. He's won three terms as a Republican governor in a Democratic state, he has a great civil rights record, he steals labor and Negro votes from the Democrats, and he's strengthened the Michigan GOP.[8] The problem is that he started running for president before he mastered the big issues, and he believed all his early rave notices. He can give twenty-second answers to the obvious questions like Vietnam and inflation and crime, but once experienced reporters drill down into the specifics on national issues, they see an empty suit.[9] Since I hit the road with this guy, it's been one embarrassing gaffe after another as his crumbling poll numbers show."[10]

"I was with RN in a Tempe hotel room when we saw his 'brainwash' interview on TV. When Nixon heard it, he recognized the gift potential immediately. How the hell did that happen?"

"Romney went to Detroit to do some local TV news show. On the way to the studio I tried to prep him on how to handle the latest dispatches from Vietnam. He wouldn't listen—he thinks he's smarter than everyone else.[11] Besides, he told me, don't worry—the reporter was an old friend—famous last words, right? Anyway, when I heard Romney say during the interview that our generals 'brainwashed' him during his Vietnam visit, I almost had a stroke in the engineer's booth.[12] During the ride back to the hotel, I laid into him. I knew the headlines would be brutal, so I told him to backtrack on that comment immediately.[13] He just shrugged like it was no big deal."

"When the story hit," Jason continued, "believe it or not—the reporters gave him an out and asked if he had been misunderstood. Instead of taking the gift and wiggling out from under this, he said it again—he started babbling that we've all been brainwashed—that everyone in America is brainwashed—and he's glad he called attention to it.[14] If I see one more editorial cartoon of Romney with a headful of soapsuds, I'm going to shoot the bastard that drew it.[15] Then, as the press beatings escalated,[16] Romney gets mad and tells the reporters he won't answer any more Vietnam questions—the number-one issue in the campaign, for Christ's sake!"[17]

"Did you hear Gene McCarthy's line? When a reporter asked about Romney's brainwashing comment, Gene said, 'Romney didn't need a complete brainwashing—for him, a light rinse would have done the job!'"[18]

"Fuck him, too," Jason snapped. Then, putting down his sandwich, he leaned across the table and asked in a near-whisper, "Seriously—do you know how we recover from all this?"

"How?"

"We don't. We're toast. Romney flew in today to beg Rocky to get into the race so he can quit. Rocky told him to stick it out. This has turned into a goddamn train wreck, but Rocky's insisting we all keep riding in the club car while Romney derails the engine, crashes it through the fence, and plunges everyone aboard into the river below. Rocky's so blinded by his dislike of Nixon that he doesn't see the obvious—Nixon will murder us if he challenges Romney in New Hampshire."

Wayne polished off a bottle of Stroh's and then ordered another round. "Expect to get murdered, buddy. I'm heading up there tomorrow for a month or so of advance work, and then RN will arrive sometime in January to announce formally. In fact, our fear now is that Romney will get out. We need him to stay in so we can start shedding our 'loser' image by kicking his ass."

"You know," Jason said with grudging admiration, "when I heard Nixon declare his six-month moratorium on politics after the '66 mid-terms, I thought he was an idiot to turn over the field to us. Now I think he was brilliant—with Nixon going underground, Romney became the only game in town for the press to chew up."[19]

"That's my boss! After the midterms, Nixon told us he didn't want to be the lead horse coming out of the gate. He felt that if he spent 1967 campaigning for himself, people would tire of him and want a new face.[20] I thought the move was risky, but now I think it was genius. And speaking of geniuses, why in hell did you guys decide to run Romney in New Hampshire first? You should've known we'd own that state—it's rock-ribbed and they love Nixon there. When Romney entered there, I thought maybe you were losing your edge."

"Another Rockefeller idea—he didn't want to give Nixon a free ride in the first primary. He worried that if Nixon won big there he'd build momentum. Of course, Romney agreed back when he thought he was Superman. He was sure he could take Nixon. I warned them both that New Hampshire is fool's gold—we needed to fight in Wisconsin first—it's more liberal and hospitable. They both shot me down, and now Romney's sniveling that he's going to lose, and he wants out altogether."[21]

"With all the other libs Rocky could have pushed—guys like Percy, Hatfield, Lindsay***—why did he bet the farm on Romney?"

"Early on, Romney dominated the polls. Plus, he was a governor,

---

***   Mark Hatfield (1922-2011), governor of Oregon (1959-1967), US senator (1967-1997); John V. Lindsay (1921-2000), mayor of New York City (1966-1973).

he looks like a movie star, he was Horatio Alger, and he and Rocky are close. On paper, he's the perfect candidate. Rocky didn't even consider anyone else. Besides, this really isn't just about Romney. Rocky saw this as a chance to engineer a GOP White House victory and earn back his credibility with the Party. He could have picked among half a dozen credible moderates. Now it's too late. The Republican governors have started lobbying Rocky to dump Romney and to get in himself. But he's firm—or stubborn—Romney's still his man."

"Did it ever dawn on you that Rocky shoved Romney out there to take the early flak and then fold, so Rocky could step in later as the savior of the Party from that 'loser' Nixon?"

"Rocky's very smart and, when he needs to be, he's manipulative, but he's not that manipulative—I am, but he's not."

"RN thinks he is, and he expects the final Miami showdown will be us and Rockefeller, not Romney."

It was getting late, and both men needed to return to their battle stations. When the waitress left the check, Jason pushed the bill over to Wayne.

"Hey, it's your turn—I got the last one," Wayne reminded him.

The Romney-induced gloom that dominated Jason's expression dissipated, and his typical imperious, cocksure disposition flickered momentarily. "I gave you my valuable political insight. That's worth more than a sandwich and a few beers—you're getting a bargain."

"Your insight wouldn't be a bargain if the waitress gave me a 'half-off-for-assholes' coupon to pay for you." Then, after momentary reflection, Wayne picked up the bill.

"I'm glad you see it my way," Jason said victoriously.

Wayne smiled. "This is charity. Since you're sinking Romney's campaign faster than the iceberg sank the Titanic, I want you to save your money—after New Hampshire, you'll need it."

"If Romney does lose, Nixon will hire me—as your boss."

"Listen, tough guy, the only opening you'll find with us is the door—when our security guards toss you through it!"

Jason pushed back his chair and stood. "Give me a dime for the pay phone so I can do you a favor."

"What?"

"I'm calling Ted Mack—and book you on Amateur Hour."[22]

As Jason headed for the exit, Wayne called across the near-empty deli to him, "Hey, General—drinks in Manchester this weekend?"

Jason pushed open the door onto Seventh Avenue. "The Midland hotel bar, Saturday night at eleven," he replied with his back to Wayne—

"—and bring your wallet. I'm sure you'll need my advice again."

Time magazine cover, October 20, 1967, suggesting a potential Republican ticket of Governor Nelson Rockefeller for president and Governor Ronald Reagan for vice president (Author's collection)

CHAPTER 25

"DID YOU KNOW that Cary Grant and Deborah Kerr filmed *An Affair to Remember* on this ship?" the reporter asked.

The man to whom he posed the question smiled. "Well, I may not know much about ad valorem taxes,"[1] came the reply, "but I know my movie trivia."

Indeed he did. Although Ronald Wilson Reagan was now ten months into his term as governor of California—his first elective office—Reagan preceded his new political career with over a quarter-century in

Hollywood as a film and television actor. After working for five years as a radio sports announcer, Reagan landed a contract with Warner Brothers Studios in 1937 where they assigned him to the B-film division (the lower-budget movies distributed as the bottom half of double features). Years later he joked that with B-movies, the studios "didn't want them good; they wanted them Thursday."* He played opposite legendary stars such as Errol Flynn and Humphrey Bogart, but his performance as football player George Gipp in *Knute Rockne, All American* later earned him a nickname—*The Gipper*—that attached for the rest of his life. He continued in films and television into the 1960s, but his additional employment as General Electric's goodwill ambassador crystalized his political orthodoxy. During Barry Goldwater's faltering 1964 presidential campaign, Reagan gave a nationally broadcast speech in defense of conservatism, entitled "A Time for Choosing," which catapulted Reagan onto the political stage. In 1966, Reagan ran for California governor successfully, beating the Democratic incumbent by a million votes and becoming overnight the darling of Republican conservatives nationwide. Despite his limited political experience, center-right voters increasingly favored a Reagan presidential candidacy over that of the moderate Nixon, or the liberal Rockefeller-Romney alliance. Although Reagan denied publicly any presidential ambitions, as 1968 drew near, Reagan embarked on a speaking tour of Southern states, raising money for local GOP coffers and helping candidates in a region teeming with hundreds of convention-bound delegates.

Now, having joined forty-one of his fellow governors for their 1967 National Governors' Conference aboard the luxury liner *S.S. Independence* for an eight-day cruise from New York City to the Virgin Islands and back,[2] Reagan held a press conference in the ship's Marine Lounge, where his interrogation competed with a calypso band stationed just outside the large dining room.[3] The casually dressed Californian continued his

---

*   Lou Cannon, "Actor, Governor, President, Icon," *Washington Post*, June 6, 2004. http://www. washingtonpost.com/wp-dyn/articles/A18329-2004Jun5.html

answer to the reporter who posed the movie trivia question. "In fact," Reagan added, "Cary and Deborah didn't shoot that film here on the *Independence*. They filmed it on her sister ship, the *S.S. Constitution*."[4]

"How did you know that, governor?"

"I was the stunt double on that picture."

"*You* doubled for Cary Grant?" asked the surprised newsman.

With perfect comedic timing, Reagan deadpanned, "No—for Deborah Kerr!"

The howling laughter drowned out the music momentarily, and as Reagan stood to leave, another reporter called out a final question: "When he boarded earlier, Governor Rockefeller told us flatly that under no circumstance does he want to be president.[5] Any comment?"

With a cock of his head and a wide grin, Reagan replied, "Well, I have a carry-over rule from my previous occupation—I never step on another actor's lines!"[6] More laughter as the veteran performer smiled and returned to his stateroom to prepare for the scheduled lifeboat drill.[7]

To the press traveling with the governors on the *Independence*, George Romney radiated confidence. Early each morning, in sweat pants and sneakers, he jogged the Promenade Deck while taunting the torpid, hung-over reporters strewn about on deck chairs—their condition a consequence of the unending shipboard supply of free fru-fru rum drinks and rich food.[8] "Come on and join me!" Romney challenged them. "I'm up and exercising while you lazy guys are still sleeping!"[9] Behind the scenes, however, his vitality turned to despair abruptly.

On the third day at sea, and after finishing his run, Romney went down to his stateroom and saw a steward sliding the latest copy of *Time* magazine, dated October 20, 1967, under each cabin door. Entering his room, he bent down and retrieved the complimentary copy. The cover art stunned him like a rabbit punch. He slumped despondently into a chair to read the 4,802-word lead story. When he finished, he rolled up the magazine, trudged up to the A Deck and knocked quietly on S-25, the Bolivar Suite.

Nelson Rockefeller, clad in a wrinkled, loud-patterned, open-neck print shirt, cotton slacks, and with his full head of hair mussed, opened the door holding a glass of water in one hand and a pill bottle in the other. "Come on in, George. Happy's** topside playing ping-pong or something. I thought I'd sleep a little later this morning since the breakout session I'm addressing isn't until the afternoon."

George stepped inside and closed the door to the spacious cabin. "What are you taking?" George asked as he nodded to the pill bottle. "If it's an ulcer remedy, give me a fistful of them."

"It's Bonamine. I love sailing, but believe it or not, I get seasick. I take these so I won't throw up on Wally Hickel's*** shoes."[10]

The two allies settled into chairs on the suite's balcony. As Rocky gazed out at the vast blue Atlantic, he remarked, "For a guy who loves the ocean as much as I do, you'd think I'd have gotten over it long ago, but if I don't take these pills, I'll be queasy all day."

"I wish there was a pill to get over my nausea from this," George replied solemnly and then handed him the magazine. As Rocky studied its dramatic design, his face betrayed first surprise and then a glint of satisfaction, which disturbed George more than the initial shock he felt seeing the artwork. Millions of subscribers around the world now saw what Rocky saw: a magazine cover mocked up to look like a Nineteenth Century campaign poster. Festooned with a bald eagle and draped American flag were two sepia-toned images encased in ornamental ovals, and from golden scrolls blared the legend, "FOR PRESIDENT— ROCKEFELLER OF NEW YORK / FOR VICE PRESIDENT—REAGAN OF CALIFORNIA." The magazine touted the duo as the "Dream Ticket" for Republicans in 1968.[11] Worse, the cover story related how more and more Republicans now clamored for a Rocky-Reagan pairing as a neces- sary alternative to Romney's dismal, failing candidacy.

"Nelson, this is unbearable. The press crucifies me daily and Party leaders are fleeing." George took back the magazine, turned to the lead

---

**   Margaretta "Happy" Rockefeller (1926-2015), the second wife of Nelson Rockefeller.

***   Walter J. Hickel (1919-2010), governor of Alaska (1966-1969; 1990-1994).

story, and read aloud. "Listen to this—'No candidate is so far ahead that he can't be beaten, or so far behind that he can't catch up—*except Romney*,' and 'Romney's dead,' and 'Republicans are looking for a reason to turn away from Romney.' These shots aren't coming from enemies. They're coming from friends—from establishment Party leaders. Even my own home-state delegation is slipping away.[12] Please, Nelson, this has failed. I need to get out, and you need to get in."

"Jesus, George, we've been at sea for three days, and this is the third time you've come to see me about quitting. You're the consensus choice of the Republican governors—they're counting on you to stick it out. I promise—things will turn around eventually. Just wait until Nixon gets in—I know him—he'll screw it up. Besides, you've made a commitment to the governors, and you need to honor it. They don't want to pick someone else—they want you. And I can't be a candidate, as you know."[13]

"But you're the most electable. You have the highest poll numbers of any Republican in America—"

"—Yeah, and the greatest liabilities. The right-wing nuts have an almost pathological hatred of me. I don't think they'd vote for me if I picked Saint Peter as my running mate."[14]

"When I agreed to do this, I told the governors that if I couldn't get the job done, I'd withdraw. Between that brainwashing statement, the dropping polls, and everyone begging you to step in, my chances are over. I need to pull out. Believe me—I *want* to keep fighting. But this is useless. The governors need to pick someone."[15]

"They have, George," Rocky said firmly. "They picked you."

The cabin door opened. "Hi boys!" Happy Rockefeller, Nelson's trim, bubbly wife, entered and greeted the two men. "Why don't you come up on deck with me? The breeze and sun are magnificent!"

"That's a good idea, honey," Rocky agreed quickly, wanting to extricate himself from Romney's melancholia. "I'll join you. George was just leaving anyway. Thanks, George—I'll see you at lunch."

"When you see Lenore, tell her we're still on for shopping this afternoon," Happy said to her departing guest, "while you governors have your boring meetings."[16]

"I'll tell her, Happy. See you both later."

George left the suite and descended the stairs to his deck. The morning vigor of his jogging stride had disintegrated into a slow plod, akin to the ambulation expected of a prisoner approaching the execution chamber. A few minutes after reaching his stateroom and lying down on his bed, the nearby telephone rang.

"Governor Romney, this is the ship-to-shore operator. We have your call ready to France. Go ahead, please."[17]

A young, solemn voice on the other end greeted the dejected governor. "Hi, Dad. Are you and Mother doing okay?"

"We're both fine, Mitt. Your mother has stepped out, but she sends her love. She'll want to call you when we dock. Listen—we only have a couple of minutes. This shipboard connection won't last long. Tell me how are things in France?"[18]

"I just mailed a letter this morning telling you and Mother about my mission. Things are going well, and I'm even learning the language. But Dad, I've been reading the press over here. I wish there was some way I could help."

"You'll help me most by ignoring the press and focusing on your ministry. There's nothing you can do about what's happening here, so don't worry about it. I'll be all right.

"Dad, you don't deserve this. You're a great public servant and a great man."

George sighed. "I don't know about being a 'great' public servant, but I think I'm a devoted one. But no matter how good or dedicated a man might be, when the press and the voters make up their mind about him, that decision tends to be final."

"People can change their mind when they hear the truth—"

"No, son, they won't—not when they become fixed in their opinion. And in my case, the American people seem to have come to a conclusive judgment—"

"—They think your dad is just too dumb to be the president of the United States."[19]

CHAPTER 26

DANA ALICE HAD AN EAR FOR VOICES.

The perky twenty-five-year-old college co-ed's talent came from her hobby—collecting tapes of vintage old radio dramas from the 1930s and 1940s. She developed the passion from her father, a state court judge who entertained his twin daughters when they were little girls by turning off all the lights and creating a spooky atmosphere while they listened to mystery shows like *The Shadow*, *The Whistler*, and *Murder at Midnight*. To his dying day, the judge had little use for television.

Dana also credited her lifelong "theater of the mind" exposure to developing an active imagination, one which she indulged playfully at her part-time job—desk clerk at the Manchester, New Hampshire, Holiday Inn. As travelers checked in, she often amused herself by deducing occupations, passions, foibles, and travails for the arriving strangers.

During the evening of January 31, 1968, while behind the counter on a dark, wet, near-freezing night, Dana saw five men—one middle-aged, and the others appeared to be in their late twenties, enter the hotel lobby. The approaching group ignited her amateur sleuthing streak as she synthesized the clues: "All are wearing the same outfit—long beige raincoat, black hat, aviator sunglasses. I get the raincoats and hats, but why dark glasses? It's pitch-black outside. Also, why does everyone's clothing match? And no luggage—don't they plan to stay?" Dana concluded they arrived in disguise to avoid identification, and they intended very brief business.

The older man led the pack, one hand concealed in his coat pocket when they approached the front desk. The other men stood behind him and, strangely, kept looking back toward the entrance.

"Oh, my gosh," she deduced silently, "robbers!" Dana stood motionless, her heart racing, as the older man—the ringleader she was now convinced—spoke:

"Good evening. I have a reservation for five rooms."

Once she heard his voice, Dana's tension dissolved. She tried not to grin.

"May I have the name, please?"

"Chapman. Benjamin Chapman."

She flipped through the card file, found the reservation, and asked Mr. Chapman to sign the guest register.

"Do you gentlemen have luggage?"

"Yes—it's in the Plymouth parked out front—the rental," one of the younger companions said.

"I'll have a boy bring your suitcases up to your rooms. Will there be anything else, Mr. Chapman?"

"No, thank you."

As Dana handed over the room keys, she leaned across the counter and spoke quietly. "I'd know your voice anywhere. It's such an honor to meet you."

Mr. Chapman looked back at a companion nervously and then pulled out his wallet. Laying a twenty-dollar bill on the counter, he said earnestly, "Young lady, my presence here is for important business, and I *really* don't want people to find out. I'm counting on you to honor my privacy."

"You can trust me—I promise." Then, returning the money, she told him, "I couldn't possibly take this. I'm a huge fan. My sister and I love you—and so do my folks—my dad's a judge."

Mr. Chapman smiled now. "I hope he's a good law-and-order judge!"

"Yes, sir—he was a district attorney before that. The only tip I'd like from you is an autograph for my sister Claire and me—would you mind?"

Mr. Chapman asked her for pen and paper, which she handed over. As he started writing, Dana gushed, "We watch you on *Dragnet* every week! When I tell my dad that I met Jack Webb in New Hampshire, he'll never believe it!" The incognito star stopped writing, glanced back at his group, and then finished the sentiment: "To Dana and Claire, models of loveliness—and discretion! With best wishes, Jack Webb."* He handed back the autograph and the cash, which he insisted Dana accept.

"Thank you so much," Dana gushed, "and goodnight, *Mr. Chapman!* Please let me know if there's anything we can do to make your stay more comfortable."

The men proceeded to the elevators and boarded an empty one. The doors closed, and as it started moving, one of the young companions standing to the rear hummed aloud the *Dragnet* theme music: *"Dum—de-DUM-DUM."* The men all laughed, and none harder than Mr. Chapman, who was still chuckling by the time he reached his fourth-floor room.

"Mr. Chapman, the rest of us are going down to the bar for a drink," an aide said. "Would you like us to bring you back a beer?"

"That's fine. No hurry—I'll be working on my speech for tomorrow."[1]

"The speech you are about to write is true," chimed in Wayne Paugh, reciting a takeoff on the television show's weekly opening line. *"Only the pronouns have been changed to protect the innocent!"*** More laughter

---

*   Actor Jack Webb (1920-1982) was most famous for portraying Los Angeles Police Department Sgt. Joe Friday on NBC's *Dragnet* from 1949-1957 (radio) and 1952-1959 (television). Webb reprised his role when *Dragnet* returned to network television from 1967-1970.

**   The show *Dragnet* traditionally opened with the announcement: "The story you are about to see is true. Only the names have been changed to protect the innocent."

as Wayne, Pat Buchanan, Ray Price and Dwight Chapin returned to the lobby in search of a nightcap, leaving behind "Benjamin Chapman"—aka "Jack Webb"—to work on his revisions.[2]

The next day, February 1, at a press conference in a downstairs meeting room of the same Holiday Inn, Richard Nixon, age fifty-five, stood before a bank of microphones. After making a joking reference to his premature 1962 retirement from politics ("Gentlemen, this is *not* my last press conference!"), he announced his candidacy for the presidency of the United States.[3]

Dana Alice was not at the hotel during the day's political excitement. When her morning classes ended at Wilshire College, she went to the local Walgreens and bought a trim black frame to display her prized "Jack Webb" autograph, which thereafter hung on the wall of every home in which she lived. She never learned the true identity of the man signing that autograph for her, which was just as well. Had she known it was Richard Nixon, and not Jack Webb, she might have been disappointed.

She, along with her father the judge, were ardent supporters of Ronald Reagan for president in 1968.

"Did you know the Russians and Japanese signed the Treaty of Portsmouth here in 1905?" George Romney asked Jason Roe as his campaign director entered the candidate's suite at New Hampshire's landmark Hotel Wentworth on the New England coastline.[4]

"Does that information raise us money or get us votes?" Jason replied tartly.

"No, it's just an interesting historical fact."

"If it doesn't help beat Nixon, then it's not interesting. Stop wasting your time looking up shit like that."

"Jason," remonstrated Romney, a devout member of the Mormon Church, "your language—"

"Governor, since you started running, I've heard more 'hells' and 'damns' coming from you than Hubert Humphrey's heard coming from

Lyndon Johnson,[5] so don't worry about my language—worry about the primary. You've read the morning papers?"

"Yes. I had to look for it, though. At least it was no surprise."

Romney was right. His team expected Nixon's February 1 entry into the New Hampshire presidential primary. A few days earlier, the former vice president mailed advance notice of his decision to every GOP voter in the state.[6] However, on the day of his announcement, many newspapers across the country pushed the Nixon story off the front page, making room for a startlingly graphic photograph of South Vietnamese General Nguyen Ngoc Loan executing a Vietcong prisoner with a single pistol shot to the head.[7]

While discussing Nixon's entry, Jason felt annoyed by Romney's apparent indifference to drawing a formal challenger. "I wish I could be as bored about this as you are," he said. "At least one of us understands what this means."

Romney reached over and grabbed a newspaper off the nearby table, turned to page three, and then handed it to Jason. "It isn't the Nixon story that bothers me. Did you see this yet?" Romney asked as he pointed to an article he had circled, captioned "Rocky Still Backs Romney."

"I didn't read it. So what? Did you think he might endorse Nixon?"

"No, but I didn't think he'd endorse himself, either."

A quizzical look crossed Jason's face, who read the offending story. Speaking at a press conference last night, after saying he stood by Romney, a reporter asked if Rocky would accept a draft at the convention. Instead of minimalizing that speculation and reiterating his unwavering Romney support, Rocky replied—enthusiastically—yes.[8]

"Why on earth would Nelson undercut me like this again?"

"I'm sure he didn't mean to, governor. My guess is that he just answered a hypothetical question. He's for you to the end."

"To the end, all right—I just don't like the *end* he's giving me. I thought Nelson and I were friends. He got me into this, and then he keeps doing things to keep his name alive at my expense. This isn't the first time, as you know."[9]

"Governor, I'll talk to him again. I'm sure it's not—"

"That's the problem," Romney interrupted sadly. *"I'm sure it is."*

Romney stood, put on his suit jacket, and walked to the door. "Come on," he said listlessly, "or we'll be late for our tour of another damned milk plant."

A few weeks later, Gabriela Cervantes worked at her desk outside Governor Rockefeller's office when her phone rang.

"Is he in, Gabby?"

"Oh, hi, Jason. He's meeting with Congressman Goodell right now. Shall I interrupt him?"

"Yeah—tell him we need to talk."

Gabby put Jason on hold for a few minutes. When the call reconnected, Nelson Rockefeller sounded contrite immediately. "Jason, *I know*—George is pissed at me again. I heard from him already. I wasn't trying to undermine him. I said it as a joke—"

"A joke? A reporter asks you to explain Romney's campaign gaffes, and you tell him, 'I can't explain them—go ask a psychiatrist!'[10] That's a joke? You're fucking killing us up here. And I told you weeks ago to knock off that 'draft' talk when they ask you about it."

"I'm sorry. I've told the press I'm *for* George, I'm *not* a candidate, but if the convention deadlocked and then turned to me, of course I'd accept the nomination. What the hell am I supposed to say—I'd turn it down? Everyone on earth would know that's a goddamn lie. The reporters think I'm using Romney as a stalking horse—"

"—They don't *think* it—they *know* it, and you've given them good reason for it," Jason interjected. "That includes Nixon, by the way,[11] who's probably pivoted his strategy to run against you by now. Despite Romney's campaign going down the drain, and unlike you ducking the fight because right-wingers are mad at you—this guy fights. Nixon comes up here and he packs his rallies with thousands of people. Romney shows up at events and draws crowds so small that it's embarrassing—but he still shows up.[12] He campaigns eighteen hours a day. I don't think there's a gas station, coffee shop, factory, or union hall we haven't visited.[13] Our internal polls show Nixon clobbering him 70 to 11 percent, and thanks to your buddy Governor Gregg starting a write-in campaign for you, now we might come in third—behind a write-in for a guy not running. The press ridicules him, the donations have dried up, he's facing humiliation,[14] and yet he fights *knowing* he can't change the outcome. He doesn't deserve these whacks from you."[15]

Taking a breath, Jason took a step back and spoke dispassionately. "Look, governor, I took on Romney's cause because you asked me. Your constant remarks haven't been helpful, but it doesn't matter. Romney's campaign never got off the ground, and it crashed into Shit Mountain once the spotlight hit him. The bottom line is that Nixon's going to murder him in two weeks. Unless you're ready to hand over the reins of the Republican Party to Nixon, then you're going to need to reassess your position."

"Maybe the Party deserves Nixon as its nominee."

"Bullshit. Romney's campaign died when he made his brainwashing comment, but his death gave you new life. So get ready, because after this primary, you won't be able to say you're for Romney anymore—he'll be irrelevant. The Republican governors, and every moderate Republican in America, will start screaming for you."

"Even if I wanted to get in now, how could we stop Dick's momentum with the huge win he'll have coming out of New Hampshire?"

"We can claim that Nixon basically ran unopposed here which, by the way, he might as well be. Our latest private poll shows him beating Romney six-to-one.[16] That's ironic since our polling also shows these same Republicans still believe he was a big drag on Ike's ticket in '52 and '56, and that he's a loser when he runs on his own. Everywhere I go, people tell me they like Nixon personally, but they think the Democrats will bury him in November."[17]

"I'd have no organization, and Nixon's been campaigning in the primary states for two years."

"The contested primaries will only pick about 150 of the 1,333 delegates needed to win the nomination. Even if Nixon runs the table in the primaries, he can be stopped. Republicans want a winner this time, and Nixon doesn't fit that profile."[18]

"Are you coming to D.C. tomorrow with George for the Republican governors' conference?"

"Yeah, there are a couple of big donors I'm meeting. I'm trying to get them to finance some last-minute TV ads. If we can exceed minimal expectations on election night, we can spin Nixon's win as unimpressive."

"Call me when you get in so we can discuss how to proceed when George implodes."

"I won't have time to call you. We fly into D.C. late morning, and then George is doing a quick speech and meeting at your governors' conference while I take the donors to lunch, and then we're flying back for the final push."

"When can we have a serious discussion about the future?"

"After New Hampshire, I'll have all the time in the world to talk, since by then Romney won't be a presidential candidate—he'll be a contestant on *What's My Line?*"****

Late that night, and after another long campaign slog through snow and rain, Jason climbed into some motel bed—he no longer remembered in which New England burg he awoke in the mornings or bedded down at night; they all blurred now. When the phone rang, at first he ignored it, but the caller's persistence wore him down.

"Hey, buddy, are you ready to start your job search?" Wayne Paugh had tracked down his friend to gloat over Nixon's impending victory. Wayne expected one of Jason's trademark expletive-laced replies, so the

---

*** *What's My Line?* was a television quiz game where celebrity panelists tried to determine the occupation of a mystery guest by asking only yes-no questions. It ran on CBS from 1950 to 1967 and then in syndication from 1968 to 1975. See https://en.wikipedia.org/wiki/What%27s_My_Line%3F.

tempered response caught Wayne off guard.

"You know, I'm actually proud of the Mormon. I've learned a lot about him these last three months. He has great integrity, and despite everyone hitting him from all directions, he doesn't quit. In that regard I think he's more like Nixon than like Rockefeller who, by the way, has done his share of screwing us—much worse than Nixon."

"Nixon hasn't laid a glove on Romney," Wayne replied. "He hasn't needed to. This state has taken off for us like panties on prom night. Come on, man, it's not Rocky's fault your boy's crashing to earth. Romney's the worst candidate in history. That stiff couldn't sell pussy on a troop ship."[19]

Getting no reply, Wayne worried that he had pushed one button too many. "Hey, Jason, look, I know you guys fought against the odds. Actually, RN speaks highly of Romney privately. If we win, he'll probably get a Cabinet slot."

Jason ignored the olive branch and instead transitioned to an unrelated issue: "Did you see the bowling alley thing?"

"I heard about it, but I didn't want to kick you any more while you're down—even though I get so few opportunities to do it that it's hard to resist."

"It's symbolic of our campaign. George visits some goddamn bowling alley to shake hands. Someone gives him a ball. He throws it and knocks down seven pins—not too bad, I thought, for a guy that doesn't bowl. Then he throws *thirty-six* more to knock down the last three pins. Jesus Christ—nobody could make him quit.[20] I tried to get the press to give him a break and write a story about his tenacity.[21] Instead, they reamed him. One prick from the Detroit Free Press told me that watching Romney trying to run for president is like watching a duck trying to fuck a football."[22]

Wanting to cheer up an exhausted and deflated friend, Wayne began a soliloquy of compliments, telling Jason what an outstanding job he did under tough circumstances. When he finished, he expected an appreciative reaction, but the honoree didn't reply.

"Hey, Jason—hello. Hello? Jason? *You asshole!*" Wayne hung up the phone.

Jason had fallen asleep in his motel bed, the telephone handset still cradled next to his ear.

The next morning, a weary Romney and a small campaign contingent arrived at Washington National Airport for his brief appearance at the midwinter Republican Governors' Conference at the Statler Hotel on Sixteenth Street. When they landed at the TWA gate, several reporters awaited. "Governor," one asked, "do you have any comment on Governor Rockefeller's statement that he would accept a draft at the convention?"

"Governor Rockefeller supports my candidacy," Romney replied. "He made that 'draft' comment a couple of weeks ago, and we've already addressed that misunderstanding."

"Respectfully, sir, I'm not asking about when he said it before—I'm asking you to comment on him saying it again this morning at the governors' conference. He reiterated that he would accept a draft."

Romney looked at Jason, whose jaw tightened at the news. "Boys, I have nothing new to add," Romney said. "Please excuse me—we're on a tight schedule."

Jason walked in silence with Romney through the small terminal to a waiting sedan. After Romney climbed into the rear seat and closed the door, he rolled down the window. Jason tried not to notice the expression of pain and betrayal in Romney's eyes. "I'll meet you back here at three," he told Jason quietly, and then his car disappeared into airport traffic.

With time before his meeting, Jason found an airport cocktail lounge, had a few drinks, and then flagged a taxi for the Cosmos Club and his donor luncheon. A minor accident caused heavier-than-usual traffic crossing Memorial Bridge. During the ride, Jason couldn't shake the anger he felt over Rocky once again pulling out the rug from under Romney. He tried to justify, or at least understand, this latest "draft" statement.

Was this Rocky's way to euthanize an already terminal patient? Or was it just more Rockefeller candor—supporting George, but also giving an honest answer? Either way, the "draft" angle promised to dominate the news cycle—again—at the expense of Romney's perishing campaign.

By the time the taxi pulled in front of the private club on Massachusetts Avenue, Jason was almost thirty minutes late. Upon entering, he asked the maître d' where he'd find Mr. Poochigian's and Mr. Pringle's table.

"Are you Mr. Roe?" the host asked?

"Yes."

"They both left ten minutes ago—Mr. Poochigian said you would understand."

Jason's pent-up anger broke loose. "Understand? I flew down here to meet them at their suggestion, I interrupted a presidential campaign to do it, and because I'm a few goddamn minutes late they left? Are you kidding?"

The maître d' straightened up. "Beg pardon, sir, but they didn't leave because you were late. It came over the radio in the kitchen—everyone in the club is talking about it. When Mr. Poochigian heard the news, he left, saying you'd understand."

"Understand what?"

"Governor Romney just announced he's withdrawing from the race. It seemed to be big news to Mr. Poochigian and Mr. Pringle."[23]

It took a minute for Jason to absorb the shock, and then he asked to use the house phone. "Operator, connect me to the Statler Hotel please." The desk clerk answered on the second ring.

"Do you have a Miss Cervantes registered? She's with Governor Rockefeller's party."

"We do, sir—I'll connect you." After two more rings, Gabby answered.

"It's me. Is Rocky in?"

"No, he's downstairs at the conference. Did you hear about Romney?"

"I heard—the hard way."

"Do you want me to get the boss a message, or will you just call back?"

"Yeah, give him a message. First, tell Nellie I said 'well done' on fucking over a good guy."

"I can't tell him that!"

"Tell him, Gabby."

"Is that it?"

"No. Tell him one more thing—"

"—it looks like we'll have time to discuss the future after all."

Late that night, after catching a shuttle back to New York, Jason dropped his bags in the doorway of his flat. He downed a couple shots of Jack Daniel's and then entered the darkened living room, where he lay on the couch and closed his eyes before the telephone rang.

"Well, Mr. Manager, do you forgive me?" George Romney asked.

"You could have given me a warning."

"I couldn't, Jason, because I hadn't planned it. When I heard at the airport that Nelson was promoting himself—again—it was the last straw. I made the decision in the car before I reached the hotel. Had I stayed in the race, Nixon would have murdered me in the primary, and that would wipe out any influence I might have in Miami over platform negotiations. Besides, I knew that if I told you, you'd talk me out of it—and then use some vulgarity to describe me. My Mormon ears have endured your vocabulary ever since Nelson teamed us up."

"You're right. I wouldn't have let you quit—and by the way, in case you don't know it, you're a big pussy."

"That aside, this might amuse you. Tonight Mrs. Romney ran into Nelson in the hotel lobby. He put his arm around her and said, 'Oh, hi, Lenore, how are you? Gee, I'm so sorry to hear that George withdrew.' Lenore glowered at him and said—in front of about ten other governors—'He withdrew because of you. *You* caused it, and you *know* you caused it.'"[24]

"What did Rocky say?"

"You know Nelson—he turned scarlet and muttered something

about all of us getting together soon, and then rushed off."

"Lenore's tough—not like you. We should have run her in New Hampshire. How are you both doing?"

"She and I are fine—we're not at all distressed. The truth is, we're both very relieved."[25]

As Jason groped through his fatigue and frayed emotions, George added a postscript to the day. "Hey, this other story might redeem me in your eyes because it shows how much you've rubbed off on me. Do you know Ted Agnew?"

"Spiro Agnew—Maryland governor."

"Yes. Anyway, about an hour ago he called my hotel room, congratulated me on my effort, and said I made the right decision. Then he told me he was organizing a national 'Draft Rockefeller' effort. He asked me to be the first governor to sign on."

"What did you tell him?"

"At first I didn't know how to respond. I thought the timing of his request was quite insensitive, especially given what I've been through these last couple of weeks. So I thought, 'How would Jason handle this?' and then I answered accordingly—

"—I told him to go to hell!"[26]

Jason listened while George laughed at his own propriety lapse and then replied, "Governor, I've had no influence on you at all, otherwise you'd have told him to go fuck himself."

For once, George didn't remonstrate with Jason over his language. "Well, let's say that in the LDS church, telling a man to 'go to hell' is the officially sanctioned alternative of your version!" George's innocent Mormon joke broke the stress, and Jason laughed along with him.

Growing serious, George said, "You know, Jason, it's no secret that I wasn't ready for all of this. I've learned that being a good governor—even being a good leader—is far different than being a good presidential candidate. Before I got into politics, I spent my entire professional life in sales. I guess I'm good at selling any product except myself. I'm just sorry I disappointed everyone, especially you." On the lowest day of

George Romney's professional life, he sought to comfort his manager, not the other way around. Jason started to respond but found his words constricted as his throat tightened with emotion.

"Lenore and I will never forget all you've done for us," George continued. "We think of you as part of the family, and I've come to think of you as a son—well, not exactly a son, because if you were my son I'd wash out your mouth with soap. When things settle down and you finish what you'll need to do for Nelson, we want you to come and stay with us on Mackinac Island. Will you promise to do that?"

Jason wiped his eyes before answering the man that he once dismissed as a lightweight and now viewed as one of the finest gentlemen he knew.

"I'll come, but when I arrive it will be after nightfall. It would hurt my reputation to be seen hanging out with a guy who got his ass kicked by a big loser like Dick Nixon."

"Okay," George laughed. "Come at nighttime! We might even build a tunnel for you. Goodnight, Jason—

"—goodnight, son."

Badge reminding Republicans that Richard Nixon was a two-time loser; distributed by supporters of Nelson Rockefeller and Ronald Reagan at the 1968 Republican National Convention (Author's collection)

CHAPTER 27

"THE BASTARD CHEATED ME."

Wayne heard the boss' voice coming from inside the nearby study when he arrived at Richard Nixon's Fifth Avenue apartment on the night of the New Hampshire primary. The living room, which looked out on Central Park, was crowded with senior campaign staff, along with a sprinkling of RN's law firm partners. Rather than celebrating in the Granite State, Nixon decided to remain in New York tonight and claim victory at his newly opened national campaign headquarters, located in a five-story building on Park Avenue recently vacated by the American Bible Society.[1] "This place seems fitting," Nixon commented when he signed the lease. "After all, the Bible's central theme is resurrection."

Wayne peeked inside Nixon's open study door. There he found RN, looking strangely somber, seated in an overstuffed velvet brown chair and holding a can of Fresca in one hand and a pen in another while watching election returns.[2] A yellow legal pad covered in handwritten notes rested on his lap. RN saw Wayne and waved him in. Expecting to find the boss elated over a landslide victory, RN's grumpy demeanor and the "cheating" complaint baffled him.

"Mr. Nixon, I heard you say someone 'cheated' you—who?"

"Romney."

"But NBC just projected you winning the primary tonight with about 80 percent of the vote. If that's cheating, we need more of it!"[3]

"It's a hollow victory," RN lamented.[4] "Our polling since last year showed that Republican voters view me as the most qualified man for the presidency, but they also think I'm like Harold Stassen—a perennial loser.[5] We based our entire primary strategy on entering and winning all of them. The only way to bury this 'loser' rap is to kick the shit out of my opponents in every region."

"My dad told me never turn down a free meal or a free ride."

"Romney's exit isn't a gift—he was always a hopeless candidate. A year ago the pundits all thought he was the man to beat, but I knew he couldn't hit big league pitching and that he'd crack once the national press sunk their teeth in him. That's why I kept talking him up. I wanted Romney's candidacy kept alive so that his collapse would make our win even more dramatic. When he dropped out at the last minute he cheated me out of a meaningful victory. Well, that's just like a businessman—no goddamn guts."[6]

"Do you think this brings in Rocky?"

Nixon took a sip of his diet soft drink. "Maybe. With Romney out, I think tonight's results put great pressure on him to shit or get off the pot.[7] Either way, I'm not worried about him."[8]

"Isn't he your toughest obstacle?"

"No, for several reasons. He has the same problem Romney had. Party loyalists don't object to a couple of whores rejoining the church, but they hate like hell to see them leading the choir the first night.[9] Conservatives won't forgive either of them for hiding in the tall grass in '64 and not backing Goldwater.[10] I think they'd rather vote for Johnson than vote for a traitor. The other reason is more subtle—I hear he has a girlfriend—a Spanish or Mexican woman he imported from California. He put her on his staff, if you know what I mean—very pretty, by the way. Divorcing the first wife to marry his girlfriend a few years ago almost ruined him. A new sex scandal will kill him for good."[11]

"I don't know if this new one is his girlfriend, but I've met her. You're right—she's a looker."

"I've known Rocky for twenty years. Does she have large breasts?"

"Yeah—they're magnificent."

"Then she's his girlfriend. Anyway, to answer your question, no—I'm not worried about Rocky. He can't beat me *mano a mano*, and he knows it."[12]

"I hope you're right," interjected Leonard Garment, one of Nixon's law partners who joined the conversation. "Pat Buchanan just gave me a poll showing Rocky's gained *thirty* points on Johnson—from fifteen points behind to fifteen points ahead. That's a huge swing. We can't ignore it."

"Rocky does well in the polls when he's not a candidate," Nixon countered. "Right now he's stolen our playbook from last year and declared his own moratorium on politics. Every time he insists he has no interest in the presidency and that he only wants to be a good governor, the press buys it and his numbers go up.[13] That will end very quickly if he jumps into the race. Besides, that poll sampling you mentioned included Democrats and independents. When it comes to a Rockefeller versus Nixon matchup in Miami, with Republican delegates voting, Rocky gets slaughtered, so I'm not worried about him—standing alone. My concern is that he'll team up with Reagan. That could create problems."

"Reagan's only been in office for fourteen months," Wayne noted. "Doesn't it take that long to figure out where the bathrooms are in the capitol?"

Nixon walked over to a telephone and buzzed his longtime secretary Rose Mary Woods. "Rose, tell everyone I want to leave in five minutes." After hanging up, he responded to Wayne's minimization of a Reagan threat. "Last summer Reagan and I ended up in the same encampment at the Bohemian Grove.[14] He told me he had tentative plans to enter the California primary as a favorite son. Then he gave me an 'ah, shucks' explanation about how surprised and flattered he was by all the talk about his presidential chances. He assured me that the only reason he might run as a favorite son was to preserve Party unity."[15]

"How does that help Party unity?"

"He claims it prevents a bloody California primary like we had in '64. What it really does is send Ronnie to Miami with eighty-six delegates in his hip pocket."

"It will take a lot more than eighty-six delegates to stop your nomination."

"True, but the South is the key. Southerners prefer me to Rocky or Romney because they see me as the more electable conservative, but my support there is soft. Their hearts are with Reagan and his brand of hard-core conservatism. If he holds the California votes as a favorite son, and then picks up traction in the South, and if Rocky gets in and holds the Northeast, they could deadlock the convention and block me on the first ballot. The threat isn't from either of them individually—it's from them combining. If they block me on the first ballot, the 'loser' reputation will kick in. That could knock me out of the competition, and then the final showdown will be between them."[16]

"Southerners *liking* Reagan is one thing, but if he wants to lock down those delegates, won't he have to say he's running—soon?"

"Watch what Reagan does, not what he says. Ever since he became governor, he's been knocking the hell out of all those Berkeley-type radicals, and he's the Vietnam War's biggest cheerleader. Last summer he started touring the Deep South—all the states Goldwater won—raising money for candidates and the Party. They love him.[17] Forget about Rockefeller—he's just the one the press is ginning up. The guy to watch is Reagan. If he surges, he could push us to a second or third ballot. If that happens, the 'loser' reputation resurfaces, and we're dead."[18]

The three men left the study and joined the other Nixon staffers in the foyer. "The cars are ready downstairs, Dick," said Leonard Garment, now in his role as conscripted campaign assistant. "There's a large crowd—very enthusiastic, and lots of press. The family's already en route—time to go."

"I just came from there," added Dwight Chapin, another young Nixon campaign aide who advanced the event. "You'll enter from the back and walk past an honor guard of go-go girls—"

"Go-go girls?" RN interrupted. "What kind of party are we throwing?"

"They're *Go-Go Girls for Nixon.* They're waving pom-poms and dressed in campaign outfits."[19]

"Oh, for a minute I thought you meant bikini girls dancing *The Twist* in giant bird cages."

"Mr. Nixon, nobody dances *The Twist* these days—they're doing *The Monkey* now," Wayne said, smiling at RN's squareness. "And I'm curious—where did you see bikini girls dancing in giant bird cages?"

"In a Peter Sellers movie," RN replied. He then led his entourage to the door. "Okay, everyone, let's go claim our first eight delegates—

"—Eight down, 659 to go."[20]

Early 1962 campaign card promoting Baltimore attorney Spiro T. Agnew for county executive, autographed by Agnew for the author in 1987 (Author's collection)

Ted Agnew did things his way.

Born Spiro Theodore Agnew in Baltimore, the son of an immigrant Greek restaurateur, he served in World War II as an Army officer before returning home and earning a law degree. Active in local service clubs, he won election as Baltimore County executive in 1962—the first Republican to win the position in the twentieth century. Building an early reputation as a political moderate and civil rights supporter, Agnew ran four years later for governor and defeated the segregationist Democratic nominee in a nine-point landslide despite the state's strong Democratic registration advantage. Although barely a year in office, political pundits viewed Agnew as a future vice president or Cabinet member in a Nelson Rockefeller administration, because nobody outside of Rocky's immediate staff worked harder or longer to put the New York governor in the White House. Agnew's enthusiasm for Rocky started as early as 1965, after winning his first county race. Once he became governor, Agnew promoted Rocky ceaselessly, and George Romney's alternative candidacy did nothing to dull his enthusiasm.

"How did it go?"

"I spent half an hour with him. He basically told me to get lost."

When Jason Roe returned from his half-day political mission to Annapolis and reported to Governor Rockefeller in Albany, Rocky leaned back in his chair and laughed at the result. "That sounds like Ted! He can be a stubborn, tough bastard. He's only the fourth Republican Maryland governor in this century. But you know, he's the future of the Party. He's a true progressive, especially on civil rights."

"Of course he looks progressive—he ran against a goddamn segregationist. John Birch would have looked progressive in '66 running against George Mahoney.* Anyway, I told him that you're not a candidate, and that the 'Draft Rockefeller' movement he's started is nothing you want promoted, and that you'd like it stopped."

"And?"

"He said that Johnson will kick Nixon's ass in November, and that the only hope the Party has to capture the White House is to block

---

* George P. Mahoney (1901-1989), the 1966 Democratic nominee for Maryland governor. In defiance of anti-discrimination laws, Mahoney's pro-segregation campaign slogan was, "Your home is your castle—protect it!"

Nixon and nominate you. He said you made a mistake promoting Romney, and now that he's crashed and burned, you have a moral obligation to run—and he has a moral obligation to push you.[21] So he's going forward with his effort, with or without your blessing. Besides, now that Romney's out, he knows the pressure is building for you to get in, and he said you gave him hope when you spoke a week ago."[22]

"Did you tell him I'm reconsidering?"

"Not directly, but I hinted strongly at it, and I told him that in the meantime, all these one-man 'drafts' and 'write-in' things just cause embarrassments—like that jackass Hugh Gregg did to us with his New Hampshire write-in campaign against Nixon. What did that get you up there—5 percent?"[23]

"Ten."

"Anyway, I told Agnew that when we move forward, we need to move as a unit. I invited him up for the meeting this Sunday. He said he'd come, but he's not stopping his effort."

"It's hard to be mad at a guy who's more for you than you are for yourself."

On Sunday, March 10, two days before the New Hampshire primary made Richard Nixon the undisputed front-runner, Nelson Rockefeller gathered at the Fifth Avenue apartment his "war council"— a dozen assorted GOP governors, congressional leaders, former Republican National Committee chairmen, and New York Mayor John Lindsay. Although that three-hour meeting left open the decision whether Rocky should challenge Nixon, a strong consensus developed favoring his entry.[24] Now, one week later, the same brain trust reassembled at Fifth Avenue. With the clock ticking, and Nixon coming off his big victory, Rocky knew that if he wanted to run, he must decide.

"Dick Nixon deserved his New Hampshire win," Rocky said as he kicked off the session. "He worked hard for it, but politically I think it's insignificant. Since he had no competition, it wasn't a true test of his strength as a candidate."[25]

"He won't roll up those numbers in my state primary if you run," said Oregon Governor Tom McCall.** "You could make a great showing against Nixon there, and beating him in the West will send a meaningful signal to delegates that you have strong support beyond the East, but to do it you'll need to get boots on the ground—now."

"Well, Tom, I know you're in my corner, but—"

"It's not just me," McCall interrupted with a smile, "it's them, too!" McCall pushed a box toward Rocky, who opened it and found petitions signed by 51,000 Oregonians urging him to run for president.[26]

"Too bad George Romney couldn't get this kind of outpouring," Rocky lamented.

"Nelson, that wasn't going to happen. We all like George, but he's not you. That's why so many of the Republican governors withheld endorsing him."[27]

Rhode Island Governor John Chafee,*** a longtime Rocky friend and supporter, added, "Unless we want to let Nixon take the entire Republican ticket down with him in November, I guess the only real question is how to stage a draft for you at the convention."

As Chafee laid out his "Draft Rocky" blueprint, Jason Roe whispered an unvarnished opinion to his boss: "This guy's a dipshit—you have as much chance of getting drafted at the convention as you have of getting a blowjob from the pope."

Rocky stood and paced as he talked: "I'm very skeptical about the primary route—there'd be lots of bloodletting. That puts me in a damned box, because if I sit back and wait for a draft, I might as well endorse Nixon right now. A draft will never happen."

"But your poll numbers are stratospheric," countered Mayor Lindsay. "Isn't this the time to strike?"

"Mr. Mayor, you're right about the polls," Jason replied. "The governor does great in the polls when he's a non-candidate." Turning

---

** Tom McCall (1913-1983), governor of Oregon (1967-1975).

*** John Chafee (1922-1999), governor of Rhode Island (1963-1969), US secretary of the Navy (1969-1972), US senator (1976-1999).

to Rocky, Jason said, "If you could win the nomination, you'd win the White House. You're very popular with all voters generally, but rank-and-file Republican leaders don't share that love—and it's from their ranks that the convention delegates will come.[28] If you challenge Nixon in the primaries, conservatives will rush into his arms. If you don't run, he'll win the nomination in a cakewalk. And if Nixon is really unelectable, as most people here believe, then he'll likely drag down every state and congressional candidate in a tight race."

"Nelson," pleaded Tom McCall, "like it or not, the only thing standing between Richard Nixon and the collapse of the Republican ticket in November is you. I think you owe it to the Party—and to your country—to do it."

Jason walked over and handed Rocky two pieces of paper. "As expected, once again you've turned this into another coffee klatch. Here—the first one is a draft statement announcing your candidacy, the other one says you are not running. Either sit out the fight or get into it. Pick one."

Rocky reviewed both pieces of paper and then handed back to Jason the one announcing he'd run. With dramatic flair, he tore up the withdrawal draft, buzzed his secretary on the intercom, and told her, "Gabby, block out Thursday morning for a press conference. Tell our media shop there'll be a major announcement. Jason has the details."[29] The council burst into applause as Rocky told Governor McCall, "Tom, I think it's time for your team to assemble a strategy for Oregon."

"Before you jump into Oregon, shouldn't we analyze the primary states between now and then?" Jason asked.

"You can do that over the next couple of days," Rocky replied before drafting Senator Thruston Morton into service. "Thrus, put together a group of our congressional friends in Washington to meet me in the next couple of days. Let's take their final temperature before Thursday."

"We're in session this week," Morton replied, "so it will be easy. I'll set it up for Tuesday morning at the Capitol. That still gives you time for Thursday's announcement."

Rocky walked over and shook hands with Spiro Agnew while expressing esteem for the Maryland governor: "Ted, you're the father of this thing. You never gave up on me."

Agnew beamed. "I *knew* that if I shook the tree long enough, Nelson Rockefeller would fall out!"[30]

Everyone laughed, stood, and applauded again—everyone except Jason Roe. The strategist sat in his chair in the corner of the living room, knowing the coming days were fraught with landmines. Ignoring his gloomy adviser, Rocky beamed as he accepted congratulations from all before declaring, to another round of applause: "Gentlemen, the coffee klatch is over—

"—let's go save the Republic from Dick Nixon."

Campaign "tab" buttons reminding Republican voters that Nelson Rockefeller was a proven winner—and suggesting in comparison that Richard Nixon was unelectable (Author's collection)

CHAPTER 28

"HEY, TED, WHERE ARE YOU HEADING?"

After holding his final strategy meetings in Washington, Nelson Rockefeller entered the United Airlines VIP lounge of Friendship International Airport in Baltimore. While awaiting the shuttle flight back to New York, he spied Governor Agnew, who was seated alone sipping tea and working the *New York Times* crossword puzzle.

"Nelson! This is a surprise."

"I hope you aren't going far—after tomorrow's announcement, we're putting you to work!"

"I'm on my way to keynote a Greek Lodge convention in New York. I planned to call you tonight to see how the congressional meetings went."

"They couldn't have gone better. We're set to go tomorrow with a two o'clock press conference in Manhattan.[1] Can you make it?"

"I can't. I have a noon speech in Annapolis tomorrow followed by a press briefing, so I'll have to be with you in spirit. Anyway—tell me about the Washington meetings."

"I flew in on Monday and had dinner with Thrus Morton. He's agreed to be my national campaign chairman.[2] I didn't ask you to do it, Ted, because if this thing takes off, I may have other plans for you. Yesterday he hosted a private meeting with sixteen Republican senators. Each of them seemed very eager for me to run. Honestly, it was hard not to get caught up in the excitement."[3]

"Excuse me, Governor Agnew," interrupted an attendant. "They're ready to board you now."

"Okay, thanks." As Ted stood to leave, the two governors shook hands heartily. "Nelson, are you *sure* this is a go?"

"It's a go—we're in. I'll have my secretary confirm it for you just before tomorrow's announcement."

"This is great news for the Party and for America. I'll do whatever you need to help."

Rocky smiled. "Be careful saying things like that, Ted. If I win the nomination, a promise like that could change your life—profoundly!"

After his parents divorced five years earlier, custody of Michael Acosta went to his mother, but when she later moved to New York to take a government job, he lobbied her successfully to stay behind with his father so he could complete high school in Southern California. At 10:00 a.m. on Thursday morning, March 21, the eighteen-year-old team captain and first baseman for the *Brea Wildcats* stepped to the plate at his school's athletic field for batting practice. The second pitch beaned him, and he lost consciousness briefly. He felt sick when he revived, so his coach drove him to the nearby hospital. After admitting Michael to the emergency room, and unable to reach his father, a nurse tracked down his mother, working in the New York City office of Governor Rockefeller.

"Miss Cervantes, this is Dr. Frank Ambrose calling from St. Jude Hospital in Fullerton."

Gabby panicked. "Oh, my God—is Michael all right?"

"He's fine. He has a mild concussion—he tells me a southpaw with no control hit him with a ball during practice this morning."

"Have you contacted his father?"

"Mr. Acosta isn't answering his phone, but Michael's aunt is on her way here to take him home."

As they spoke, Rockefeller's private office door opened, and he walked over to his assistant's desk. "Gabby, I need you to handle something important."

"Doctor, just a moment," said the agitated, concerned parent. "Yes, governor?"

"Call Ted Agnew and give him this message—it's important. He'll know what it means. Tell him I'm leaving for the press conference." Rocky handed her a piece of paper.

"Yes, sir. I'm on the phone with my son's doctor. He was hurt at school."

"Is he okay?"

"It sounds like it. I'll call Governor Agnew in a moment."

After Rocky left, Gabby spoke to Michael briefly. Once assured he felt fine, she called Agnew's office and learned that the governor had not returned from his speech. A secretary put her through to Agnew's administrative assistant, Curtis Iaukea.

"Mr. Iaukea, this is Gabriela from Governor Rockefeller's office. He asked me to get an important message to Governor Agnew."

"Of course—what is it?"

"Governor Rockefeller said to tell Governor Agnew 'it's a go,' and that he just left for the press conference. He said Governor Agnew would know what that meant."

"He should be here any moment. I'll give it to him immediately—and I think we all know what that means! Please congratulate Governor Rockefeller and wish him luck from all of us here."

"Thank you. I will."

Her task completed, Gabby turned her attention to locating her ex-husband on the West Coast.

A few minutes later, Curtis Iaukea intercepted Governor Agnew when he returned to the capitol. After delivering the message from Rockefeller, Curtis had an idea. "Governor, the reporters are waiting for your weekly press briefing in the conference room. Why don't you invite them to watch Governor Rockefeller's announcement with you? It's set for the same time—in about five minutes."

"That's a great idea, Curt—wheel in a TV set so we can all watch it together."

Agnew entered the conference room and greeted the reporters. "Gentlemen, before we discuss this week's areas of interest, I've asked Mr. Iaukea to bring in a TV. I thought you'd all like to join me and watch Governor Rockefeller declare his candidacy for president."

"Governor, this may prove as big for you as for him," suggested Robert Wyatt of the *Baltimore Sun.*

"This day belongs to Governor Rockefeller—and to America. He'll make a great president."

"Does that mean you'll make a great vice president?" asked Bret Muncy of the *Frederick Post,* evoking laughter at the columnist's bold question.

Agnew grinned widely. "I'm only interested in serving Maryland as her governor, but if Governor Rockefeller needs me in this campaign, I'll do whatever I can to help him win the White House."

"Are you *sure* he's running—or is that a stupid question?" queried Andre Manssourian of WBAL.

Agnew picked up that morning's edition of the *New York Times* and pointed to an article reporting conclusively that Rockefeller would enter the presidential race today. "This may be the only occasion where I agree with the *Times!*" Agnew replied.[4]

Muncy followed up: "If Governor Rockefeller becomes president, I'm assuming your very close relationship with him will be of great benefit to Maryland."

"Well, it won't hurt."

Curtis turned on the television as Agnew pulled up a chair in front of it, obviously savoring this moment for which he had worked so hard. The dozen-plus reporters gathered for his press briefing stood behind Agnew; some took pictures of him watching the broadcast to record the moment for posterity. The images from the New York Hilton's West Ballroom, now crammed with 500 reporters, projected onto the small TV. Then, on time, Nelson Rockefeller appeared, looking calm and purposeful as he strode to the lectern.[5]

"Here we go!" Agnew said enthusiastically.

Agnew and the press watched as Rocky smiled, pulled some notes from his coat pocket, put on his glasses, and read a brief statement:

> I have decided today to reiterate unequivocally that I am not a candidate for the presidency of the United States. I shall do nothing by word or deed, to encourage a draft, although I would accept one if offered. Please spare me any suspicion or distrust. I mean—and I shall abide by—precisely what I say.[6]

A look of disbelief engulfed Agnew's face as he heard it. From the press, there was dead silence—before the snickers.

"It sure helps Maryland to have a governor who's in the know!" one reporter said in a stage whisper.

Agnew stood and turned off the television, trying to mask his humiliation.[7] "I'm greatly disappointed and tremendously surprised, but this hasn't changed my position about Governor Rockefeller. I still think he is the best possible candidate the Republican Party can offer the voters."

"Will you continue your 'Draft Rockefeller' efforts?" another asked.

"I'll need time to analyze the situation as it has developed. This comes as a complete surprise. I have to think it over—

"—Thank you, gentlemen."[8]

With that, the crestfallen and angry governor stalked out. As he closed the door behind him, the cackle of laughter from inside mocked him all the way down the hallway.[9]

Moments before Nelson Rockefeller stepped before the cameras for his nationally televised press conference at the New York Hilton, Richard Nixon occupied another hotel suite a few miles across town. Wayne Paugh knocked on the door and found RN dressed in a suit, sitting on his bed reviewing briefing materials.

"Mr. Nixon, Rockefeller is about to go on. Do you want to come and watch?"

"No—you guys watch it, and then come in and give me a complete report. I want your immediate impressions." Wayne closed the door and retreated to the living room. Standing around the television set with Pat Buchanan and Dwight Chapin, they saw the startling announcement unfold. Avoiding the temptation to rush back and tell the boss the news immediately upon hearing the revelation, they followed orders and watched the entire statement. Once Rocky stepped away from the microphones, the three men broke toward the bedroom door.

"He's not running!" Dwight cried out. "He even filed an affidavit to remove his name from the Oregon primary ballot!"

Nixon listened without showing emotion. Then he stood, smoothed down his suit, and picked up his notes. "I guess that proves it," he said casually.

"Proves what?" asked Pat.

"I told you before—he's got a girlfriend."[10]

Late that evening, Jason met Wayne for drinks at Toots Shor's. "Nixon turned me on to this place when I joined his firm," Wayne said. "Before the campaign started, he liked to hang out here on Saturday nights and talk sports."[11]

"I'm fascinated. Shall I take a sleeping pill for my insomnia, or will you just keep sharing irrelevant trivia?"

"That's pretty funny coming from the father of this year's two greatest political fubars."

"The Agnew one wasn't my fault," Jason protested. "After all his big supporters pumped up Rocky a few days ago, he went to D.C. for meetings while I stayed behind to crunch the numbers. This morning, when he flew back for the press conference, I gave him the bad news. The Oregon primary was supposed to be his big launch pad, but I found out that Governor McCall's statewide poll was two months old. As of today, Nixon's crushing Rocky there.[12] I also studied the primary calendar. If Rocky declared today, he'd have to face Nixon in Indiana on May 7, and then in Nebraska on May 14—and both states are solid Nixon country. By the time we limped into Oregon there'd be nothing left. The kicker was the meeting he had a day or so ago with those jackass senators. They all urged him to run, but I found out from someone in the Senate who owes me a favor that they did it just so Nixon could beat him and shake off his loser image.[13] I told him that challenging Nixon in the primaries was suicide."[14]

"How did Rocky handle the news?"

"He was livid. He said he wasn't going to be some goddamn sacrificial lamb to make Nixon look stronger. So he backed out at the last minute. Now he's reverted to his 'You can draft me or lose with Nixon' theme."

"Why didn't you guys give your big dogs a head's up? I hear Agnew's on the warpath over the screw-up."

"As we were leaving for the press conference, Rocky told a couple of staffers to get the 'A Team' on a conference call, but there wasn't time to reach everybody. The Agnew thing was a total fluke. I told Rocky to call him personally, since Agnew's done so much for us, but he wasn't in. Rocky had Gabby call and make sure Agnew learned that it was off, but she flubbed the message—she told Agnew's staffer it was on.[15] Her kid got hurt at school, she was flustered, and she probably misread the note he gave her. She swears she delivered it properly, but Agnew's guy said she very clearly told him that the campaign was *on*—he even told Gabby to congratulate Rocky."

"My former college roommate works as one of Spiro's Annapolis legislative aides. He said Agnew's calling you guys every name in the book."

"Rocky will spend forever trying to make it right with Agnew. I hear his local press is killing him—we've seen the bulldog editions of the Maryland papers—cartoons, editorial hit-pieces. They all make Agnew look like an out-of-the-loop fool."

"Impressive—you guys have the magic touch. First you make an enemy out of Romney and now Agnew.[16] Thank your boss for putting the Michigan and Maryland delegates in play for us—they should be low-hanging fruit for RN to pick. I heard Agnew plans to drop his 'Draft Rockefeller' committee and will now run as a favorite son to control Maryland's twenty-six delegates at the convention. RN's already invited him up for lunch—we want to catch him on the first bounce."[17]

"He's all yours. Rocky conceded to the press today that Nixon will be the nominee."[18]

"Nixon won't trust Rocky until we count the last delegate, and probably not then, either. Just because your boy's out of the primaries doesn't mean he still won't try to gin up a draft. RN thinks Rocky's 'personal sacrifice for Party unity' is all bullshit. You guys tried using Romney to block us. Now he thinks you'll use Reagan."[19]

The friends finished a final round, flipped for the check, and then they went out on West 52nd Street so Jason could hail a cab.

"So," Wayne asked, "did Gabby get fired?"

"No, she'll never get fired. She has unemployment insurance."

"So do I, but it doesn't keep me from getting fired if I screw up like she did."

"Her unemployment insurance is different from yours, buddy. Yours comes from the government."

"Where does hers come from?"

"From a couple of D-cups."

Campaign button with Uncle Sam and Richard Nixon: "He's good enough for me in '68" (Author's collection)

CHAPTER 29

"SO, WHAT DO YOU THINK about the White Sox selling Colavito to the Dodgers this week?"*

Wayne Paugh welcomed the question. When he started flying in 1967 with Richard Nixon, he learned his duties as official traveling companion from RN's speechwriter Ray Price: flying time is work time, and if RN's not working, he's thinking—he doesn't want idle chatter unless he initiates it.[1] When they flew commercial, Nixon's aide also served as a professional buffer, taking the aisle seat between the Boss and other passengers who recognized him and wanted to chat.[2] The campaign's new charter jet solved the unwanted visitor problem, but the "speak-not" rule still held. However, once Nixon tired of work and wanted to relax, Wayne enjoyed picking the brain of this historical figure who was, in such moments, very down-to-earth.[3]

"Colavito's been on the downswing since '65," Wayne replied. "I

---

* On March 26, 1968, the Chicago White Sox sold pitcher Rocky Colavito to the Los Angeles Dodgers.

wouldn't be surprised if they cut him before the end of the season."

"I agree, I think this is probably it for him—a good player in his day. But keep your eye on Cincinnati's rookie catcher—a kid named Johnny Bench—he's a comer."

For the next ten minutes, RN amazed Wayne with an encyclopedic knowledge of baseball trivia and statistics that matched his vast knowledge of world affairs. Pat Buchanan interrupted the performance: "Mr. Nixon, it's almost time, and we have the radio hooked up to hear Johnson's speech. Shall we pipe it through the speakers?"

"That'll be fine."

While Pat instructed the cabin to play President Johnson's Vietnam speech through the Convair, Wayne asked if RN still planned to deliver the Vietnam speech he had helped draft and that RN was scheduled to give today before he shelved it. "I wanted to ice that speech until after Johnson's, in case we need to adapt to changing circumstances," RN explained.

A few minutes later, although the radio crackled a bit, the unmistakable Texas drawl filled the cabin: "Good evening, my fellow Americans: Tonight I want to speak to you of peace in Vietnam." For the next thirty-eight minutes, Nixon listened and scribbled on his yellow legal pads while LBJ announced various Vietnam de-escalation initiatives.[4] Only when LBJ reached the penultimate lines did RN's pen stop scratching against the paper: "I shall not seek, and I will not accept, the nomination of my Party for another term as your president."[5]

"Holy shit!" Wayne blurted. RN's staff looked at each other gape-mouthed. Only Nixon showed no reaction as he listened in silence until the broadcast concluded. "First, Romney, then Rockefeller, and now Johnson," RN noted. "I guess this is the year of the dropouts."[6]

"Did you see this coming, sir?" Dwight Chapin asked.

"No—I thought he'd be my opponent, and I looked forward to it. He's so vulnerable on so many fronts. In '64, Republicans had to run against Kennedy's ghost and Johnson's promises. This time, we had Kennedy's ghost running against him, and if Lyndon beat Bobby in

Chicago, we'd get to run against him on performance, not promises.[7] Besides, I'm the one Republican who can goad Lyndon into overreacting.[8] Well, I guess I shouldn't be too surprised by this—Gallup shows his approval ratings have dropped from 80 percent when he became president to around 38 percent now.[9] No wonder he quit."

"What's your read on how this shakes out?"

"It's a new dynamic. When it was Lyndon versus Bobby, whoever won the nomination would have come out of Chicago bloodied up pretty good. Now Humphrey will probably get in, and it will still be bloody, but not like it would have been with Lyndon and Bobby going at it."[10]

"Between Humphrey and Kennedy, isn't Bobby the hardest to beat?" asked Wayne.

RN looked at him paternalistically, as if about to correct a child's foolish question: "Bobby's the *best* Democrat to run against—I can beat him. He's nothing like his brother. He doesn't have Jack's charisma, and he has none of his centrist-conservative appeal. He's moved so far to the left to attract the hippies and the college kids, and he's savaged the president of his own Party to do it. He'll never unite the Democrats.[11] If he wins the nomination, we'll sweep the South, as well as hold all the GOP and pro-war states. Also, he's a single–issue candidate. Johnson can kneecap his entire campaign before November by announcing peace. That takes the war issue away from him—what's left? On top of all that, if he's the nominee, I'll indict him right back to the Bay of Pigs."[12]

RN stared out the airplane window as if deep in thought and then volunteered, "You have no idea what a mean, classless, nasty guy Bobby is. I remember attending a banquet some years ago, and he was there. The waiter brought out his food, and Bobby didn't like it, so he threw his meal on the floor—and at the waiter. Everybody at the event stared in horror, but nobody said anything to him."

"It's hard to believe a public figure could behave that way and get away with it," Wayne explained.

"The press always covers for the Kennedys," RN replied irritably. "When we're in Key Biscayne next week, ask Bebe Rebozo. He knows all of them—their families socialized down in Florida. He'll tell you—the Kennedys treat the help like crap wherever they go. They're not nice people. The legend of Jack being gracious and charming is bull. He'd spit on waiters and scream at the help, but Bobby's the worst. He's a no-good little bastard."[13]

"If Johnson had stayed in, would he have beat Kennedy?"

"No question. Lyndon's tough, and he's got guts—look how he's stayed and fought those goddamned North Vietnamese. A lesser man like Bobby would have packed it in once the going got rough."[14]

"You make LBJ sound like a patriot in comparison."

"Johnson *is* a patriot—even if he is a calculating bastard.[15] He's not a good man, but he makes decisions from his gut, and he tries.[16] Next to the Kennedys, he's a saint."

"Mr. Nixon," Ray Price interrupted, "we'll need to get something ready for the press. Shall we put it together for you?"

"How long before we land at LaGuardia?" RN asked Pat Buchanan.

Pat checked his watch. "About half an hour."

"That gives us time to craft a response. You and Ray draft it. Make it complimentary of Lyndon. If Kennedy ends up as the nominee, it might help start laying the groundwork to enlist Johnson's private help. I think he'd rather see a Republican win than have Bobby succeed him."[17]

RN paused in thought, grinned, and then nodded his head. "If I run against Bobby, I think Lyndon would turn cartwheels over the chance to knife that little shit."

Richard Nixon's theory that President Johnson might want to provide covert help to a Republican presidential candidate was correct—but he misjudged for which contender LBJ aimed his largesse.

On April 23, 1968, a sleek black limousine with tinted windows pulled up to the guard station on East Executive Avenue in Washington. Three weeks after eliminating himself from presidential consideration, Nelson Rockefeller stepped quickly from the vehicle and entered a White House side door for a private dinner with the occupant.

After cocktails, stewards served the two men in the Family Dining Room, where LBJ got down to business before the first course arrived. "Goddamn it, Nelson, I'm in a hell of a fix. Look at my choices for president: Gene McCarthy—who's more interested in reciting poetry than in governing, Hubert—who's as weak as a bled calf,[18] and Bobby—who's unfit for the presidency. And I can't sleep at night thinking about Dick Nixon becoming president. I hear you're taking a second look at getting into the race, and I'm telling you to take a *very hard* look at it. I want to leave this office in the hands of a man competent to handle it—and that's you, not any of these other jackasses."[19]

Nelson smiled. "Well, Mr. President, as one who followed your lead in stepping away from 1968, I hear you're reconsidering as well!"

"Never mind that, Nelson—I'm out. As your president, and as your friend, I'm asking you to reconsider. I'm afraid Bobby might steamroll Hubert in Chicago, and if that happens, you may be the only man in America who can beat him. You know I think the world of you—you're a sensible moderate who understands power and how to use it."[20]

"This almost sounds like an endorsement, Mr. President."

"I can't do that publicly, but by God, if you get into this race, I'll support you quietly, and I will *never* campaign against you."[21]

"To be honest, I have been rethinking it. Since I got out, I've been contacted by most of the old-line major donors who fear Nixon will lead Republicans to defeat. They've been pledging big amounts if I reconsider, and they started funding a new—and more muscular—draft movement. These last few weeks they've spread out around the country and put together the money, the manpower, and a skeleton organization in every key state.[22] I've run for president—or come close to running—three times in the last ten years, but this is the first time I'm being *asked* to run, and being asked by a widespread national network."[23]

"So do it!"

"I'd have to draw away delegates already pledged to Nixon. I'm too late to enter and win delegates through the primaries—"

"—That doesn't matter," LBJ interrupted. "Nixon can be beaten.

He's like a Spanish horse who runs faster than all the other horses for the first nine lengths, and then turns around and runs backward. You'll see, he'll do something wrong in the end. He always does.[24] Besides, there are primaries in only a dozen states, and half of them are tied up by favorite-son governors—including Reagan in California—so most of your delegates will get picked in the smoke-filled rooms, where politicians understand the meaning of winners and losers."[25]

"It'll be tough to turn those people around. Nixon campaigned all over the country for candidates in the '66 midterms, and he picked up countless chits, and those people will all be delegates. They feel they owe him. I was stuck back home that year fighting in a tough reelect. After the Goldwater fight, those people at best don't think they owe me anything, and at worst will do whatever they can to screw me."

"You need to disabuse those folks of the notion that they owe Nixon something. Look at the goddamn map of his travels—he picked carefully where to campaign. He went to traditional Republican districts that were lost in a fluke by my landslide over Goldwater. Those seats were going back to the Republicans in '66 with or without Nixon, so he showed up, and then he took the bow for their win."[26]

"If you were in my situation, how would you go about it?"

"You need to do two things. First, convince the delegates you can beat Bobby or Hubert in November. Second, convince them Nixon can't. The polls will prove the first thing for you—easy—and common sense will prove the second."

As a steward served coffee, LBJ poured cream and sugar into a white china cup emblazoned with a small gold presidential eagle: "You know, all those sonsabitches in my Party that wanted to run me out of town a few months ago now are wetting their britches over Bobby or Hubert winning the nomination and losing to Nixon. If you play this smart, the same bastards that booed you in '64 might turn over the keys to you in '68." Then, taking a sip, the president looked at his guest and grinned:

"Rocky, it's a hell of a business we're in, ain't it?"

Late that night, back in Albany, Rocky huddled with several key advisers, including Jason Roe, who just returned from a nationwide four-day canvass of donors and opinion leaders. He reported that everyone he contacted pleaded for Nelson to run.

"Nixon's got a big lead, and most of the delegates would prefer to take him over you," Jason said as he hunched over the conference table, reports and graphs spread before him. "But that preference is qualified—they only prefer him *if* he can win in November. It's too late to get on the ballot and challenge him directly in any of the remaining primaries, but it's not too late to change the delegates' minds. You'd need to take your case to the people—and I don't mean just Republicans. You need to campaign to all segments—Dems and independents—to move public opinion. In twelve weeks, if we can head into Miami with all the mainstream polls showing that you can win and Nixon can't, you could yank this nomination right out of his clenched fist."[27]

"How do you recommend we do it?"

"Three campaigns: one geared toward the Republican base, with you barnstorming to as many states as we can squeeze in between now and August to show the locals that you aren't Lucifer. You don't have to ask delegates to commit—just try and get them to stay loose. The second part is to influence public opinion directly, and that is with an unrelenting media buy. Sixty-second TV spots twice a day in the key media markets and weekly national network TV spots. With the budget that Whitney** thinks he can help us raise, by opening day of the convention, we will have brought you into 90 percent of every American home. It's a longshot, but it could work."[28]

"That's only two parts," Rocky replied. "You said there were three."

"The third part is in Sacramento, and he doesn't know yet that he'll be

---

** After Rockefeller announced at his March 31 press conference he would not seek the presidency, the prime financier of the new Draft Rockefeller movement was John Hay Whitney (1904-1982), one of America's wealthiest men, who raised for Rocky vast sums of both WASP old-money, as well as pledges from the liberal Jewish business leaders around the country. Lewis Chester et al., *An American Melodrama: The Presidential Campaign of 1968* (New York: Viking Press, 1969), 379-380.

the guy who hands us the nomination if we win. If things work out, you could arrive in Miami with upwards of 400 delegates. We'd need almost three hundred more to block Nixon on the first ballot. We get them from Reagan. He'll go to Miami with almost one hundred votes automatically as a favorite son from California. We need him to freeze about 180 votes from the Southern delegates—they absolutely love him."[29]

"Why would Ronnie do this to help me?"

"He won't do it to help you, but he'd do it to help himself. He needs you as much as you need him. If we don't combine to block Nixon, then Nixon wins—period. If we can stop him, then the gloves come off between you and the actor; but right now, he's our closest ally."

As Rocky nodded and took notes, Jason reached into a folder and produced the *Time* magazine from last October—the one with the cover depicting the old-style campaign poster touting Rocky for president and Reagan for vice president as the GOP's 1968 "Dream Ticket." "Here," Jason said as he slid the periodical across the table to Rocky. "Autograph this for me. If you pull this off, I'll get Reagan to sign it after you pick him as your running mate."

Rocky inscribed the cover and then drew an "X" mirthfully across Reagan's portrait. "You won't need his autograph on this," Rocky replied. "If I do get into this thing and win, there's one guy I really like for VP, and it isn't Ronnie—it's Ted Agnew. He'd satisfy the South—he's governor of a Border State that was part of the Confederacy, he's solid on law and order, yet he has a good civil rights record. If I win the nomination, I think Kennedy's my likely opponent, so a guy like Agnew can rally conservatives without scaring off the moderates and liberals the way Reagan would. Besides that, he's the most loyal supporter I had out there—he kept at it for me even when we told him to stop. Most of all, after I humiliated him during my press conference, I owe him. Even if I don't pick him, I'll leak at the proper time he's on my short list. That will make those press bastards in Annapolis stop laughing at him."[30]

Rocky settled back into his chair. "You know, Jason, I was thinking earlier about how most presidential nominees never get a chance to consider a running mate until the last minute at the convention, and then they make the biggest political decision of their life in a few hurried hours. I've had a decade to think seriously about the presidency, and I like Ted Agnew. Since we have the time and the resources, I want you to handle something delicate for me—take the next four or five days and run the traps on him now. Go down to Baltimore and get the boys to help you."

"*The Baltimore Boys?*" Jason asked.

"Yeah—they're wired pretty extensively. Tell them this is for me, it's very secret, and if it isn't handled quietly it will embarrass all of us."

"Isn't this premature? You're about to create a campaign from scratch and embark on a nearly impossible race."

"No, I want you to do this. You won't miss anything. The next few days will be figuring out where we need to go over the next three months. You can rejoin me on the campaign next week. I know my winning is a longshot, but if things fall into place, I want to be ready—and this time, I have a feeling things could break our way."

"Do you want me to talk to Agnew?"

"No—keep him out of this. I don't want to set him up for another embarrassment or disappointment. Handle this quietly, collect what you can, and then put the information in the safe that Gabby keeps for me. When we get to Miami, if we're still in the game, we can approach the running mate issue more formally. For now, dig around and see if there's anything from his early Baltimore days that we should know. Don't waste time on the public stuff—we'll put political researchers on that later if we need it."

Rocky walked Jason out the door and to the elevator. "You know," he told his adviser, "it's the damnedest thing. In 1960 they said I dropped out too soon, and in 1964 they said I stayed in too long. Well, this year they'll say I've done both!"[31]

Badge urging the Republican Party to draft Nelson Rockefeller for president in 1968 (Author's collection)

One week later, on April 30, 1968, less than six weeks after telling America categorically that he would not seek the White House, Nelson Rockefeller held another nationally televised press conference. At this one, he asked America to ignore his earlier disclaimer—and then declared himself a candidate.[32] Lest anyone not take his candidacy seriously, within a day of announcing, and without appearing on the ballot, Rocky beat both Nixon and favorite son candidate, Governor John Volpe, in the Massachusetts Republican presidential primary—and he did it with write-in votes. Rocky's victory margin allowed him to pocket every one of the thirty-four delegates the Bay State would send to the Republican National Convention.[33]

The New York governor was off to a very good start.

1966 Spiro Agnew for Maryland governor campaign button (Author's collection)

CHAPTER 30

"TRY THE CRAB CAKES. They're the best in town."

Jason Roe accepted the recommendation without question, since John and Pat Rogan knew Baltimore better than any parade of city fathers. The Rogan brothers made an imposing duo: both stood well over six feet, with beefy frames, goatees, permanent scowls, and deep, authoritative voices. Back in the 1930s, as young apprentice members of Baltimore's International Union of Operating Engineers Local 37, their favorite Friday night activity was hitting the local Irish bars, getting hammered, and then joining in any available drunken brawl. Now in their mid-and-late fifties, their rowdy pub days were over, but nobody with sense tested their mettle.

Pat worked as director of engineering operations at Memorial Stadium, home of the Baltimore Orioles, with John across town as chief engineer for Maryland National Bank's main headquarters. Whenever people needed favors done in Baltimore—or things kept quiet there—the Rogans were potent allies. They knew everyone worth knowing in town: elected and appointed officials, police and fire brass, and the highest ranking members of every trade union. When Governor

Rockefeller attended an Orioles-Yankees game in 1962, "My Baltimore Boys" (as Rocky called them) handled all the logistics. Rocky had such a good time, especially when they gave him an unofficial tour of Baltimore's nightlife, that a friendship began. Now, when Rocky needed private help in the Washington-Baltimore area, he bypassed traditional channels and called upon them.

After the three men grabbed a table at Connolly's Seafood House on the waterfront, Jason shared his purpose in code so that nearby diners would not overhear the sensitive assignment. "Your good friend in New York asked me to come and see you. As you know, he may be moving to another location next year, and if he does, he's interested in inviting your former county executive to join him."

"You mean our friend that's now in Annapolis?" John asked.

"Yes."

The brothers looked at each other and then turned back to their visitor. Shaking his head, John said, "That's a bad idea right now."

"Are you on the outs with him?"

"Just the opposite—we're old friends. I knew him back in our Kiwanis days when he was a local lawyer. But it's a bad idea right now."

Pat flagged down the waiter: "Hey, Manny, we'll be back. Hold our table and our food order."

They exited the restaurant and walked along Pratt Street, not stopping to talk until they made it halfway across the now-deserted Jones Falls Bridge. Turning to Jason, John asked, "Ever heard of Dale Anderson?"

"No—who is he?"

"He's the Democrat who took Ted Agnew's place as Baltimore County executive. He's in hot water with the feds right now. The US Attorney here is investigating him for shaking down local engineering companies for kickbacks after he steered county contracts to them."

"The federal prosecutors here are all Dem appointees," Jason noted. "Why do they want to destroy one of their own?"

"Dale's small potatoes. The feds don't care about him. They want a

Democrat back in the governor's office. If they can use this to take down Agnew, then the Democratic lieutenant governor takes over. That's the long game here. Remember, before Agnew won last year, Democrats held the governorship for most of the last sixty years. They want it back, and they'll do what it takes to get it."

"How does a corrupt local Democrat shaking down personal bribes hurt Agnew?"

"When the feds started digging," Pat explained, "they noticed that the three engineering firms paying the heavyest bribes to Dale were owned by Republican bigshots with close ties to Agnew. Jerry Wolff was once Agnew's aide. Lester Matz was Agnew's business partner years ago, and Bud Hammerman's his longtime friend. The US Attorney is bulldozing them. They've been told they're facing prison for conspiracy and bribery unless they cooperate, and the prosecutors aren't interested in them laying out Dale. They want these guys to say they also paid kickbacks to Agnew."

"How reliable is your information?"

"From the horse's mouth, buddy. One of the federal investigators likes to come to the stadium for games. It's good for business—I bring him and his girlfriend into the park, get them seats behind home plate, load them up with free beer and food, and then I have a friend at the courthouse. Sometimes when he's drinking he talks, and sometimes the information is helpful to guys I know. I pass it along, and maybe if I need a favor down the road, they help me. That's how it works in this town. But it's not just beer talk here. When he told me about their investigation, it turned out I knew these three Agnew pals. When we built the stadium I threw some contracts to Lester's firm, and I got to know Jerry and Bud through him. After hearing about this I went over to warn Lester, but he already knew. He started crying and told me what they were trying to make him say about Agnew."

"Do you think they'll roll over on Agnew?"

"They're in a fix, because all three of them are caught dead-bang on trading kickbacks for contracts. When Lester offered to testify about paying bribes to Dale, the feds laughed at him—they already have enough to bury Dale. They told Lester that if he wants any kind of deal, he has to say he paid kickbacks to Agnew—as governor—because the statute of limitations had passed on most of the old contracts Ted awarded them when he was Baltimore County exec."

"Do you think Agnew knows about any of this?"

"He knows, but I don't think he appreciates the danger he's in. Lester told me that he and Jerry went to see Ted and told him about the feds threatening them. They asked Ted to step in and kill it. When Ted said he couldn't do anything about a federal investigation, they got pissed and told Ted the feds offered them immunity to testify that they paid him bribes."

"How did Agnew handle that?"

"He got angry. He told them that all they ever gave him were contributions that went directly into his campaign account, not his pocket. But once Ted told them he couldn't help, they ran across the street and started cutting their deals with the feds. From what I hear, Ted's not taking this very seriously—but I'm telling you, the shit's gonna hit the fan eventually. It's only a question of when."

"You know how it goes," John said. "It doesn't have to be true to be believable. When the feds have you in their grip, they'll squeeze until you pop. They tell these guys there are two choices: thirty years in federal prison—never see your kids grow up and lose everything you have defending yourself, or tell us how you bribed Agnew. What would you do? I like Ted a lot, but if those are my choices, I'll tell them whatever they want to hear, whether it's true or not. And I know these three guys, too. They'll crack like dry plaster. They'll serve up Ted eventually."[1]

"This was very helpful," Jason said grimly. "I owe you guys."

"Listen," Pat told him, "all I want from you is a promise. This info is on a need-to-know basis, okay? If Rocky is about to go out on a limb with Ted, then tell him. Otherwise, deep-six this conversation—we know how Rocky likes to gab. This information is hot, and it could screw us with lots of people. We can't have this traced back to us."

"When I get back, I'll write a memo of our discussion and put it in the safe. I won't show it to Rocky or anyone else unless I absolutely need to."

"Thanks, Jason—

"—Now, let's get back to those crab cakes."

NIXON'S THE ONE! badge worn by a delegate to the 1968 Republican National Convention (Author's collection)

CHAPTER 31

"ASIANS—I LOVE THOSE LITTLE BROWN PEOPLE!"[1]

On June 21, the second of a two-day break from the campaign, Richard Nixon and his senior staff relaxed on the veranda of Villa 41 at the Key Biscayne Hotel. Wearing Hawaiian shirts, smoking cigars, drinking, and enjoying the evening ocean breeze off the Atlantic, they strategized over their final push to Miami. When Wayne Paugh heard the slurred "little brown people" remark come from RN, his convulsive laughter almost caused him to spew the beer he had just gulped. "Please tell me I didn't just hear what I heard," Wayne cracked to the tall man seated next to him.

Robert H. Finch, lieutenant governor of California, smiled. "You heard it," he chuckled. "It sounds like Dick's in his cups, although with him, I should say his cup-and-a-half. It doesn't take much to get him loose, because he drinks very little."[2]

Of everyone inside the Nixon campaign "bubble," Bob Finch knew the candidate best. A Marine Corps officer in World War II and Korea, his relationship with RN dated back to the mid-1940s when the two young Southern California lawyers were budding politicos. After Nixon went to Washington as vice president, Bob joined his staff and later managed his near-successful 1960 presidential campaign against John F. Kennedy. Elected lieutenant governor in 1966 on the same day Ronald Reagan won the governorship, Bob outpolled the popular Reagan—much to the amusement of his running mate but to the unending consternation of California's new first lady, Nancy Reagan. Following this year's California GOP presidential primary, Bob was pledged (technically) as a Reagan "favorite son" delegate, but everyone in Sacramento knew he remained a Nixon adviser and loyalist.[3]

During their Florida respite, Wayne appreciated this downtime with Bob. It gave him time with a man so close to RN that the boss referred to Bob as his younger brother. "I came on board with him during the '66 midterms," Wayne told Bob. "All of us on the campaign are twenty years younger. You've known him for decades—what's he really like with old friends when he lets his hair down?"

Bob lit yet another cigarette from the two packs he would smoke before day's end. "On the personal side, he's kind, considerate, and even sentimental. But in political battle, he can be very cold and calculating. Those traits, by the way, are not necessarily bad—they're essential tools of the trade. On either level, when he's upset or depressed, he can be impatient, vindictive, angry."[4]

"I haven't seen much of that, and I've been traveling with him for a year. I've really never experienced him losing his cool in public."

"That's because he learned a lesson after his disastrous 1962 'last press conference.'"

"The only time I've seen what staffers call the 'dark side' is when he thinks the press is holding him to a double standard—crucifying him for something and then giving the Democrats a pass for doing the same thing. He can brood for days over it."

"That's been a longtime source of resentment for Dick, and those resentments have accumulated over the years. You're right—he keeps it in check generally. Sometimes it boils over."[5]

Looking out at the ocean, Bob reminisced. "When I think of old resentments and double standards, this hotel comes to mind. I'm surprised Dick likes to come here."[6]

"Why this hotel?"

"In 1960 we knew Kennedy had stolen the election from us with voter fraud in Texas and Illinois. A week after the election, Dick came down here to rest. Kennedy called and wanted to fly over from Palm Beach to see him. They met here at this hotel in Villa 69, the one right behind us.[7] Kennedy told the press it was a social visit with an old congressional colleague, but the real purpose was to insure that Dick wouldn't contest the election results and demand a recount. Kennedy was worried about that, and there was lots of pressure on Dick to challenge the votes in those states. Even Kennedy admitted during their private meeting that he wasn't sure who really won the election."

"Why didn't he contest it? He could have saved America a hell of a lot of grief."

"Dick didn't want to put the country through that kind of uncertainty, especially with an ongoing precarious military situation with the Soviets. So he let Kennedy take the White House from him, fairly or unfairly, but the press never once gave him any credit for perhaps the most magnanimous act of statesmanship of my lifetime. Maybe now you understand why this unending double standard gnaws at him."[8]

"You had a ringside seat in 1960—what are the big mistakes we need to avoid this time?"

"There are always mistakes in a campaign—it's unavoidable. Sidestepping the obvious ones from that race is easy. The trick is to avoid making new ones. The two big lessons we learned from 1960 are, first, don't run him ragged, and, two, understand the importance of television. Back then, we dragged Dick through unending eighteen-hour days across fifty states to fulfill a stupid pledge when two minutes on the network evening news would have exposed him to more voters than all those personal appearances combined.[9] As to the second, Dick's been gun-shy about TV since that first debate where he looked gaunt and pale next to Kennedy. Dick's always hated TV and never did very well on it. Now we're going to use it to our advantage. Have you met Roger Ailes yet?"

"I heard the boss talk about him with Buchanan, but I don't know him."

"Until recently he produced *The Mike Douglas Show.** We've hired him to handle our TV ads this year. Instead of putting Dick in front of hostile reporters every day, Roger's going to shoot footage of town hall meetings with a small number of citizens asking questions. No press, no crowds, just Dick standing in the middle of a dozen or so people taking whatever questions they toss at him. It's the type of environment where he excels, and with professional lighting, makeup, and the ability to edit the footage, Roger will cut the best segments into thirty and sixty-second commercials to run throughout the campaign. Roger calls them the *Man in the Arena* ads."[10] Bob butted out his cigarette and then lit another. "Of course, after tomorrow's meeting all the TV ads in the world won't help if we don't come away with what we need."

"You mean the endorsement? I went to Atlanta with the boss a few weeks ago when he met with the Southern leaders. I thought that was locked down."

"Dick met with the leadership of the Southern states there, and he's picked up some good support from it, but there was only one man in that meeting that counted. If we get his endorsement tomorrow, then he'll bring the Southern delegates with him. If that happens, we win the nomination on the first ballot. We should get it, but as a former campaign manager, I'm a worrier by nature—"

"—That's why tomorrow Dick needs to hook ole' Strom."

Strom Thurmond didn't impress easily.

Born in 1902, the former South Carolina state legislator and county

---

*   *The Mike Douglas Show* was a Philadelphia-based daytime television talk and variety show hosted by Mike Douglas that ran in syndication from 1963 until 1981. See https://en.wikipedia.org/wiki/The_Mike_Douglas_Show.

judge resigned from the bench to enlist in the Army during World War II, where he fought in Normandy on D-Day. Returning home as a decorated combat veteran, and running as a Democrat, he won the governorship. In 1948 he bolted from the Democratic Party over civil rights and challenged Harry Truman for the presidency as a third-party candidate. Although Truman won the election that November, Thurmond carried four states and received thirty-nine electoral votes. In 1954, he became the first man in US history to win a contested US Senate seat as a write-in candidate.** In 1964, after President Johnson signed the 1964 Civil Rights Act, Thurmond abandoned LBJ and the Democratic Party and supported Republican Barry Goldwater (who voted against the act reluctantly on constitutional grounds). Like most Southern politicians of his era who remained in office, Thurmond later relented on his earlier staunch segregationist position. Unlike most others, he never apologized for it.[11] By 1968, although no longer advocating segregation, he had become an icon in the South for his unwavering support of states' rights, a strong national defense, and virulent anticommunism.[12] The slim, courtly senator was fitter than many men half his age—and proved it repeatedly. That year, at age sixty-six, he married his second wife—a twenty-two-year-old former Miss South Carolina with whom he later sired four children. During the debate on the 1964 Civil Rights Act, Thurmond refused to attend Senator Ralph Yarborough's committee hearing on the legislation in an effort to block a quorum. Later, tiring of Yarborough's pleas and tricks to get him to attend, Thurmond offered to settle the matter by wrestling Yarborough in the hall of the Old Senate Office Building. Yarborough accepted the challenge, and Thurmond immediately threw and pinned him to the marble floor. When Yarborough complained that Thurmond

---

** Except for a six-month break in 1956, Strom Thurmond served in the United States Senate from 1954 to 2003. He was the only member of Congress in American history to reach the age of 100 while still in service. At the time of his retirement in 2003, he held the record as the longest-serving member of the United States Senate.

had a head start, Thurmond agreed to a redo. With lightening speed, Thurmond again threw and pinned Yarborough to the ground, helped him up, brushed him off, and walked away.[13]

In 1968, Thurmond's importance rested on geography. The Southern states would send to the Republican National Convention half of the delegates necessary to win the presidential nomination (334 of the 667 needed for a majority).[14] Almost uniformly, those delegates revered Strom Thurmond.[15] Where he led, Southern delegates followed, and in his heart, he knew into whose arms he wanted them pointed.

Early in the campaign season, when a presidential hopeful addressed the annual South Carolina GOP state convention, Strom watched intently from the head table as 3,000 Party faithful inside the Columbia Township Auditorium cheered wildly over almost every sentence. "By God," Strom whispered to his longtime aide Harry Dent, "I love that man! Have you ever seen anyone motivate the troops like him?"

"Yes, senator, I have," Harry replied with a grin. "In fact, I work for him."

Strom laughed, slapped his knee, and then returned to his observation. "This man's the best hope we've got for America, and he can stop George Wallace from bleeding Republican and independent Southern voters in November. Look at those people—they're mesmerized! In one night, he's retired the debt of the entire state Party. He's our next president if I have any say in it."[16] Leaning in closer, Strom whispered, "When dinner's over, I'm going to slip away so it isn't obvious. Bring him to my room. I'll line up the boys by tomorrow for him."

At the end of the evening, Harry escorted the state Party's honored guest up a service elevator to the suite. "Young man," Strom declared as he strode across the room, grabbed the visitor's hand and pumped it heartily, "you are the future of this Party. I'm for you, and I'll do all I can to put you in the White House next year."

"That's very flattering senator, but I'm not a candidate, at least not now. To be honest, I'm not sure I'm ready to be president. Let's wait and see what happens. Of course, if the Republican convention beats on my door, I won't say, 'Get lost, fellas.'"[17]

And, with that expression of modest indecision, California Governor Ronald Reagan let Strom Thurmond slip through his fingers in 1968.[18] By contrast, when Richard Nixon traveled to Atlanta to meet Thurmond, he demonstrated none of Reagan's hesitancy:

Nixon came to close the deal.

On June 1, aboard RN's chartered campaign jet, the Nixon team brimmed with cautious optimism when it landed at Atlanta Municipal Airport for the Southern GOP leaders' workshop. A waiting sedan whisked Nixon, Pat Buchanan, and Ray Price to the downtown hotel, while Wayne Paugh remained behind working on a speech draft scheduled for delivery tomorrow in Cleveland. Ninety minutes later, Wayne looked out the window of the aircraft and saw the sedan return, along with another car carrying Pat and Ray. "Why didn't they ride back with the old man?" he wondered. He learned the answer when Nixon stepped from his car with Strom Thurmond, who rode with him to the airport and now bid Nixon a warm goodbye on the tarmac.[19]

A few minutes later, Pat took the seat next to Wayne. "That was quick," Wayne said.

"Why waste time when you got what you came for?" Pat replied.

"Did Strom endorse the old man formally?"

"Not yet.[20] He wants to talk with the South Carolina delegation as a courtesy. They're meeting in a few weeks. But his chief of staff told me Strom will deliver for us."[21]

"It sounds like the trip was a success."

"In spades—while there we picked up endorsements from the Tennessee and Oklahoma state Party chairmen, so there's another fifty delegates.[22] If we get Strom this month, then that means we may have wrapped up the nomination at this meeting today."

"How come you say 'may have'? If Strom comes through, doesn't that make the race over in the delegate count?"

Pat tossed his jacket in the overhead bin as the plane taxied for takeoff. "Sure—if he can hold the fort."[23]

Three weeks after that Atlanta meeting, on June 22, Strom Thurmond declared publicly his support for Richard Nixon.[24] Everyone on Nixon's team received the news with elation—everyone except RN. He understood that the hard part lay ahead: forcing Southern convention delegates to choose between the past or the future—

—to choose Strom Thurmond or Ronald Reagan.

Next stop: Miami.

THE SWITCH IS ON TO RON campaign button worn by Ronald Reagan supporter at the 1968 Republican National Convention (Author's collection)

CHAPTER 32

BILL KNOWLAND WOKE UP CRANKY.

The night before, Saturday, August 3, the "California Special" carrying Governor Ronald Reagan and other members of his state's delegation landed at Miami International Airport's Concourse One well past its 8:30 p.m. scheduled arrival. Stepping off the plane into the muggy summer air, Reagan never wilted as he bounded down the stairs, crossed over to the hundreds of waiting fans and plunged into a sea of outstretched hands as a Dixieland band played. After the speeches, the Californians boarded buses for the oceanfront Deauville hotel on Collins Avenue, which was their delegation's headquarters for convention week.[1]

When Bill checked into his room, he splashed water on his face, changed into a fresh shirt, and then used a convention volunteer to taxi him around Miami for late-night meetings with various Southern and Western delegates. Working with other members of Reagan's stealth presidential campaign team, they hoped to expand their governor's pledges beyond California's eighty-six favorite son delegates committed to him. It was well after 4:00 a.m. on Sunday before he fell exhausted into his hotel bed.

A few hours later, the alarm clock rang. After showering, he turned on the television and watched Reagan's interview on the Sunday CBS News show *Face the Nation*, airing live the day before the opening gavel of the 1968 Republican National Convention.[2] While shaving, he heard Reagan's oft-repeated claim that he was not running against Nixon or Rockefeller for the nomination and only sought to hold California's delegates as a favorite son. "I much prefer being governor of America's number one state to the presidency or vice presidency," Reagan declared.[3]

"What a bunch of bullshit," Bill scoffed, because he knew that for almost eighteen months senior Reagan aides—with the governor's knowledge and occasional personal participation—had been plotting a way to engineer a convention draft to deny Nixon the nomination.[4] Part of that plot involved hiring staff to work potential delegates surreptitiously throughout 1967 and 1968, while Reagan traveled throughout the South charming activists, raising money for the GOP, and denying all presidential ambitions.[5] In the Western states, campaign aides Frank Whetstone and Anderson Carter engaged in a recurring example of this subterfuge, repeated by other operatives in other regions. Whetstone and Carter traveled around for various Republican causes whispering to activists and reporters that Reagan was running. When reporters called the governor's Sacramento press secretary, Lyn Nofziger, for confirmation, he denied it vehemently, knowing the press would write stories that Reagan was indeed running. Lyn would then call Frank and Andy and tell them to keep up the good work.[6]

Bill turned off the TV, picked up the phone and dialed the hotel operator. "This is Senator William F. Knowland. Put me through to Governor Reagan's suite."

"Right away, sir." A few moments later Allen Brandstater, Reagan's young deputy press aide, took the call.

"This is Knowland—is he there?"

"Good morning senator. He just left the CBS taping at the Fountainbleau. He's on his way to breakfast with the Mississippi delegation, and then he has at least six more delegations he's seeing back to back. We're adding more as we go along. He's scheduled to return to the hotel about five to freshen up for tonight's meetings."

"I've got seven different delegations I'm visiting myself and also a dozen national committeemen from around the country once they check into their hotels. Find a time when I can see him tonight so we can compare notes."

"Yes sir."

It never dawned on Allen to say no to Bill Knowland. By 1968, the elective office days of the current *Oakland Tribune* publisher were a decade in the past, but his influence in the conservative community hadn't waned. In 1945, California Governor Earl Warren appointed the then-state assemblyman to the United States Senate. Later elected to two terms, at age forty-four he became the Senate's youngest majority leader in history (at the time, the minority leader was Texas Senator Lyndon B. Johnson). In 1958, with an eye on challenging fellow Californian Richard Nixon for the GOP presidential nomination two years later, Knowland engineered a political switch with California Governor Goodwin Knight. Knowland pushed Knight out of his reelection plan and forced him to run for the Senate while Knowland ran for governor, believing Sacramento was a better launching pad for a 1960 White House run. That November, both men lost in a Democratic landslide, so Knowland returned to publishing the family's newspaper and never again sought elective office. This year he went to Miami as a Reagan delegate, but now, on the eve of the convention, he developed an impulsive idea for his candidate and friend—derail the Nixon nomination train openly, rather than furtively.

Bill's problems with Nixon dated back to when they served as California's senior and junior US senators—with Bill senior to newly elected Dick Nixon. At the 1952 GOP Convention, both men were pledged to California's favorite son, Governor Warren. During the

Robert Taft-Dwight D. Eisenhower battle for delegates, the Taft forces approached Bill and offered the vice presidential nomination if he broke ranks with Warren and delivered California to them. Although Bill aligned philosophically with the conservative Taft, not the liberal Warren or the moderate Eisenhower, he stood honor-bound by his pledge. Ike's forces offered the same deal to Nixon: while remaining committed to Warren publicly, Nixon worked behind the scenes to undermine his state's governor and carry California for Eisenhower. This turned the tide: Ike beat Taft and picked Nixon as his running mate. Neither Earl Warren nor Bill Knowland ever forgave or trusted Richard Nixon again.[7]

Late Sunday night, after Bill met with Reagan and his senior advisers, he went down to his room and opened the bulldog edition of Monday morning's *New York Times*. Something on page two gave him an idea to bleed votes away from front-runner Nixon. The *Times* reported that Nixon would choose a liberal running mate—either Rocky, Mayor Lindsay, or Senator Percy. Armed with news of this left-wing switcheroo, he ordered a thousand copies of the newspaper for delivery to Pat Nolan, an eighteen-year-old conservative activist manning both the "Youth for Reagan" operation out of the hotel's Regency Room, and the YAF[*] headquarters at the Hotel Monte Carlo. After waking Pat and giving him marching orders, he also awakened Allen Brandstater and told him not to let Reagan go downstairs Monday morning for the scheduled California delegation breakfast until he and the governor spoke.

The next morning, Monday, August 5, an hour before the private California caucus, Bill took the elevator to Reagan's suite on the sixteenth floor of the Deauville.[8] There he met with Reagan, Lyn Nofziger, and senior aide Clif White. Bill handed a copy of the *Times* story to the governor. "Ron, you've got a huge opening here. This Nixon story

---

[*] YAF: Young Americans for Freedom, founded on September 11, 1960, at the home of William F. Buckley Jr. Its purpose is to inspire young Americans to understand and value the ideas of individual freedom, a strong national defense, free enterprise, and traditional values. See http://www.yaf.org.

is spreading like an epidemic, and we're doing the spreading. We've got Youth for Reagan and the YAF'ers passing out copies of this to every Southern delegation hotel. They're warning that Nixon is about to screw the South by picking a lefty VP. We can stop Nixon with this, but only if you drop this 'favorite son' façade. You'll need to throw your hat in the ring."

"Bill, why do I need to become an active candidate? Isn't this news about Nixon just as devastating if I remain a favorite son?"

"No—I'm hearing from Southern delegates that they'd consider switching to you, but not unless you announce. They won't buck their state Party leadership to throw in with a guy who's only a favorite son."[9]

For once, Ronald Reagan didn't default to his "I'm not a candidate" soundtrack. "Lyn," he asked, "what do you think?"

The short, rumpled, balding former reporter for the Copley News Service didn't hesitate to offer his opinion. "Governor, my mind hasn't changed since we first met at your house a month after you were elected governor. I've been telling you since December '66 that Nixon's vulnerable, and had you said the word, you could have been turned overnight into a major contender with 300 or more delegates.[10] The question now is whether you're too late, but we won't know that unless you try. If you take a pass on this and a Republican wins in November, you'll have to wait until 1976 to run. And by that time, you'll be sixty-five and carrying ten years of political scars. You'll be too old, and it will be too late. Right now you're hot, and you're the natural successor to Goldwater. I say do it."[11]

Ron turned to Clif White, Barry Goldwater's chief delegate hunter at the 1964 GOP convention and now serving in the same capacity for him. "Clif, can we stop Nixon on the first ballot with this story if I announce?"

Wearing his trademark tweed jacket and bow tie, Clif opened his notebook and rifled through some papers. "The winner needs 667 votes. Nixon is claiming 700 first-ballot delegates, but I count only 550 hard votes for him. Rocky has about 400.[12] You have eighty-six out of

California automatically. If you run, and if we can bring your delegate count to 300, we'll combine that with Rockefeller's Northeastern support. Most delegates still worry that Nixon will lose in November. Since New Hampshire, he's been on the ballot in ten primaries. He won all ten—*running unopposed*—yet you're the top vote getter in the 1968 Republican primaries. California gave you more votes than Nixon got in ten states combined. So he can't exactly claim he's the people's choice. Finally, the South and the West, where you're strongest, have more delegates than the Midwestern and Northeastern states that favor either Nixon or Rockefeller—682 to 634 votes.[13] To answer your question—sure, it can be done. Will it be easy? No, because you've waited too long. We'll have to convince pledged Southern delegates to peel away from Nixon or their state's favorite sons, but they're our lowest hanging fruit. All we'd need is just one break—one state switching to you—and we've got it."[14]

"I've been saying since I ran for governor that I'm not interested in the presidency. For the last year, I've told everyone I'm not a candidate—I'm only running as a favorite son to prevent a bloody and divisive California primary. How do I reverse my position now and not appear phony?"

"*You* don't," Bill replied. "I'll handle that issue. That's why I told Allen not to let you downstairs until we talked." Looking at his wristwatch, he reminded everyone that the California caucus was meeting in fifteen minutes. "Ron, you stay here—*do not* come down to the meeting. Lyn, don't let anyone answer the phone until I get back."

Without awaiting a response to his directives, Bill left the suite, went back to his room and scribbled on a piece of paper. When he finished, he tore it from the tablet and went downstairs to the Napoleon Room where he joined the other California delegates for the closed-door meeting.[15] When Lieutenant Governor Bob Finch, the delegation vice-chairman, called the meeting to order, Bill rose and addressed the group:

"Mr. Chairman, I wish to present a motion for immediate consideration. It reads as follows: 'Resolved, that the members of the California delegation urge Governor Ronald Reagan to end his favorite son campaign status and become an active candidate for the 1968 Republican presidential nomination.'"[16]

Finch, a stalwart Nixon supporter placed in the awkward position of being Reagan's lieutenant governor and home-state bound delegate, surveyed the room uncomfortably. "Is there any discussion on the motion?" No hands raised.

"I call for the question!" someone shouted from the audience. On a voice vote, the resolution passed unanimously.

Bill bolted from his seat, rushed to the nearest elevator, and returned to the sixteenth floor. After relaying what just happened, he told the governor, "There's your cover, Ron. Go down and tell the press you're running so we can start scooping up delegates."

Reagan looked at Clif and Lyn, and then grinned broadly. "Oh, hell—why not?"[17]

Later that morning, at a hastily called press conference, Ronald Reagan stepped before the microphones. "Well, everyone," he declared on this opening day of the 1968 GOP Convention, "this is the year of political surprises.[18] As of this moment, I am no longer running as a favorite son. I am a candidate before this convention for the presidential nomination."[19] He explained that his action was in response to his state delegation's unanimous urging. When questioned about the late switch, Reagan told reporters that this was not a preconceived plan: "I want you to know that the resolution came as a complete surprise to me—totally out of the blue."[20]

Bill Knowland, standing off to the side of the room with other Reagan aides, drove an elbow into Lyn Nofziger's ribs. "Like I said before—what a bunch of bullshit!" he whispered.

Then, for the first time since landing in Miami, Bill Knowland smiled.

Placard welcoming delegates to Miami Beach for the 1968 Republican National Convention (Author's collection)

CHAPTER 33

"WHEN YOU HAVE 700 FIRM VOTES, you don't need to be there."

As Pat Buchanan and Wayne Paugh walked from Nixon's temporary residence at Skipper's Cottage to their car, Wayne answered reporters staking out the compound on why Richard Nixon—unlike Reagan and Rockefeller—didn't arrive in Miami early. Four days before Miami, and believing he had wrapped up the nomination, Nixon cleared his schedule of all public appearances and went into seclusion at Gurney's

Inn at Montauk, New York,[1] remaining alone in a private beach cottage while his staff hunkered down at the inn.

"What's Mr. Nixon doing in there?" another reporter asked Pat.

"He's drafting his acceptance speech."[2]

"Is he working with speechwriters?"

"No—he wants this to be his own."

"Have you been in to see him?"

"Not since we arrived. He wants time to think, to walk along the beach, and write his address for Thursday night. When he needs something, he calls on the phone."

"Has he called you today?"

"Only once—he told me to bring him more legal pads."[3]

The reporters laughed as Pat and Wayne got into their rental and drove into town for lunch. With the car radio tuned to the news on station WOR, they listened to the updated reports of Reagan's late entry into the race that day.

"When I talked to the old man this morning," Wayne said, "I asked about Reagan's announcement. He seemed pretty indifferent."[4]

"I don't think it matters," Pat replied. "What's the worst thing that could happen? We fall short—barely—on the first ballot. Right now there are 666 votes locked up on the first ballot by favorite son pledges— just one vote short of a majority.[5] If we don't go over the top on the first ballot, all those pledges to favorite sons end, and those delegates are up for grabs. We have loyalists in every one of those states, so if we hold our current total and then pick up enough freed ones, we win on the second ballot."

"What happens if Reagan starts peeling off Southern votes from us?"

"The odds still favor us. Even if Rocky and Reagan join forces to block us on every ballot and we start dropping, at some point it will become nuclear war between them. Ultimately, Reagan's people will *never* vote for Rocky and vice versa. If Rocky starts inching ahead, Reagan's people will panic and run back to us. If Reagan starts moving up, Rocky's people will do the same to block him. Either way, on a first ballot win or as a compromise centrist candidate on a later ballot, I think we win. That's the irony. If Rocky and Reagan combine to stop Nixon, in the end—

"—They get Nixon."[6]

Handbill inviting supporters to greet Richard Nixon upon his arrival in Miami Beach for the 1968 Republican National Convention (Author's collection)

"Is Agnew there yet?"

As Nixon's plane approached Miami Airport on Monday night, with the first day of the convention well underway, he asked Chief of Staff Bob Haldeman if Maryland's governor would be there to greet him when they landed.

"He's on the tarmac waiting for you. There's lots of press covering your arrival, and he'll make the announcement when we land."

"Was he bringing any Maryland delegates with him?"

"He said he didn't know—I checked before we left."

"When I gave him the chance to give one of my seconding speeches on prime-time national television for his support, I thought he'd deliver most of his delegation to me—not just hand over his solo endorsement."

"He told me he'd keep working on his people, but as of now, he's given us no names."

"Make sure he knows I expect that of him. If things get tight, we'll need those twenty-six Maryland delegates. Has he told Rocky yet?"

"Yeah, this morning. He said Rocky begged him to remain a favorite son. From the way he told the story, I got the feeling Agnew enjoyed sticking the knife in Rocky as payback."

When RN's chartered jet landed, a dozen governors, scores of congressmen, hundreds of cheering fans, and a high school marching band greeted him. Governor Agnew announced the end of his favorite son status and endorsed RN.[7] The Nixon party then motorcaded through downtown Miami to his convention headquarters, the Hilton Plaza on Collins Avenue, where 600 supporters cheered him and his family.[8] Through it all, RN smiled broadly, projecting confidence in his victory as he surveyed the scene before him: a young man dressed as Uncle Sam walking through the crowd on stilts, a line of pretty "Nixonettes" dancing and waving pom-poms, another band, lines of dignitaries, and a live elephant.[9] Leaning over to Wayne, and speaking through a frozen smile, Nixon growled, "I thought I told you guys no goddamn elephants at the hotel."

Wayne smiled. "Relax, sir—we paid the handler to give it an enema before they brought it over—another lesson learned from the '60 campaign!"[10]

Once inside the Hilton, the Secret Service escorted RN to his eighteenth floor suite, Penthouse B, while the campaign staff scattered across the top four floors.[11] Fifteen minutes later, senior aides joined him in the penthouse's solarium, a circular-shaped living room. After taking a seat in an overstuffed chair facing the sofas along the rear wall, RN turned to his law partner and convention manager John Mitchell, who had been in Miami overseeing operations the last few days: "John, what's the count?"

"Don't worry, Dick," John chuckled. "We have everything under control."[12]

California Lieutenant Governor Bob Finch now joined the meeting. "Sorry I'm late," he said. "I couldn't get past your Wackenhut security guards—I didn't have the right color pass. They thought I was a spy!"[13]

"You *are* a spy!" cracked John, and everyone laughed at the California delegate's dilemma—longtime Nixon friend and supporter, but technically a Reagan favorite son delegate.

"Bob, what's the consensus among your delegation with Reagan's announcement? Since he's now abandoned his favorite son status, will this free up our California people to go with us on the first ballot?"

"That's undecided as yet. Right after he announced, I told the press that this should eliminate our delegation's commitment to support him as a favorite son. Many of our guys feel that way, but we'll discuss it at tomorrow's caucus. Ronnie's people know that our supporters are restless,[14] so they'll do everything they can to hold them in line, and they'll probably succeed. There's not much of a future in politics for people who screw their home-state governor."[15]

"Well," RN mused, "at least we've smoked out Reagan. With Goldwater supporting me, I don't see Barry's people flocking to him. Goldwater called him and urged him not to run—he said the Democrats would destroy him. I guess that didn't mean much. Don't you love it? He doesn't enter any primary, and now he asks the convention to nominate him on a glossy image."[16]

Lighting his pipe, Mitchell told RN, "You're in your mother's arms. Like I said, don't worry."

A reedy drawl came from the doorway: "You'd better rethink that advice, son." Senator Strom Thurmond entered without uttering any greeting. "Dick," he said, "we have a big problem."

RN's relaxed demeanor evaporated. "What's wrong, Strom?"

"This *New York Times* story about you picking a liberal running mate is spreading fast. My phone won't stop ringing. Everywhere I go our folks are telling me that you're about to double-cross us.[17] Reagan's people are fanning the flame in every Southern delegation. Have you seen this?" Strom asked as he handed RN a copy of the newspaper.

"I saw it this morning and ignored it—it's just gossip."

"You better stop ignoring it and start taking it seriously—it's thrown Southerners into a panic about you."

"The goddamn *Times!*" RN spat. "Where did this come from—some Rockefeller plant?"

"I suspect it came from that horse's ass Governor Bartlett. When he endorsed you yesterday, he started guessing for the reporters your VP pick, and the press ran with those names. Since he's a governor, they figured he had the inside track."

"Yesterday that goddamn idiot was for Rockefeller. What would he know about my running mate? There's no basis for this."

"Dick, I just needed to hear that from you personally. When I leave here, I'm sending this telegram to every Southern delegate—it will be under their hotel room doors when they wake up tomorrow morning." Strom reached into his coat pocket, unfolded a Western Union form, put on his glasses, and read his message:

> Richard Nixon's position is sound on law and order, Vietnam, the Supreme Court, military superiority, fiscal sanity, and decentralization of power. He will pick a vice president who will make all of us proud. He is best for unity and victory in 1968. Our country needs him, and he needs our support in Miami. See you at the convention—Strom Thurmond, U.S. Senator.[18]

"I can add to the senator's observations," Bob Finch said. "Since this *Times* story broke, Rocky and Reagan have been working together trying to convince delegates you're hemmoraghing votes. The press has started picking up the word Rocky's people are using—*erosion*—to claim you're slipping.[19] They're also dredging up the 'loser' issue."

Nixon walked over to the bar and poured a drink. "*Loser*—I'm so sick of hearing that," he fumed. "If I'm such a loser, how come neither one of these clowns ran against me in the primaries?[20] I scared Romney out of the race before the first votes were cast. Rocky was so indecisive about taking me on that he made Pa Kettle look like Alexander the Great. When I blew out Reagan's slate with 70 percent of the vote in Nebraska, all the goddamn press wanted to talk about was his 23 percent.[21] I've beaten them all, and now these carping bastards still say I can't win—that they need to nominate someone else. I went through the fire of every primary,[22] and now I have two guys trying to replace me who spent all year swearing they had no interest in the job. What else can I do—paint my ass white and run with the antelopes?"[23]

Everyone in the room sat silently as RN walked over to the alcove and stared down at the darkened beach below. Finally, he called out firmly, "Strom, here's what I need you to do—shadow Reagan tomorrow and Wednesday. Wherever he goes, you show up and speak to each delegation right after him. Bob Finch will get you Reagan's schedule—Bob, update it for Strom as soon as Reagan's people update it for him."

"Will do," Bob replied.

"Every time Reagan walks off the stage, Strom, I need you to walk in and set those people straight. You make sure they know my VP will not be someone who divides this Party—and tell them I said you'll be in on the final choice.[24] I'll send some guys with you. If there are any Shaky Jakes out there, have my staff bring them over to see me personally. I need you to hold that Southern line for me. I'll keep visiting as many delegations as I can between now and the balloting Wednesday night."

"Mr. Nixon, maybe it's time to take off the gloves with Reagan and Rocky and start hitting back hard," Wayne suggested.

"No, I'll need to unify the Party when this is done. We don't want to end up like the Democrats this year. I'll keep my guns trained on

Johnson, Humphrey, and Kennedy for giving aid and comfort to rioters and protesters."[25] RN finished his drink and looked around at the people in the room. His tense face relaxed, and the anger in his voice disappeared. With a wry smile, he said, "Of course, *I* won't say anything negative about Nelson or Ronnie—*but some of my friends might*—

"—Good night, *friends*."

STROM THURMOND FOR PRESIDENT campaign button worn by member of the South Carolina delegation to the 1968 Republican National Convention (Author's collection)

CHAPTER 34

"FOR ALL HIS SO-CALLED EXPERTISE, Dick sure was slow to see this coming. I'll bet he's in panic mode."

Sitting on the balcony of his fourteenth floor suite of Miami's Americana hotel with a few close advisers late Tuesday afternoon, the convention's second day, Nelson Rockefeller appeared surprised that Reagan's entry caught Nixon flat-footed.

"I don't think he was slow," Jason Roe replied. "A friend on his staff told me months ago that Nixon thought Reagan was the man to watch. I think what's rattling him now is that for two years he's run an almost textbook-perfect campaign, and now it might get upended by a guy who's been in the race for less than a day."

"I hear he's using Thurmond to keep his ship from capsizing," added Arkansas Governor Winthrop Rockefeller—"Winrock"—Nelson's younger brother.

"That old coot is amazing," Jason said. "He's spent all day yesterday and today visiting every Southern delegation, and in between he's collaring state chairmen, groups or individual delegates, and he's putting it in no uncertain words—it's a matter of honor for them to stand by their commitment to Nixon. I snuck into the Florida delegation meeting a couple of hours ago and caught his act." Then, slipping into a Southern drawl, Jason mimicked Strom's plea to Southern honor: *"Ah tell y'all that a vote fo' Reagan is a vote fo' Rockefeller! We have no choice if we want to win—no suh! Quit thinkin' with yo' hearts and start thinkin' with yo' heads! I love Reagan—we can all be fo' him next time. This year, Nixon's the one! I'm layin' my prestige on the line over this—my record of forty years in public life—I'm beggin' y'all—stand by me now...."*[1]

"Before Strom started beating back these defections, we saw significant slippage in Nixon's Southern flank," added Rocky's longtime adviser George Humphreys. "I've been monitoring these delegations since Saturday. By my count, there are 334 delegates from the South. If left to their own preferences, I'd bet 300 of them would go with Reagan.[2] If we could stop Strom, Reagan might pull at least 250 of them, and that's enough to deadlock the convention on the first ballot. But governor, if we can't stop Strom, we might as well close up shop."

"How can we stop him? The balloting is tomorrow, and it sounds like he's using his personal prestige to hold these delegations for Dick."

"We don't need to stop him," Jason interjected. "We just need to slow him down."

"Can it be done?" Nelson asked.

"Sure—but you won't like it. I'd have to call Monty."

"Who's Monty?" Winrock asked.

"Let's just say he's chairman of our 'Little Things Committee,'" Jason replied elusively. "When we need something done politically and we don't want it traced back to us, I turn it over to Monty—and I don't ask questions, before or after."

"Does he play by the rules?"

"Does Nixon?"

Turning to Nelson, Jason asked, "Tomorrow the Party chooses its nominee. We're running out of time and options. It's your last chance, but if I bring in Monty, it might get ugly. It's your call."

"Do I want to know what he might have in mind?"

"No. And if I knew, I wouldn't tell you."

Rocky sat silently, nodding his head and rubbing his chin in deep thought. Then he replied:

"Call him."

"Oh my goodness!"

The secretary of the South Carolina delegation passing out credentials looked up from her paperwork. A smiling man stood before her on the mezzanine of the Versailles Hotel, her state's convention headquarters. "Good evening, young lady. I'm Ronald Reagan. I'm here to see Senator Thurmond."

"I—I didn't expect to run into you! It's an honor to meet you, governor. I'll call Mr. Dent—he'll bring you to the senator's room." After relaying the information, she told Reagan he'd be right down. "And governor," she whispered as she looked both ways to make sure nobody overheard, "we all love Senator Thurmond, but we're rooting for you."

A few minutes later Harry Dent, the chairman of the South Carolina delegation, exited an elevator. "Hi, Harry, good to see you again. I hear I've been keeping you and the senator busy."

"Good to see you, governor. Believe me when I say we'd rather it not be this way. Come with me—the senator's waiting for you." Taking the elevator to the thirteenth floor, Dent accompanied Reagan into Thurmond's suite.

"Hello, senator," Reagan smiled. "I wish we were meeting under different circumstances."

"Young man," Thurmond replied, "one day we *will* meet under different circumstances, but this is not that day. Have a seat, please."

"Harry," Reagan said, "I'm wondering if you would mind leaving Senator Thurmond and me so we can chat privately?"

"Senator?"

"It's all right, Harry—I don't think this California boy will slicker me!"

Dent left the room, leaving the two conservative titans alone. Thurmond wasted no time in delivering a firm message. "Governor, nothing would please me more than to see you president someday. In fact, I believe you *will* be president someday, but this is not your day, and this is not your year. It's too soon. I'll support you next time, but I've given my word to Dick Nixon. Did you come here to ask me to break my pledge?"[3]

Reagan smiled. "When you put it that way, senator, then the answer is no. I won't ask that. Thank you for your time."

Reagan stood, shook Thurmond's hand, and walked toward the door. Before leaving, he turned and looked back. "You know, with you following me into every caucus meeting, we're getting pretty good at our dog-and-pony show. When this convention is over, maybe we should take it on the road!"

"Thurmond laughed. "We won't have time to do that, governor—we'll both be too busy campaigning for Dick Nixon!"

Collection of admission tickets (with original stubs attached) to the 1968 Republican National Convention
(Author's collection)

CHAPTER 35

ON WEDNESDAY MORNING, AUGUST 7, delegates to the Republican National Convention awoke in Miami to the serious task that lay ahead that evening—selecting a presidential nominee. By this, the third day, delegates had grown accustomed to finding all manner of schedules, invitations, flyers, polling data, candidate biographies, and other propaganda slid under their hotel room doors during the night. Wednesday morning was no different, with one stark exception. Left in each Southern delegate's room was a large flyer, printed on heavy cardstock. At the top, it featured a prominent photograph of a middle-aged black woman. Below her portrait, in bold letters, it read:

Meet Essie May Washington

You don't know her, but you know her daddy!

When Senator Strom Thurmond visits your delegation caucus today, ask him about Essie Mae.

Essie Mae's momma, Carrie, was the Thurmond family's servant back in the early 1920s. When Carrie was 16 and Strom was 22, she gave birth to Essie Mae.

Although Strom has kept the existence of his mixed-race daughter quiet for 43 years, he paid for her schooling and helps support her financially. He also has four grandchildren from Essie Mae's marriage.[1]

The flyer contained no source of origin. During the morning and afternoon, as Thurmond made the rounds pleading for Southern delegates to stand firm with Nixon, not one person with whom he met raised the issue—they had too much respect for the legendary senator and too much civility to dignify the slur. Strom never mentioned it, either, but he was perceptive enough to know it would cause some injury to Nixon's tally. The question: How much?

With Reagan still working the South, Rockefeller waited until Wednesday morning to launch his final missile.

Since declaring his candidacy on April 30, Rocky's twelve-week national PR blitz to drive up his poll numbers ended this day in Miami. During that three-month period, his committees ran national newspaper, television, and radio ads, and dropped millions of pieces of direct mail. Rocky gave hundreds of speeches and interviews, and held countless private meetings with delegates and Party leaders while traveling 65,000 miles and to forty-six states.[2] He never asked anyone committed to abandon Nixon. Instead, he urged them to remain open so that if, by convention time, it appeared Nixon couldn't win in November, they would consider nominating the GOP candidate best able to take back the White House.[3]

Having laid his foundation as best he could, Rocky scheduled a 10:00 a.m. press conference at his hotel. The previous night his team leaked to the *Washington Post* the result of the final Lou Harris poll; the *Post's* Wednesday morning edition headlined it "Rocky Tops All Candidates." At the press conference, he also planned to release the Crossley poll he commissioned, which showed Nixon running only two points ahead nationally, but with Rocky enjoying substantial leads in seven of the nine swing states.[4]

In his suite half an hour before the press conference, Rocky reviewed his talking points. When Jason Roe arrived, Rocky tried out the opening line for him: "These polls show I'm ahead of Humphrey, McCarthy, and Kennedy without running in any primaries and having just gotten into the race. Nixon's been running for four years, and he's in a dead heat with all of them." Looking up from his notes, he knew from his strategist's demeanor there was a problem.

"Governor, you'd better take a look at this."

Taking the paper Jason carried, Rocky read it, then sighed deeply. "Has this been released?"

"Nixon's people are passing it out all over Miami—and to every reporter setting up for your press conference right now."

The final Gallup poll, released at the same time as the Harris and Crossley polls, had a conflicting message: Nixon Overtakes All Democrats; Rocky Only Runs Even with Them.[5]

Disappointment bathed Rocky's face. "You know," he said fatalistically, "my entire campaign was based on using polling data to convince delegates that I can win and Nixon can't. With Gallup and Harris pointing in different directions, this press conference won't convince anybody of anything. Delegates will pick the poll they want to believe and disregard the other one."[6]

"I agree. The problem is that there are more delegates that want to believe Nixon's polls than want to believe yours."

Tossing his notes on the coffee table, Rocky opened the nearby sliding glass door and walked out onto the balcony overlooking the pool area. Looking down at perhaps a hundred guests baking under the late morning Miami sun, he said resignedly, "Maybe I made a mistake by not getting into this earlier.[7] With no Republican race in the primaries, the press focused on the Democrats. Maybe things might be different had I contested a few key primaries.[8] Well, let's go put the best possible face we can on this."

Leaving the hotel room and becoming encircled immediately by a phalanx of Secret Service and aides, Rocky put his arm around Jason's shoulder after they entered the elevator and whispered, "You know, I feel like the general who mounted the greatest offensive in wartime history, only to learn when the smoke cleared that the enemy marched on another road.[9] You might as well tell our people to relax and take it easy tonight. There's nothing left for us to do. Now it's up to our California friend to get enough Southern votes to stop Nixon. The nomination's in Ronnie's hands, not ours."

"Jesus," he added with a smirk, "can you think of anything scarier?"

"We still need eighteen."

Richard Nixon had spent all Wednesday morning and into the lunch hour shuttling between delegation meetings up and down Collins Avenue. Now, for the last three hours, he sat in his Hilton Plaza suite burning up the telephone lines calling governors, senators, low-and-high level Party officials, iffy delegates—anyone who might throw or round up an extra vote his way.

At 3:00 p.m., with only two hours until the convention reconvened to begin the nominations and vote, Nixon joined his senior advisers seated in the spacious solarium. Richard Kleindienst,[*] the Arizona attorney Nixon put in charge of his overall delegate operation, also attended. Kleindienst did whatever he needed to get delegates to commit to RN and, once committed, hold them to it. Among RN's staff, he earned the nickname "The Genghis Khan of Miami."[10]

"Dick, where are we?" RN asked him.

---

[*]   Richard Kleindienst (1923-2000) later served as United States attorney general from 1972 to 1973.

"Six-sixty-seven is the magic number," Kleindienst reminded everyone. "When the convention started Monday, we had 674—seven more than needed. After Thurmond's Negro baby smear, we lost forty-six. As of now, we're at 628. The networks are projecting that you're between 619 and 657.[11] I think my count is more current and reliable. That means we still need eighteen votes—"

"Eighteen?" RN snapped. If we're short by almost forty votes, how does eighteen put us over the top?

"Pennsylvania is the key. Even though Governor Shafer is going to nominate Rocky tonight, we've identified twenty-one Pennsylvania delegates who will break with Shafer and throw in with you and be the kingmakers—on the condition you are within twenty-one votes of victory by the time the roll call reaches Pennsylvania. So we need an eighteen-vote pick-up somewhere between Alabama and Oregon. If we don't have those eighteen votes by the time the secretary calls Pennsylvania, we'll lose those twenty-one votes, and that's the end of our first-ballot chance. The problem is we've run out of places to find the last eighteen. I've basically promised some of these favorite sons—in your name, I might add—everything from federal judgeships to national parks to Cabinet slots, but right now we've picked clean all we can get. They all smell blood in the water, and they all see themselves as possible compromise choices if the Big Three deadlock the convention.[12] We're frozen at 628. We need eighteen votes before the roll reaches Pennsylvania."[13]

"What about a second ballot?" Wayne asked Kleindienst.

"All bets are off. Governor Nunn just told me he's holding twenty-two of Kentucky's twenty-four delegates for us, but if we don't win on the first ballot, most of those votes will move to Reagan. I've heard the same thing from Texas, Florida, and other key states. Of course, if we drop and the battle becomes Rocky versus Reagan, and one of them starts advancing, it's possible that the delegates on one side or the other will panic and rush back to us. It's also possible that all three of you lose and the convention turns around and picks another guy as a compromise. That's why we need to put this away on the first ballot, or your chances might melt like a scoop of ice cream dropped on a hot Miami sidewalk."[14]

"Where's Agnew now?" RN asked. "He's got twenty-six Maryland delegates. I gave him a prime-time speaking slot tonight—has he turned any of them our way?"

"He's says he might be able to bring three more."

"He's been saying that for two days," RN fumed. "Doesn't he have any control over his fucking delegation?"

"He's been very vague. Since we can't count on him, I haven't included any of his people in my total."

"I can't believe this shit!" Nixon snapped. "I run in ten primaries and win every goddamn one. Romney comes after me with both guns blazing and I wipe him out before any votes are cast. Reagan spends a year denying he's a candidate, and then he announces two days ago. Rockefeller spends the year making a fool of himself with his indecisiveness, and then he jumps in late and launches this absurd 'battle of the polls' strategy.[15] He spends ten million dollars on a national campaign to drive up his poll numbers.[16] He drove up his popularity all right—with Kennedy and McCarthy voters! The last time I looked, they're not delegates here.

"I beat them all, damn it. Am I supposed to believe, now, after all it took to get here, that because some asshole slides a Negro woman's picture under a few hotel room doors that the presidency will be stolen from me—again?" Slamming his hand on the table, Nixon exploded, *"I'm telling you it's not going to happen."*

RN stood and paced. His staff remained silent, leaving the boss to his thoughts. Suddenly, he turned and jabbed a finger at Wayne Paugh. "Where are Agnew and the Maryland delegates staying?"

"They're at the Sans Souci."[17]

"Does Strom like Agnew?"[18]

"When Senator Thurmond gave us his list, he ranked Agnew as 'acceptable,' but he's not in Strom's top tier."

"He doesn't need to be."

Turning to Dwight Chapin, RN ordered, "I want you to have our people start leaking that I just offered Reagan the vice presidency and that he's accepted. Push that story all over Miami. That will slow things down for Reagan.[19] Get going on it." As Dwight hurried out of the room, RN ordered Wayne: "Get Agnew on the phone for me—now. I'm going to get those eighteen votes, and he's going to give them to me."

"Sir, shouldn't we run the traps on him before you call?" Pat Buchanan asked anxiously. "We could get our people—"

"—There's no time for that," Nixon interjected. "He's been a county official and elected governor. If Agnew had dirt, the Democrats would have dug it up and flung it at him when he ran in '66. Wayne—get me Agnew."[20] With that emphatic order, RN spun on his heels and stalked into the bedroom, slamming the door behind him.

Pat Buchanan sat shaking his head sadly. "You know what this means?" he asked Wayne.

"What?"

"It means when you call Agnew, be polite—

"—you'll be talking to the next vice president of the United States."

A few minutes later, Wayne rapped on the closed bedroom door.

"Sir, I have Governor Agnew on line two."

"All right," came RN's voice from the other side.

Alone in the bedroom, Nixon picked up the phone and cut to the chase. "Ted, as of right now, I'm eighteen short. You're holding enough delegates to put me over the top, and so are four other favorite sons. The first guy who delivers those eighteen votes to me will make my formal nominating speech tonight. He'll do that so I can introduce him to a national television audience, because tomorrow I'll pick him for vice president. My people already have drafted the speech for him. I have five names on my list in alphabetical order. You're at the top, so you're getting the first call. Deliver those eighteen votes to me within ten minutes or I go to the next name. It's nut-cutting time, Ted. I'm not screwing around with this any longer. If I don't hear from you in ten minutes, I'll move on."

"Dick, I'll get right back to you," Ted replied and hung up the phone abruptly.

RN opened the bedroom door and asked Wayne, "If Agnew doesn't come through, who's the next guy on the list?"

"Governor Carlson of Kansas—twenty-two delegates."

"Line him up on the phone right now and ask him to stand by for me. If I have to speak to Carlson, I want you to get the next guy on the list after Carlson is in the queue. If Carlson can't deliver, we go directly to number three."

Wayne never needed to put Carlson on hold. Within five minutes, Agnew called back. "Dick, send the speech over. I've got your eighteen Maryland votes."

"That's great, Ted, but just to make sure there are no slip-ups, be ready to cast those votes as soon as the roll call starts. Arizona is the third state on the list. When the chairman recognizes Arizona, I'll have Governor Williams yield to you. If any of your delegates piss backward on me, I'll want to know early so I can move to Plan B."

"There'll be no slip-ups, Dick. You won't need a Plan B."

"Fine. And Ted—

"—You'll make a great vice president."

1968 campaign button promoting Richard Nixon for president and Spiro Agnew for vice president (Author's collection)

CHAPTER 36

JASON ROE EXPECTED A LONG, BORING NIGHT.

At 5:04 p.m. on Wednesday, August 7, the chairman of the 1968 Republican National Convention, Congressman Gerald Ford of Michigan, banged his gavel and called to order the delegates so the Grand Old Party, for the twenty-ninth time, could choose its presidential nominee. Sitting in Governor Rockefeller's suite at the Americana with the candidate, his family, and a dozen senior aides, Happy Rockefeller asked Jason how long the speeches would take before the delegates voted. "Who knows? There are twelve names going into nomination tonight—three serious candidates and nine idiot favorite sons who want their moment on television.[1] That means twelve nominating speeches—and between two to four seconding speeches for each candidate—not to mention the floor demonstrations for each. I checked with the convention secretary. She said there are forty-five speeches lined up.[2] I'm guessing it will take at least eight hours.[3] We'll need to order lots of strong coffee to get through this."

And so the night dragged on, with hour after hour of speeches, parades, delegates chanting and marching for their favorite contenders, band numbers, and more speeches. Almost three hours after Reagan's nomination started the procession, and after watching Pennsylvania Governor Raymond Shafer nominate Rocky, a bored Jason told everyone he'd be back later.[4] He went downstairs to the Club Gigi, ordered a drink, and half-listened as the lounge television (brought into the club to appease convention-goers this week) droned on with gavel-to-gavel coverage.

An hour and three drinks later, Jason leaned his head back in the small booth, eyes closed, head nodding slightly, and daydreaming of Friday night—when he would climb into his own bed for the first time in a month, disconnect his phone, and sleep for a week. Just a few more hours, he told himself, and 1968 would be over—at least for him and the Rockefeller campaign. Right now, he felt too exhausted to care.

"Hey, Roe, is this where you're holding Rocky's wake? I thought you guys would be down the street at Memorial Gardens!" Norman Mailer,[*] the celebrated novelist, slid into Jason's booth and ordered two of whatever his near-comatose friend was drinking.

"What the hell are you doing here, Mailer? You aren't even a Republican."

"I'm going to do a book on both conventions. I've been here all week. I'll head out to Chicago for the Democrats later this month. They'll have a lot more action. You Republican corpses have kept this one pretty boring."

"Not by choice."

The waitress brought the drinks, the two men clinked glasses, and then Mailer nodded toward the televised image of a man speaking before the convention. "What do you think about Agnew?"

Jason looked over and saw the Maryland governor now extolling

---

[*]   Norman Mailer (1923–2007) was a Pulitzer Prize-winning American writer. His book on the 1968 Republican and Democratic National Conventions, *Miami and the Siege of Chicago*, was published that same year.

Nixon's virtues—after opposing his nomination all year. "What am I supposed to think? He flipped us his vote."

"No—I mean what do you think about Agnew getting *The Speech*? Do you think Nixon will pick him?"

"It's just a seconding speech. Nixon threw him a bone for his support."

"Wrong, buddy. Your intelligence is old. Haven't you been watching? Nixon reshuffled the deck at the last minute. This isn't the seconding speech—Agnew's giving Nixon's formal nomination speech."

A jolt of adrenaline shook loose Jason's lethargy. He stared at the screen as the nasally voice intoned, "It is my privilege to place in nomination for president of the United States the one man whom history has so clearly thrust forward—the one whom all America will recognize as a man whose time has come—the man for 1968, the Honorable Richard M. Nixon."[5]

"Oh, shit," exclaimed Jason. Throwing a five-dollar bill on the table, Jason pushed his way out of the booth. "I gotta go, Norman, see you later."

"Hey, Roe," Mailer called as Jason bolted for the door, "You're wasting your time. Nixon won't pick Rocky for veep—I think it's Agnew!"

Jason rushed upstairs to his hotel room, picked up the phone, and told the operator to connect him to the Hilton Plaza, where they patched him through to the campaign's special eighteenth floor switchboard. "This is Jason Roe with Governor Rockefeller. I need to speak to Wayne Paugh. It's an emergency."

"I'm sorry, sir. Mr. Paugh is in a meeting. I can take a message."

"Please get him for me—it's important."

"I'm sorry, sir."

"Okay—put me through to Rose Mary Woods."

"One moment, please."

When Nixon's longtime secretary answered, Jason sounded almost as if he were hyperventilating. "Rose, this is Jason Roe with Governor

Rockefeller. We've met before—I'm a friend of Wayne's."

"Of course, Jason. What can I do for you?"

"I need to speak to Wayne. It's an emergency."

"He's in a meeting with Mr. Nixon right now. I can have him call you when he comes out."

"That will be too late. I need to speak to Wayne this minute, and I can't tell you why. Please, Rose, trust me on this."

"Hang on, Jason." Rose put him on hold for what seemed like forever.

It was almost five minutes before Wayne came on the line. "Listen, if you pulled me out of my meeting to beg for a job, send a resume—we may need precinct walkers in Amarillo this fall."

Ignoring the usual banter, Jason sounded grim. "I'm at the Americana right now. I'm grabbing a cab in two minutes. Meet me in the lobby of the Hilton in ten."

"Why? So you can cry that we stole your lunch in Maryland? Forget it—we're busy over here."

"Are you through with your bullshit? I said to meet me in ten minutes."

Sensing Jason's distress, Wayne grew serious, too. "I can't, buddy, I'm meeting with the old man right now."

"I don't care if you're humping him. Ten minutes—or you're on your own." Jason hung up and rushed downstairs to the cabstand.

Entering the Hilton Plaza's lobby, Jason saw Wayne approaching from an elevator bank. "This better be good, you jackass," Wayne said.

"Come on," Jason called, and pulled him into the nearby Palladium Room. Finding seats in a private corner, Jason stared at Wayne intently. "I have just one question. Did you guys offer the VP slot to Agnew?"

"Wouldn't you like to know!" Wayne laughed. "Is that what you called me down here to ask? Why? So you can get five-to-one odds with your bookie? Watch the old man's press conference tomorrow morning and see who gets picked—like everyone else." When Wayne stood to leave, Jason grabbed his arm and yanked him back into his chair.

"Sit down, asshole. I'm only going to ask you one more time. If I don't like the answer I get, I'm leaving. *Did Nixon pick Agnew?*"

"All right, you little bastard, I shouldn't trust you with this one, but I will. We needed eighteen more votes to stop Reagan. Agnew had them. He's from a Border State, and Strom Thurmond said he's okay.[6] So it's Agnew."

"That's what I thought."

Jason handed Wayne a sealed large envelope. "Rocky hasn't seen what's in here. You need to show this to Nixon *and to nobody else.* Tell him not to disclose the source of the information. He'll burn me if he does." Wayne opened the envelope and read Jason's memorandum of his meeting with Rocky's "Baltimore Boys," the Rogan brothers, and about the federal bribery and corruption probe of Agnew. Wayne's jaw slackened as he read the incendiary contents. "Is this on the level?" he asked incredulously.

"I've done my job—and you're welcome." Jason got up and walked out.

Wayne returned to Penthouse B. It was now shortly after 1:00 a.m. Thursday morning. The nominating speeches were almost over, and the balloting was about to begin. Nixon sat in the overstuffed chair he had favored during these meetings, with family and senior staffers occupying the nearby couches.

"Mr. Nixon, I need to see you for a minute—alone. It's important."

Chief of Staff Bob Haldeman looked irritated at the young lawyer's presumptuous request, especially moments away from the balloting. "Uh, Wayne, I'm sure it can wait—or you can say what you need to say in front of all of us."

"No. It can't wait, Bob." Turning to RN, he said quietly," Mr. Nixon—please—now."

"All right," said RN as he stood and motioned Wayne toward the bedroom. "Bob, let me know when they start the roll call." RN closed the door behind Wayne and him.

"What's so important?" he asked brusquely.

"You remember my friend Jason Roe—Rockefeller's strategist. He just gave me this and told me to show it to you. He said even Rocky hasn't seen it. He's asking that you protect his sources in this report."

Nixon picked up his reading glasses off the nightstand, sat on the edge of the bed, and read the memo. When he finished, he looked up at Wayne. "This is coming from Rockefeller," he scoffed. "It's probably all bullshit."

"Mr. Nixon, it's not coming from Rockefeller. It's coming from Jason—that's how I know it isn't bullshit. He and I go way back. You can trust him."

"Why would he be giving this to me? He's the enemy. It doesn't make sense."

"If you knew Jason, you wouldn't ask that. He works for Rockefeller, but he's a loyal Republican, and I'll never say this in front of him, but he's a goddamn patriot. He knows we have this won. He's trying to protect you from a terrible mistake."

Nixon nodded silently, and then folded the report and put it in his breast pocket. "Okay," he said. "I'll trust your judgment on this. I hope this is true—for your sake."

"Shall I get Agnew on the phone so you can give him the bad news?" Wayne asked.

Nixon shook his head. "That's not necessary right now. We'll call after the balloting ends and I'm the nominee. There's no reason to tell him right now. It doesn't change his problems back home."

"I understand."

The two men walked toward the door to rejoin the group. RN stopped and looked at Wayne. "What's your friend's name again?"

"Jason Roe."

"Bring him up to see me."

"Right now?"

"Later—

"—Right now, let's go watch the reason we've come this far."

Gavel used by Michigan Congressman Gerald R. Ford to chair the 1968 Republican National Convention
(Author's collection)

CHAPTER 37

"WISCONSIN."

It took fifty-one minutes. The convention secretary, Consuelo Bailey, began calling the roll of states Thursday at 1:19 a.m., with most televisions in America turned off to the momentous proceedings inside the hall. That did not apply to the TV set inside the solarium of the Hilton's Penthouse B. After polishing off a cheese omelet, ice cream, and a glass of milk, Richard Nixon popped open a can of Seven-Up[1] while keeping score of his vote tally on a yellow legal pad.[2]

With forty-eight states now polled, his total delegate count was agonizingly short. Secretary Bailey reached Wisconsin, the next-to-the-last state in the Union. Governor Warren Knowles rose. "Mr. Chairman," he said, "Wisconsin is proud to cast all of its thirty votes, which will make a majority for the nominee of this convention—Richard Nixon!"[3] Cheers erupted throughout the arena, drowning out the handful of scattered boos.

It was over. Eight years after losing to JFK, and six years after his home-state humiliation, Richard Nixon again stood within reach of the presidency. Curiously, in his victorious moment, he did not join the celebrants in cheers, hugs, and handshakes. When the TV screen flashed the announcement NIXON WINS, he remained in his chair and buried his forehead in his hand. "You know," he said to nobody in particular, "it's a bit galling that we had to go all the way to Wisconsin before I put this away."[4]

Patricia Nixon, the nominee's wife, walked over and gripped his arm. "You did it. That's what counts. How far down the roll we had to wait doesn't matter."

Somebody handed a glass of champagne to RN, who raised his drink aloft and thanked everyone for fighting alongside him on this long path to victory. Then, before taking a sip, he added one more expression of gratitude—

—"To Strom."[5]

The moment Richard Nixon went over 667 votes and secured the nomination, a depressing pall fell over the throngs of Reagan supporters in the auditorium galleries. Perhaps none felt it more than the Youth for Reagan coordinator, Pat Nolan. While the Nixon delegates danced and celebrated in the aisles, Pat shuffled dejectedly through the auditorium as he headed to the hotel shuttle buses. CBS News reporter Mike Wallace spied the young man, walking with his head down and carrying a now-obsolete "I'm Gone for Ron" rally sign. Sticking a microphone in front of Pat, he asked for reaction to his hero's loss. Pat said that Youth for Reagan would work hard for a GOP victory in November. Once the interview ended and the cameraman turned off his equipment, Pat asked, "Mr. Wallace, you've covered quite a few of these things. Do you think there's a chance Governor Reagan can ever be elected president in the future?"

Wallace looked at the disappointed youth and answered with the solemn authority that his position and experience warranted. "Not a chance, kid. Reagan's as dead as a three–day old cadaver. He's finished. He's way too old to run for anything but reelection as governor."[6]

Pat looked down at his sign, now bent and battered from four days of waving. "Mr. Wallace," he replied with the same degree of certainty that the reporter projected, "you may know a lot about politics, but I think you'll eat those words someday."

"Well, I guess we should make it unanimous."

Moments after Nixon won his majority, Ronald Reagan, sitting just outside the convention hall watching the proceedings in his communications trailer,[7] told campaign aide Clif White he wanted to ask the delegates to proclaim Nixon the nominee by acclamation. The two men entered the auditorium and made their way to the stage. Congressman Gerald Ford, the convention chairman, eyed Reagan's approach warily as he and Clif reached the rostrum. Ford signaled to Republican National Committee Chairman Ray Bliss to intercept Reagan and see what he wanted.

Ford, a Nixon supporter, a Midwestern congressman from a swing state, and the House Minority Leader, harbored a slim hope that Nixon might pick him as a running mate. It wasn't the first time Ford coveted RN's vice-presidential favor. At the 1960 GOP Convention, Ford lobbied unsuccessfully for the nod, and the Michigan delegation backed up his play by producing and distributing black-on-yellow "Ford for Vice President" campaign buttons.

Badge worn by Michigan delegates to the 1960 Republican National Convention in Chicago promoting
Congressman Gerald R. Ford for the vice-presidential nomination (Author's collection)

Now, with Nixon again needing a second banana, Ford viewed
Reagan as a potential competitor for the slot—and he wasn't looking
to give a rival any unwarranted exposure. With the band blaring, and
with the delegates on the floor cheering and celebrating Nixon's triumph, Ford watched as Bliss stopped Reagan just behind the platform.
"Governor," Bliss asked, "may I help you with something?"

"Yes, Ray, I'd like to come out and make a motion that we name
Nixon the nominee unanimously."

"Wait here for a minute."

Bliss walked over to Ford and told him Reagan's purpose. Ford left
Reagan standing offstage and ignored the vanquished candidate seeking
Party harmony while the floor demonstration continued. Ten minutes
later, Ford advised the delegates, "Under the rules of the convention,
now that the alphabetical call of the states has concluded, I will recognize any delegates or states that wish to change their votes." Reagan
waited—and fumed—while Ford returned to calling the roll of states
lining up to jump on the Nixon bandwagon.

After recognizing seven states randomly, each of which switched
their votes to Nixon, Ford recognized California, which also gave its
votes to RN.[8] Then the delegation spokesman asked, on behalf of his

state, that Ford allow Reagan to address the convention briefly. "There is no provision in the rules of the convention for anyone to come to the platform and be recognized at this time,"[9] Ford replied. Again ignoring Reagan, who remained standing in the wings, he returned to recognizing those wishing to change their votes.

William French Smith, Reagan's fellow California delegate, grew angry at this discourtesy. He waved his state banner and shouted repeatedly, "Mr. Chairman! Mr. Chairman!" as Ford ignored his plea for recognition. After calling twenty-seven more states, Ford acknowledged Smith. "Mr. Chairman," Smith pleaded, "California believes that it is time to unify the Republican Party. Therefore, I move that the convention suspend the rules and allow Governor Reagan to speak briefly." A great cheer of approval rose, but Ford ignored it. Still balking at the request, he required two states to second the motion before considering it. Maine and Virginia called out their seconds.

Finally, after an overwhelming voice-vote of approval, Ford recognized Reagan, who walked to the platform amid a great ovation.[10] Reagan waved for silence and then made his brief request: "Mr. Chairman, delegates, and my fellow Republicans, on behalf of our California delegation, I ask this convention declare itself unanimously behind Richard Nixon as our nominee for president of the United States, and I so move."[11]

Instead of putting the question to a vote, Ford thanked Reagan for his motion, announced the total final vote, and then adjourned the convention following a benediction.[12] Although this parliamentary nuance was lost on most of the media, Ford technically precluded Nixon from receiving the unanimous nomination that Reagan requested. However, the snub was not lost on the California governor.

Thus, two politicians—Ford, a Nixon loyalist thinking Reagan a grandstander, and Reagan—wanting to show magnanimity and unity, and blocked by Ford from doing it—developed a mutual disdain from that Miami interaction. The settling of scores between them would wait to another day.[13]

"Mr. Nixon," Wayne said as he held a telephone receiver, "Governor Rockefeller's on the line." Wayne handed the phone over to the boss, who still sat in his armchair in front of the TV a few minutes after going over the top.

"Congratulations, Dick," Rocky exclaimed. "I sure tried to give you a good run."

"Thanks, Nelson. Yes, it was a good fight. I'm just glad it's over."

"Ronnie didn't come through for us as we thought. Oh, well—anyway, congratulations again."

"Thanks Nelson—you were good to call."[14]

RN hung up from the very brief concession. "You know," he reflected, "Rocky has an impressive resume, but he never had any hope of winning the nomination. If he had, Goldwater and his people would have walked out of the convention."[15] RN returned to the TV coverage in time to see Reagan's acclamation motion. Then, with a gavel bang and a final balloon drop, it ended.

A few minutes later, Reagan also called to congratulate RN. "Ron," he told him sympathetically, "you'll get another shot at this. After all, you're still a young man."

Reagan laughed. "Dick, thanks for the vote of confidence. But you forget—I'm two years older than you!"[16]

"Well, that reinforces my opinion."

"Seriously, Dick, I'm not disappointed that I didn't get it. To be honest, I'm not sure I was ready for it. We got caught in the excitement of the convention. Anyway, you can count on my campaigning for you—enthusiastically, because I'll be able to go back to Sacramento a happy and relieved man."[17]

After thanking Reagan for the call, Nixon told Pat Buchanan, "Get the tribal chiefs up here in forty-five minutes."

"We can have them here sooner," Pat volunteered.

"No, I have to handle something first. Wayne, call Agnew and tell him to come over immediately. Meet him downstairs and bring him through the back to avoid the press. Take him to Penthouse D down the hall—don't bring him here. I want to meet with him privately."

"Like I said," Pat whispered to Wayne, "be polite—we might end up working for him some day."

"I'll be polite, Pat, but I don't think there's any danger of that."

Wayne called Agnew's suite at the Sans Souci hotel, and the Maryland governor answered on the first ring—as if awaiting the late-night summons. "Governor, this is Wayne Paugh. Mr. Nixon is asking that you come to his suite immediately. Please drive to the back of the Hilton to loading dock number two. I'll meet you there and escort you up to the penthouse. Mr. Nixon would like you to arrive with as little attention as possible."

"I understand completely," Agnew said, grinning broadly. "Shall I bring my family with me?"

"Mr. Nixon wants this to be a principals-only meeting."

Within minutes, Agnew sat in the rear of his chauffeured car rushing down Collins Avenue for the two-mile drive to the Hilton Plaza. Wayne greeted Agnew at the loading dock, and then escorted him and his chief of staff, Curtis Iaukea, to the upper floors and through the multiple layers of security. Only a few staffers recognized the man who nominated Nixon a few hours ago. An occasional "Great speech, governor" brought a smile and thanks from the beaming Marylander. As Agnew navigated through these hallways, he wanted to savor every moment of the experience—a memory to share with his grandchildren someday, he thought.

Wayne rapped on the door of Penthouse D. RN greeted Agnew, and then asked Wayne and Curtis (carrying a camera) to wait outside. RN closed the door behind him. "The governor will be disappointed," Curtis told Wayne. "He wanted me to take pictures of their meeting for posterity." Wayne only nodded in reply.

Ten minutes later, Agnew emerged from the room, grim-faced and alone. Curtis asked his boss, "Shall we get the pictures now?"

"Let's go," Agnew replied stiffly.

Wayne had a final task. RN had asked him to give Agnew a message after their meeting but not to identify Nixon as its source. "Governor," Wayne whispered as he put his hand on Agnew's shoulder, "I know this is disappointing, but if he wins, he'll control the Justice Department. He'll be able to help. It's in your interest to show discretion over the change of plans." Agnew stared at Wayne in silence, and then he turned to Curtis, nodded his head toward the elevators, and the two men disappeared down the hall.

With Agnew dispatched, Wayne entered RN's room and found him pouring a cup of coffee. "How did it go, sir?"

"About as you might expect," Nixon sighed. "I told him what I heard about the investigation—he seemed surprised that I knew. I assured him that I thought this was a political hatchet job against him and that I had faith in his integrity, but I asked him if he felt he could be an effective vice presidential candidate once the story broke in the press. Unbelievable—he told me yes! He said voters would understand it was just a bunch of ex-business associates trying to get themselves out of trouble by dragging him in. I told him that if an indictment hits him— even one politically motivated—voters will assume corruption, and the entire GOP ticket would suffer with him on the ticket. He argued, and then he begged me to reconsider. He even threw in my face that I owed my nomination to him. I told him I was sorry, and then I walked him to the door. Jesus, I thought he'd never leave."[18]

"I'm sure it was pretty uncomfortable."

"It was, but it had to be done. Any effective leader has to be ruthless.[19] Gladstone once said that to be a good prime minister, one must be a good butcher, so—

"—We just butchered Agnew."[20]

Lapel pin of Republican elephant wearing Senator Barry Goldwater's horn-rimmed glasses, produced and distributed during Goldwater's 1964 presidential campaign (Author's collection)

CHAPTER 38

THIS WAS SHAWN STEEL'S LUCKY DAY.

Midway through the presidential balloting roll call, the convention operations manager called together fourteen high school and college student volunteers working as floor pages. As he passed out one envelope to each of them, he said, "Track down the person whose name is on your envelope and give this to him. Don't give it to anyone else except the man listed." When Shawn took his envelope, he couldn't believe whom he drew: "Mr. Conservative," his boyhood hero—Senator Barry Goldwater, the 1964 Republican presidential nominee. "Listen, everyone, this is important," the manager emphasized. "Don't screw around. Get these delivered to your person in five minutes, and then get right back here and confirm delivery."

After surveying the states' seating chart map hanging on the backstage wall, Shawn rushed onto the floor and over to the Arizona delegation, situated in the first three rows to the left of the podium. Sitting alongside the large silver and blue state standard mounted atop an eight-foot pole sat his objective, now keeping track of the ongoing vote on a *Newsweek* magazine complimentary tally sheet.

"Excuse me, Senator, but this is for you. They said it's important."

Goldwater looked up through his trademark black horn-rimmed glasses and took the message. "Thanks, son," he said as he put aside his clipboard and started opening the envelope.

Shawn took a deep breath. "Senator, it's an honor to meet you. I was a YR passing out your campaign buttons at the Cow Palace in '64."*

Goldwater smiled as he gripped the boy's hand. Reaching into his pocket, he pulled out a small gold metal lapel pin—a GOP elephant wearing Goldwater-styled eyeglasses. "Here, this is for you. Thanks for helping me four years ago. Now, go out and do the same for Dick Nixon this year."

"Yes, sir!"

Shawn pinned the elephant to his shirt, and then ran back to report his success and show off his treasure to fellow pages. (Many decades later, as California Republican Party state chairman and as a member of the Republican National Committee, Shawn still wore in his lapel the elephant-with-eyeglasses pin).

Goldwater opened the envelope and removed the mimeographed slip of paper that read, "Please come to the Hilton-Plaza hotel immediately after the end of the balloting. Mr. Paugh will meet you at the reception desk on the fifteenth floor and bring you to my room. It is a matter of great importance. Thanks, Dick Nixon."[1] As soon as Chairman Gerald Ford declared Nixon the nominee, Goldwater left for the Hilton.

---

* "YR": Young Republican (now the Young Republican National Federation). See http://yrnf.gop. In 1964, the Republicans held their national convention at the Cow Palace in San Francisco.

"Mr. Nixon, this is Jason Roe."

Before Goldwater and the Republican éminence grise arrived in response to RN's invitations, Wayne Paugh escorted his longtime friend and (until a couple of hours ago) Rockefeller strategist into Penthouse B. "Jason, you saved me—and the Party—a huge headache," RN said as they met. "I'm surprised you'd do that, especially since you're in the other camp."

"Mr. Vice President, when that gavel banged down tonight, that put us all in the same camp."

RN smiled. "Okay, good. We're going to build a new team for the general election. I'd like you aboard. If you have any loose ends with Rocky, I can call him and try to ease the way. What do you say?"

"I'd be honored, but there's one condition—wherever you assign me, you have to make me Wayne's boss."

RN looked perplexed, as he was not in on the private joke between the two friends. "Well, Wayne's role in the fall campaign—and most everyone else's, hasn't been defined yet. I'm not sure—"

Wayne interrupted. "Mr. Nixon, I think you're missing the point. It doesn't matter what job you give me. Jason wants to be my boss. It's his way of stepping on my neck. He's been doing it since we were in the College Young Republicans together. You might as well say yes, because he'll end up telling me he's my boss anyway."

"Okay," RN replied, "but whatever it is you're bossing him to do, make sure you both get it done right."

Pat Buchanan walked in. "Sir, everyone's here—whenever you're ready."

"Welcome aboard," RN told Jason. "We'll work out the organizational structure after the convention. Stick around—it's going to be a long night."

After making his new hire, Nixon turned to the first round of meetings with GOP kingpins summoned to his suite. Over the next four hours—from 2:30 to 6:30 a.m., RN held three such sessions—each one populated by different Party honchos. The express purpose of these meetings was to solicit running mate suggestions, but in truth, RN just wanted to create the impression of seeking advice. When it came to the real decision he wanted very limited counsel, and the choice was contingent on Strom Thurmond's approval—the cost of having the Southern delegations held in line for him.

As RN entered the solarium, his guests rose and applauded, and then cigars, bourbon, and Scotch passed among them before everyone took their seats on the sofas along the walls.[2] RN sat in his easy chair, now turned to face them. In each meeting he brought together a careful mix of conservative, moderate, and liberal Republican leaders for input.[3] Those now joining Thurmond and Goldwater in the suite were Bill Knowland, Bob Finch, Thomas Dewey (the 1944 and 1948 GOP presidential nominee), and seven other senators, governors, and Party elders.[4]

"Gentlemen," RN began, "the hour is late, and I appreciate all of you coming on short notice. I need to make a critical decision, and I don't have much time. I want your input on a running mate. In making this selection, forget the accepted wisdom that we need to identify the man who helps me the most. In my decades in politics I've learned that a running mate can't help you. He can only hurt you. To be honest, I wish I could do this without one—I think I'd run stronger.[5] So let's keep the discussion focused on who hurts me the least."[6]

Once RN opened the conversation, battle lines drew quickly. The liberal Republicans tossed out a handful of names, but the one upon which they all agreed was New York City Mayor John Lindsay, the telegenic former congressman. "Dick, let me make this easy for you," Barry Goldwater chimed in when the liberals finished their Lindsay pitch. "Under no circumstance will conservatives accept Lindsay, and I'll lead a floor fight against him if he's picked. Lindsay's a left-wing Democrat masquerading as a Republican. He is absolutely unacceptable."[7] RN looked over at Strom Thurmond, who said nothing but shook his

head from side-to-side. With that, the group dropped Lindsay's name.**
The liberals threw out other suggestions—Percy of Illinois, Hatfield of
Oregon, Agnew of Maryland ("He's unavailable," Nixon said tersely),
and even former rival George Romney (to that suggestion Nixon said
dismissively, "Let's not waste time on that one.").[8]

After dispatching those suggestions, it became evident that the
conservatives dominated the meeting, both in numbers and in volume.
When their turn came, they also tossed out names for discussion, like
Baker of Tennessee and Tower of Texas. But one man topped their list
unanimously—Ronald Reagan. They lobbied hard for the California
governor, and even though the liberals pushed back ("Reagan is just
as unacceptable to the Northern and industrial states as Lindsay is to
the South"),[9] the conservative Reagan consensus jelled quickly.[10] Most
significantly, his two biggest backers were the men whose early support
was critical to Nixon's victory—Thurmond and Goldwater.[11]

Nixon listened to the deadlock for an hour, thanked everyone for
coming, and then excused himself to attend the next meeting down the
hallway. It was now almost 3:00 a.m., and this new session was a reprise
of the last one.[12] Conservatives wouldn't support Lindsay, and liberals
were hostile to Reagan. Nixon listened, nodded, made notes. Finally,
at 6:30 a.m., he returned to Penthouse B for a brief nap.

Two hours later, at 8:30 a.m., he went downstairs to the "Jackie-
of-Hearts Room," named after Miami's favorite television star, Jackie
Gleason, whose CBS network comedy show broadcast from the same
Miami auditorium where the Republicans now held their convention.
Here RN met his third and final group of ersatz "advisers," who again
raised the same names—and the same objections.[13]

Having now endured the parade of a broad spectrum of Party elders,

---

**   Conservative distrust of John Lindsay was well founded. Three years later, in 1971, Lindsay left
the Republican Party, re-registered as a Democrat, and ran for the 1972 Democratic presidential
nomination to challenge Richard Nixon for reelection that year. After losing every primary and
caucus he entered, Lindsay abandoned his campaign four months before the Democratic National
Convention.

he retired to Penthouse B with his senior campaign staff to finalize the selection. Cold cans of Seven-Up and Coca-Cola had replaced the hard liquor and cigars of the all-night and morning meetings.[14] Meanwhile, the clock ticked: he promised earlier to announce his choice at an 11:00 a.m. press conference. It was now 10:00, and he was no closer to having a running mate than he was last night.

"All right, everyone," RN commanded. "We need to come to a decision. Size up my options for me."

"As I see it, Mr. Nixon," Pat Buchanan began, "you have a bigger consideration than merely deciding who hurts you the least. You need to worry about the guy who hurts you the most—and that's George Wallace. He'll sweep the Southern states if we can't compete there, and if that happens, you'll lose in November. Humphrey or Kennedy will run strong in the North and Northeast. We need to offset that strength in the South and West. Wallace has locked up South Carolina, Georgia, Alabama, Mississippi, and Louisiana—the Goldwater states. The fight in the other six Southern states—Texas, Florida, North Carolina, Virginia, Tennessee, Arkansas—will likely be between you and Wallace. We'll need our Southern flank braced, and it has to come from your VP.[15] The best man to help you there is Reagan. He can peel away Wallace voters, and he'll draw the fire and spare your prestige at the top of the ticket.[16] Plus, Reagan can free you up in the South so you can concentrate on other key regions."[17]

John Tower, the first Republican US senator from Texas since Reconstruction, agreed. "I reckon Reagan could shear away half of Wallace's strength in these states, and he's the only conservative who can do it."[18]

"Goddamn it, John," RN replied, "I've been listening all night long to people trying to shove Reagan down my throat. I've had polls done on Glamour Boy. If he helps me in one place, he hurts me in others."[19]

"I don't think Reagan would accept even if you offered it," Bob Finch opined.[20] "He told the press when we floated the VP rumor about him that he wouldn't accept if you tied him down and gagged him—and he said if you did that he'd signal 'no' by wiggling his ears.[21] Pretty funny line, by the way."

"Hilarious," Nixon said sarcastically.

"They all say that when they go for the top slot," Pat countered. "I don't think that means much now that the race is over. The idea of Humphrey or Kennedy in the White House would overcome his reluctance. Reagan's a good Republican, and both his base and Party loyalty would force him to say yes."

Wayne Paugh shared the results of his state-by-state analysis of a Nixon-Reagan ticket versus a Democratic ticket led by Humphrey or Kennedy. "I agree with Pat," he said. "This year, the South will be where we win or lose. Your running mate needs to be someone who can out-campaign Wallace down there. Reagan can do that, plus pull ethnic and blue-collar workers gravitating to Wallace in the industrial states. Remember, too, that you need Thurmond's sign-off. So, if it's not Reagan, then whom? Goldwater's too old. Bill Buckley's too high-brow. Senator Tower would make a great VP, but the Dem governor in Texas would appoint his successor, and we'd lose a key Senate seat. It all lines up for Reagan."

"If Reagan's on the ticket, there's no guarantee he can even carry California," Nixon insisted, "especially if Kennedy's on the ticket."

"True, but even if he can't, he'll force the Dems to spend huge resources in California. As Pat said, Reagan will cover your Southern flank while you focus on the eight or so must-win swing states. He's your best hope for victory."[22]

Pat continued tag-teaming for Reagan with Wayne, adding, "After Labor Day, we'll have to fight a two-front war. We're going to have to stave off Wallace's assaults from the right, and then keep Humphrey or Kennedy from moving to occupy the center. It's almost impossible for you to do both of these things at the same time. Reagan will free you from the burden of fighting Wallace and give you a chance to run a centrist campaign."[23]

RN grew irritable. "Reagan's just a goddamn actor—he's a glamour boy.[24] Aside from his lack of experience, he'll try to upstage the president at every opportunity.[25] A vice president needs to be loyal—like I was to Ike. I want one who's equipped for the job, loyal, and absolutely trustworthy." As RN spoke, he motioned with his hand toward his old friend on the sofa. "Someone like Bob Finch. Yeah—a guy like—

"—*Bob! Will you do it?*" Bob Finch—and everyone else—looked shell-shocked over Nixon's impulsive question.

"Dick," Bob stammered, "you—you can't be serious."

"I'm serious. I want you."

"But—but I'm only a lieutenant governor. You can't make the jump from that job to the vice presidency."

"Most can't. You can. You got more votes in '66 than Glamour Boy, for Christ's sake, and for that matter, more votes than every sitting governor and senator in America. You're the future of the Republican Party. Let's make the future *now*."

"A lieutenant governor, even from a big state, gives the ticket no heft. I'm an unknown, and the selection would reek of cronyism."

"You're the number two man of the biggest state in the union and one of the largest economies in the world. You have many of Lindsay's best qualities—you'd bring youth and freshness to the ticket, and you'd have great appeal to Party regulars and to independents. Besides, you know politics, you know policy, and you're the one man out of all of them that I trust completely. You're my man."[26]

As the campaign staff eyed each other nervously while sensing a runaway train was about to career off the rails, RN asked Bob to step out of the room so he and the others could discuss it freely. Bob left the solarium, walked into the entryway, picked up the phone to warn his wife Carol about the unexpected development, and then thought better of it. "This will blow over in a few minutes," he told himself. "No reason to shock or upset her." Putting a fresh cigarette in his mouth, he noticed the match's flame shaking in his hand when he tried to light up.

Fifteen minutes later, RN came out and walked over to his old friend. "We discussed it," he told Bob. "You're my choice."

"Dick," Bob pleaded, "this should have been settled hours or days ago. You're not thinking clearly. You're under stress—the press is clamoring for your choice, and time is running out. That's not how you should make this decision. I'm just not ready to carry the other end of the stick in a presidential campaign. I'm your friend, and you know I'll do anything I can to make you president. And because I'm your friend, my answer is irrevocable and absolute—*no*.

"Now," Bob added, "let's get back to the meeting and pick your *real* running mate."[27] Disgruntled but yielding, RN returned to the solarium with Bob.

"Finch is out," Nixon reported. "We need to get this done." Turning to his latest hire, Jason Roe, who had remained silent throughout tonight's marathon discussions, he said, "You're a Californian. What kind of president do you think Reagan would make?"

Introducing Team Nixon to the trademark sarcasm usually reserved for Wayne, and at a time when he might otherwise have shown discretion, Jason replied off-handedly to his new boss, "What fucking difference does it make?"

RN's eyes glowered at the smart-aleck ex-Rockefeller staffer—now on a quick trajectory to becoming an ex-Nixon staffer. "What the hell does that crack mean?" he shot back angrily.

"You asked me what kind of a president Reagan would make. Who cares? I thought *you* were going to be the president. I didn't know *Reagan* was going to be the president. That's why I asked what fucking difference it makes."[28]

Silence enveloped the room.

The other aides, eyebrows raised atop their stunned facial expressions, avoided eye contact with either the boss or the new guy. Having recommended Jason to RN, Wayne stared at his shoes, certain that his pal had just shot to hell his own credibility with the boss. Only RN looked at Jason, who never broke eye contact with the nominee. After a few tense moments, Nixon nodded:

"You're right."

Wayne didn't realize he had been holding his breath until he exhaled. Looking around the room, he saw grins replacing grimaces. Opening another Seven-Up, RN looked at his watch. "It's almost one," he grumped. "This thing took us all night." He stood and tossed aside his yellow legal pad and started giving orders. "Pat, get Reagan on the phone. And since you helped lead the charge for the actor, you damn well better talk him into doing it."

"Don't you want to call him personally?" Pat asked.

"No, you do it. If I call him, I might change my mind mid-offer. This is still against my instincts." Pat rushed to the alcove and placed the historic call.[29] "Wayne—you call the Secret Service command center and tell them we have a pope—have them dispatch a detail to Reagan ASAP and tell them to confirm it's in place before I go downstairs to make the announcement."[30]

"I'm on it, sir."

"Jason—welcome aboard. I think I'll have you help babysit Reagan. Attach yourself to him and tell his people I want you there to coordinate our campaigns. Report to me through Bob Haldeman and Pat Buchanan. I'll probably need two guys keeping Reagan in line, so take Wayne with you."

"Wayne who?" Jason asked.

"Wayne Paugh."

"Oh, you mean my underling. Okay."

"Don't press your luck, dickhead," Wayne whispered to his new "boss." "And be glad Haldeman wasn't in the room to hear your stupid 'what fucking difference' comment. If he were, you'd be on your way back to Loser Land right now."

"Hey Wayne, swing by my room at the Americana and pack my clothes. There may be a tip in it for you."

"Come on, jackass—let's get going."

Dwight Chapin answered the ringing phone and then reported, "Sir, confirmed from the Secret Service. A detail will deploy in three minutes at the Deauville."

"Fine," RN said as he stood before a mirror and ran a comb through his hair. "If some hippie shot Reagan now, I'd have to start this god-damn process all over, so I don't want anything to happen to him." Then, turning to face Wayne and Jason, RN added, "But you two guys had better do your job and make sure he toes the line, or I might feel differently about him—

"—and about both of you."

Badge distributed at the 1968 Republican National Convention promoting Richard Nixon for president and Ronald Reagan for vice president (Author's collection)

Two weeks later, and after the Republicans had selected their Nixon-Reagan ticket, the GOP nominees and their joint teams held a private retreat at the Bahia Resort at San Diego's Mission Bay. Campaign staff told the press it was to plot strategy, but actually their playbook was in the can already. The candidates wanted to cede the media limelight to the Democrats in Chicago, knowing that the inevitable protests and discord plaguing the eventual nominee would highlight the network news programs each night.[31]

The plan worked.

Richard Nixon sat in his suite watching on television Vice President Hubert Humphrey, his old Senate colleague, best Bobby Kennedy and Eugene McCarthy for the Democratic nomination. What surprised him was Hubert's last-minute selection of RFK as his running mate, combined with Humphrey's abandonment of President Lyndon Johnson's—and his own—Vietnam policies. He knew LBJ would make Humphrey pay a stiff price to break free of the president to appease the Party's left wing. "Poor Hubert," RN said mockingly as he saw Humphrey raise Kennedy's arm in victory after their acceptance speeches. "He had to choose between loyalty to Lyndon and a convention demanding Bobby—

"—If I know Lyndon Johnson, he'll make Hubert regret this choice for the rest of his life."

PART THREE

PRELUDE TO NOVEMBER

Photograph of FBI Director J. Edgar Hoover autographed for the author, September 22, 1971 (Author's collection)

CHAPTER 39

"MR. HOOVER, when you meet with the president this morning, will you need anything from the file cabinets?"

Now in her fifty-first year as private secretary to legendary FBI Director J. Edgar Hoover, Miss Helen Gandy knew the man as well as anyone, and she understood how he operated. He hired her as a bureau[1] clerk-typist in 1918; she became his personal assistant when President Coolidge appointed him the first director in 1924. Both remained single, dedicating their entire lives to the FBI. Curiously, and despite the over half-century of professional intimacy between them, Hoover never once called Miss Gandy by her first name.[2]

By 1968, with well over forty years at the bureau's helm, Hoover had long ago passed from establishment bureaucrat to law-enforcement icon. On his watch, Hoover's FBI brought to justice a *Who's Who* of infamous mobsters, spies, assassins, and traitors.[3] To most Americans, J. Edgar Hoover deserved the credit directly—his name became synonymous with law and order. Hollywood actors portrayed him in movies and radio dramas, books and magazines profiled his genuine and fictionalized exploits, and police departments viewed his organizational structure and scientific investigatory techniques as the law-enforcement gold standard. A long-running network television series glorified the professionalism and courage of Hoover and his agents (with Hoover and senior aides approving every script personally).[4]

There was another side to Hoover that remained hidden from public view during his tenure. After his death in 1972, the secret of his unprecedented longevity was revealed:

It was the file cabinets.

Hoover satisfied his mania for personal information on high-ranking officials and celebrities with decades of legal and illegal wiretaps, buggings, video and audio surveillances, and mail intercepts. He kept records on everybody in power, and he buried the scandalous evidence in his secret files. One senior FBI official described the private dossiers on government leaders as "drawers full of political cancer."[5] At Hoover's discretion, or on a whim, that cancerous information might metastasize quickly—and publicly.

Hoover's technique of squeezing a recalcitrant target was more subtle than crude. He or a top aide would visit the source of his irritation or interest. After advising that his agents came across something personally or politically embarrassing to the target or his family, Hoover offered assurances that he would take steps to protect them from disclosure.[6] When Robert Kennedy was attorney general in his brother's administration, these visits to reveal the latest salacious tidbits about

JFK or another family member became, as Bobby recalled later, almost a monthly ritual.[7] Journalist Victor Navasky noted, "Hoover's genius was to let everybody believe that he knew all your indiscretions, whether or not he knew them. And you had to assume, since he would tell you what he had on other people, that he was capable of telling other people what he had on you."[8]

The Kennedy family knew Hoover had enough information buried in his files to destroy them and that his evidence reached back decades. FBI surveillance tapes and files on President Kennedy dated to JFK's naval service during World War II. In 1941, a Harvard-educated FBI agent taped a sexual encounter in the next hotel room between suspected Nazi spy Inga Arvad (whom he was surveilling) and her current paramour, whose voice he recognized as his university classmate—JFK. The agent followed orders and delivered into Hoover's hands personally each report on the Kennedy-Arvad liaisons. The FBI monitored Kennedy's later sessions with Arvad, which extended to other dates and cities. Once, in South Carolina, the FBI had the hotel desk clerk maneuver Arvad and JFK into a pre-bugged bedroom.[9]

If Hoover was the collector of the skeletons and scandals, Miss Gandy was their keeper. She buried his secret files—his "insurance policies"—in the scores of locked cabinets crowded throughout her private office. She even adopted a coded system of mislabeling files, so if anyone ever picked the locks and rifled through her cabinets, they likely would overlook the explosive information they sought.[10]

Someone besides the Kennedys knew Hoover maintained these files. President Lyndon Johnson also knew, and after Vice President Hubert Humphrey betrayed him at the 1968 Democratic Convention by jettisoning his Vietnam policies, and then picking Robert Kennedy as his running mate, LBJ drafted Hoover—and his files—into service.

Johnson and Hoover had a longstanding social and personal relationship dating back to when LBJ served in Congress. They shared a mutual respect and friendship, and they often dined in each other's homes. When Hoover reached the mandatory retirement age of seventy on January 1, 1965, LBJ signed the needed waiver to keep Hoover on the job and thereafter renewed it annually. Since Hoover depended on Johnson's grace to retain his directorship, he never hesitated to put the FBI's services at the president's disposal when requested.[11]

A few days after the Democratic Convention, when LBJ returned to Washington, he summoned Hoover to the White House for what promised to be a mutually gratifying assignment—destroy the political aspirations of a man they both hated—Robert F. Kennedy.[12]

Hoover's dislike for Bobby Kennedy started early. After operating for decades with presidents deferring to him, and with virtually no supervision from any attorney general or the US Department of Justice, Attorney General Kennedy treated him as an underling. RFK appeared to enjoy irritating and humiliating the man who became FBI director a year before Bobby's birth. The new attorney general installed a buzzer on Hoover's desk and ordered him to report immediately to Bobby's office whenever it signaled. When a secretary once answered the direct line Bobby had installed on Hoover's desk, he chewed her out and commanded that when he called on that phone, only Hoover was permitted—and expected—to answer it. When the formal Hoover did report as summoned, he often found Bobby in shirtsleeves, and with his necktie askew and his feet on the desk. While speaking to Hoover, Bobby remained slumped in his chair and throwing darts at a target hanging on the wood-paneled office wall. Each time Bobby missed the target, the dart stuck into the paneling, which defaced government property and made Hoover simmer even more over Bobby's utter disrespect. President Kennedy's assassination liberated Hoover from the pressure of RFK's heavy thumb: the day after Dallas, Hoover ordered the buzzer and direct line connecting him to the attorney general removed from his office, and thereafter he ignored Kennedy and dealt directly with President Johnson.[13] Within a few days of JFK's death, Hoover went to the White House and gave to LBJ's top aides his security dossiers on senior Kennedy administration appointees.[14]

Hoover's contempt for Bobby was mutual. In early 1961, Hoover sent him a report regarding communists in the government. Bobby mocked him as he showed the report to Kenny O'Donnell, a longtime aide and member of JFK's *Irish Mafia*. "Look at this shit," Bobby told O'Donnell. "Hoover's gone mad. All this nonsense about the Communist Party in America. What a supreme and utter waste of time." Kennedy then added his opinion of the director personally: "He's a fucking asshole. Any day I expect him to show up for work wearing one of Jackie's *Dior* dresses."[15] Near the end of his tenure as attorney general, Bobby told reporters he thought Hoover was dangerous, senile, and something of a psycho.[16] Word of these and other insults got back to Hoover, who bided his time in settling his score.

"Edgar, good to see you. Come on, let's sit over here."

As Hoover entered the Oval Office that Monday morning, President Lyndon Johnson steered him to a sofa near the fireplace, and then he settled his huge frame into his rocking chair and got down to business quickly. "You know, Edgar, I always expect a backstabbing from Bobby Kennedy, but I never thought he'd get my own vice president to hold the knife for him."

"Mr. President, watching Vice President Humphrey abandon your courageous battle against the spread of communism in Southeast Asia was shocking. I never thought he would betray you, especially after all you have done for him."

"Hubert doesn't have the balls to betray me—or to be president, for that matter.[17] Kennedy's scent is all over this, and then he manipulated Hubert's weakness to land himself a spot on the ticket. Edgar, listen to me—there is no way in hell I'll stand by and let Bobby Kennedy take over this country.[18] If they win in November, Hubert will be his stooge—a placeholder until the Kennedy machine tramples him on their way back to the White House. I'm prepared to do whatever needs to be done to end that little bastard for keeps, and I want your help."

"I will assist any way I can, but to stop him might mean the Republicans winning instead of your own Party's nominees. Are you prepared for that eventuality?"

"Christ—at least Nixon and Reagan stand *with me* on Vietnam![19] After four years of playing head cheerleader for my policies, Humphrey deserted me in a single afternoon to throw in with Bobby and the hippies. Now he's ready to abandon our boys fighting over there— including my own sons-in-law.[20] I've devoted my presidency to winning this goddamn war, and I won't let these fucking appeasers tell 50,000 American mothers that their boys fought and died for nothing.[21] If Humphrey and Kennedy win, on their first day in office Bobby will get Hubert to walk away from three presidential commitments to a demo- cratic Vietnam. They'll let the commies run wild through Saigon, and they'll do what Chamberlain did in World War II—reward aggression. They'll sweep away everything I've stood for as president, and they don't give a damn about the carnage they'll inflict on our country or to our prestige—as long as it pleases all those draft-dodging shit-bags that go to their rallies." After taking a gulp from a root beer can, LBJ continued: "Do you know what will happen then? After Bobby gets Hubert to order an American military defeat in Vietnam, that little prick will go on TV and blame the defeat on me. He'll say I betrayed his brother's promise to South Vietnamese democracy—that I was an unmanly coward who wouldn't fight and couldn't win. Oh, I can see it coming, all right!"[22]

"If we suffer defeat in Vietnam, Mr. President, the Soviets and the Red Chinese will exploit our weakness and fill the vacuum of power we leave when we abandon the battlefield. That could start the dominos falling—"

"—Falling toward World War III," LBJ interrupted, "and then Kennedy and those cock-sucking Harvard professors who write all the history books will trace the blame straight back to me.[23] I'm already seeing what Hubert's cowardice a few days ago has cost us militarily. Thanks to his betrayal, now the North Vietnamese are dragging their feet with our peace negotiators—they think they can hold out for a better deal from these two traitors."[24]

LBJ looked somber as he glowered at his guest. "Edgar, I want to end this war if possible before my term ends in January. I don't want to leave it for the next president to finish. But whoever finishes it, I want it ending in victory for us, not for the communists. That's why we need to let the North Vietnamese know they won't get a better deal later—and they'll know it if they think that Nixon's gonna be the next president. They'll figure out they're better off dealing with me now than with Nixon next January."[25]

"Sir, I've been fighting communism for fifty years. This battle isn't just your life's work—it is mine as well. I can assure you that the bureau will not let you or the American people down." Then, leaning forward and speaking in a near-whisper, Hoover asked his host, "Would you like me to have Deke* bring over some materials for your review? I think it would be quite helpful to you in dealing with the vice president, and especially with Senator Kennedy."

"No—and no. Despite my purges, this place is still lousy with Kennedy loyalists—from the maids to the window-washers. I don't want any files in the mansion where someone could see them and tip our hand. Also, I'm not interested in Hubert. He's just the dummy in this act. Bobby's the shot-caller. Ever since Dallas, he's been living off PR and sympathy. People think he's some sort of Greek martyr. You and I know what he really is. It's time America came to know it as well—but they need to hear it at just the right time."

"In your opinion, when might that time arrive?"

"Well," LBJ said as he rubbed his chin, "I've always thought late October was a good opportunity to let the voters know the truth about a candidate. They pay far more attention to flaws just before they vote. So—we understand each other?"

"We do indeed." Hoover rose from the sofa and nodded, a slight grin crossing his thin lips. "Mr. President, you can count on the bureau

---

*   Cartha "Deke" DeLoach (1920-2013), the third-ranking official at the FBI, was "almost like a son" to Director J. Edgar Hoover, who named DeLoach as his personal liaison to President Johnson. See William C. Sullivan and Bill Brown, *The Bureau: My Thirty Years in Hoover's FBI* (New York: W.W. Norton & Company, 1979), 61.

to continue as your partner in the fight for freedom. There are ways to put that sneaky little son-of-a-bitch's true nature in perspective—and to give the voters an accurate understanding of the man who wants to raise the surrender flag.[26] Shall I use the usual channel of communications?"

"How wide is Drew Pearson's syndication now?"**

"He's in more than 650 newspapers, and he has over sixty million readers."[27]

"I think that will be more than enough to get the ball rolling. Thank you, Edgar—this will be yet another great service you are doing for the Republic."

"Mr. President, believe me when I say that this assignment will be a pleasure. I consider it an obligation to my country to prevent a communist dupe and a moral degenerate like Robert Kennedy from ever entering the White House."

** Drew Pearson (1897-1969), was one of America's premiere "muckraking" columnists from the 1930s through the 1960s. For almost forty years he wrote *Washington Merry-Go-Round*, in which he attacked mercilessly (and often with unsubstantiated claims) American politicians and other notables that were the subject of his investigative journalism. See generally https://en.wikipedia.org/wiki/Drew_Pearson_(journalist).

Anti-George Wallace campaign buttons from the 1968 presidential election (Author's collection)

CHAPTER 40

IN THE EARLY 1960S, the repeated violent police confrontations with peaceful civil rights marchers in the South shocked voters; they responded by supporting President Lyndon Johnson's "Great Society," which poured billions of dollars into welfare programs to help the poor and minorities work their way out of the ghettos. However, starting with the Watts riots of 1965, nonviolent protests increasingly gave way to militancy. Over the next three tense years, the evening news broadcasts showed black communities in over one hundred major cities in flames, along with armies of black rioters beating and killing innocents and threatening to "burn down America." In 1968, many of those previously sympathetic white voters were scared—and fed up. Just as abuses against earlier nonviolent civil rights marchers shocked them into demanding an end to segregation, now the violent protesters shocked these voters once again—and they responded to presidential candidates promising to restore law and order.

They responded to former Alabama Governor George Wallace.

In January 1963, the short, wiry farm boy from Clio, Alabama, (who grew up so poor that the first home he and his new bride Lurleen shared was a converted chicken coop)[1] became the symbol of Southern defiance. As the newly-installed Alabama governor, he proclaimed in his inaugural address "segregation now, segregation tomorrow, segregation forever." He then backed up his pledge by challenging the US Justice Department's attempt to integrate the University of Alabama when he stood in the college's doorway and blocked the entrance in a temporary standoff with federal agents and troops. Wanting to test his strength outside the South, Wallace parlayed his feisty notoriety into three strong showings in the 1964 Democratic presidential primaries he entered: Indiana, Wisconsin, and Maryland, which gave him 34 percent, 30 percent, and 43 percent of the vote, respectively.

By 1968, when Wallace declared his presidential candidacy as the nominee of the American Independent Party,[2] he jettisoned his earlier segregationist message and instead banged away on states' rights, a strong national defense, victory in Vietnam, and law and order to combat violent racial and campus protests.[3] One writer noted that "in his harangues against liberals and radicals [Wallace] frequently catalogued the 'plain people'... the wage earners sprung from working-class origins and lately arrived in the lower, shaky regions of the American middle class. The cocky ex-truck driver, his hair slicked down like a drugstore cowboy, chin thrust forward defiantly, spoke [with an] electric rapport between speaker and audience."[*]

Wallace used the same campaign template for his fifty-state campaign: if elected, he promised to gather all the bureaucrats in Washington and throw their briefcases in the Potomac River. "When I'm president, you good people will be able to walk any street in Washington, DC safely, even if I have to keep 30,000 troops standing on those streets two feet apart with two-foot-long bayonets. And I'll throw in jail every rioter and every treasonous college professor supporting our enemies in Vietnam. The day for these anarchists, revolutionaries, and communists is coming to an end."[4]

---

[*]   Richard J. Whalen, *Catch the Falling Flag: A Republican's Challenge to His Party* (Boston: Houghton Mifflin Company, 1972), 170.

How did this message resonate with a national audience? In October 1967, polls showed him with 10 percent of the vote. By summer 1968 he hit 16 percent, and pollster George Gallup reported, "If the presidential election were being held today, the strong possibility exists that . . . George Wallace would deny either major Party candidate the electoral votes needed to win."[5] Gallup's warning proved prescient: by the end of the 1968 Democratic National Convention in late August, his new poll reported that a surging Wallace ran only seven points behind the Democratic nominee, Hubert Humphrey—and closing the gap—which meant that nobody could ignore him any longer.

"If you liked Hitler, you'll love Wallace!"

The student heckler in the upper rafters of Harvard University's Sanders Theatre screamed out the insult to the speaker standing behind a lectern on the historic stage below. Most of the students in the packed venue cheered the protester's lack of Chesterfieldian politeness, and then they booed louder when they saw their guest's reaction to it. Instead of appearing startled or humbled by the outcry, he smirked at the taunting demonstrator and replied in a thick Alabama drawl, "Somebody needs to show that child where the little boys' room is!"[6] That set the galleries afire—now hundreds of students hissed, booed, and shook their fists angrily toward the stage. From the front rows, a handful of students stood and hurled vegetables. The candidate, a two-time state Golden Gloves boxing champion, ducked effortlessly as the missiles sailed past their mark. Pointing to their ranks, he shouted back, "These young punks are the ones that decent people are sick and tired of. They're giving y'all a good lesson in what we've been saying in this campaign. They talk about free speech but won't allow it to others.[7] The people of Alabama are intelligent, refined, and cultured—why don't you little Nazis come down there, and we'll teach y'all some manners!" Surprisingly, from the vast Harvard audience, a smattering of enthusiastic applause broke out, so he drove home his point. "I want to thank you people who just applauded. There are more good folks like you in this country than there are these little pinkos running around Harvard, but we'll band together—and when you and I start marching and demonstrating and carrying signs like they do, we'll shut down every highway in this country!"[8]

"Besides," he added with a sneer, "you can't really blame these kids. This is what their draft-dodging professors are teaching them. So let me tell all you commie professors something—y'all better get your protestin' in right now, because when I become president, I'm going to ask my attorney general to seek an indictment against any one of you who calls for a communist victory in Vietnam. That's not dissent. That's not free speech. That's treason—and we're seeing the fruits of it here at Harvard."[9] When the obscenities from the crowd reached a fever pitch, he pointed down to a group of bearded students giving him the middle finger from the front of the hall: "Hey, when my speech is over, why don't you smelly hippies come on up here on stage—I'll autograph your sandals for you!"

George Wallace glanced over his shoulder to the stocky, sandy-haired man in his early fifties wearing black horn-rimmed glasses, who nodded and smiled back from the stage's wings. David Azbell took a leave of absence from his Alabama political consulting firm when his father, Wallace campaign press secretary and noted Montgomery reporter Joe Azbell, became ill. Now filling in for his dad, David shot the boss a thumb's-up over yet another near-riot developing at a Wallace campaign rally held in enemy territory. Wallace winked at him, and then turned back to his audience and continued ginning up the anarchy.

Lilith James, a thirty-year-old conservative activist and university researcher, joined the campaign recently as David's green but enthusiastic deputy press secretary and speechwriter. She did not share in the private, bizarre satisfaction her two bosses enjoyed at the current insurrection. Miss Lil (as the governor called her) was beautiful to the point of distraction. Tall (five-eight)—and that was before she slid into her signature stiletto-heeled, open-toed mini-boots—she had waist-length blonde hair, porcelain skin, the longest legs in Montgomery County, and smoky eye makeup adorning her deep blue-green eyes. This transplanted Alabaman seemed out of place inside the Wallace team. Her native Canadian accent and her fitted, elegant dresses accentuating every curve of her slender body contrasted sharply against Wallace's remaining contingent of twangy, portly, rumpled aides.

"Why on earth did you bring him here?" she asked David—with rising agitation in her voice.

"Darlin,' *I* didn't *bring* him. He planned this speech when he announced his candidacy last February. We scheduled Harvard and the other commie colleges before we scheduled anything else."

"Didn't you realize how hostile these crowds would be?"

David pulled a cigar from his suit jacket and lit it. "This crowd? Oh, they ain't nothing. At Dartmouth they threw bags of urine at him.[10] Wait till you see what happens when he heads out back to his car—which reminds me, you'll need to stay behind and drive to the hotel with that trooper standing over there," he said while pointing to a nearby plainclothes bodyguard. "When we hustle the guv off the stage and out the back door, there'll probably be a riot. They'll spit on him and whack him on the head with their protest signs, and then they'll try to smash the windows and turn the car over before we can get the hell out of here."[11]

"This is crazy—"

"—Everything about this campaign's crazy," he interrupted. "Whenever he tells these creeps to get a haircut and take a bath, or warns that if any protester ever lies down in front of his car that it'll be the last car he ever lies down in front of,[12] these hippies and their professors go nuts. But millions of blue-collar people see him wading into these beatnik lairs and taking the fight right to 'em. If they attack him when he leaves—and they will—the press will film it, and that footage will lead off tonight's network news. It'll be him staring down these ass-hats. Every time they show film like that, we get so many thousands of donations pouring into Montgomery—from cops, beauticians, cab drivers, shopkeepers—you name it—that we literally can't get enough people in our headquarters to tear open the envelopes and count the money.

It sits for days in mail sacks until we can get to it—"[13]

David stopped mid-sentence and put his finger to his lips to silence any reply, telling Lilith, "Okay, here it comes—you'll see what I mean. I've heard this wrap-up a hundred times, and I never get tired of it. Listen—"

Now raising both his fist and voice, Wallace shouted into the microphones: "You can take all the Democratic and Republican candidates, put them in a sack and shake them up—because there's not a dime's worth of difference between them.[14] Now, I know you pampered Harvard elitists like it that way—you like the way the federal government has been abusing the common folks in this country. But I'm here to tell you that the people of Cleveland and Chicago and St. Louis are so sick of y'all interfering in their lives and in their local schools that they'll be voting for Wallace by the millions come November. The real people are done with your pointy-headed bureaucrats who can't park their bicycles straight but keep trifling with their children and telling them which teachers to have teach in which schools.[15] They've had a bellyful of you people telling them we need to bus their little children halfway across their state just to achieve what your professors think is the proper racial mix. They've had it with all you mooching welfare loafers, and they're fed up with the sissy attitude of Lyndon Johnson and all the dummies and theoreticians that surround him. And they're damned tired of that sorry, no-account Supreme Court that lets criminals run wild. These morons have created a court system where if you're knocked on the head today, the man who assaulted you is out of jail before you get to the hospital.[16] And when that Court banned prayer in public schools, they cast their lot with the worldwide socialist conspiracy. They've made a mockery of the Bill of Rights in a decision as deadly as any ever issued by any dictator. There's a reason why the US Communist Party platform's been demanding the abolition of religious instruction in schools for forty years. If you don't believe me, just ask your professors—they probably wrote it.[17] And when it comes to the Vietnam War, all you draft-dodgers here better get your short haircuts now, because when I win, your student deferments are over—we're shipping you overseas where you can learn to quit being sissies and fight for your country."[18]

After taking a long draw on his cigar, David pulled it from his mouth. "You know why regular people respond to him? It's because when they watch him on TV speaking at one of these rallies, they think, 'That's what I'd say if I were up there.'[19] And by the way—look where all the applause in the theater is coming from."

Lilith peered out over the stage lights and saw the sources of unbridled enthusiasm for Wallace's message:

It came from the three dozen Boston police officers providing security at the event.

"You know," David said with a grin, "if these peckerwoods damn near kill him tonight, we could probably raise enough cash to finance not only this entire campaign—we'd have money left over to pay for his 1972 reelect!"

"David, what are you smoking there?"

Forty-five minutes after having survived the gauntlet from the Sanders Theatre's rear exit to his waiting sedan, George Wallace paced in a holding area next to the Commonwealth Room of Boston's Copley Plaza hotel, where he would hold his third press conference of the day. Patting his breast pocket and finding he was out of cigars, and seeing his press secretary with a lit stub in his mouth, George decided to bum one.

"*Garcia y Vega*, of course," David replied. "I thought it was part of my job description to smoke only your brand."[20]

Taking one from David, George smiled at his new press assistant, "You know why he smokes only my brand, Miss Lil? It's because he steals them from my cigar box!"

"He means his cigar *boxes*," David told Lil through teeth still gripping the remnant. "We get five boxes delivered each week from the local tobacco wholesaler. If I have to lug them around for him, I figure I'm entitled to one now and then. I call it 'carrying charges.'"

Lighting his seventh of the day, taking a long puff, and then continuing his nervous pacing, George asked, "How do you like the show so far, Miss Lil?"[21]

"Governor, I knew you stirred up the crowds, but I didn't think you were suicidal. I'm surprised you got out of there alive."

"We're just getting started," he said with a grin. "Wait till I hit 20 percent in the polls—that's when we'll send all these liberals into a psychiatric meltdown."

"They'd better start making their doctor appointments now, governor," said campaign manager Seymore Trammell, who rushed into the holding room waving a sheet of paper. "Here's the latest Gallup poll coming out tomorrow. You just cleared 21 percent!"[22]

As his staff let out a whoop of excitement, George held his cigar in his hand and nodded in silent satisfaction. "Here we are in mid-September at 21 percent," he said. "We were at 9 in April, and 16 in June. Hell, if we continue on this trend, we could—"

Seymore finished the thought: "—Our pollster says if this continues, we'll hit 30 percent by Election Day. Congratulations, governor. You're on your way"[23]

"David," Lil whispered to her supervisor, "I know 30 percent is great, but it's not a win. Why the congratulations?"

"Actually, it *is* a win. If we can reach 25 to 30 percent by November 5th, no candidate will have a majority of the Electoral College, so we can deadlock the election."

"But if nobody wins in the Electoral College, the election goes to the House of Representatives—and the Democrats have a huge majority there. Doesn't that put Humphrey and Kennedy in the White House?"

"First, even with a deadlock," David said, "don't be too sure the Electoral College won't pick the new president. The guv swears that if we stop Nixon and Humphrey from getting a majority of electoral votes, the decision will never reach the House of Representatives. He'll order his electors to cast their votes for the candidate who lets him pick the next couple of Supreme Court nominees."[24]

"How can he force his electors to vote for Nixon or Humphrey?" Lil asked.

"We screened our electors very carefully, and before we named any of them to our slates in each state, we had them sign a pledge to cast their vote for president in the Electoral College for the candidate Governor Wallace wants. Those votes will go to the man who deals with us on cutting the size of government and—most importantly—giving us a say in any Supreme Court vacancies.[25] On Election Day, if we carry the South and grab a couple of Border States, we'll hold all the aces."

"What happens if the electors break their pledge?"

"We may still have a winning hand. If the electors deadlock, then the House of Representatives gets to pick the next president. Although the Democrats control the House, many of them are Southern Democrats—and they're a hell of a lot different from those New York and California Democrats. The South holds a quarter of the entire national population—that's a huge voting bloc.[26] If we win or run strong in their state, and then those Southern congressmen ignore our wishes, their careers will be over. Besides, if we win enough states to deadlock this race, we'll so terrify those boys that at the next midterm election in 1970 they'll line up to run with us.[27] So, yeah, we're probably not going to win the White House, but if the stars line up for us, we'll choose the next president and help set policy for decades. Once we became the first third party campaign in history to qualify for the ballot in all fifty states, the big boys took notice.[28] Now that we've moved up to 21 percent in the polls with six weeks to go, they'll have to do more than that—they'll have to, as we say back home, *come a-callin.'* All we'll need to do is sit back and wait for the courting to begin."

The sudden backstage movement signaled it was time to start the press conference. "Have you ever seen him at one of these?" David asked her.

"Only snippets on TV. This will be my first time seeing one live."

"You're in for a treat," he said. "He'll give you a graduate degree on how a politician should handle these jackals. Follow me." The two press aides stepped from behind the curtain and stood along the back of the riser, facing a room filled with seventy-five reporters and photographers.

"They look hungry," Lil whispered.

"They're not the hunters," David replied with a grin. "They're the quarry."

A few moments later Wallace strode through the curtain backdrop. When the harsh television camera lights clicked on, Lil noticed how they reflected off the governor's slick hair pomade. Her candidate wasted no time laying down his marker with the Fourth Estate:

"Good afternoon, everybody. We had a good time at Harvard this afternoon. All the misfits that couldn't get jobs as network news reporters were there representing your interests—throwing their trash and trying to shout me down. I noticed that you reporters call those people who throw rocks and bottles at me 'demonstrators.' When they do the same thing to Humphrey or Nixon, you call them hoodlums and thugs.[29]

"Well, I see the reporter from *Life* magazine is here. I remember how you attacked my wife while she was battling cancer, and then you treated the good people of Alabama who voted for Lurleen and me like they were a bunch of degenerates.[30] Oh, and the *Saturday Evening Post* is with us, too. You people sure take lots of pictures, and then you pick out the worst one of me and put it in your magazine. And right down in front is the guy from the *Wall Street Journal*—you're the boy who made fun of my wife on your front page because she used to be a dime-store clerk and her daddy was a shipyard worker. Well, I've got some bad news for you reporters and your socialist editors that decided you're not gonna have any more of George Wallace. You think you can band together and repudiate this movement, but the people will show you differently. They know I'm fighting you and your outlaw, beatnik crowd in Washington and New York that has just about destroyed America. They know I'll save this country, and I'll do it without help from y'all."[31]

"Governor," interrupted Jeff Ferguson of the *Christian Science Monitor*, "how do you respond to the NAACP issuing a press release today calling you a racist and a bigot for your virulent opposition to court-ordered busing?"

"It's a sad situation in America that anyone who disagrees with these communist-manipulated groups is called a racist. I do not dislike any person because of their color, and I'm not calling for segregation anywhere in this country. I believe that the states should determine the policies of their domestic institutions—and the bureaucrats in Washington ought to let the people in Massachusetts and New York decide for themselves what type of school system they are going to have."[32]

"When you say 'domestic institutions,'" Ferguson countered, "don't you mean *segregated* institutions?"

George's chin jutted out. "Mr. Ferguson, I know that you and your newspaper look down your noses at every working man in the United States and think they're all a bunch of rednecks. When I'm talking about domestic institutions, I'm talking about the seniority of working men in their labor unions. I'm talking ownership of private property and the right of a homeowner to rent a room to anybody they choose. I'm talking about the local schools of every community in America. I want to say this about the schools of Massachusetts—the folks from Alabama don't have any recommendations to make in your state about what kind of schools you ought to have here in Boston. You people are intelligent enough in this city to decide for yourselves what's in the best interest of your child and where he should go to school. If you people here want to bus your child to some other school across your town or across your state just to meet the plans of some bean-counting racial engineer, then I don't object to that if that's what you want to do. But you people here in Massachusetts ought to decide that for yourselves, and not have that decision made by some bureaucrat or some unelected judge ordering you to do it. And we sure don't need to send to Washington half a billion dollars of your hard-earned tax money so some worthless bureaucrat can harass every school system, every hospital, and every seniority list of every labor union to see if they have what he thinks is an acceptable percentage of any particular race."[33]

"If you reject the racist label," asked Alicia DuBois of the Copley News Service, "then how do you explain your continued opposition to the 1964 Civil Rights Act and the backlash against Negro rights you keep stirring up?"

Wallace shook his head in dismay at the reporter. "See? That's what I mean—you liberals come up with a high-sounding name for a bill that guts individual freedom, and then everyone who stands up to your power grab is a racist or a bigot. I didn't oppose the so-called 1964 Civil Rights Act to hurt Negroes. I opposed it because it was a massive power grab by federal bureaucrats against our states and communities. There isn't any backlash in America against people because of their color. There's a backlash against big government in this country. I'm not even fighting the federal government—I'm fighting this beatnik mob in Washington that's destroying our federal government. Anytime you stand up to these liberal bums, they call you a racist.[34] Thanks to these leeches and a bunch of out-of-control federal judges who protect them, every businessman in America will have to keep records on the race, color, religion, and creed of his employees to prove that he's not discriminating. If he has 100 employees and only two of them are Chinese Baptists, but there are 4 percent Chinese Baptists where he lives, some Washington bureaucrat's gonna make him fire two of you and give those jobs to some unqualified Chinese Baptists."[35]

"What's your solution for ending all the urban riots in America?" asked Michael Leversen of Gannett News.

"I'll end that problem on my first day in the White House—I'll ask every police officer in America to shoot looters and arsonists on the spot.[36] We don't have riots in Alabama. They start a riot down there, the first rioter to pick up a brick gets a bullet in the head, and then we tell the next rioter, 'All right, let's see you pick up one of them bricks now.[37] When I win, I'm gonna give the moral support of the presidency to the police and firemen in our cities."[38]

Scott Steiner of the *Pittsburgh Post-Gazette* asked, "How can you ask people to trust you with the American economy when you presided as governor over one of our poorest states?"

"Let me tell all you liberal crybabies who never report the facts something—back when I was governor, we built more schools, more colleges, more hospitals, more mental institutions, and more nursing homes and clinics than any other governor in Alabama history. We gave out more free textbooks, more state employee benefits, and we finished more road building programs than any other state in this country per capita.[39] So when you write about George Wallace, why don't you try writing that for a change, instead of saying all our supporters are a bunch of hicks."[40]

Looking back at Lilith, Wallace winked, and then reached into his wallet, pulled out a dollar bill, and held it aloft for the photographers. "Here you go," he added, "I'll pay this dollar—cash money—to the first one of you reporters who puts in your story that in the last Gallup poll of America's most admired men, I came in seventh place—just below the pope and just ahead of Nixon—and Humphrey didn't even make the list! I'm offering you money, because the only way you'll ever print that story is if I bribe you!"[41]

Satisfied that his boss had given the press what he wanted for the lead soundbites in the Boston-New York media market, David tapped the governor on the elbow, signaling time to wrap it up. "Let me just tell you people one more thing," Wallace continued. "You press people are going to be in for a bigger shock than all those bureaucrats and pinkos you love so much. The American people are sick of all you newspaper and TV dudes who get on your soapboxes and slant and distort the news to malign people like me and brainwash this country. Your day is coming."

As Wallace turned to leave, Dan Rather of CBS News rushed forward and called to him, "Governor, if you ever have an instance where CBS has distorted news about you in any way, I want you to call me—collect—and let me know. I will see that we correct the record."

Wallace stopped, looked back over his shoulder, and replied, "I just can't do that."

"Why not?" asked Rather.

Wallace smiled. "Because, Mr. Rather, if I did, I'd bankrupt CBS."[42]

Campaign buttons worn by supporters of Senator Robert F. Kennedy and Governor Ronald Reagan during the 1968 presidential campaign (Author's collection)

CHAPTER 41

"I BEG YOUR PARDON?"

As Richard Nixon emerged from the side door of the International Center at the Broadmoor Hotel in Colorado Springs after addressing a Labor Day luncheon, Don Oliver* of NBC News blindsided him. With a television camera whirring and a microphone thrust in front of the candidate, Oliver repeated his unexpected question: "Mr. Nixon, given your earlier refusal to accept Vice President Humphrey's debate challenge, are you now reconsidering after Governor Reagan's announcement a few minutes ago that he's agreed to debate Senator Kennedy?" For the American politician perhaps most practiced in answering press questions, Nixon appeared dumbfounded by the revelation. Standing alongside RN, Pat Buchanan saw the boss' usual poker face contort at the news, with an unmistakable fury in his eyes.

"I haven't spoken to Governor Reagan since the challenge was issued this morning, so I have no information that he or a member of his staff

---

*   Don Oliver (1936-2013) was an NBC News political reporter from the mid-1960s until 1992.

accepted what I think to be a Democrat publicity stunt and a waste of—"

"—Governor Reagan just told the press about ten minutes ago when he deplaned in Memphis that he accepts Senator Kennedy's challenge. We're already flying the film of his remarks to New York to lead off tonight's network news broadcast."

"Of course, if Governor Reagan has made that decision, I have every confidence that he will do well. I also—"

Oliver again interrupted the nominee to press his query. "Does this mean you will change your mind and accept the vice president's challenge?"

Forcing a smile for the camera, Nixon replied deftly, "Mr. Humphrey has been on both sides of every important issue since he became a candidate for the presidency. In fact, Mr. Oliver, the 'Great Debate' at the top of this ticket should be Humphrey versus Humphrey—and with all of his flip-flops that debate will take so long that I'll probably have to ask for equal time from the networks.[1] I would suggest that the same is true for Senator Kennedy. His inconsistencies on everything from Vietnam to welfare to riots in our cities will make any debate between him and Governor Reagan a waste of time. Why doesn't NBC invite Senator Kennedy to debate himself, and then he can explain how he keeps coming down on all sides of every issue?"

Ignoring the taunt, Oliver lobbed the question he hoped would provoke a reaction. "A few minutes ago Vice President Humphrey used Governor Reagan's acceptance to brand you as afraid to debate. He called you 'Richard the Chicken-Hearted' and urged you to show the same guts that Governor Reagan has displayed. Doesn't your continued refusal make this criticism legitimate?"[2]

Nixon's face flushed in anger. With a finger now jabbing toward Oliver's chest, Nixon snapped, "I'm not afraid to debate. I'm not afraid of anybody, so don't put words in my mouth that I'm afraid to debate anyone, especially Mr. Humphrey. I've debated before in all my campaigns, and I'll do it again—and we'll win."[3]

"When you say *I'll do it again,* does that—"

Sensing disaster, Pat grabbed Nixon's arm. "Sir, we need to go. We're already fifteen minutes behind schedule." Pat and the staff moved in to extricate Nixon from the reporter and then hustled him into the nearby Secret Service sedan.

As soon as the doors closed and the motorcade left the hotel, Nixon demanded, "What the hell is this all about?"

Riding in the jump seat directly in front of RN, Pat shook his head. "I have no idea. We've heard nothing of this from Reagan's plane."

"Where is he right now? Didn't you guys clear my statement on debates with his people this morning?"

"Sir," Pat said apologetically, "they were in flight when we put out our press release trashing Humphrey's challenge, and the operator couldn't get us a connection. I gave instructions to an aide on the ground in Memphis to brief Wayne and Jason once the plane landed and before anyone disembarked. It sounds like the press got to Reagan before we did."

"This is just great," RN replied. "Now what the hell do we do? And how does this make me look? They'll say Reagan's brave, and they'll brand me a coward. And that dumb bastard will get his ass handed to him by Kennedy. We could lose this race if they debate. Jesus Christ! Once we get back to the plane, get me Reagan on the phone. You guys better find a way to unwind this." Hitting his fist in frustration on the seat cushion, Nixon growled, "I can't believe this shit."

Within the hour, Reagan called Nixon's campaign plane from his suite at the Sheraton-Peabody. "Dick," he said apologetically, "I'm sorry we got our wires crossed. When the press confronted me with the challenge, I thought Kennedy directed it to me. It never dawned on me to run it by anyone first. I didn't know Humphrey also challenged you."

Trying to mask his simmering anger and lack of confidence in his running mate, Nixon explained, "Ron, the problem is this. First, debates are for losers,[4] and since Humphrey and Kennedy are behind in key swing states, they have everything to gain by debating us, and we have everything to lose. Besides, if I agree to debate Humphrey, he'll turn around and insist that Wallace be included, because Wallace is bleeding Republican votes from us far more than he's taking them from the Democrats. Anything we do to elevate Humphrey and Wallace will be self-destructive to our efforts."[5]

"Well, I think those are all very good reasons for you to refuse to debate Humphrey, but I'm in a different position. Wallace doesn't even have a running mate yet. So it will be just Bobby and me, and I think when the voters see a contrast between our side and his appeasement of communists and rioters, it will be a good thing."

"It won't be that easy. Bobby is a dirty street-fighting little prick who will do whatever it takes to win, and the press will bend over backwards for him—just as they've done for all the Kennedys over the years."

"I guess they'd do that for him no matter what we do. But to be honest, I think the format will work for me. It will be a—"

"—Wait—you guys already have a format? How did that happen so fast?"

"CBS News is hosting a one-hour international town hall forum with college students in Europe. Bobby challenged me to debate him in front of those kids. The format is that the students will be in London, and they'll ask us questions by satellite."[6]

"You haven't already agreed to this rigged set-up, have you?" RN pleaded.

Chuckling as a little boy might do when caught sneaking candy, Ron replied, "Well, I guess I did. It seemed like a natural for me. I've been debating these students and their peacenik professors on the California university campuses since I became governor. I know how to handle them, Dick. It'll be fine."

"All right," RN growled while still trying to conceal his seething anger. "We're backed into a corner. Let's make the best of this. I'll have Wayne assemble a team of experts to start working with you on the issues so we—"

"I'm afraid there won't be much time for that," Ron interrupted. "The debate is in three days."

"*What?* Oh, for Christ's sake," RN blurted, no longer able to maintain his composure.

"Bobby will be in a New York studio, and I'll be in California. CBS will air the program live in prime time on Thursday night and then rebroadcast it in their Sunday morning *Face the Nation* time slot."

"I can't believe I'm hearing this."

"Relax, Dick, I promise—I won't let you down."

When the call ended, RN told Pat, "When this slaughter is over on Friday, I want you to fire every son-of-a-bitch on Reagan's staff who allowed this cluster-fuck to happen—

"—That is, if they haven't already quit by the time Bobby gets done mopping the floor with this stupid jackass."

After Reagan hung up, he walked over to the conference table in his suite and joined his campaign staff to relate the substance of the conversation. "How bad was it?" Wayne Paugh asked the vice presidential nominee to whose campaign Nixon ordered him detailed.

"Well, you know Dick," Reagan replied with a crooked grin. "He holds his cards pretty close. Let's just say I think he was perturbed."

"*Perturbed*—that's a euphemism. I've worked for him almost two years. He doesn't get 'perturbed'—he gets royally pissed. Did he tell you to cancel?"

"No. He knows it's too late for that. Besides, I wouldn't cancel even if he did tell me."[7]

"Governor," Jason Roe interjected, "why didn't you clear this with the Nixon people first? You knew better than to just accept. They must be going bat-shit on his staff right now."

Reagan folded his hands on the table in front of him. "Jason, I learned when I was making pictures in Hollywood that when you want to shoot a scene different from what the director tells you, it's better to just do it and then apologize later. Besides, if it comes out okay, the director will use the footage—and he'll take credit for it. I know I should have gotten Dick's blessing, but I also knew that if I asked him, he'd say no, and there's no way I'll pass up a chance to take a whack at Bobby Kennedy."

"Not meaning to bathe you in negativity, but you didn't do so well against him at the Gridiron Club last year,"[8] added campaign aide Clif White.

Wayne cut in. "The Gridiron? Did you and Kennedy debate there?"

"No," Reagan added, "nothing like that. The Gridiron is an annual roast held by the Washington press corps. They put on skits and make fun of politicians, and the politicians are supposed to go along with it. Last year they invited Bobby and me to speak at their shindig. The speeches are supposed to be funny, and the press grades you on how well you do. Well, the consensus was that Bobby was funnier than I, but let's face it—that was a Washington insider audience. They laughed like hell at everything that came out of his mouth, no matter how lame, and they stiffed me on most of my lines. The next day the press made Kennedy into another Jack Benny, and they treated me like I was some low-rent Borscht-Belt comic."**

"The press treated him that way because he *was* funnier than you," campaign aide Tom Reed said. "I was there."[9]

"So you agreed to debate Kennedy on live worldwide TV in front of a bunch of commie university students to get even with him for one-upping you at the Gridiron?" Jason asked sarcastically.

"I have a score to settle with that fellow," Reagan said as his eyes narrowed, "but it has nothing to do with the Gridiron. In 1954, when my Hollywood career was on the skids, General Electric signed me to host their weekly television show, *General Electric Theater*. Aside from reviving my career, over the next six years I traveled the country visiting GE plants and giving motivational speeches to their employees about

---

**   "The Gridiron Club is best known for its annual dinner which features satirical musical skits, remarks by the president of the United States, and a representative of each political party. Politicians participating in the skits and speeches are expected to be self-deprecating or funny." https://en.wikipedia.org/wiki/Gridiron_Club.

free enterprise, innovation, and all the things that make a country prosperous. Plus, whenever I visited their plants, GE management booked me for local service club speeches and interviews with local radio and TV stations. It really was my early training for politics.

"Anyway, in 1960, I campaigned hard for Nixon when he ran against JFK. I headed 'Democrats for Nixon.' After Nixon lost, and Kennedy made Bobby his attorney general, Bobby decided to get even with me for not supporting his brother. Bobby had the Justice Department file antitrust charges against GE, who was still my employer, and then he tried to bring charges against me for my time as president of the Screen Actors Guild. Bobby convened a grand jury and dragged me before it. They grilled me for hours under oath. After I testified, Bobby ordered an IRS audit of my taxes—and Nancy's—going back to 1952. When he still couldn't prove any wrongdoing, he settled the antitrust case with GE—and then told the execs that unless they canceled *General Electric Theater* and fired me as host, he'd see to it that GE never got another government contract. So GE canceled my show that year and left me unemployed."[10]

"How do you know Bobby was behind the cancelation?" Wayne asked.

"When the president of GE, Ralph Cordiner, called to fire me, he apologized and said Bobby told him personally, 'If you want any more government contracts, get Reagan off the air.' So, yeah—I've got a score to settle with this bastard—and I don't care whether Dick Nixon likes it or not."[11]

Reagan started to get up from his chair, stopped midway, and then slid back into his seat as the familiar grin returned. "You know," he said, "it just dawned on me. If GE hadn't fired me, I probably never would have run for governor of California or gone into politics. Maybe I've been looking at this all wrong! I guess, in a strange twist, if I become vice president in January, I'll owe it all to Bobby Kennedy—

"—and on Thursday night, I'm going to get the chance to pay him back."[12]

"You should take it easy on the aspirin, Bob. The doctor warned you those things will rot out your stomach lining."

In his hotel suite at Portland's Benson hotel, Bobby Kennedy downed a handful of Excedrin to ease the recurring headaches that plagued him since his release from the hospital. "They've already destroyed it," he replied to Press Secretary Frank Mankiewicz. "I can campaign with a screwed-up stomach. I can't campaign with a throbbing migraine. Sometimes my head hurts worse now than after getting shot. The headaches always seem to hit hardest at night. Anyway, I'll worry about my stomach lining after November 5th. Until then, I'll keep going any way I can."

Putting down his water glass on the end table next to the sofa on which he stretched his lean frame, Bobby asked, "Have they finalized the format for tomorrow night?"

"They have," campaign manager Fred Dutton replied, "I just got off the phone a few minutes ago with Don Hewitt at CBS."****[13]

"Don's a good guy—he produced Jack's first debate with Nixon in 1960. Is he doing ours?"

"Yes, he'll be in New York at the studio with you. It'll be a bunch of college kids, and they'll be in London. They have one American kid for the panel and the rest are foreign students. Charles Collingwood**** will moderate and take the students' questions, and then you and Reagan will answer them."

"Bob," Frank interrupted, "why don't we postpone this thing. You look like shit, and you've been driving yourself too hard since you got out of the hospital. If we reschedule it, nobody will criticize you. You're

---

***   Don Hewitt (1922–2009) was a CBS News producer and executive who, in late 1968, created the CBS television magazine *60 Minutes*. In 1960, he produced the first Kennedy-Nixon presidential campaign debate, and in 1967, he produced the RWR-RFK debate. See https://en.wikipedia.org/wiki/Don_Hewitt; Paul Kengor, "The Great Forgotten Debate," *National Review*, May 22, 2007.

****   Charles Collingwood (1917–1985) was a longtime CBS News reporter. He joined the network during World War II and continued at CBS until his retirement in 1982.

still recovering. People will understand."

"That's not happening," Bobby snapped. "It's like the doctor told me—recurring headaches are the cost of being alive. I can deal with it. And the last thing I want is for people to think I'm not healthy enough to campaign—and I especially don't want them to think I'm not up to handling that boob Reagan. Besides, why give him more time to prepare? He's been governor for what—eight months? I've been doing this most of my life. He's a failed B-movie actor who stumbled into the governorship. I'll show America that Nixon's first major decision—his selection of a potential successor—is a disaster. I'll bet Nixon already regrets putting that lightweight on the ticket, but he'll regret it even more after this debate. There's no downside for me.[14] So that's it—we're on for tomorrow night—period." After taking a large gulp from the chocolate milkshake a staffer brought him from a nearby soda fountain, Bobby added, "Eighteen European college students—Jesus, this audience is tailor-made for me. All I'll probably need to do is sit back and hold their coats while they rip Reagan a new asshole over Vietnam and civil rights." Then, putting down his milkshake, Bobby looked around the room at everyone:

"Remind me," he said with a broad smile, "to put Don Hewitt on my Christmas card list."

ROBERT F. KENNEDY FOR VICE PRESIDENT campaign button worn at the 1964 Democratic National Convention by supporters of RFK as President Johnson's running mate that year, and Ronald Reagan campaign button from the 1968 presidential election (Author's collection)

CHAPTER 42*

"GOVERNOR, CAN YOU HEAR ME?"

The voice coming through Ronald Reagan's earpiece broke his final moments of pre-debate concentration.[1] For the last day and a half he had been studying a twelve-page issues memorandum[2] compiled for him by Jason Roe and Wayne Paugh, and with additional input from a secret but highly experienced coach—former President Dwight D. Eisenhower. Unbeknownst to almost everyone, Ike struck up a quiet relationship with Reagan prior to his running for governor. Since the election, the two men met a few times, and they spoke over the telephone regularly. What began as an acquaintance developed into both a friendship and a tutor-student association, with the retired five-star general schooling the

---

*   In this chapter, the debate dialogue between RWR and RFK is adapted from their actual debate transcript: *Town Meeting of the World:* "The Image of America and the Youth of the World" with Senator Robert F. Kennedy and Governor Ronald Reagan, as broadcast over the CBS television and radio network, Monday, May 15, 1967, 10:00-11:00 pm. EDT, Charles Collingwood, moderator. See http://reagan2020.us/speeches/reagan_kennedy_debate.asp.

rookie governor on complex foreign policy issues—especially America's historic and military role in Vietnam.[3] This was a sensitive relationship that Ike wanted kept quiet: Ike expected Reagan to run for president in 1968, and if he did, Reagan would challenge for the nomination Ike's two-term vice president—Richard Nixon.

Sitting in a chair and facing a television camera in a small studio at Sacramento's CBS affiliate, station KXTV,[4] Reagan folded his research memorandum, slid it back into his breast coat pocket, and replied to the voice in his earpiece, "Yes, I hear you loud and clear."

"Great—thank you for agreeing to appear. This is Don Hewitt in Washington. We'll go live in about five minutes. We have eighteen students in London, and Senator Kennedy is here in our DC studio. When we go up on the satellite, you'll be able to see the senator and the students on your nearby TV monitor. You and he will be in color, but the London studio will be in black and white—so when you see the contrast, it isn't a problem with your screen. We still haven't perfected transatlantic satellite reception."[5]

"Can Senator Kennedy hear me now?"

"No, sir, not until we begin the program. Are there any last-minute questions I can answer?"

"No—I'm ready on this end."

"Okay, governor. The next voice you'll hear will be the moderator, Charles Collingwood, when he opens the program. Thank you again for joining us, and have a great debate."

After the earpiece went silent, Jacki Brown, the local affiliate's news producer, turned on the television monitor resting on a table off to the side of the camera trained on Reagan. "Jacki," he asked, "will you turn that off and keep it off for me during the program?"

"Of course, governor," she replied, "but if it's off, you won't be able to see Senator Kennedy or the questioners."

"Don't worry—I know what Bobby looks like, and when you've seen one college student you've seen them all! I don't want the screen to distract me." Jacki clicked off the monitor, stopped to listen to a message in her earpiece, and then told her guest:

"Two minutes thirty seconds to air, governor. When I throw the cue, you'll be live."

In the nearby engineer's booth, Jason, Wayne, Press Secretary Lyn Nofziger, and policy adviser Ed Meese watched the TV screen as Reagan applied ChapStick while the seconds ticked down.

"Hey Ed, how did he do today?" Jason asked about Reagan's only debate practice session held a few hours earlier at the hotel.

"As expected—once he believes in the righteousness of a cause, he has an uncanny ability to communicate his ideas with great forcefulness, and Ike's help has been invaluable. The governor's a quick study when he's engaged, and on Vietnam, he truly believes that America is doing the right thing—and he believes Kennedy is cowardly for wanting to cut-and-run. I think he'll be fine."[6]

"Either way, we're in a *Catch-22* with this debate," Wayne noted wryly. "If he does poorly, aside from the damage it will inflict on the campaign, Nixon will go on the warpath and want our scalps."

"What's the *Catch-22*?" Ed asked.

Wayne laughed. "If he does well, Nixon will go on the warpath and want our scalps."

Twenty-four hundred miles away, and fifteen minutes earlier, Senator Robert Kennedy and his entourage arrived at WTOP studios in Northwest Washington. Don Hewitt greeted RFK in the lobby and then escorted his party up to the greenroom adjacent to the television studio. Although he told Bobby he looked great, Don was surprised at how thin and fatigued the candidate appeared since last seeing him before the assassination attempt over four months ago. After getting his guests settled, Don brought Bobby over to makeup. While the studio cosmetologist applied the heavy pancake and powder needed to diffuse the harsh studio lighting, Don briefed Bobby on the format.

"How many kids will you have on the panel?" Bobby asked.

"Eighteen—they're all at our London studio with Charlie Collingwood."

"Any American students?"

"Just one. He studied over there as a Rhodes Scholar—Bill Bradley from Princeton."**

"The basketball player?"

"Yep."

"What's he doing on the panel?"

"A couple of years ago he interned at our London office when he did the Rhodes program. Because he joined the NBA early, he never finished it, so he worked out a deal with Oxford to return for a couple of months this fall and take his final exams. Since he's the only American student our London producer knew, he invited Bill on the panel. Do you know him?"[7]

"I met him after the '64 Olympics at a reception for our gold medal winners, and I've talked to him a few times since. He's smart—and he's a Democrat. Good call."

After taking his place on the set, a technician miked Bobby while the makeup artist took a brush to his still-short hair as she tried to tame a slight cowlick. Bobby watched the nearby TV monitor that showed the students taking their seats on the two-row set erected in the London studio. "Senator Kennedy, welcome," a female voice said in Bobby's earpiece. "We're a few minutes to air." Bobby nodded silently at the time signal. "Now I know how Jack felt eight years ago," he thought in the final moments before the start of what the press already billed as "The Great Debate of '68."

In the greenroom, Ethel Kennedy studied her husband's image alongside that of Reagan's on the split screen as they awaited the start of the live broadcast. "Reagan looks tense," Ethel told Frank Mankiewicz. "Do you think he realizes what a huge mistake he's made in agreeing to this?"

** Bill Bradley (born 1943) played professional basketball for the New York Knicks from 1965-1977. In 1978, he won election to the United States Senate and represented New Jersey for three terms until 1997. In 2000, he ran unsuccessfully for the Democratic presidential nomination. While finishing his Rhodes Scholar program at Oxford, he was one of the eighteen student panelists participating in the May 15, 1967 RWR-RFK debate.

"If he doesn't know it yet, he will in about four minutes. Bob's going to destroy him."[8]

Ethel smiled and nodded. "This will be like watching a Central Park mugging," she replied. "Only this time, I'm rooting for the mugger."

"Quiet on the set, please. We're live in thirty seconds."

At London's BBC studio in the Alexandra Park district, Charles Collingwood stood in front of the center television camera and rolled his neck from side-to-side to loosen up as he awaited the director's cue. Behind him sat the group of college students CBS selected to question the two vice presidential nominees. With an anticipated estimated audience of 101 million viewers in the United States alone,[9] and millions more around the world watching, this promised to be a highlight of his lengthy journalism career.

London was familiar turf to Collingwood, who went to work at CBS during World War II and joined Edward R. Murrow's team stationed there during the German blitzkrieg. As one of "Murrow's Boys," Collingwood risked his life daily to present the news live from the front lines to radio listeners back home. Now, during the final debate countdown, he found himself—surprisingly—more nervous than he remembered feeling when Nazi bombs dropped around him.

"And we are live in—five—four—three—two—one—" With that, the director pointed his index finger at Collingwood who, when the red light illuminated on Camera Two, read his introductory remarks from a cue card held underneath the lens. "I'm Charles Collingwood, and this is *Town Meeting of the World*, a transatlantic confrontation that satellite communication now makes possible. With me here in the BBC studio in London are a group of young university students—one from the United States, and the rest from Europe, Africa, and Asia. They are all attending universities in Great Britain, and they have provocative ideas about the United States and its role in the world. For the next hour, they will participate in a global dialogue with the Democratic vice presidential nominee, Senator Robert F. Kennedy of New York, and the Republican vice presidential nominee, Governor Ronald Reagan of California. The first question will go to Senator Kennedy from student Anna Ford."

The haughty lead-off student didn't ask a question. Instead, she made a brief, indignant speech: "I believe the war in Vietnam is illegal, immoral, politically unjustifiable and economically motivated. Do you agree with me?"

RFK looked pensive as he replied quietly and without emotion, "I don't agree with that. I have reservations about the war, but the United States is trying to let the people of South Vietnam choose their own destiny. I think Governor Reagan would agree with me that if North Vietnam would let the people of South Vietnam decide what kind of government they want, then we would leave the region. That's all we're interested in accomplishing. We have no colonial aspirations there. So I think the situation is quite different than you've described it."

Collingwood gave Reagan a chance to reply. "Well, Senator Kennedy and I are in agreement on this issue. Our country has a long history of nonaggression and a willingness to aid those who want the freedom to determine their own future. Unlike a family quarrel, it doesn't take two to make a war—it only takes one. Our participation in Vietnam is justified by our goal of giving the South Vietnamese the right to choose their way of life and not have a totalitarian communist government forced upon them."

Back in the greenroom, Kennedy's aides started keeping preliminary score on the combatants. "That's a good way for them to start," Frank told the others, "but I would have preferred to see Bob be a little less confrontational with the girl. After all, she speaks for our base—and for all those McCarthy kids we'll need to bring home in the next few weeks." They continued watching as Collingwood let student David Jenkins give the next question to Reagan.

"Mr. Reagan, you said before that every man has the right of dissent. If you really believe this, then why do you attack those young Americans who show their opposition to the Vietnam War by opposing the draft?

Why do you keep calling them draft dodgers?"

"I support the right of dissent," Reagan said firmly, "but people also have a responsibility to obey the law. Citizens give up certain individual freedoms in the interest of preserving the legal rights of all. I do not support—or respect—those who are resisting the draft. They are disobeying the law and weakening our country. Every American is born with the right to life, liberty, and the pursuit of happiness. But if my pursuit of happiness comes from swinging my arm, my right to swing it ends before it reaches the tip of your nose."

Eyeing the split screen monitor, and reading her husband's body language, Ethel saw RFK stiffen. "Here it comes—Bob's going to let him have it," she said in hopeful anticipation.

Looking away from the camera, RFK responded, "I don't think that either morality or God is on our side just because we're in a war. If there are those who oppose the war, then they should make their views known. They aren't less patriotic just because they disagree with Governor Reagan. Those who have a different point of view about President Johnson's policies have a responsibility and a right to state those views."

Ethel turned to Frank and smiled. "Bingo!" she called, provoking laughter among the staff.

Their enthusiasm was premature. When Reagan replied, his eyes remained locked on the camera lens, making it appear he was addressing RFK directly: "Let me make this plain for Senator Kennedy. People have the right to dissent, but when their dissent takes the form of helping an enemy actively engaged in killing our troops—aiding the enemy by avoiding the draft, refusing to serve, blocking troop trains and shipments of munitions as some demonstrators have done, this goes beyond dissent. It is lending aid and comfort to an enemy engaged in killing young Americans who are fighting to preserve freedom. I draw the line at that, senator, and so should you."[10] Kennedy sat mute and did not respond.

"Shit—that hurt," Frank muttered.[11]

When student Steven Marks asked whether the nominees agreed with Secretary of State Dean Rusk's claim that the ongoing antiwar protests on college campuses in the US hurt the war effort, Kennedy defended the student activists. "The war continues in Vietnam," he replied, "because of our adversaries' determination to continue it. The protests here in the United States have no influence on that. If all the protests on college campuses and elsewhere ended tomorrow, the war in Vietnam would continue."

Once again, Reagan fired back. "Of course these demonstrations lengthen the war. They encourage our enemy to believe that the division created by these protests in America will give them the chance to grab victory. That is an unfortunate cost of free speech, which we continue to guard jealously."

Next, a Pakistani student, Arshad Mahmood, asked the candidates whether they agreed that the Vietcong, an armed band of South Vietnamese guerilla insurgents fighting for the communist North, should be included in any peace negotiations. After Kennedy said that he favored their participation in the peace talks, Reagan pounced again. "The Vietcong are a rebel and illegal force fighting against the duly authorized government of its own nation. To sit them down at the peace talks between North and South Vietnam is tipping the scales in favor of the communists. I don't understand why Senator Kennedy thinks this is in the interest of peace or freedom."[12]

Irritated that Reagan landed another blow, Kennedy shot back, "Well, if the Vietcong shouldn't be involved in negotiations to end the war between North and South Vietnam, why should the United States be there, for that matter?"

"I don't see any parallel between a band of treasonous rebel murderers and the United States of America," Reagan responded coolly.

For the rest of the hour, it got worse for Kennedy—and better for Reagan. As almost every student teed up a new anti-American rant over Vietnam,[13] RFK grew deferential and apologetic, while Reagan defended US military policy and challenged any interrogators' false statistics used to bolster their arguments.[14] When Jeff Jordan accused the US of using its immense power to destroy freedom in Vietnam and other hot spots around the globe, and Kennedy didn't challenge the comment, Reagan jumped in, telling the student, "I challenge your history." He then walked the student through a comprehensive Vietnam chronology leading to the current popularly elected government in the South.[15] When Jordan interrupted—repeatedly—and made the outlandish claim that America installed a puppet regime in South Vietnam that sent six million people to forced prison camps, Reagan countered, "I challenge your history again. There is absolutely no record of them sending six million people to concentration camps—South Vietnam has only sixteen million people in the entire country. And America could hardly install a puppet regime when we had less than seven hundred unarmed military advisers there teaching the South Vietnamese how to organize an army to protect their country from guerilla attacks."

With Reagan dominating the debate, Collingwood interrupted, saying "Governor, let's get Senator Kennedy in on this. We haven't heard from him in a while. Why don't you answer Mr. Jordan's question, senator?"

Again, Kennedy demurred. "Well, let somebody ask me a question directly, and then I'll answer it."

In the WTOP greenroom, the earlier spirit of impending victory and joviality had long ago disappeared. Grimaces replaced grins as Kennedy's staff watched Reagan, an experienced television actor who knew how to find a camera and look into it directly, and contrasted that to the weak performance of their man, who continued to gaze off into empty space. Reagan appeared forceful and in command, while Kennedy looked lost and sounded weak.[16] When he again declined to respond to Reagan's latest powerful salvo in defense of America, Ethel had seen enough. She stood and shouted at the TV monitor angrily, "Hit him back, Bob—he's killing you!"[17]

In challenging Reagan to debate, Kennedy and his team assumed the format favored RFK overwhelmingly. Instead, Bobby found himself caught in an untenable position—either defend the United States against these anti-American students by defending Lyndon Johnson's war policies, or appease his domestic college-student base by sympathizing with the hostile questions of angry young foreigners.[18] To the chagrin of his campaign staff, and to the delight of Republican partisans, he chose apology and conciliation. When Collingwood announced—mercifully—that the hour was up and the debate concluded, there were sighs of relief among the Kennedy party. However, relief turned to nervousness when Kennedy interrupted the moderator and asked if he could say a final word. Thrown by the request, Collingwood stammered, "Yes—say a word."

In fashioning what he thought was an elegant closing commentary, Kennedy again slipped into an apologia for America, reiterating, "We recognize that we make major mistakes within the United States. Perhaps we don't remedy them as rapidly as you would like, and we recognize that we are obviously far from perfect. But the world belongs to you, that what we do and the decisions that we make have an effect on your lives. When you see us make mistakes, you must continue to criticize."

Collingwood then gave Reagan a chance to close. Speaking directly to his audience, Reagan said, "Since I'm the oldest person here, I take the liberty of giving a little advice to the young people. The highest aspiration of man should be individual freedom. As you pursue your future, weigh everything proposed to you on this one scale—does it make you free? Never trade sanctuary or security for your right to fly as high and as far as your own strength and ability will take you as an individual. Reserve your right to be free."[19]

"Thank you very much," Collingwood concluded with the sign-off. "This is *Town Meeting of the World*. I'm Charles Collingwood. Good night."

In Sacramento a few moments later, Jacki Brown called, "All clear," and a technician stepped forward to remove Reagan's lapel microphone. Looking off camera to his four assembled staffers, Reagan smiled. "Well," he said cheerfully, "I guess this was one time woodshedding paid off.[20] Come on—let's go."

"Let's go?" Jason asked incredulously. "Don't you want to know how you did?"

Reagan patted his aide on the shoulder. "I already know how I did, Jason. I was there."[21]

"You don't even want to talk about it?"

"Okay, if it makes you feel better—how did I do, Jason."

Now it was Jason's turn to smile. "You were *just fair,*" he deadpanned.

When Wayne and Ed started laughing at Jason's blasé interpretation of Reagan's utter domination of the debate, the nominee laughed. "Well, if The Little General thinks I was only *fair*, I guess that means it was a home run.[22] That'll satisfy me. I only hope it satisfies the other fellow."

At that same moment on the other side of the continent, the TV monitor went black in WTOP's greenroom as the Kennedy team sat in silence. Campaign manager Fred Dutton leaned over to Frank and whispered, "What do you think?"

"What do I think?" Frank asked morosely. "I think it was a goddamn disaster. It was the most one-sided, awful debate I've ever seen. Reagan was polished, and Bob looked disinterested and rambled. It was chaos."[23]

"Should we tell him?"

"Don't you think he knows?"

He knew.

When Bobby entered the greenroom, his staff started telling him he did a good job. Ignoring the forced compliments, Bobby said angrily, "All right, who the fuck got me into this?" Spying Frank, Bobby walked toward him with an accusing finger pointed in his direction. "*You're* the guy who thought this would be a great idea." Before Frank could answer, Bobby stalked toward the room next door to have his makeup removed. He stopped suddenly and turned toward Frank. "Listen," he snapped—

"—don't you *ever* put me on the same stage with that son-of-a-bitch again."[24]

The next morning, Wayne Paugh reached Pat Buchanan by phone at his Carson City hotel room before the Nixon entourage embarked on a one-day, five-state campaign swing. "What did you think?" Wayne asked his fellow RN staffer.

"Reagan killed it," Pat said blandly.

"You might sound a little more enthusiastic."

"Believe me—I'm probably more enthused about it than you—we all are, but we don't want the boss to see it. He's been red hot over this issue since he learned Reagan agreed to debate, so we're not talking about it on our end. It's bugged him since the convention that Reagan draws bigger crowds, and now they'll be bigger and more fervent than ever. After tonight, Reagan's the GOP's biggest rock star, and it'll grind on RN."

"Is he that jealous?"

"It's more insecurity than jealousy. Last night on the plane, he had a couple of beers, and then he grumbled that in Miami the convention's heart belonged to Reagan, not him. He said that if he had stumbled in his delegate count, they would have run from him and into Ronnie's arms.[25] He also knows that between now and November the press will use this to call him a coward for refusing to debate Humphrey. He tries not to show it publicly, but that whole *Richard the Chicken-Hearted* thing is getting under his skin.[26] Since Bobby gave a shitty performance, Humphrey will press it harder to get people to stop talking about how good Reagan was and how bad Bobby looked."

"Any reaction from the campaign committee?"

"Yeah—it's already buried in an avalanche of telegrams and morning mail—checks, cash, thousands of calls, letters, and wires thanking Reagan for standing up for America. A large number of them are messages saying they wish Reagan were the presidential nominee. I can't imagine the old man's reaction if he saw those—and I don't want to."[27]

"What did he say when he saw the press clips?"

"Not much. By the way, a friend at *Newsweek* told me they're coming out in two days with a two-page story on it, and they're going to say Ronnie crushed Kennedy."

"No surprise there—just about every daily and editorial I've seen says that Reagan nailed it.[28] Did you hear what happened with CBS?"

"No—what?"

"I called Hewitt at the network and asked if we could get a copy of the show. Our media guys thought we could use the clips of Kennedy apologizing for America in our TV commercials. Hewitt told me he'd have to run it by their legal department. When he got back to me today, he turned me down. He said Kennedy didn't want the debate film shown anywhere, so he was honoring that request."[29]

"I guess that's the best compliment of all. Tell the governor congratulations from all of us on this end—

"—But for God's sake, don't *ever* tell the boss I said that."

CHAPTER 43

"I HOPE YOU AREN'T PLANNING to wear this at the rally today."

As Air Force Two jetted to Maryland from Michigan, where Vice President Hubert Humphrey toured the nearby Ford Motor Company plant and spoke at a morning trade union conference, he studied the small campaign button with the uninspiring message handed him by aide Ted Van Dyk:

DEMOCRACY DEMANDS • STOP HUMPHREY

"No sir," Ted laughed. "Not today. I already have a hole in my lapel from a DUMP THE HUMP badge."

"Very funny. Of course, after my speech at the Ford factory nothing would surprise me. You know, I've devoted my entire public life to helping organized labor. It hurt like hell seeing all those union workers on the assembly line wearing WALLACE FOR PRESIDENT stickers on their hard hats.[1] So forgive me if I expect the worst today."

"I understand why some frustrated blue-collar guys are for Wallace. What I can't understand is why so many of Senator McCarthy's supporters are for him. How do you go from 'Clean Gene' to a segregationist and racist?"[2]

"That just shows you the level of madness this race has produced," HHH said sullenly. "In the end, I guess they want change—and they don't care who gives it to them."

Ted opened a file folder and handed a piece of paper to the vice president, telling him, "Maybe this will help inject a degree of sanity into your day."

"What is it?" HHH asked while reaching for his reading glasses on the seat next to him.

"It's the letter that came with that STOP HUMPHREY button. The writer dropped them both off at the DNC after Senator Kennedy's debate a couple of weeks ago. Chairman O'Brien sent it over in the mail pouch—he thought you'd like to see it."*

HHH unfolded the message and read it silently:

September 15, 1968

Dear Mr. Vice President:

Ever since you declared your candidacy for president, I have been wearing this "Stop Humphrey" badge. I supported Senator McCarthy in the primaries, and I have participated in many antiwar and anti-Humphrey efforts. I attended the convention in Chicago to protest your candidacy, and I received twelve stitches in the emergency room after Mayor Daley's gestapo beat me in Grant Park during a peaceful demonstration. I left Chicago vowing never to vote for you, even though the alternatives to your candidacy are horrible.[3]

After listening to Senator Kennedy debate Reagan last night, and listening to his heartfelt expressions of concern over our continuing course in Vietnam—compared to Reagan's jingoistic bromides that will cost thousands more lives needlessly, I have realized how wrong I am to oppose you. It took guts for you to choose Senator Kennedy

---

* DNC: Democratic National Committee, located in Washington, DC. Following his victory at the Chicago convention, HHH selected Postmaster General Lawrence F. O'Brien as chairman of the DNC.

as a running mate, and even more guts to repudiate Johnson's war policies. So I am turning in this button today at the front desk of the Democratic National Committee—I don't need it anymore. I'll ask them to exchange it for a Humphrey-Kennedy button, which I will wear proudly between now and November 5th. I'll do all I can to help you defeat Nixon and Wallace so you can bring peace to America and to Vietnam.

Sincerely,

John Vargo

Humphrey's face relaxed. "That made my day," he nodded. "Let's send this over to Bob—I'll do a note to go with it. Maybe this will get him to stop kicking himself over his debate performance."

"I still can't understand this ongoing 'Reagan was great' narrative."

"He *was* great—if you're a warmonger and a simpleton. Bob did a hell of a job. I think everyone is fawning over Reagan because the press expected him to fall flat on his face, and instead he memorized his spoon-fed script and got through it. The only thing Reagan did better than Bob was remembering to look into the TV camera directly. That's a hell of a basis on which to pick a potential president."

Taking back the letter and badge, Ted said, "I'll messenger these to the senator when we hit DC this afternoon."

"Have you lined up that meeting with Johnson for today?"

"Sir, they're still yanking my chain at the White House, but as of now, I'm told the president will give you seven minutes at three this afternoon."

"Seven minutes," HHH sighed resignedly, "for the vice president of the United States and the Democratic Party's presidential nominee. Ever since the convention, Johnson's been screwing me at every opportunity, including freezing me out from every traditional major Democratic Party donor."[4]

"That's true, but since the convention, you've got a lot of pluses in your favor. We're creeping up in the polls, the war protesters have all but disappeared from your rallies, and the crowd enthusiasm since the convention is electric.[5] Before Chicago, you couldn't get local elected officials to show up at your events. Now they're pushing their way onto the stage to get in the picture with you, and O'Brien told me the small contributions are pouring in by the tens of thousands. So things are moving in the right direction, which makes me wonder why you're jumping through hoops to get a seven-minute meeting."

"Because it's time for the president and me to make up, if for no other reason than for the sake of the Party. And let's face it—I'm also going to need his help in Texas to counter Wallace's strength."

"Did he ever get back to you about appearing at our Astrodome rally on election eve?"

"No. We haven't spoken since the convention. He won't return any of my calls. When is that rally again?"

"November 3rd—two days before the election—during our final push through the Border States. Shall I try Marv Watson again?"

"Don't bother. I called him this week and told him our polling shows we'll need a big push in Texas or else we'll lose it to Nixon, especially since Governor Connally** still hasn't endorsed me—no doubt on Johnson's orders. Connally doesn't shit unless Johnson tells him to squat. I nearly begged Watson to ask Johnson to nail down Connally for me, and that I need them both at the Astrodome or else we won't carry the president's own home state."

"What did he say?"

"Watson waited three days before calling me back, and then he told me, 'The president suggested you bring Bobby Kennedy to the Astrodome and let him carry Texas for you.' So that's where we stand now. I keep hoping he's just squeezing out his pound of flesh for my picking Kennedy and changing the Vietnam plank, but who knows? When Johnson first threw me over after Chicago, I assumed it was

---

** John B. Connally (1917-1993), who began his political career as a protégé of Lyndon Johnson (dating back to LBJ's days as a young congressman), served as governor of Texas from 1963 to 1969.

temporary. But with only three weeks to go before Election Day, I'm beginning to think the screw job might be permanent. One of my White House spies told me Johnson's maintaining back-channel communications with Nixon.[6] Of course, with Lyndon, you never know if he's really helping Nixon, or just stringing him along, too. I only know we're running out of time. If we lose Texas, the ballgame's over. *President Richard Nixon*—that's a hell of a price for America to pay just because Lyndon Johnson's pissed that I picked my own running mate and campaign platform. Well, if seven minutes is all he'll give me, then I'll take it—even if I have to spend six-and-a-half of those minutes kissing his big ugly ass."

Ted nodded and left the cabin. Alone again, Hubert turned and looked out the airplane window. "Seven minutes," he muttered to himself. "Seven minutes to enlist a Democratic president's help in electing a Democratic successor—

"—Lyndon, you bastard."

After Humphrey's plane landed, he addressed an outdoor rally at a Silver Springs, Maryland, shopping center just outside of Washington. The crowd was boisterous and enthusiastic, but Humphrey got soaked in an unexpected downpour. On the way to the White House, he asked his driver to stop by his Southwest Washington apartment so he could change into dry clothes. This detour delayed Humphrey's schedule by ten minutes.

When his motorcade pulled into the White House gate and came to a stop in the West Wing driveway, Hubert checked his wristwatch: 3:01 p.m. He hurried inside, where an usher awaited his arrival. Entering the president's reception area, Hubert noticed the Oval Office door cracked open slightly. Inside he saw Lyndon Johnson seated behind his desk reading a document. It was now 3:03. "Welcome back, Mr. Vice President," the secretary said. "I'll let him know you're here." Picking up the phone, she announced his arrival.

Jim Jones, LBJ's aide, exited the Oval Office and blocked the door.

"I'm sorry, sir," he said with a voice tinged in embarrassment. "You're three minutes late. The president asked me to convey that he is now unable to see you. The meeting is canceled." As Jones spoke, Hubert looked back through the door and saw LBJ get up from his desk and walk to the other side of the office and out of view.

Hubert's reaction was instantaneous and visceral. "Jim, are you goddamn kidding me? I'm trying to run a presidential campaign as our Party's nominee! Are you telling me Lyndon Johnson doesn't care?"

"I'm sorry, sir. He's moving on with his schedule."

"Listen, Jim, I want you to give the president a message from me."

"Yes?"

In a voice loud enough for Johnson to hear, HHH said, "Tell him I said to take his meeting and shove it up his ass."[7]

Humphrey's expression of exasperation with President Johnson may have felt therapeutic, at least momentarily, but the relief didn't last: The next day, the White House issued a press release announcing that the president invited Richard Nixon—*only* Richard Nixon—to the LBJ Ranch in Texas for a private briefing on Vietnam.

"Mr. Nixon, what's the political significance of this invitation?"

Richard Nixon stood under a gray October sky at Bergstrom Air Force Base and in the shadow of the olive-green military helicopter that, when used by LBJ, flew under the call sign of *Marine One.* A group of reporters gathered trying to pry information about the unusual Johnson-Nixon meeting less than a month before Election Day.[8] "There is no *political* significance to the invitation," the nominee responded, "at least not in the partisan sense. The president has been keeping all three major candidates briefed on developments in Vietnam, and he has often given those briefings personally. I presume today's invitation is a courtesy he's extended because of my planned two-day Texas trip. Besides, the president and I are former congressional colleagues who go back more than twenty years, so I look forward to seeing an old friend in a relaxed setting."

"He and Mr. Humphrey go back at least as far," a reporter said. "Do you see any message in the fact that he invited you and not his own vice president?"

"As I said, I assume it is because my visit to the president's home state coincides with his ranch stay."

"Sir," another asked, "with only a few weeks to go before the election, is this meant as a signal to Mr. Humphrey that the president's still mad over what happened in Chicago?"[9]

"If I could predict and interpret internal Democratic signals, I'd be a bookmaker, not a presidential candidate. Anyway, I don't want to keep the president waiting. Thank you, gentlemen." With that, RN boarded the helicopter, took a seat next to the pilot, waved to the photographers, and then lifted off for the fifty-mile hop to the LBJ Ranch.[10]

After flying for twenty minutes over mostly uninhabited hill country, they reached the brown Pedernales River. As the chopper began descending, RN saw in the clearing a ranch house with a pool, a few nearby buildings, a dozen sedans scattered about, a small airplane hangar, and even a cemetery. Scattered around the property were men in dark suits and sunglasses looking in all directions away from the house. The American and presidential flags flew from a tall pole on the lawn. A dust cloud kicked up as the pilot touched down on the small airstrip constructed a couple hundred yards from the main building. At landing, two men exited the house and walked toward the strip. Nixon waved to his host, stepped from the helicopter, and walked along the gravel path to greet LBJ, who wore a short-sleeved khaki shirt, tan pants, black cowboy boots, and a large tan Stetson cowboy hat.

"Mr. President, you look more relaxed than I've seen you in a long time."

"It's the ranch air, Dick. You and Pat should come out here and stay a spell after November." As the two old foes shook hands, LBJ apologized for Lady Bird's absence. "She's up in New York for a charity affair," he said. "She baked an apple cake for your bride. Don't let me forget to give it to you when you leave, or she'll tack my hide to the wall." RN introduced his two aides, Ray Price and Pat Buchanan, and LBJ turned them over to ranch foreman Dale Malechek.*** "Dale, fix up these boys with some Texas grub while I give Dick a tour of the place."

LBJ escorted RN to a large white Continental convertible. Reaching into the cooler propped on the back seat, Johnson grabbed two beer bottles, popped off the caps and gave one to Nixon. Then, pointing to a large box on the seat cushion as he got behind the wheel, he told his guest, "There's a present in there for you. It's a tradition to give these to visitors. Open it." Nixon climbed into the passenger side and lifted the lid. Inside was a gray five-gallon cowboy hat.[11] "Put it on, Dick—if you want to *win* Texas, you gotta *look* Texas!" Appearing about as uncomfortable and stiff as Pat Buchanan ever saw the boss, Nixon (in a dark blue business suit) put the oversized hat on his head. Johnson revved the motor and took off while drinking from his beer bottle, and with a Secret Service chase car in pursuit.

LBJ's tour of his 2,700-acre ranch might have qualified as a Disneyland "E ticket ride." They hit bumps, ruts, mud holes, and gravel at speeds often over eighty miles an hour.[12] Driving past his livestock pens, he quipped, "That's where the cattle go in—and the money comes out!"[13] Occasionally Johnson pulled his car alongside one of his Herefords and blasted the dashboard-activated bullhorn at the animal (making a loud *ah-oooo-gah* sound) to get a reaction.[14] When one of his prized cattle remained unintimidated by the horn and kept grazing, LBJ climbed out and patted him on its hindquarters. "Look here, Dick," he said. "This is where the best steaks come from, but I didn't buy this boy for eating." Then, with a broad smile, he lifted the bull's tail and revealed its giant testicles. "I call this big fellow with all the social standing *Lyndon!*" LBJ then walked over to a nearby steer and lifted his tail, which showed his castration scars.[15] "Since this one's got no balls, I named him *Hubert!*" Still laughing at his own joke, LBJ climbed back

*** Vernon Dale Malecheck (1930-1985) served as manager and foreman of the LBJ Ranch beginning in 1961 and remained throughout Johnson's life.

in the car, spun it around, and headed back toward the ranch.

Returning to the main house, a steward served cocktails before both men settled in the comfortably appointed living room. Johnson sat in his Carolina rocker (a replica of the one he kept in the Oval Office) positioned in front of the large fireplace, while Nixon sat to his left on a red floral-patterned sofa.

"Dick, I appreciate all your support on Vietnam. I wish I could say the same for Hubert and Bobby. Of course," he added with a wink, "if you hadn't supported me on Vietnam, I might be sittin' here meeting with presidential nominee Ronald Reagan instead of with you!"[16]

RN laughed and added, "Well, you might be more right about that than you know!" and then changed the subject: "Is there any favorable movement at the peace talks?"

"No. The North Vietnamese are still giving us shit in Paris. Our negotiators haven't been able to get them to the table. Too many pre-conditions, and they won't sit down if the South comes. I've been trying like hell to finish this before the next president takes over, but this may land on your plate come January."

"Mr. President, I know you have done everything a leader can do to bring peace. If it falls upon me to conclude the war because the North decides they can wait you out, I can assure you they will get no benefit for stalling. I will continue your policies until we achieve peace with honor."

"I know that, Dick, and I appreciate the support and restraint on Vietnam you've shown in the campaign. That's more than I can say for my own vice president, or that little bastard he picked as a running mate. Hubert and Bobby are out there calling for a withdrawal from Vietnam, and now Bobby's telling audiences that his brother would have pulled out our forces years ago—what a crock of bullshit. After Yalta and China, there is no way Jack Kennedy would have allowed himself to become the third Democratic president in twenty years to be accused of surrendering a democratic government to the communists."[17]

"I was probably as shocked as you when Hubert picked Kennedy.

In his acceptance speech, when he said he was for both a bombing halt *and* supporting your hardline peace efforts in Paris, it made me wonder what the hell side he's on."[18]

"I'll tell you what side Hubert's on—he's gone over to the side of the college professors and the peaceniks, and he's turned his goddamn back on every man fighting over there. I can't forgive him for that."[19]

"I notice that since the convention he's using Bobby's line that Vietnam is fighting 'a civil war.'"

"Every time he says it it pisses me off—he knows better. It's a 'civil war' when citizens of the same nation fight each other. He knows damn well that North and South Vietnam are separate countries recognized by the Geneva Accords. When the North attacks the South, it's not a civil war any more than if a stranger walks into your house and shoots at you. It's aggression, for Christ's sake."[20]

Leaning forward toward his host, and emphasizing his point by tapping his index finger against the sofa armrest, RN looked at LBJ intently. "Mr. President, we understand the rules of political engagement. For the next few weeks, you know I'm obliged to point out certain weaknesses in your administration. But I want you to know I will stand with you on Vietnam to the end, and I will never say anything in this campaign to embarrass you personally. I think you're the hardest working and most dedicated president since Lincoln, and I've said so publicly. I respect you—as a man and as a president—and if I win this election, when this war ends, I'll give you the lion's share of credit. I'll want a close working relationship with you, and I'll seek your advice continually. I'll want to use you for special assignments to foreign countries. And I will do everything I can to give you a revered place in history—because you deserve it."[21]

Lyndon reached over and squeezed RN's forearm with his big hand. "You'll never know what those words mean to me, Dick. And I know you appreciate that even though I've kept a low profile since Chicago, at some point I'll have to indicate my support for Humphrey.[22] But there are many levels of 'support,' if you know what I mean. For example,

Texas might well decide this election, and you've noticed that Governor Connally hasn't endorsed Hubert so far. I think you know his silence isn't accidental."

"I know that, and I'm very grateful."

"Anyway, Dick, I give you my word—I won't use a Vietnam peace maneuver as some last minute ploy to help elect Humphrey, especially after the way he betrayed me."[23]

"I understand completely. Of course, if you did announce some last-minute bombing halt of the North, it will help Humphrey and Kennedy whether you like it or not."

LBJ scoffed. "Well, I can goddamn assure you there will be no unilateral bombing halt of the North between now and the election. Bobby's bombing halt promise would guarantee that all those North Vietnamese and Vietcong ammo trucks can keep pouring over the border into the South carrying weapons to kill American boys—

"—*And that will never happen on my watch.*"[24]

When it was time to go, LBJ walked Nixon to the helipad. After the two men shook hands, RN boarded the aircraft and then turned to say a final goodbye. As he did, LBJ's little mixed-breed dog Yuki ran up the stairs and stood underneath RN's legs.

"Goddamn you, Dick!" LBJ laughed. "First you take my helicopter, then you're fixin' to take my job, and now you want my dog!"

RN handed his Stetson hat and boxed apple cake to a Navy steward, bent down and picked up the dog, and carried him back to LBJ. "That's okay, Mr. President," he said with a smile. "You can have him back—

"—I'll settle for two out of three!"[25]

Later that night, in an Austin hotel suite, RN briefed his senior staff on his meeting with Johnson. "It sounds like it was a huge success," Ray Price noted optimistically.

"It depends on how you define success," RN replied. "Lyndon succeeded in giving me the impression he wants to help me crush Humphrey and Kennedy without leaving any evidence at the crime scene."

"You sound skeptical."

"That's because I've known Lyndon Johnson for decades, and that's long enough to expect a last-minute double-cross. You wait and see. Between now and November 5th, it'll come."

"It's good to be cautious, but at this point I only see a couple of ways we lose the election. The first is that we make a critical campaign mistake."

"There's little chance of that," Pat Buchanan added. "Right now we're like a basketball team that's sitting on their lead by freezing the ball and running out the clock. Of course, that strategy only works so long as Hubert doesn't get his act together."[26]

"I'm not worried about Hubert getting his act together," RN said. "I'm worried about Johnson waiting until the last minute and then putting it together for him."

"The only way Johnson can do that is to announce some dramatic Vietnam breakthrough."[27]

"If Johnson decides to stab me, he'll time it perfectly—and Johnson has pitch-perfect timing. Humphrey's still behind, but he's creeping up slowly. You watch—I expect Johnson will pull a late-October surprise and order a last-minute bombing halt, or announce a Soviet summit, or that North and South Vietnam have agreed to negotiate—and the Democrats will claim that the war is over. If that happens, Humphrey will surge and win. Our friends in South Vietnam should be wary of any last-minute White House initiative—they need to push back if it comes."[28] Taking a sip of his drink, RN mused, "Of course, there is another more obvious way for him to fuck us—and it doesn't have nearly as many variables involved—it's Johnson deciding to rally his Democratic base to stand by their nominees."

"But you said Johnson called Humphrey and Kennedy traitors," Ray noted.

"He did say that, and he may have meant it when he said it, or he may have said it to lull me into a false sense of security. Make no mistake—Lyndon's still the leader of the Democratic Party, and I don't believe for a minute—no matter how much bullshit he feeds me—that he wants the election of a Republican president to be his legacy. So there are several ways for Johnson to sucker-punch me between now and November 5th, and I expect him to use every trick at his disposal. Remember—they're the same team that stole the 1960 election from me, and they'll try it again. Johnson once told me that every effective leader has to be a son-of-a-bitch. And trust me—Lyndon Johnson is the biggest son-of-a-bitch I have ever known."[29]

Putting down his drink on the coffee table, RN walked across the room and shut off the TV. Looking back at his staff, he added, "Never forget that, in this campaign, there's one name that unifies the Democrats more than any other."

"You mean the name Kennedy?" Ray asked.

RN shook his head. "No—

"—I mean the name *Nixon*."[30]

Button worn by Vietnam War protester, 1968 (Author's collection)

CHAPTER 44

RICHARD NIXON'S PREDICTION of White House-generated sabotage began taking root less than thirty-six hours after making his gloomy prophecy, and it started with a 4:00 a.m. call from Paris on October 9, 1968.

The telephone rang four times before the hand of the sleeping man in the large four-poster bed started fumbling for it in the pitch-black bedroom. "*What?*" he barked with irritation when answering.

"Mr. President, this is the White House operator. I'm sorry to awaken you, but Ambassador Cyrus Vance* is calling. He said it was urgent."

"Give me thirty seconds and then put him through." LBJ turned on a lamp and rubbed his eyes until they adjusted to the light. Moments later, the crackling voice of Vance came over the scrambled, secure line.

"Mr. President, forgive me for calling now, but we may have substantial movement in Vietnam."

---

*   Cyrus Vance (1917-2002), a former secretary of the Army and former deputy secretary of defense, served as an American delegate to the Vietnam War peace negotiations held at the Majestic Hotel in Paris in 1968. He later served as US secretary of state under President Jimmy Carter (1977-1980).

Upon hearing those words, any annoyance LBJ felt over his interrupted sleep vanished. Since the so-called "Paris Peace Talks" began last May, negotiations between the US (on behalf of South Vietnam) and representatives of the communist North Vietnamese government remained stalemated during their meetings at the Majestic Hotel in France. The North refused to meet with the South until the US agreed to an unconditional bombing halt of their country. Further, the North demanded that any negotiations include the South Vietnamese communist rebels—the Vietcong.[1] On the other side, South Vietnam refused to include the Vietcong (whom they viewed as rebellious traitors), and they also refused to talk with the North until they ended all attacks on the South. Now, unexpectedly, on October 9, the North cracked open the door by asking US negotiators in Paris if America would halt the bombing of their country if the North agreed to negotiate in good faith with the South.[2]

When Vance reported this development, LBJ's pleasure brimmed over.[3] "Cy," he told his ambassador, "I lay awake at night over not being able to bring an end to this war during my administration. If the next president ends the war after I did all the heavy lifting, it will dull my place in history. So you tell our people in Paris that hell yes—I'd consider a bombing halt if the North is serious. This could be the development that I've been praying for. I do have a question, though—why now?"

"This is all Soviet driven. After financing and supplying North Vietnam for years, with their recent invasion and occupation of Czechoslovakia, and their new tensions with Red China, it appears the Russians want Vietnam off their plate. When the North Vietnamese representative contacted our delegation this morning, I received a simultaneous signal through a Soviet back channel that if we'll announce a bombing halt, the Soviets will guarantee a favorable negotiating response from North Vietnam."

"I'll have Marv Watson round up the secretaries of state and defense, the NSA, and the Joint Chiefs. They'll all be in my office by 7:00 a.m. If this works out, it means I can end this war during my term of office, or at least finish my presidency with the promise of pending peace. Great job, Cy."

"Thank you, Mr. President."

"Cy—*thank you.*"

For the next three weeks, LBJ's attention shifted away from the presidential campaign to securing his place in history. Throughout October, he conferred unendingly with Secretary of State Rusk, Secretary of Defense Clifford, his field generals, the Joint Chiefs of Staff, National Security Adviser Walt Rostow, US Ambassador to South Vietnam Ellsworth Bunker, and his Paris negotiators (Vance and Ambassador W. Averell Harriman). If North Vietnam proved willing to negotiate, the unanimous consensus was to take the deal. Throughout this period, Vance and Harriman cabled to Washington their increasingly optimistic reports with each high-level sign-off. Surprisingly, by late October, the only significant pushback came from South Vietnamese President Nguyen Van Thieu, who told the American delegation he would participate in talks with the North only if Johnson kept bombing the North's "infiltration routes" into the South during the cease-fire. After days of arm-twisting and pleading, Thieu agreed—reluctantly— to participate.[4] Further, both sides compromised on the Vietcong: the VC would attend the discussions but have no official recognition as an independent entity.[5]

When word of the final agreement reached LBJ on Wednesday, October 30, he requested airtime on each network for a major address to the nation the following evening at 8:00 p.m. Eastern.[6] Then, in strict secrecy, he went to the White House Family Theater and taped his speech scheduled for the broadcast tomorrow night.[7] As Richard Nixon lamented suspiciously after his ranch visit with the president a few weeks earlier, Lyndon Johnson had perfect political timing: America would hear the news of peace in Vietnam exactly 100 hours before the 1968 presidential election.

The day of his scheduled speech broadcast, Thursday, October 31,

Johnson remained holed up with key military and policy advisers, and stayed in constant communication with his Paris delegation. Although everyone else showed an increasing sense of exhilaration, LBJ kept his enthusiasm in check. He knew all too well that it could fall apart, especially with Thieu's grudging acceptance—and his continued waffling on his commitment to join the talks. By 5:00 p.m.—three hours before the broadcast—the deal remained firm. LBJ held a conference call with the three presidential candidates—Nixon, Wallace, and Humphrey—and advised them formally of the diplomatic breakthrough. Under the circumstances, all three candidates promised to support the bombing-halt decision.[8]

Lyndon Johnson's triumph was within reach. Settling the war in the waning days of his contentious administration would salvage his presidency and his reputation for the ages.[9]

In the euphoria of the moment, Johnson overlooked on his calendar an unrelated appointment that evening, which had been on his schedule for over a month. At 6:00 p.m., a secretary entered the Oval Office and advised that FBI Director J. Edgar Hoover awaited him in the Cabinet Room. "I forgot about this," he told her. "We've been so damned busy the last few days that this fell off my radar. What does he need to see me about?"

"He said you'd know."

Johnson walked down the hallway and entered the Cabinet Room, where he found Hoover seated at the foot of the table with a film projector in front of him and a portable movie screen across the room. "Edgar, what are we doing—watching home movies from your last California vacation?"

"Good evening, Mr. President. No, this doesn't involve any vacation. It involves our discussion after the Democratic Convention when Vice President Humphrey selected Senator Kennedy—and then abandoned your battle against communism. When we last met, you enlisted the FBI's help in protecting the integrity of the presidency from two quislings, and you suggested that the end of October was the appropriate time for me to bring you what we have on Senator Kennedy. I'm prepared to proceed with that request now."

LBJ heaved a sigh. "Jesus, Edgar, we're about to announce a possible settlement in Vietnam. As you know, we've worked the whole month on this."

"I know, sir. The CIA director has kept me apprised. Congratulations on your diplomatic victory. My purpose here is to help you insure that America chooses a successor who will battle the communist threat with the same vigor and resolve you have shown so nobly. May I continue?" LBJ walked over to his Cabinet chair and took a seat. Hoover nodded to FBI Deputy Director Deek DeLoach, who switched off the lights. A few moments later, the image that projected on the screen, in grainy black-and-white, shocked Johnson. The film depicted a readily identifiable blonde woman performing oral sex on a man whose face was just out of camera range.

"What the hell is this all about?" Johnson demanded.

"Mr. President, this is surveillance film we took at the home of Miss Marilyn Monroe shortly before her suicide. Although her male partner's face is turned from the camera, I think you will recognize his features if you study him." Hoover was right: the man receiving fellatio appeared to be Robert F. Kennedy.[10]

"Edgar, turn this shit off." Hoover stopped the projector, and Deek turned on the lights. "What the hell am I supposed to do with this?" LBJ asked the director.

"Respectfully, don't you think the American people should know the type of hypocritical degenerate that Mr. Humphrey selected, who could one day sit in the Oval Office if he is not stopped?"

"Listen, I can't use this movie against Bobby. First, how do we explain getting it? Second, America would never see it. Do you think Walter Cronkite's gonna play it on the *CBS Evening News* tomorrow night?"

"No, but in the right hands, the media and public will know it exists, and Senator Kennedy will be hard-pressed to deny it. There are reliable patriots in the press who will disseminate the truth of his behavior in a most effective manner."

"If people learn that Bobby got a blow job from Marilyn Monroe, with his luck, his goddamn poll numbers will go up, not down. The only people who'll find this offensive are the blue-haired old ladies already voting for Nixon. Forget it. This is no good."

Hoover reached into his briefcase, removed a gusset file, and walked over to LBJ. "Perhaps his relationship with Miss Monroe might create some sort of fantasy fascination around his behavior, but I suspect what's in this file will negate any positive aura around his cavorting with a movie star." Hoover handed the gusset to LBJ, who reached in and pulled out a stack of documents and photographs. After seeing the first picture on the top of the pile, the president uttered a spontaneous comment without examining any additional ones:

"*Holy shit.*"

McCarthy Supporters for Humphrey Now campaign button urging Eugene McCarthy supporters to stand with the 1968 Democratic Presidential Nominee, Hubert Humphrey (Author's collection)

CHAPTER 45

My fellow Americans:

I now report very important developments in our search for peace in Vietnam. After months of deadlock in our discussions with the North Vietnamese in Paris, they have accepted our terms for peace talks with South Vietnam. As a result, I have ordered that all air, naval, and artillery bombardment of North Vietnam cease. I have reached this decision believing it will lead to a peaceful settlement of the Vietnam War. With full participation of both sides, the peace talks will begin next Wednesday, November 6.

PRESIDENT LYNDON B. JOHNSON
REMARKS TO THE NATION, OCTOBER 31, 1968, 8:00 P.M.

IRONICALLY, WHEN PRESIDENT JOHNSON DELIVERED his blockbuster announcement that promised—or threatened—to change the dynamic of the campaign in its final days, none of the three presidential contenders watched as it aired on television. George Wallace was in flight to a rally in Wilkes-Barre, Pennsylvania. Hubert Humphrey and Robert Kennedy appeared on a two-hour fundraising telethon aired across four Midwestern states, while Richard Nixon and Ronald Reagan both addressed their largest rally of the campaign at Madison Square Garden.

When HHH watched the replay of Johnson's remarks in his hotel room that night, he could barely contain his ebullience. "This will allow me to unify the Party," he told his staff excitedly. "For the first time since I became the nominee, I think we can win this damned thing—if we don't run out of time before the momentum from this news carries us over the top. Lyndon Johnson just lifted an enormous weight off of my shoulders."[1]

"Do you think the president announcing that peace talks will begin the morning after the election might look too contrived?" asked his executive assistant, Bill Connell.

"Well, yes, to the Republicans. Too damned bad—for them. Maybe with this announcement Gene McCarthy will get off his ass and endorse me properly."

"His so-called endorsement the other day was about as anemic as it gets," complained Ted Van Dyk. "First he announces that he's leaving the Senate and political life at the end of his term, and then, with only a week left in the campaign, he tosses out casually that he'll vote for you next week—and says his supporters should 'suffer' with him in doing the same thing.[2] What the hell kind of endorsement is that? I don't understand why he can't bring himself to say the magic words and urge his supporters to get behind you enthusiastically. With Nixon and Wallace as the only alternatives out there, his behavior is inexcusable."

"I learned a long time ago that Gene does things his own way. Right now I'll take whatever I can get from him. There's a big chunk of his supporters still licking their wounds and sitting on their hands, or worse—they're voting for Wallace or Nixon. In a tight election, we'll need every one of them."

Press pass issued to reporter covering Richard Nixon's campaign rally at Madison Square Garden, October 31, 1968—the night that President Lyndon Johnson announced a bombing halt in Vietnam (Author's collection)

Halfway across the country, while Nixon attended a post-rally private cocktail reception for major donors at the Sherry-Netherland hotel near Central Park, his aides Jason Roe, Wayne Paugh, and Bryce Harlow sat hunched on stools over bourbon and pretzels in a corner bar two blocks away. Campaign manager John Mitchell had recalled Jason and Wayne from the Reagan staff three days earlier to help advance the Garden rally. For this final drive, Wayne would remain with the Nixon team, and Jason would rejoin the Reagan staff in Albuquerque tomorrow.

"Well, despite Johnson's speech, we had a hell of a rally," Bryce told Wayne and Jason. "Nice job, you guys. With twenty thousand people attending, I thought we'd have our hands full of protesters. In the car ride back to the hotel, the old man said it was the biggest pro-Nixon crowd he'd ever seen—and he was surprised that he never heard a single heckler during the rally."

"We were just lucky, I guess," Jason grinned.

"Luck had nothing to do with it," Wayne laughed. "It was all Jason's doing." Wayne then explained to Bryce the system Jason set up for screening entry into the Garden. "When people arrived with general admission tickets, he funneled them into one of two lines. We sent anyone looking like a hippie or a troublemaker into the left line. Anyone looking like a Disneyland employee or a tenor with the Mormon Tabernacle Choir went to the right line. The jerks in the left line passed through a doorway, which took them down a flight of stairs, down a long corridor, and to a door manned by a few burly staffers ushering them through it. When they went out that door, they found themselves outside of the building and on the street! There, we had a team of people to intercept them when they tried to get back inside. We examined their tickets and told them there had been a problem with counterfeit tickets. We apologized and sent them to an office we rented for the day three blocks away. The inside was set up with Nixon posters and flags so it looked like a real campaign headquarters. After we kept them waiting in there for half an hour or so, an older staffer in a suit came out, apologized profusely, gave them a dummy "Golden Circle" ticket, and then told them to return to Gate 4 at the Garden for preferred seating. When they finally got back to the Garden at our specially manned Gate 4, they handed over their 'special' ticket. Our people told them, 'Oh, sorry—the Garden's full. The city fire marshal just ordered us not to admit any more people.' It was brilliant."[3]

"All in a day's work," said Jason. "Speaking of which, Johnson sure did a day's work on us tonight."

"The boss knew for days that he would pull this," Bryce said. "We have a mole working in the West Wing who warned me last week that this was coming. We started planting press stories last Tuesday that LBJ planned a bombing halt as a cynical last-minute attempt to push Humphrey over the finish line.[4] I'm surprised that, for all his savvy, until the last minute Nixon really wanted to believe that Johnson would keep his word and not do this. On the ride back in the car tonight he mocked Johnson's promise when they met at the ranch—complete with

Texas accent—'*Ah'll never let one ammo truck of those goddamn commies pass inta' South Viet-NAM tah' kill American boys.*' God, RN was pissed when LBJ called today."[5]

"How are we handling it?"

"Right now Nixon wants us to wait—he thinks there's a good chance that today's euphoria will turn to disappointment in the next forty-eight hours when voters see through this phony peace initiative.[6] But if that doesn't happen, then tonight's news will be catastrophic for us next Tuesday."[7]

"What makes him think this is a phony deal?"

"The boss heard that Thieu was going back and forth about participating in the peace talks.[8] Johnson used every threat imaginable to get him to say he'd sit with the North and the Vietcong, but now he's facing a domestic shit-storm for agreeing to it. His vice president and military leaders think he's sold out."

"What happens if Thieu backs out in the next couple of days?"

"Then the peace talks collapse, Humphrey will wet his pants, and we're back in the game." Throwing some cash on the bar, Bryce yawned. "I'm heading back to the hotel. Good job tonight, guys. Wayne—see you tomorrow. Jason—have a good trip—see you Tuesday night."

After Bryce left, Jason downed his drink in one gulp. "I've gotta go, too. My plane leaves for New Mexico before dawn." Then, leaning closer to Wayne, he whispered, "There are ways to persuade Thieu to back out of these talks."

"How?"

"Ever hear of Anna Chennault?"

"No, should I have?"

"Between now and Election Day, do everything you can to make sure you don't hear of her. Don't mention her name to anybody—no matter what you hear, and no matter who asks you." With that cryptic message, Jason stood to leave.

"Where are you going?"

"Back to the hotel to make a couple of phone calls. I have a project.

Don't ask me any more questions. And listen, if you want us both to stay out of federal prison—

"—This conversation never happened."

Before dawn the next morning, at La Guardia International Airport, Jason picked up a just-delivered copy of the Friday, November 1, *New York Times*. A three-inch black banner headline screamed across the front page:

VIET PEACE TODAY!

"This day's not quite over yet," he muttered to himself, and then boarded a plane for Albuquerque.

Campaign buttons promoting Hubert Humphrey for president and Robert Kennedy for vice president (issued in early 1968); Richard Nixon for president and Ronald Reagan for vice president (distributed at the 1968 Republican National Convention); and George Wallace for president and Curtis LeMay for vice president (issued by the 1968 Wallace-LeMay campaign) (Author's collection)

CHAPTER 46

ON FRIDAY, and with only four days before America went to the polls to choose his successor, LBJ sat at his desk in the Oval Office looking through stacks of newspaper headlines declaring his diplomatic accomplishment. PEACE! was emblazoned across the front page of every major metropolitan daily, and an overnight tracking poll showed both his own popularity, along with Hubert Humphrey's, soaring. For the first time in the 1968 campaign, Humphrey pulled ahead of Nixon in the polls and registered a three-point lead.

Although LBJ pursued his momentous announcement to cement his own legacy, an unintended byproduct was that it now helped—significantly—the Humphrey-Kennedy ticket. True, the president had refused to assist his Party's nominees since the Chicago convention, but savoring his triumph helped dilute his lingering anger toward them. Conversely, his earlier appreciation for Nixon's hard-line Vietnam support waned greatly. Nixon aided in this reversal by funding a barrage of television commercials depicting demolished Vietnamese cities, with RN's recorded voiceover promising to rectify all of LBJ's war "mistakes." This angered Johnson,[1] but not nearly as much as the GOP nominee's behavior over the last week. As LBJ neared a peace deal with North and South Vietnam, Nixon launched a preemptive media offensive by suggesting that any forthcoming bombing halt announcement was a contrived attempt to boost Humphrey.[2] LBJ's growing fury with Nixon in these final days of the campaign made a Johnson-Humphrey rapprochement easier. Besides, with the bombing halt now ordered, a peace conference beginning in a few days, and the promise of American GIs returning home soon, the once vast chasm between LBJ's Vietnam policies and those of the Humphrey-Kennedy ticket became transposable.

In the vernacular of the intelligence community, Dick Helms* was a good spook.

His spying career began during World War II with the Office of Strategic Services (OSS). After the war, and with the creation of the CIA, Helms joined the agency. Over the next twenty years, he moved up the management chairs during four presidential administrations until LBJ named him director in 1966.

Helms may have attended more White House meetings in the two

---

* Richard Helms (1913-2002) served as director of the Central Intelligence Agency from 1966 to 1973.

weeks leading up to the bombing halt decision than he had in the last two decades. When he and Secretary of State Dean Rusk arrived there to see the president on Saturday morning, November 2, given the frequency of their recent visits, nobody thought their arrival unusual.

A secretary ushered both men into the Oval Office, where they found LBJ still buoyed by the press and polling data from the last thirty-six hours. The president greeted his advisers cheerfully as they entered, but the jauntiness in his voice didn't last.

"Mr. President," Rusk said gravely, "this morning President Thieu called our ambassador in Saigon and stated that he will not participate in next week's meeting with the North Vietnamese. Thieu also issued a simultaneous public statement of withdrawal from these negotiations. He told Ambassador Bunker that he faced a coup d'état if he joined these talks, and that Vice President Ky threatened a political and military revolt unless he withdrew."[3]

LBJ rose from his desk with dark fury in his eyes. "Just yesterday that lying bastard gave me his word he'd attend."

"Sir," Helms said, "that's not all. We have intercepted cable traffic and telephone calls to and from Thieu's office. It appears that the Nixon campaign contacted Thieu and other high-level South Vietnamese officials and urged them to boycott the talks. This contact promised that Nixon will demand tougher terms on North Vietnam if he wins on Tuesday. Thieu told the caller this would quell the threat to his presidency caused by his agreeing to participate."[4]

"Who's responsible for this?" Johnson demanded. "This is goddamn treason, and I bet Nixon's behind it personally."[5]

"Our intercepts show the contact is Mrs. Anna Chennault—"

"Who the hell is she?" Johnson interrupted angrily.

"She's Chinese, a naturalized American citizen and the widow of General Claire Chennault—he led the *Flying Tigers* squadron in World War II."[6]

"I know who he was, but what's his wife's connection to Nixon?"

"When the general died, she took over his international business affairs and maintains all of her professional and personal contacts throughout the Orient. She's active in various Asian-Republican organizations. This year she's heading a group called Concerned Asians for Nixon, and she co-chairs Women for Nixon. She's raised about a quarter-million dollars for the Nixon campaign—mostly Chinese money. She is also very close to South Vietnamese Ambassador Bui Diem."[7]

LBJ slammed a newspaper down on his desk. "Do you know what this means?" he shouted. "Every fucking newspaper in America tomorrow will say there's no peace agreement—people won't know what to think. This will throw the election into chaos.[8] I want to catch these bastards in the act. Get Hoover and tell him I want round-the-clock physical and electronic surveillance on all of them—Nixon, Chenault, that ambassador friend of hers, and the entire South Vietnamese Embassy.[9] Is there any way we can connect Nixon to this directly?"

"We intercepted a call between Thieu and Mrs. Chennault. He asked if Nixon knew about this. She told him no, but then she said "our friend in New Mexico does.'"

"Who's the friend?"

"That is still unknown, but curiously, Governor Reagan's plane was in Albuquerque yesterday."[10]

"I want the CIA and FBI to check every telephone record and see if Reagan or any of his staff called Chennault. These Republicans are trying to delay this war for political reasons, and if we catch them in the act, I'll order the attorney general to convene a grand jury and we'll indict them. Dean, you call our ambassador in Saigon and tell him I said to lean on Thieu to cooperate—and lean hard. Tell Thieu if he doesn't change his mind fast, and if Humphrey wins the election, he'll be up shit creek for keeps. A coup will be the least of his worries."[11]

Jabbing an index finger angrily, Johnson snapped at his two advisers. "I need you both to get on this—*now, goddamn it.*"

After Rusk and Helms left, LBJ paced his office in thought for a few minutes. Finally, he buzzed his appointments secretary, Jim Jones. "Jim, tell Lady Bird and the Secret Service we're heading to Texas. I want to leave about five o'clock this afternoon with as little notice as possible. Make no statement to the press about it."

"Yes, sir. Are we going to the ranch?"

"No, to Houston. And it will be a quick turnaround. Tell Colonel Thornhill he'll have Air Force One on the ground for about ninety minutes, and then we're flying back to DC."

"What's in Houston tonight?"

"A big *fuck you* to Richard Nixon."[12]

"Is John Connally coming?"

Hubert Humphrey and Robert Kennedy sat on the stage of the Houston Astrodome, with tens of thousands of cheering fans surrounding them at the indoor rally. As the preliminary speeches of state officials wrapped up, HHH leaned over and asked Senator Ralph Yarborough if he had any last-minute indication whether John Connally, the Texas governor who had not yet endorsed the ticket, would attend.[13]

"No word yet, Hubert." Ralph told him. "You know that Big John and I don't get along, so I'd be the last person to know anyway."

"I phoned him three times over the weekend, but he never returned my calls. I begged his chief of staff to get him here. If we don't carry Texas on Tuesday, Lyndon might as well hand the White House key to Nixon right now."

As a choir from a local college sang a medley of patriotic songs, Hubert scanned the printed program. "You're up next, Bob," he told his running mate. "Hit it out of the park for us."

"So Connally's a no-show?" Bobby asked. When Hubert nodded, RFK said sadly, "You know, he and I served together in Jack's Cabinet. What a disappointment."

"There's nothing we can do about it. He's doing Johnson's bidding. Just keep smiling and fire up the crowd. We need them to leave here tonight with as much enthusiasm as we can generate."

As the emcee, Congressman Bob Eckhardt, stepped to the microphone to introduce RFK, a security guard walked over and handed him a note. Eckhardt unfolded the paper, beamed at Humphrey, and gave him a thumb's up signal. "Before we proceed with the program," Eckhardt told the crowd, "we have a surprise guest who has just arrived and wants to say a few words in support of our great ticket!"

As the audience cheered, Hubert beamed as he patted Bobby's arm and shouted excitedly, "Connally came through for us after all!"

"—And so, ladies and gentlemen," Eckhardt said, "please give a big Houston greeting—a big Texas welcome—to one of our own sons—

"—The president of the United States, Lyndon Baines Johnson!"

Humphrey and Kennedy both looked stunned as LBJ charged into the stadium from the northwestern tunnel, crossed the field waving to the screaming crowd, and made his way to the stage. Humphrey shouted something to Kennedy, but the comment was lost amid the deafening applause and cheers. Johnson bounded up the steps, shook hands with Eckhardt, and then turned to the microphone bank on the lectern without greeting Hubert, Bobby, or the other dignitaries. He raised his hands and signaled for silence, and then spoke to the audience—and to the rest of the country—the words that Democratic Party loyalists had waited to hear since Chicago:

> Distinguished platform guests, fellow Texans, and my fellow Americans: I return home to Texas today to proclaim that my dear friends Hubert Humphrey and Robert Kennedy are going to be the next president and vice president of the United States!
>
> They are men who have united Southerners and Northerners, laborers and teachers, city dwellers and farmers, small bankers and businessmen, and the people who make up the majority of our land.
>
> There is divisiveness in America's house this afternoon—a bitter narrowness of mind that threatens to set one American against another. Divisive men are, this very hour, trying to play upon fear and griev- ances in this country. If they succeed, then the great struggle of 100 years toward one country, toward one union, will all have been in vain.
>
> In the last few days, after working day and night, I have taken a big step toward peace. The election on Tuesday offers a choice

over which direction will we take in 1969. Unlike their opponents, Hubert Humphrey and Bobby Kennedy have worked all their lives not to generate fear, but to inspire. Unlike their opponents, they are progressive and compassionate. So I beg you—I beg you—for the sake of America, these men must become the next president and vice president of the United States! And my dear, beloved friends, I pray that on Tuesday, Texas will lead the way!

And now, it is my high honor and privilege to present to you the next president and vice president of the United States, my friends and your friends, and the friends of people all over the world, Hubert H. Humphrey and Robert F. Kennedy![14]

"You know, Lyndon, that may have been one of your finest hours."

As the presidential motorcade raced down a dark Houston freeway to the airport, Lady Bird Johnson leaned over and kissed her husband on the cheek. "After all you've been through with them, especially with Bobby over the years, you showed tremendous grace tonight. I'm very proud of you."

"I was surprised at how emotional it was. I had to fight tears when I embraced Hubert", LBJ said. "Of course, Hubert was crying—I expected that from him. He's always been sentimental."[15]

"He has a warm and tender heart, dear—and he's always loved and respected you."

"I wasn't prepared to see Bobby Kennedy choke up with tears when I put my arm around him."

"I don't think there was a dry eye there. I saw reporters wiping their eyes."

"Bobby hugged me back and thanked me—*really* thanked me. By God, I think he actually meant it. Maybe that shooting changed him. Hell, maybe this year's changed all of us. That boy may surprise us and wind up a hell of a vice president after all. One thing's for sure—he'll help stiffen Hubert's spine. Bobby's tough. He'll do for Hubert what I did for Jack."

"What made you decide to do it?"

"A lot of things. This damn war has divided everyone. I never wanted to be a president sending boys to die in some God-forsaken jungle swamp. Before Vietnam, we passed my Great Society program. That's why I wanted this job—to be a builder and a healer. I wanted the Great Society as my epitaph—Medicare, Medicaid, the War on Poverty, aid to education—all of it. When I signed those bills, I thought the Great Society would grow into a permanent part of American life. I realize now that if Nixon wins, he'll destroy my life's finest work. He'll wake up in the White House every morning and figure a way to slash funding for each of my programs. It would be a terrible thing for me to sit by and watch him starve my Great Society to death, because when it dies, I'll die, too.[16] Besides, if Humphrey loses, Democrats will blame the loss on me, and future historians will call it a complete repudiation of my administration."[17]

"What are you going to do with the information about Mrs. Chennault?"

"Nothing. When I told Hubert about it in the back room before we left tonight, he exploded in rage. He wanted to denounce Nixon publicly as a traitor. I told him no—we can't prove it, and we'd have to disclose all of our wiretaps to reveal it.[18] So we have to just let it go."

Lady Bird took her husband's hand. "You gave a beautiful speech tonight, darling. I hope every person in America gets a chance to see it."

Lady Bird Johnson got her wish.

Millions of Americans did see on the TV news her husband's Astrodome speech, especially the Johnson-Humphrey-Kennedy lovefest. One of them watched it from his basement recreation room at 4936 Thirtieth Place in Northwest Washington, DC.[19] After seeing LBJ's ringing endorsement of both Democratic nominees, he picked up the phone and called his deputy, Cartha DeLoach.

"Deke," he said, "come right over."

Fifteen minutes later, DeLoach arrived and met his chief in the caller's living room. "The president has gone wobbly on us," J. Edgar Hoover told Deke. "It looks like he cares more about pleasing that crowd of college professors than he cares about the security of this nation. We have a responsibility to save America from a political and moral disaster—and save the president from his own foolishness." Pointing to an open file containing photographs and documents Hoover brought to show LBJ in the Cabinet Room a few days earlier, along with the Marilyn-RFK surveillance film, he told his trusted aide, "I think it's time we air out this musty closet."

"I understand, sir. Shall I use the usual source?" As Hoover nodded affirmatively, DeLoach picked up the file and then left to perform his task.

Hoover poured himself a drink and then settled into his recliner. "Oh, Mr. President," he chuckled as he rocked a snifter in his hand, swirling the brandy inside to warm it, "you aren't the only one in this town with an October Surprise."[20]

1968 Robert Kennedy campaign button referencing the memory of his assassinated brother, President John F. Kennedy (Author's collection)

CHAPTER 47

WHEN IT CAME TO THROWING political Molotov cocktails, Drew Pearson was an equal opportunity arsonist.

The muckraking journalist, who inaugurated the *Washington Merry-Go-Round* newspaper column in 1932, knew no political loyalties when it came to exposing or humiliating powerful people fixed in his crosshairs.[1] As historian Richard Norton Smith noted, sixty million Americans began their day with his column, which outstripped every competitor.[*] By the late 1960s, with some 650 newspapers carrying his byline, *Time* magazine named him America's best-known columnist.[2]

When Pearson put his lash to public figures, they felt the sting. President Franklin Roosevelt called him "a chronic liar."[3] In the midst of World War II, General George Patton told aides he wanted to hang him for an unfavorable disclosure.[4] General Douglas MacArthur sued Pearson for defamation but later dropped the suit when Pearson threatened to publish MacArthur's love letters to his mistress.[5] He drove one Cabinet member to instability and suicide;[6] a US senator suffered a fatal

---

[*]   Richard Norton Smith (foreward): Drew Pearson, Peter Hannaford (editor), *Washington Merry-Go-Round: The Drew Pearson Diaries, 1960-1969* (Lincoln: Potomac Books, 2015), ix.

stroke after reading an unfavorable column,[7] and another, Senator Joseph McCarthy, kneed him in the groin and slapped him to the ground in a nightclub restroom.[8] When Pearson alleged on an ABC news show that Senator John F. Kennedy's best-selling book, *Profiles in Courage*, was ghostwritten, Kennedy threatened to sue ABC and him unless the network issued a retraction (it did).[9] As Pat Buchanan later noted, Pearson "trafficked in scandals other columnists would not touch."**

Perhaps one reason Pearson drew such ire is that he wouldn't pass up a good story on grounds of limited or poor corroboration. As his protégé and later *Washington Merry-Go-Round* successor Jack Anderson noted, truth for Drew Pearson "'was often a subjective matter.' When forced to choose between publishing a story that was accurate and one that damaged [his subject], Pearson did not hesitate" to publish it.[10] Anderson said Pearson had "a Machiavellian toughness that did not shrink at using blackmail and bribery to further his goals. He put eavesdropping waiters and chauffeurs on his payroll, bribed a Navy clerk to leak classified documents, and ordered an assistant to break into the desk of a prominent Washington attorney to search for incriminating financial records. He . . . waged unconditional war on his enemies[.]"[11]

During the final hours of the 1968 presidential campaign, with LBJ's bombing halt and peace conference announcement—and President Thieu's later repudiation of these talks—Americans faced chaotic uncertainty: had we achieved peace in Vietnam, or did bloody war persist? Short of a ballistic missile attack, it appeared inconceivable that any topic could replace this question in the national consciousness on Monday, November 4—the day before voters elected the thirty-seventh president of the United States.

Yet on that morning, on the front pages of 650 American newspapers, Drew Pearson blew Vietnam off the headlines when he detonated his nuclear device.[12]

** Patrick J. Buchanan, *The Greatest Comeback: How Richard Nixon Rose from Defeat to Create the New Majority* (New York: Crown Forum, 2014), 143.

"Miss Shaw, this is Senator Kennedy calling. Let me speak to Mrs. Kennedy, please."

Maud Shaw, the longtime nanny for Caroline and John F. Kennedy Jr. answered the phone at Jacqueline Kennedy's 1040 Fifth Avenue apartment in Manhattan. "I'm sorry, senator, but she's gone. She and the children left last night. She told me to pack their bags."

"Oh, Christ—where did they go?"

"Greece."

"Greece? Are you kidding me?"

"No, sir. Last night after dinner, Mr. Drew Pearson called for her. She was on the phone with him for a minute or two. When she hung up, she looked white as a sheet. She put in a call to Mr. Onassis in Greece and then told me to pack for the children. The driver took them to the airport late in the evening. Mr. Onassis chartered a private jet for her." Pausing to wipe away a tear, Miss Shaw continued, "Senator, I've never seen her like this, not even after the president's death. When she hung up from Mr. Pearson, she started yelling that she hates America—that America's a country that kills and hurts Kennedys, and she doesn't want her children to live here because they might be the next victims.[13] I didn't know what it was all about until I saw the morning newspaper. I—I'm sorry, senator. I don't know what else to say."

Bobby's face tightened in anger. "When you hear from her, please tell her to call me right away. I must speak to her."

Hanging up the phone in his hotel bedroom, Bobby rejoined his campaign aides. "She's gone," he told them, "and I can't get ahold of her. I don't know when—or if—I'll hear back."

"Bob, we've got to move on this," said Press Secretary Frank Mankiewicz, a rising urgency in his voice. "Here's the final draft. We need this out in the next few minutes. The reporters downstairs are howling. We need this approved right away." Bobby walked over to the couch, put on his glasses, and read silently:

CITIZENS FOR HUMPHREY-KENNEDY

FOR IMMEDIATE RELEASE

Monday, November 4, 1968, 8:30 a.m. (Eastern)

Senator Robert F. Kennedy (D-NY), the Democratic vice presidential nominee, issued the following statement in response to Drew Pearson's *Washington Merry-Go-Round* column published this morning:

"The habitual lies and reckless smears of Drew Pearson continue. This is another example of the lengths to which he will go in his current efforts to vilify and defeat me.[14]

"I absolutely and categorically deny his allegation that I have had a sexual relationship with Mrs. John F. Kennedy. This slander on President Kennedy's memory and on his widow's reputation is unforgivable. He has inflicted incalculable injury on her, on her children, on my own wife and children, and on our entire family. His viciousness will not go unchallenged.

"I have instructed my attorneys to file a multi-million dollar libel and defamation suit against Mr. Pearson, his syndicate, and every newspaper that carried this malicious falsehood. I have ordered that this action commence unless Mr. Pearson issues a public retraction and apology by 3:00 P.M. today.

"If Mr. Pearson is attempting to influence tomorrow's election with this outrage, I trust the American people will see this for what it is—a desperate smear by a cruel man—and reject it. Mr. Pearson is the same man that President Franklin D. Roosevelt labeled, correctly, 'a chronic liar.' This is the same man who accused President Kennedy of having his best-selling book, *Profiles in Courage*, ghostwritten—and then he retracted the claim long after he inflicted the damage to President Kennedy's reputation and honor.

"Finally, I call on Mr. Nixon and Governor Reagan to condemn Mr. Pearson and his last-minute character assassination designed to influence this election."

Bobby inked a few minor changes in his tight, cramped handwriting. Handing the paper back, he instructed Frank, "Release it."

"They want you to come down and make a statement in person."

"Forget it." Then, turning to campaign manager Fred Dutton, he instructed, "Cancel my public schedule for the rest of the day."

"We can't do that, Bob," Fred protested. "For Christ sake, it's the last day of the campaign! We can't cancel now. We have three rallies today, and then we need to meet Humphrey in Los Angeles for tonight's telethon. You can't go into hiding. If you do that, everyone will believe it's true. You've got to stare this down now or you'll regret it the rest of your life."

"The goddamn press won't cover anything I say unrelated to Jackie, and they'll swarm every event and shout questions about this. Why should I let that image lead off every news report on our last campaign day?"

"Because if you don't, you'll mire the last campaign day with the bulletin 'Kennedy in Hiding.'"

"All right—fine. I'll go down and face the bastards. Frank, don't pass out the statement until after I speak, but have our people Teletype copies of it right now to every newspaper, radio, and TV station on our call list."

"Got it," Frank replied, and left the room to circulate the release.

As Bobby slid on his jacket, Ted Sorensen approached him and whispered, "We both went to law school. Remember what they taught us in torts class—when a plaintiff files a defamation or libel lawsuit, *truth* is a complete defense."

"Fuck it," Bobby growled angrily as he banged his fist into the palm of his other hand. "Do you think the old prick is bluffing?"

"Maybe, but how far do you want to test him? My guess is that he went to print with innuendo and rumors from unnamed people. No responsible person would attach his name to this allegation. If he did, Pearson would have printed it."

"What if Hoover or Jimmy Hoffa*** is behind this?" Bobby asked, with concern now infiltrating his demeanor. "That means there could be surveillance photos or recordings."

"Then you may have a serious problem."

"It doesn't matter. If he claims he has any proof, we'll deny it. Everyone knows photos and recordings can be faked."

"I think people will want to give you—and especially Jackie—the benefit of the doubt. It would help to get a statement from her."

"It would help if I could get ahold of her. She's with that Greek bastard by now. I won't be able to get through to her—he'll see to that. I've hated him since the first time I met him."

Pierre Salinger entered from an adjoining bedroom. "Bob, Ethel's on the line. She wants to talk to you—now. She told me she didn't want to hear any excuses." Bobby looked around the room and saw his aides avoiding eye contact with him.

"I'll take it in the bedroom," he said quietly, and then stepped inside and closed the door.

"Ethel, I'm sorry we have to deal with this. Tell the children it's not true."

"I've already told them that, but just because you're lying to them, don't think you can lie to me. Maybe you're used to seeing Kennedy wives pretend away these things, but I won't—not anymore. You're just like your brothers—maybe worse—and what kills me is your mother really thinks you're the choirboy in the family. I've suspected for years that you've been cheating with your little groupies,[15] but now you've graduated to doing it with your own family. I feel sick to my stomach just thinking about this."

*** James Riddle Hoffa (1913-1975), president of the International Brotherhood of the Teamsters from 1958-1961. As attorney general, RFK headed the so-called "Get Hoffa" squad that led to Hoffa's lengthy prison sentence.

"Will you let me explain? I've—"

"—I don't need an explanation," she shouted. "Save your breath. If you're only worried about bad publicity, then have no fear. I'll go along with the denials for the sake of our kids, but I'm not stupid, and don't insult me by saying it's all a lie."

"Ethel, I—"

"—When we go and vote tomorrow, I'll hold your hand, I'll smile for the cameras, and I'll stand by you when you deny all this. But don't you dare tell me it's not true. I've known for a long time. And I don't want to see that two-faced bitch ever again. I never faulted her for cheating on Jack, given what he did to her.[16] But now she's attacked my children and their home, and you're as guilty as she is."

"Please, just let me—"

"Oh, and by the way, if you and Hubert lose tomorrow because of this, I'll be sorry for him. He's a good man and deserves to be president. Right now I couldn't care less what happens to you."

Click.[17]

That morning, on Bryant Street—a low-income blue-collar neighborhood in San Francisco's Mission District—Helen Kleupfer, a longshoreman's widow, opened the front door and picked up her copy of the *San Francisco Chronicle.* After pouring a cup of tea, she sat to read the morning edition. When she saw the Pearson story, disbelief set in. The sixty-year old Irish-Catholic widow and her entire family revered the Kennedys. Like most Irish-Catholics in her neighborhood, two framed photographs hung in the living area of her cramped flat: one of Pope Paul VI and the other of President John F. Kennedy. She called her older sister Della Glover, sixty-seven, a spinster living in a small apartment in nearby Daly City. Like Helen, Della was Irish, Roman Catholic, adored the Kennedy family, and always voted the straight Democratic ticket.

"Della, did you see this thing about Jackie and Bobby today?"

"I just turned on the TV—it was on the news. He came on and said it's all a lie. He looked very angry."

"I think it's disgraceful that they publish a story like this, after all that family has suffered."

"I can't believe they'd put out a filthy story like that where poor Ethel and her kids could see it. They have about ten children?"

"Eleven—one's due next month."

"The Kennedys are good Catholics—their mother Rose goes to Mass every morning, and President Kennedy was a saint. I don't believe Bobby would ever do anything like that."

"I don't either—but who knows? After all they've been through, I can't imagine the pain and emptiness they felt. I remember both of them at the funeral. She was so dignified—so brave, and with those small children. She had to be strong for them. Bobby looked like a little boy—so lost and hopeless. I wanted to see someone just hug him and let him cry on their shoulder. Maybe they needed each other to get through that horrible time—who knows?"

"But if he did have an affair with her—if he could do that against his beautiful wife and all their children, I don't think I'd want anything more to do with him." Then after lighting her fourth Bel Air cigarette of the morning, Della asked her younger sister, "So, when you vote tomorrow, what are you going to do?"

"The same thing you'll do—give him the benefit of the doubt."

Taking a puff, Della changed the channel on her television to her favorite soap opera. "My programs are starting, so I'd better go. But you're right—

"—I'd rather give the benefit of the doubt to Bobby Kennedy," Della replied, "than give the country over to Tricky Dick."

Anti-George Wallace campaign button depicting the former Alabama governor as one who threatened to run his car over antiwar hippie protesters, and his vice presidential running mate, General Curtis LeMay, as a trigger-happy nuclear weapons enthusiast (Author's collection)

CHAPTER 48

"HEY, JA-NEEN, what do you think about Bobby Kennedy and Jackie?"

With that question, the second-worst media nightmare of the Wallace presidential campaign happened on Press Secretary David Azbell's watch. In fairness, neither one was his fault.

The first slipup came a month earlier, on October 3, when Wallace introduced his vice presidential nominee, retired Air Force General Curtis LeMay, the former US Air Force chief of staff and commander of the Strategic Air Command, at a packed news conference. The LeMay choice had an air of personal awkwardness: during World War II, Wallace served as a lowly B-29 bomber crew sergeant under General LeMay's theater command.[1]

An hour before the VP announcement, David sat down with the brusque, cigar-chomping general—nicknamed "Bombs Away LeMay" for saying a few years earlier that the solution to beating the communists in Vietnam was to "bomb them back into the Stone Ages."[2]

"Now, general," David cautioned, "as you know, Governor Wallace has pledged not to use nuclear weapons in Vietnam—you both agree they're not necessary for victory. But when you go downstairs to meet those media jackals, they're gonna try and trap you by asking questions like, 'Would you use them if America faced annihilation?' Don't take the bait—just tell them that under President Wallace, our military will be so strong that we won't need to use nuclear weapons. Whatever you do, *don't say you'd use nukes*."[3] LeMay grunted his assent and said he understood.

Half an hour later, in the number three ballroom of the Pittsburg Hilton hotel, George Wallace stepped before a large bank of microphones: "I am extremely pleased to present to you my vice presidential running mate, General Curtis LeMay."[4] After that, it took seven minutes for the historic event to unravel.[5] As David predicted, the first question to LeMay came from Jack Nelson of the *Los Angeles Times:* "What is your view on the use of nuclear weapons?" The man used to giving orders, not following them, answered as he pleased:

"You know, we seem to have a phobia about nuclear weapons, when in fact they can actually be very efficient. They horrify the public just because of propaganda. The world won't end if we explode a nuke. In the 1940s and 1950s, we did twenty-four nuclear bomb tests at Bikini Atoll. Guess what? The fish are back in the lagoons; the coconut trees are growing coconuts; the guava bushes have fruit on them; the birds are back. Everything is back to normal—except for the land crabs. They're a little bit 'hot,' so there's a question about whether you should eat them. But rest assured that the rats are bigger, fatter, and healthier than ever before."

David's eyes met Wallace's—and the governor looked stricken. Elbowing into the picture, Wallace leaned into the microphones and assured everyone, "Now, just to clarify, General LeMay doesn't advocate the use of nuclear weapons. He's against them, just like I am." However, instead of taking his cue to shut up, LeMay charged ahead:

"Of course I prefer not to use them. But if they're necessary to win a war, I would use anything—including nuclear weapons."

Again, Wallace tried to mop up the mess by pleading with the reporters, "All General LeMay is saying is that if the security of the country depended on using such a weapon, then he'd do it. But we both agree we can win in Vietnam without using nuclear weapons."

"Governor," David called out in a stage whisper, "it's time to go." Wallace placed a hand on his running mate's shoulder to steer him offstage, but LeMay again swallowed the microphones. "I know you reporters will misquote me," he predicted, "and make me look like a drooling idiot whose only solution to any problem is to drop atomic bombs all over the world. I assure you I'm not."[6]

From that moment until Election Day, the steadily increasing polling strength the Wallace campaign had enjoyed all year began sliding.[7]

LET THE PEOPLE SPEAK George Wallace 1968 campaign button (Author's collection)

One month later, with General LeMay safely shuffled off to Southeast Asia on a "fact-finding" mission, David and his deputy Lilith James spent the last seventy-two hours leading up to Election Day with almost no sleep. They handled press and speech logistics, background briefings, and ran interference with other campaign staff in the seemingly endless rounds of media interviews and public events crammed into the final stretch.

Now, on Election Day, November 5, 1968, a momentary distraction created another potential media train wreck.

As Wallace exited Clayton's Barbour County Courthouse (where he once served as a trial judge) after casting his ballot, he shook hands and signed autographs for the hundreds of well-wishers gathered outside. While he greeted his fans, campaign aide Charlie Snider waved David and Lilith over to confer on the schedule for tonight's final rally at Garrett Coliseum. With David's back turned away momentarily from the traveling press collected behind a rope line, a campaign hanger-on, Ja-Neen Welch, walked by the gaggle.

Ja-Neen Welch—the ex-model and ex-local beauty pageant winner—told everyone she was the actress who played "Miss Dodge Rebellion" in a popular national television marketing campaign (in truth, she merely imitated that actress for a local Dodge dealership's TV commercials).[8] Dressed in skin-tight "hot pants," cowboy boots, and a low-cut blouse with plenty of exposed cleavage, she passed around the plastic buckets for the donation pitch at Wallace rallies: "The Wallace rebellion wants youuuuuu…!" she cooed into the microphone, and the fives, tens and twenties filled the container quickly as she bounced through the crowd scooping up the cash.[9]

"Hey, Ja-Neen," a photographer called to her as she walked by the assembled reporters, "what do you think about Bobby Kennedy and Jackie?"

Ja-Neen liked the attention of having the press asking her opinion on a matter of national interest, so she offered it: "I don't see anything wrong with them having sex. Running for president is a very stressful job, and a man in that position needs a good woman who'll give him good lovin'. If Ethel's not takin' care of business and Jackie is, who are we to judge if Bobby gets a little honey on his stinger?" Enjoying the reaction she received to her frank insights, Ja-Neen continued without embarrassment: "Now you take Governor Wallace. I do for George what Jackie does for Bobby. At the end of a long campaign day, I go into his room every night for a few hours and make love to him. He's the nervous type, and sometimes he won't even take his coat off when we're making love, he's in such a hurry. Now, if I was his wife, I could calm him down and make him the best lover you ever saw!"[10]

The reporters stared at each other in disbelief and then erupted in howls of laughter. One asked teasingly, "So when will you be announcing the wedding date?"

"Well, I guess now is as good a time as any. We'll be married between the election and the inauguration. . . ."[11]

On the other side of the parking lot, as Charlie conferred with David, Lilith glanced over and saw the oversexed cowgirl talking to the pack. "David," she interrupted, and nodded her head toward Miss Rebellion engaging the press.

"Oh my God," David said in horror, and then grabbed Lil's arm and dragged her through the crowd trying to reach the still-talkative Ja-Neen. "I'll get her the hell out of there," David told his deputy as they scrambled toward her. "You find out what she was telling them."

"Come on, Ja-Neen," David said, seizing her hand and pulling so hard that he almost yanked her out of her cowboy boots. "We need everyone back on the buses."

"Thanks for the insights, Ja-Neen," a grinning reporter yelled, as more gales of laughter bathed David, who escorted his nightmare away from the scene.

After David deposited Ja-Neen into the custody of the scheduling director, he hurried back to Lilith. "What was she telling them?" he asked nervously.

"What do you think?"

"Damn. All right—listen—I'll ride back on the press bus and try to make this go away. You ride with the governor and brief him in case he gets hit with any questions later."

"Oh, thanks. Why do I get the short end of this stick?"

"Because the governor's a gentleman. When he hears the news coming from a lady, he won't say what he would say if I tell him."

As the entourage prepared to leave, Lilith asked Wallace if she could ride with him back to the house. "Sure, Miss Lil, climb in," he told her, and they both slid into the sedan's rear seat.

Once the motorcade pulled away, Lilith briefed the governor on Ja-Neen's indiscretion. "Oh, my goodness," he gasped. Then, looking humiliated, he told her, "I'm sorry you had to be the one to tell me this. You know, since Lurleen died in May, I've been under such a strain. Watching my darling waste away was something I don't wish on anyone. With the campaign on top of that, I—"

"Governor, please," she interrupted in a comforting voice. "I'm not judging you. In fact, how could I? You don't know it, but I went through a similar experience two years ago with my fiancé. I saw what cancer does to someone you love—and I know what the dying process does to those of us left behind to cope with it. Anyway, David's taking care of this with the press. They were all laughing at her—I don't think anyone took her seriously."

George lowered his head. "Thank you for that. I appreciate your understanding." Then, straightening up, he told her, "Once we get back, tell David to send that woman home—right now. And tell the Secret Service to keep her away from us—she's erratic and she's become a security concern. They'll understand."[12]

"I'll do it as soon as we arrive."

"Thank you, Miss Lil—and thank you for not being too disappointed in your old governor."

"Sir, you are not old," she said with a soft smile. "In fact, that's probably why we're having this conversation—if you *were* old, this wouldn't be an issue!"

The car pulled into the driveway of Wallace's home, a modest one-story ranch-style house. "Well, young lady," George said as he stepped from the car and held out his hand to assist his passenger, "let's go on inside and see if we can make a little history tonight."

NBC News reporter's identification badge worn at the network studio, New York City, election night, November 5, 1968 (Author's collection)

CHAPTER 49

AT 2:00 A.M. ON ELECTION MORNING, as the country slept, an exhausted Robert Kennedy did the same. The relentless ten-week vice presidential campaign he waged drained him physically and mentally, yet he soldiered on despite recurring (and sometimes near-debilitating) migraines. Meanwhile, when Drew Pearson's bombshell exploded the day before, the Kennedy PR machine attacked it at full throttle. In hundreds of calls to media owners and managing editors, they cried foul over the story, insisting it came from anonymous sources, rumors, gossip, and a couple of disgruntled ex-Kennedy family employees. If an outlet pushed back, their lawyers threatened suit. The offensive worked to isolate the scandal, keeping it off the network news and out of most of the non-syndicate major dailies. Beyond the one-day story, the claim of a Bobby-Jackie love nest—for now—remained confined.

When Bobby boarded his campaign plane for the final trip home, he curled up across two seats, closed his eyes, and was asleep before takeoff. Three hours later, he slept so deeply that it took a campaign aide several shakes to awaken him. "Senator," she whispered, "Mrs. Kennedy is on the radiophone for you."

"Tell her we land around six this morning," he answered groggily. "She'll need to have the kids ready so we can go vote at eight. The press will be waiting for us."

"I'm sorry, Senator, I didn't mean your wife. I meant your sister-in-law—Mrs. Jacqueline Kennedy." Bobby sat up quickly, tossed aside the blanket, and made his way aft. Before picking up the headset, he asked the two nearby crewmembers for privacy. When they moved away, he turned on the device.

"Jackie?"

"Bobby, I'm so sorry. When that horrid Mr. Pearson called and told me he was running that story, I just couldn't bear it. I wanted to get John and Caroline as far away from all of this as possible. With Jack dead, and after what happened to you in Los Angeles, I want to protect them from this ugliness. I needed to go someplace where I can shelter them"

"When are you coming back? After today, win or lose, I'll have downtime. We have to talk—I need to see you. *Please.*"

"How did Ethel react?"

"I told her it was all bullshit, and for the most part we've killed the story. We've gotten most of Pearson's sources to backtrack. It's blowing over. You shouldn't have run away. It doesn't look right. Please come back."

"I can't come back. I'm sorry to tell you this way—I married Ari this morning. We'll keep it a secret for as long as we can."

The news hit him like a sucker-punch. "Oh God, Jackie—I can't believe it. *Why would you do that?* You know how Jack felt about that son of a bitch, and how I feel about him—and how I feel about you."

"It's done. He gives me what I need now. You can't. Nobody else can."

Blinking his eyes to fight tears of anger and frustration, he told her, "This will knock you right off your pedestal."

"I'd rather be knocked off of it than left frozen on it. Anyway, I have to go. I'm praying for you and Hubert tonight—

"—Goodbye, Bobby, and good luck."[1]

Eight hours earlier, Vice President Hubert Humphrey and RFK finished their last formal campaign appearance—a live TV program where they answered the call-in questions of voters from around the country, rallied the faithful, and pleaded for a great turnout tomorrow.[2] When the show ended, they rode together to Los Angeles International Airport; from there Bobby flew home to New York, while Hubert boarded Air Force Two for his overnight flight to Minneapolis.

The race was too close to call as evidenced by the conflicting final national polls. Gallup had Nixon over Humphrey, 44 percent to 43 percent, while Harris had them in reverse—Humphrey 44 percent, Nixon 43 percent.[3] Since LBJ's bombing-halt announcement, Humphrey closed an eight-point deficit,[4] but now he feared that South Vietnam's sudden pullout from negotiations had slowed his momentum.

After landing in Minnesota on Election Day morning, Humphrey's Secret Service detail drove him to Marysville Township near his home on Waverly Lake, where he and Muriel voted. He returned home, slept until late afternoon, and then joined his staff for the evening's vigil at the downtown Minneapolis Leamington Hotel. Three television sets in the Summit Suite on the fourteenth floor allowed the candidate to monitor returns on CBS, ABC, and NBC.

"Well, Mr. Vice President," asked assistant Ted Van Dyk, "any regrets?"

"Mistakes are made in every campaign, but I think we ran a hell of a race given the obstacles thrown in our way. Let's say no regrets, only surprises—like our last-minute barrage of TV ads this final weekend. I thought we had burned through our media budget a week ago."

Ted smiled. "I'm not supposed to tell, so please keep this a secret—those TV spots came from Nelson Rockefeller."

"Rockefeller?"

"Yes. He paid for them. After last week's Al Smith dinner in New York, I dropped by the VIP reception. Rocky's wife saw me and came over. She said she noticed we didn't have many TV ads up against Nixon. When I told her we were out of money, she said she could get us some serious cash for more ads. When I asked her from where, she nodded toward Rocky and told me, 'Nelson will do it—because he and I both think Nixon's a total shit.'"[5]

Hubert shook his head in disbelief. "This is the damnedest campaign I've ever seen."

"So—what does your gut tell you about tonight?"

"The real question is whether our momentum this last week was in time to overtake Nixon. If not, then we'll come up short—excruciatingly short. I feel like my fingernails are scraping the top rung, but I don't have a grip on it. Maybe we'll make it. It's so damn close, and I'm so tired."[6]

Over the next few hours, Hubert, his family, and staff hovered over the television sets. With each updated state projection came either elation, optimism, nervousness, or resignation. Meanwhile, Hubert's numbers crunchers, Larry O'Brien and Max Kampelman, remained huddled with a dozen other staffers in a nearby room littered with telephones connected to key precincts and states.

It was after midnight when the two men emerged and pulled Hubert aside. Three states, they told him—Ohio, Illinois, and California—would determine the election. "Ohio's tough," Larry said, "but we can win without it. Dick Daley thinks Illinois will be with us, but it'll be close. Max and I think that by late tonight California will decide the whole enchilada."[7]

"With Bobby on the ticket, we have a strong shot there," Hubert said optimistically, "but it's also Nixon's home state—remember—he beat Jack Kennedy there in 1960. Gene McCarthy could've helped us a lot in California, but he didn't deliver. By the time he called into the telethon last night and gave me another half-ass endorsement, it was too late. I thought we had an understanding after Chicago, but apparently not."[8]

Muriel Humphrey, the nominee's wife, joined the men. "Well, mother," Hubert told her, "it looks like California will decide whether we move to a new house or get an extended vacation next year."

Looking quizzical suddenly, Hubert turned back to Larry. "Or maybe not—what's the split if I take California and Nixon wins Ohio and Illinois?"

"Don't ask," Larry replied.[9]

"It means the election deadlocks in the Electoral College," Max said. "Nobody will have the 270 electoral votes needed to win the presidency, so the decision goes to the House of Representatives, where we—"

"It may not get that far," Hubert said grimly. "It may not be the House that selects the next president."

Max took a sip of beer. "You're right—

"—It might be that goddamn George Wallace."

Original ticket to Humphrey Election Night Victory Party, Hotel Leamington, Minneapolis, November 5, 1968 (Author's collection)

"How's the old man holding up?"

On that final Monday campaign night, and at the same time Humphrey and Kennedy faced the Los Angeles television cameras, just across town, Richard Nixon and Ronald Reagan wrapped up their closing arguments to a national audience at their own telethon.[10] Standing offstage, Jason Roe—who had traveled with Reagan since the convention, asked Wayne Paugh how Nixon was facing the end of the long road.

"He hovers between depression, fatalism, and optimism," Wayne replied. "He's anxious about the close margin. He warned us two weeks ago that LBJ would pull some last-minute stunt. He thinks the Democrats are returning home and that the Wallace vote is hurting us. He warns everyone not to panic. Right now he's not looking for opinions—he's looking for reassurance."[11]

"Where are you guys heading after tonight?"

"The boss already voted by absentee, so we're leaving for Newark after this.[12] We'll spend tomorrow night in New York. Right now, I just want to get on that plane and sleep. What about Ronnie?"

"Back to Sacramento to drop the laundry, and then the Century Plaza hotel in L.A. for tomorrow night. We're going to—oh, oh—there goes our ride."

Jason never finished his thought. When the TV director signaled "all clear," a technician removed Nixon's and Reagan's lapel mikes, and the convoy of bodies swept toward the exit and the waiting motorcade. As they neared the cars that would take them in separate directions, Jason shook Wayne's hand and told him, "If we win tomorrow, be sure to call and congratulate me on the great job I did."

"What if we lose?"

"Then it's your fault."

Security badge worn by Nixon campaign worker Patrice Williams at the Waldorf Astoria Hotel, election night, November 5, 1968 (Author's collection)

Late that night, as the *Tricia* (RN's campaign plane named for his eldest daughter) took the candidate and his party back to the East Coast on a red-eye flight for Election Day returns, Nixon invited his staff inside his private compartment, thanking each one individually and seeming far more relaxed than the situation warranted.[13] By this time tomorrow night, America would either make him president or deny him the brass ring again. He told his aides he still thought he could win, but LBJ's bombing halt decision probably cost him three to five million votes.[14]

When Wayne visited with the boss, RN asked how Eugene McCarthy had responded to his quiet outreach. "He said that if you won, he would be very interested in accepting your UN ambassador offer. He thought that was a role where he could help. But you know, don't you, that he endorsed Humphrey tonight? He called into Humphrey's telethon."[15]

"That doesn't matter," Nixon shrugged. "A phone call to a TV program tonight isn't going to make any difference in the voting tomorrow.

What counts is that he didn't campaign in key states for Humphrey.[16] Hopefully, that will help depress enough of his voters to let us squeak past the Dems, especially in California. If we don't carry California, we'll have a hell of a time finding a path to victory." Then after jotting a few notes on his yellow legal pad, Nixon added reflectively, "You know, I'll bet Humphrey's saying the same thing to his staff right now."

By 7:00 p.m. on Election Day, the Nixon party commandeered the thirty-fifth floor of New York's Waldorf-Astoria Hotel. It would be here, sometime late tonight or tomorrow morning, that he would receive history's judgment. Suite 35H was reserved exclusively for the candidate, while the rest of his family and senior staff scattered in suites down the hall, which was crowded with bodies, tobacco smoke, and the cacophonous sounds of TVs, radios, bustling chatter, and ringing telephones.[17]

As the early returns trickled in, Nixon maintained a steady but slim lead. At midnight, Humphrey jumped ahead of him for the first time. Everyone now grew uneasy as the commentators attached a new word to Humphrey's incoming vote totals: *surge*.[18] Two hours later, Nixon regained his tenuous advantage. As the staff received and interpreted an avalanche of intelligence from key counties, they concluded the same thing his opponent determined: Ohio, Illinois, and California held the key.[19] When Ohio broke for Nixon, his staff could feel the walls rumble from the cheers in the downstairs ballroom. By three, Nixon led in Illinois, but Mayor Daley still held back his Chicago vote. John Mitchell, the campaign chairman, went on CBS News live, accused Daley of trying to rig the result, and demanded he throw in his cards. When Daley finally released his precinct totals, Nixon took Illinois.[20]

By 8:00 a.m. Wednesday morning, Nixon was agonizingly close. With Ohio and Illinois in his column, Nixon hit 261 electoral votes—only nine away from the prize. Humphrey remained frozen at 191, and Wallace, winning five states in the Deep South, held forty-six. California, with forty electoral votes, would either send Nixon to the White House, or send the election to the Democrat-dominated US House of Representatives. With seven million votes cast in the Golden State, Nixon now held a bare lead that seesawed back and forth for the last six hours, partly due to reported mechanical glitches in San Francisco and the Central Valley.

"Hey—here it comes!" Wayne shouted to the candidate and his colleagues, who stood nearby at a serving tray drinking yet another round of coffee. They rushed to the center television screen tuned to NBC News. The word "PROJECTION" flashed across the screen. Reporter Chet Huntley, seated at the anchor desk, finished reading the piece of paper thrust before him moments earlier, and then he looked into the camera at 8:17 a.m.:

"Ladies and gentlemen," Huntley intoned solemnly, "with almost 100 percent of California's precincts now reporting, and based on our exit data, NBC News projects that the winner of California's forty electoral votes is. . . ."

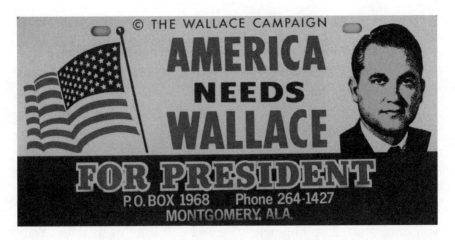

1968 campaign license plate issued by the Wallace for President national headquarters, Montgomery, Alabama (Author's collection)

CHAPTER 50

"I'VE NEVER SEEN so many reporters in one place."

Two hours after the networks called the winner in California, Lilith James peered out the window of George Wallace's Farrar Street home, tucked away in a quiet Montgomery residential neighborhood. She and Press Secretary David Azbell, along with senior campaign staff, gathered there after David notified the media that Wallace would make a statement outside his house at 10:00 a.m. After last night's rally at Garrett Coliseum, Wallace went home to sleep in his own bed (the first time in two months), while David and Lil returned to the headquarters and remained until past dawn tracking the Nixon-Humphrey vote fluctuations.

After drafting the governor's announcement, Lil and David arrived at the residence at 9:30. They found Wallace seated at his kitchen table sipping hot tea with lemon and complaining about the sore throat he developed after last night's rally. "Those folks were cheering so loudly that I had to practically shout my speech to be heard." After reviewing Lil's draft, he made no corrections. "Give me a few minutes to get ready," he told them. "I'll meet you in the foyer. And when we go out there, all I'm doing is reading this statement—and then I'm coming back inside. I'm not taking any questions. You two can handle the follow-up briefing. I want to save my voice. I may need it."

While they waited, Lil peaked out the window again. "David, have you ever seen this many reporters show up for one of his press conferences before?"

"No, but America's never had a third party campaign like this before. They're all here because of him," David said as he reached over and patted her shoulder gently, "and you helped us put him here. Ever since you came aboard, you brought style and polish to his speeches. Your words brought him from street brawler to statesman—"

"Don't exaggerate!" she interrupted with a sleepy smile.

"Okay—a statesman who likes to throw hand grenades! Seriously, you've done a remarkable job."

"I learned more from you in three months than I ever learned in four years of college and three years of grad school. You gave me this opportunity. Thank you, David." She kissed his cheek and hugged him.

David returned the hug—their first, he thought to himself, after months together. He wished it could linger, but he didn't want to cross any lines. Since she joined the campaign, he kept his growing attraction to her unspoken. She didn't know how he felt—he was sure of that. He almost dropped a hint a few times during those endless late nights, but he never did. Too many barriers in his mind separated them. She was young— almost half his age—and he assumed her beauty put her out of his league. She looked like a model on a Paris runway, and he looked like what he was—a man who abhorred exercise and enjoyed good food, good liquor, and good cigars. Besides, she talked occasionally about some boyfriend back in Canada. "Piss on Clive," he sometimes mumbled to himself when she did. "*Clive*—who the hell sticks their kid with that moniker?"

Of course, if opportunity did knock unexpectedly, those barriers would collapse—quickly. But one barrier remained unchanging, and it had a name—Mrs. Carla Azbell—his wife of twenty-five years and the mother of his two grown children. If Lil ever reciprocated his feelings—a likelihood he doubted seriously—he could never abandon his wife, no matter how intense his connection with Lil, nor how dead his marriage. He sensed that Lil would understand why he couldn't leave Carla. After all, she seemed to understand. They shared their innermost feelings with abandon, which also accentuated his intimacy deficits with Carla. He still loved his wife in his own way, but the passion they once shared fizzled years ago. More than two decades of working nights and weekends, business travel, thousands of political functions, motherhood pressures, homemaker obligations, familiarity, boredom, menopause—and all the other things that combine to suffocate matrimonial romance—took their toll on the couple. His relationship with Carla was respectful, even comfortable—like roommates and friends, but not lovers.

And then there was Lil, who saw things in David's soul that his wife never saw, or if she once had, she now dismissed as trivial or worthless. The only woman he knew that could fill the hole in his heart was unattainable.

Despite these fleeting daydreams of Lil, his protective nature toward her trumped the physical attraction. Because he never wanted to hurt her or embarrass himself, he gave no hint of his desire. If anything were to develop between them, she would need to make the first move—and probably the second, too—so scared was he of saying or doing something that would upset their relationship. That morning, when she hugged and kissed him briefly in Wallace's foyer, it may have been perfunctory to her. To him, it was sublime.

As she drew back, he heard the giggle that so endeared her to him. "I tagged you," she said, and then produced a silk handkerchief from her purse to wipe the lipstick trace from his cheek. Then, rubbing her hand across his bristly skin, she grimaced. "Ouch—when's the last time you shaved?"

"The last time I showered—I'm not even sure now—late Sunday night or Monday morning."

"No wonder we didn't carry Missouri and Kentucky yesterday!

When this press conference is over, you need to go home and clean up. That's what I did on my way over here. By the way, you didn't say if you liked my new outfit. I bought it for election night, but I never got a chance last night to run home and change into it." He stepped back and took in the view. She looked amazing in her blush-colored crepe blouse with a droopy, feminine bow beneath a moderately low neckline. The high-waisted black pencil skirt hugged every curve of her perfect hips, and between the hemline and her slingback black pumps were the best legs in Alabama—or anywhere else for his money.

"Oh, you look all right," he said, feigning nonchalance, "for someone who probably crossed the border illegally. That outfit's pretty—it might get your deportation delayed for a few extra days."

Sniffing the air around him, she replied, "At least I'll smell nice when they deport me. That's more than I can say for you. You definitely need a shave—and a shower. Sometimes I feel like your mother trying to keep you on track."

"I'm going to miss having you keep me on track when we wrap this up. When do you go back?"

"My new job starts next week at the university. I'm heading home the day after tomorrow."

"I'll let the governor know. He wants to do something for you before you leave us." Rubbing the back of his neck, David groaned, "When this thing's over today, forget the shave—I'm going home and pouring a stiff drink."

"We should have one together—we've done everything else together for months, so we should do that, too."

David eyed her suspiciously. "I thought you don't drink."

Another smile crossed Lil's face—a different smile. One he hadn't seen before—it looked, well, he wasn't sure how to describe it—*naughty?* "When I'm tired," she replied, "I do all kinds of things I wouldn't do when I'm rested."

Jesus—was that a hint? In the unlikely event it was, he asked her quickly before his nerve failed. "Well, after the press conference, do you want to come over and join me for a nightcap? I keep a small apartment for when I'm in town. It's behind my consulting offices a few blocks from here. It's nothing special."

Lil shook her head. "Nightcaps are for nighttime. This isn't nighttime. And you're right—I don't drink."

Trying to suppress the telltale redness rising in his cheeks from his obvious cue misread, he told her, "Yeah, that's what I—well, I was just—"

Lil interrupted his awkward reply. "I said I don't drink. I didn't say I don't eat. Why don't I come over and fix us breakfast?"

"Really?"

"Yes, really."

"Well, I don't know what's there. I haven't been home much. I—"

"Do you have coffee and a percolator?"

"Of course."

"Okay—I'll handle the rest."

Accompanied by several staffers, Wallace approached from down the hallway and interrupted their impromptu meal plans. "Everybody ready?" he asked.

"Sir, I just need a moment. I haven't told her yet."

"Better tell her now. I'm ready to start this thing." Wallace walked over to a hall mirror and adjusted his necktie while David led Lil to the front door. "Tell me what?" she whispered.

"I'm not handling the press briefing after his statement. You are."

"Very funny."

"It's not a joke—you're handling it. Listen, we made history last night. The world's going to watch this press conference. I discussed it with the governor. We don't want the last face of this campaign to be some twangy four-eyed redneck. We want a poised, elegant woman at the microphones—even if she does have a bizarre foreign accent. He wants you to do this, and so do I. This is your moment."

"But I'm not prepared to answer their—"

"—You're the most prepared person here. You've been in every strategy meeting, you've done most of the heavy lifting on research, you've become his chief wordsmith, and you've cleared each memo. You'll be fine."

"David, I just don't think—"

"—Listen, I know you love old movies. Did you ever see that 1930s Ruby Keeler musical, *Forty-Second Street*?"

"Yes, but—"

"Remember what the director tells the Broadway understudy after the star broke her ankle on opening night?" Feigning great seriousness, he grabbed Lil's shoulders, stared into those green eyes, and repeated the line: "*Sawyer, you're going out there a youngster, but you've got to come back a star!*"

Before giving Lil a chance for further protest, David nodded to a state trooper, who opened the front door. Into a blaze of klieg lights and flashbulbs strode Wallace confidently, followed by his senior campaign staff. David placed his hand on Lil's lower back and steered her outside with them.

"Good morning everybody," Wallace began into the jumble of microphones atop the lectern. "After I read my formal statement, my deputy press secretary, Miss James, will brief you further." With that, Wallace shared his reaction to the election results:

"When we started our third party, we had no organization and no funding. Our donations came from the working men and women all over the nation. From them we raised the money to get on the ballot in every state. We never had purse power, but we had people power.[1] These were all good people sick and tired of a government taken over by pure, brute, naked federal force, and by an out-of-control Supreme Court telling little schoolchildren they couldn't sing *America* because it has God's name in the lyrics.[2]

"Yesterday, ten million people joined our call to stand up for America. Millions more were for us, and now most of them wish they had voted their conscience. We won more popular votes, more electoral votes, and more states than any other third party campaign in history.

The two major party candidates ignored the important issues facing our country until we forced the discussion—rising taxes, inflation, welfare loafers, cutting foreign aid to our enemies, getting rid of the communists and leftists running our tax-funded universities, dismantling this dictatorial federal bureaucracy, preserving states' rights, and ending judicial activism. Now they're all talking about these issues. Listening to their speeches these last few weeks, you'd have thought there were five George Wallaces in this race instead of just one.[3] They copied us, but they couldn't steal our voters out there because the American people know the real deal from a phony.

"When the Electoral College meets on December the sixteenth to cast their ballots for the next president, forty-six of those votes will be pledged to George Wallace. With Mr. Humphrey winning California last night, neither he nor Mr. Nixon won an electoral vote majority.[4] To help break this deadlock, and before my electors vote, I will instruct them to support the candidate who meets my conditions for strengthening this Republic. I will not share those conditions with the press in advance. If one of the other candidates will commit to the reforms that millions of voters demanded yesterday, I will do all I can to help him succeed in that great cause.

"Thank you, ladies and gentlemen. Good day." Looking to his right, Wallace nodded to his deputy. He walked back inside the house, ignoring all questions shouted at him from the assembled reporters.

Stepping behind Wallace's 800-pound bullet-proof lectern[5] (the campaign transported "The Beast" from rally to rally because of constant death threats and rock-and-bottle assaults he endured), ignoring a few isolated wolf-whistles, and with David slightly behind and to her side, Lil cleared her throat and addressed the pack. "Ladies and gentlemen, I am Lilith James, deputy press secretary to the Wallace campaign. Standing next to me is our press secretary, Mr. Azbell, whom all of you know. I'll be happy to entertain any questions."

"Why isn't David answering them?" one reporter called out, evoking laughter from the gaggle. Showing no outward nerves, Lil shot back,

"We don't allow Mr. Azbell to make any public statements when he's slept in the same suit for two nights. We're concerned that such an image on TV screens might violate FCC decency regulations."

"God, I love this woman," David thought as the press howled at his rumpled expense.

The questions came with such rapidity that Lil couldn't identify their sources. "What is the legal basis that makes you think Wallace can trade away electoral votes to another candidate? Several states have passed laws making that illegal, and I'm told that a nineteenth century federal statute also suggests it can't be done."

"We have researched this issue very carefully, and it's clear that the Founders intended the Electoral College to reflect the will of its members after the fever of Election Day had passed. That's why the college meets a month after the voting. In *The Federalist 68*, Alexander Hamilton argued that *after* hearing from the people at the ballot box, the final choice of a president should go to a sober body of men capable of analyzing the needs of the country after the passions of the voters have settled down. The Founders didn't want the presidency subject to what Hamilton called 'the convulsions of the community.' The Founders wanted judgment and stability behind the final choice. This demonstrates that the Framers intended that the members of the Electoral College have a free hand.[6] We have a letter signed by over seventy law professors—Democrats, Republicans, and independents—who agree that any state or federal statute attempting to prohibit this exercise of the electors' independent judgment is unconstitutional and unenforceable."

"What can you do to compel your electors to vote the way you want if they decide to renege on their pledge to Governor Wallace?"

"Governor Wallace was very careful to select as his electors men and women of high honor. Here in the Southern states especially, honor is the coin of the realm. There is no single elector who gave their word to Governor Wallace who will renege on that pledge."

"Why should one man who is clearly a sectional candidate—after all, a huge share of his votes came from the South—choose the president for all America?"

"Calling Governor Wallace a sectional candidate is both silly and factually incorrect. Our exit data shows that almost half of his support came from labor voters in the North and West—and he earned those votes despite a vicious and dirty multimillion-dollar attack campaign from the corrupt leadership of the AFL-CIO."[7]

While Lil continued answering questions, David slipped back inside the house and joined Wallace in the study. Both men watched her flawless performance on television through the haze of their cigar smoke. "David, you were right. She needed to be the face of this campaign today. I wish I had made her the face of the campaign six months ago—I might've won this damn thing."

"I hate like hell to lose her next week. She's heading back to Toronto for her new job."

"Can't we convince her to stay? I'd sure like her help in 1970."[8]

"No, sir. I've already tried. She wants to return to her research work and her family. Plus, she left behind some boyfriend."

"What's he do?"

"He's a lawyer up there. An older guy. She says that he's pretty smart."

"Well, I don't care how smart he is. If he doesn't marry that girl, and do it soon, he's a fool. You're gonna miss her, aren't you?"

"Yes, sir, a lot."

"I don't blame you." Taking another long draw on his cigar, and studying her on his TV screen, George added, "That is one helluva woman out there. No, I don't blame you—not one goddamn bit."

An hour later, Lil knocked on David's apartment door. Opening it, he looked down at the box she carried. "No peeking—it's a surprise," she told him. "Did you make coffee?"

"No, I just got home a few minutes ago. I got waylaid by reporters."

"Well, show me the kitchen. I'll get your surprise ready."

"You need my kitchen for a surprise, eh?"

"For one of them," she smiled. "I have two. And where's your percolator? We'll need coffee for the first one." While the coffee brewed, he gave her a tour of his small apartment. Lil looked out the large living room window at the trees below. "You have a nice view from here," she told him.

"Yeah, it's great—there's nothing more romantic than looking out this window at night and watching the moon rise over the Piggly Wiggly."

Again the giggle that he loved hearing. "Nobody has ever made me laugh the way you do. I think a sense of humor is a man's sexiest attribute—far more than physical appearance."

"By that standard, I guess Jack Benny's the new Steve McQueen."

"By that standard, so are you."

She took off her coat and silk scarf and draped them on the couch. "Why don't you sit down and guard these while I'll go make the coffee and get your surprise?"

While he waited on the sofa, his thoughts raced. *Was this really going somewhere, or is she just being nice? She's dressed to kill, she called me sexy—in a Jerry Lewis sort of way—and there's a second surprise. It's possible. Oh, come on, dumb ass—you're not her type. If she knew what you were thinking she'd laugh—and then leave.* But what if this was real? If lightning struck, his Baptist upbringing guaranteed he'd feel guilty later.

But this wasn't later.

When she returned to the living room, she carried a slice of pie on a paper plate. Without diverting her eyes from his, she sauntered over and straddled his thigh, using it as a stool while lifting a bite to his mouth. "It's chocolate cream," she said in a low, sultry voice he'd never heard her use before. "You once told me this is your favorite. I hope you like it."

After swallowing, he exhaled deeply. "You know, don't you, that you're sitting on my leg."

"Am I too heavy?"

"No."

"Am I hurting you?"

"No. That's the point. I don't want to hurt you."

"The only thing about you that could hurt me is that beard stubble."

"Lil, is this really going where I think?"

"Would you like it to go there?"

"Yes—very much. But I can't imagine what you'd get out of it."

"I'd get to be with someone I respect and adore—a man who has become a part of my heart, and one I'll miss very much when I leave. I guess I'd like to take a wonderful memory with me—and also leave one behind."

"You could have any guy. I'm twice your age. I'm not exactly Cary Grant. Oh, and I'm married—and that can't change, no matter how much I might wish it otherwise. I never want you to feel hurt or used."

"I'm not looking for Cary Grant, and the age difference doesn't bother me. It's *because* you're older that I adore you. You're brilliant, witty, you have an artistic spirit, and you bring perspective to every situation. You have more energy and inner strength than anyone I know. And yes, I know you're married. I also know that relationships are more complex than they appear on paper. When I leave this weekend, you'll still be married. I respect that you don't abandon your obligations, even when they leave you unfulfilled. I know how much you care about me, and that you'd never hurt me. I'd never hurt you, either. So go take your shower and shave." She put down the plate and fork, cupped her hand behind his head, and kissed him. "When you come back," she whispered, "I promise—we won't hurt each other."

Her perfume added to the moment. *Asian cinnamon*, he thought—if such a thing existed. "Lil, I just—well—I didn't expect any of this."

"You weren't supposed to expect it. I told you it was a surprise." Lil rose from his lap and walked to the window. "Maybe I'll wait here gazing at the Piggly Wiggly until you're done. It'll create the perfect mood."

David went to the bathroom, undressed, showered and shaved so fast that he worried about slicing his throat. The *S.S. Lil* was about to sail, and if he didn't get aboard quickly, he knew this chance—or any other remotely like it—would never come again.

After slapping on some cologne, he stepped into his thick terrycloth bathrobe. Returning to the living room, he saw a trail of clothes on the floor—a coat near the sofa, a scarf in the hallway, and black pumps outside the bedroom. As he approached the partially opened door, he saw a folded skirt and blouse, nylons, a delicate nude lace bra, and black bikini panties resting atop a chair. He pushed on the door gently.

She lay on his bed, eyes closed. The white sheet covering her body displayed the contours of every mound inviting his exploration. He called her name softly—twice—but she didn't respond. The frantic final days of the presidential election campaign had caught up to her.

She was asleep.

David slumped into an empty chair and watched her in silence. Her slumber appeared to grow deeper as her chest rose and fell slowly with each peaceful breath. So many divergent feelings barraged his mind and heart, but no internal conflict existed on one point—he loved her. He knew that now. And because he loved her, if her unexpected surrender came from sleep deprivation, he wouldn't exploit her vulnerability. If she still felt this way about him later, well, maybe that was another matter.

Quietly, he retrieved a comforter from the hall closet and covered her gently. Then he dressed quietly, picked up his car keys, and slipped out the front door.

David returned to Farrar Street to help his staff handle the influx of press inquiries—and to take his mind off the biggest missed opportunity of his lifetime.

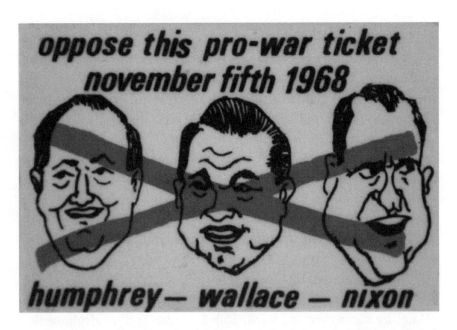

Badge worn by Vietnam War protester during the closing days of the 1968 presidential campaign (Author's collection)

CHAPTER 51

"I THOUGHT YOU'D BE COMATOSE BY NOW."

When David returned to Farrar Street, fellow Wallace aide Charlie Snider expressed surprise at his quick return. "I went home to clean up," David said. "Today's a big day. No sense missing it."

"You already missed part of it. Nixon called half an hour ago."

"Did they set up a meeting?"

"No. He invited George to New York—he also offered to fly down here and bring Reagan along, which tells me he's anxious. George suggested Nixon send an aide to meet me here in Montgomery, and then his man can carry back our message. George thought any photos of him meeting with Nixon would look like they were bartering for the presidency. He wants to handle this out of the glare of television lights."

"Do you know who's coming?"

"A couple of his guys that they said are not noticeably recognizable to the press or public. I said we'd have a driver pick them up at the airport. I'm meeting them at Chris' Hot Dog Stand in about an hour.[1] I figure that's the last place the press would stake out for a meeting that might select the next president. Want to come?"

"Sure—I've got time before I need to go home and maybe take care of some unfinished business."

Bill Jones, another senior aide, stepped from the study and interrupted them. "Humphrey's calling George right now."

"There you go, David—more history for you," Charlie said as he motioned to follow him.

"Where are we going?" David asked.

"The kitchen. A few days ago, a friendly FBI agent in the Montgomery field office came over and hooked up a speaker to the telephone line. While George is on his phone in the study, we'll hear the entire conversation in the kitchen."

"Why an FBI kitchen speaker?"

"George felt that if the election really deadlocked, both Humphrey and Nixon would call and try to cut deals. If that happened, he wanted his people to hear both sides of any conversation with them. He wants witnesses in case a screw job comes later."

When the two men reached the kitchen, Charlie signaled down the hall that they were in place. A moment later, over the speaker, they heard a click, and then this exchange:

"Hello."

"Good afternoon. Is this Governor Wallace?"

"Yes, ma'am, this is he."

"Governor, this is the White House operator. Please hold for Vice President Humphrey." A moment later, David and Charlie recognized the other voice on the line.

"Well, governor, it looks like you ended up holding a couple of aces."

"Mr. Vice President, from where I sit, I'd say my hand is more like four of a kind."

"Governor, you know there are laws on the books in several of your states requiring electors to vote for the candidate to whom they pledged originally. I know you'd like to flex your muscles here, but if any of your people vote for someone other than you when the Electoral College meets next month, we'll file lawsuits to overturn their actions."

"Is that what you called to tell me?"

"No, in fact, I called to see if we can work out something. But I also wanted you to know that I don't think your hand is a strong one."

"Well, sir, if you think I'm holding a losing hand, why don't you push in all your chips and call it? Then we'll see who wins the pot."

"I didn't call to trade poker metaphors with you. I'm calling to ask you to announce publicly that you want your electors to keep to their pledge and cast their ballots for *you.*"

"You don't need to worry about my electors keeping to their pledge. I guarantee they'll do just that—every one of them signed a pledge to vote in the Electoral College the way I tell them—and they made that pledge to me in writing before I chose them as my electors. Since these are fine Southern men and women, I can assure you they will honor their word. So if you called to threaten a lawsuit against me, I suggest you fire up your legal team."

"George, wait—no, it's nothing like that. But since we're using the metaphor, let's lay our cards on the table. When the Electoral College meets on December 16, if your electors vote for you—as I believe they must—then the election is deadlocked and the House of Representatives chooses the president.[2] With our Democratic majority there, I'll win. On the flipside, if you get your electors to vote for someone other than you, and we prevail in a lawsuit, then the House still selects the president and I get the same result. Either way, I'm the next president."

Adopting a more conciliatory tone, Humphrey pleaded with his opponent, "Come on, George, you've had your third-party fling and made your point, but you're still a Democrat, damn it. All your Southern states are heavily Democratic. Get on board now—you can go from Party pariah to the Party savior who kept Nixon out of the White House. And, don't forget, having a Democratic president who owes you a big favor won't hurt your comeback race in 1970. President Humphrey and Vice President Kennedy will be a big help to you with Negro voters back home when you challenge Governor Brewer in two years."

"Well, I certainly appreciate what sounds like an advance 1970 endorsement from you. But I must say that your House of Representatives scenario assumes an awful lot. It assumes that all those Southern Democratic congressmen and senators representing the eleven states of the Confederacy are going to vote for you and Bobby Kennedy if the election goes to the House. After both of you ran around America insulting the constituents they represent as a bunch of bigots and racists and know-nothings, as we say back home, you might find that's a bigger chaw of tobacco than you thought."[3]

"George, that's not quite—"

"—I don't wish to belabor the point. Anyway, as I started to say, I concede that some Southern congressional Democrats might vote to put you and Mr. Kennedy in the White House. It's also possible that if they do, their political careers will end at the next election. I don't know too many Southern congressional Democrats who want to throw away their careers to help advance Bobby Kennedy's."

"President Johnson's also a Southerner, and he'll do whatever it takes to force Democrats to stand by their Party. As you know, his persuasive powers are legendary."

"That may have been true before, but it's mighty hard for a president to force anybody to do anything when he only has a few weeks left in his term. Our Southern delegation members all have something in common—they want to win their next reelection, and they know my support—or my opposition—will be far more meaningful than any deep appreciation expressed by an ex-president from his ranch in Texas. So let's look at the numbers—if the election goes to the House, Nixon only needs half of the Southern states to vote for him, and then he's the new president. So I am suggesting respectfully that you shouldn't be too sure about your preordained result if the election goes to the House of Representatives."

"Okay, George. Let's stop the back and forth and get down to business. In the end, you, your entire family, your lovely late wife Lurleen, the Kennedys, myself, and Lyndon Johnson are all lifelong Democrats. Richard Nixon and Ronald Reagan stand for everything our Party opposes. We Democrats need to stick together and put a Democrat in the White House next January—that's the bottom line."

"Anyone listening to your campaign speeches—and especially to Bobby Kennedy's—might be surprised now to hear you say that we're all in the same Party. The way you boys talked about me this year, someone might think I was the nominee of the Nazi Party or the Klan Party. Nobody would know from y'alls' speeches that every political office I ever won was under the banner of the Democratic Party. Your running mate also has a very short memory of my Party loyalty—I endorsed his brother in 1960 and I campaigned throughout the entire South to help make him president. I find it ironic that since the election results of last night, both you and Bobby have now discovered we're really on the same team after all. But I'm not a bitter or vindictive man. I want what's best for my country, and what's best for my country is what ten million people voted for yesterday. So you're right, Mr. Vice President, let's get down to business. If you would like me to consider directing my electors to do as you ask, then I want three things."

"What are they?"

"First, I want you and Bobby Kennedy to call a press conference and apologize to my supporters for calling me a racist and a bigot."

"Look, I'm sure we can work this out. Things get said during a campaign on all sides that cause regrets later."

"I know that's true, and I'm sure that applies to all of us. As a Christian, the Lord tells me to forgive and to turn the other cheek. I'm prepared to do that. But I think you boys owe my supporters an apology, because when you call me a racist, you're calling them the same thing for supporting me."

"Okay, George—what's number two?"

"When I became governor in 1963, we began the process of desegregating our schools in Alabama. We chose to take it slowly to avoid violence and chaos, and to get everyone used to the changes coming. Everything was going along fine. We had no race riots in Alabama. The problems we had here came from out-of-state agitators and communists stirring up trouble. I promised everybody in the federal government that we would desegregate our schools faster than any other Southern state. As a matter fact, we did just that—and even faster than the Northern states with segregated schools—and a damn sight faster than they did in Bobby Kennedy's hometown of Boston."

"I know you did. I've always applauded your efforts there."

"That may be, but when your running mate was attorney general under the brother that I helped put in the White House, he decided that he was going to make a big public splash at our expense and force Alabama to move even faster—and he did it with no constitutional authority to do so. I told him back then that Alabama was on the desegregation path already, and I asked him to let us do it for ourselves—just as the Ninth Amendment to the Constitution requires. Instead, he sent federal troops into Alabama and forced us to desegregate on his timetable by threats of violence. When I stood on the steps of Foster Auditorium at the University of Alabama to defend our rights as a sovereign state, I did so with Bobby Kennedy's rifles and bayonets pointed at me and at the heart of every Alabama citizen—

"—So here is the second thing. I want Bobby Kennedy to fly down here, call a press conference on those same steps and apologize to every man, woman, and child in Alabama for his unconstitutional assault on their state."

"Come on, George, that's unreasonable and you know it."

"No sir, I do not know any such thing. Bobby Kennedy invaded the sovereign state of Alabama with federal troops and displayed a frightening show of force not seen down here in a hundred years. He owes every person in my state an apology for the way he treated us, and I'll be god-damned before I lift a finger to put him back in a position of power until he seeks forgiveness for his unconstitutional intrusion into our affairs."

"George, I think if our people sit down, we'll come up with something that would satisfy everyone. But for God's sake, don't put the presidency of the United States at the mercy of settling old personal vendettas."

"This isn't about settling scores. This is about making right a grave injustice committed upon our good people. I do not think a simple apology is too much to ask."

"You said there were three things. Assuming we can work out the first two, what's the third?"

A grin swept across George's face. "Well, Mr. Vice President, the third thing is written on a piece of paper in my coat pocket. It's very brief—in fact, only four words."

"What does it say?"

"Well, sir, when you deliver on the first two things, then I'll hand you that piece of paper. Until then, congratulations on your campaign effort, and I thank you for calling. Please give my regards to Mrs. Humphrey."

When the call ended, David and Charlie rejoined George in the study. "Well, governor, what do you think?" Charlie asked.

"I think my campaign did America a great service."

"How's that?"

"By pulling ten million votes from him, I did my part to make sure that Hubert Humphrey and Bobby Kennedy never spend one day as president and vice president of the United States."[4]

"Mr. Vice President, I have Senator Kennedy on the line in New York."

"Thank you, operator—put him through, please."

A few minutes after speaking to Wallace, Humphrey connected with his running mate at RFK's Manhattan apartment on United Nations

Plaza. "Hubert, how did it go?" Bobby asked.

"The son-of-a-bitch has us by the balls and he knows it. He wants me to apologize for calling him a racist during the campaign, and he wants you to stand on the steps of the University of Alabama and apologize for sending troops there in 1963."

"Did you tell him to go fuck himself, or should I call and tell him?"

"At this point, I don't think it matters which one of us tells him. Besides that, he says he has a third condition that he won't reveal until we complete the first two."

"He's playing games—even if we did apologize, he'd probably knife us and throw his votes to Nixon."

"I don't trust the bastard, either. We can't deal with him.[5] I think we need to move to Plan B and start an all-out press offensive to bring public pressure on his electors to vote for him and for nobody else."

"I agree. Pierre Salinger is already meeting with our guys to draw up the plan. It'll be expensive, but we've already got the money pledged from several major donors."

"Did you talk with Ted Sorensen and the lawyers about our chances of prevailing in a lawsuit to force his electors to vote for him?"

"I did, and they all agree—our chances are slim to none. They doubt these laws are constitutional, and it's very unlikely the local courts would enforce it. How do you *make* a voter vote a certain way? Beyond that, Ted believes any suit would tie up the election results for six months to a year, and we'd get crucified for it."

"Yes—especially after Nixon refused to contest his razor-thin loss to Jack in 1960, even with evidence of major voter fraud. The press would turn the tables on us: they'd treat Nixon as the statesman and us as the pricks."

"*Nixon as the statesman*—talk about living in a parallel universe."

"The country wants this election decided now, not next year. So that's it—we need to pressure his electors into voting for Wallace when they meet, which will force the election to the House. If we don't succeed, then our worst nightmare comes true."

"Nixon as president isn't *our* worst nightmare—it's America's worst nightmare. I'd make a deal with the devil to keep that from happening."

"Bob, I have a feeling that if we heard Wallace's mysterious third condition, even a deal with the devil might be preferable."

"I'm betting one of you fellows is Mr. Paugh."

Late that afternoon, it wasn't hard for Charlie Snider and David Azbell to spot the two Nixon emissaries at Chris' Hot Dog Stand in downtown Montgomery. Amid the long counter and booths half-filled by blue-collar workers, they were the only two men in business suits.

"I'm Wayne Paugh. Please call me Wayne, Mr. Snider—"

"It's Charlie."

"Okay, Charlie—and this is Jason Roe."

"Good to meet you. This is our press secretary, David Azbell. I hope the flight down from New York was okay."

"It was fine, although I'm going to hate it when the campaign turns in our charter airplanes," Wayne chuckled. "I've gotten spoiled flying around on them. It'll take some getting used to going back to commercial flights."

"Well, maybe tonight we'll figure out a way to get you boys flying on Air Force One for the next four years," David said. "Come on, they're holding the big round booth in the back for us. I hope everyone likes chili-covered hotdogs. If not, you'll be leaving here hungry. That's what old Chris has been serving here for the last fifty years."

"As long as a restaurant has beer on their menu," Jason said, "I never leave hungry."

After small talk and downing two rounds of hotdogs, Charlie turned to the purpose of the meeting. "Governor Wallace has great admiration for Mr. Nixon. We appreciate that he was respectful of our campaign and of our supporters. He also knows that Mr. Nixon shares his concern about an out-of-control Supreme Court under the leadership of Earl Warren, who's no better than a damned war criminal for all the harm he's brought to the country."

"Vice President Nixon and Earl Warren haven't liked each other since their days back in California politics," Wayne said. "Warren despises Nixon, and the feelings are mutual."[6]

"As they say, 'the enemy of my enemy is my friend.' Of all the issues Governor Wallace raised during this campaign, he believes the most critical one is reining in this liberal, activist Court. If we don't remake that institution with sound nominees, then we'll trade our republic for an oligarchy run by five arrogant, unelected lawyers in black robes. We Southerners have already seen what happens when federal judges dictate our lives from their marble courthouses. That needs to stop."

"Charlie," Jason added, "we can assure you that if Nixon becomes president, he'll appoint judges to the federal bench who are strict constructionists. As you know, he's not new to the dance on that issue—he made that a consistent campaign promise."

"Well, that's reassuring, but the problem is with the usual pool of Republican lawyers from where these federal judges are drawn. They all start off as conservatives and strict constructionists, but then they get on the bench and end up as lefties. We think it's because they share the same academic and regional backgrounds—raised in the East and attending Harvard, Princeton, or Yale. Eventually they stab us in the back. Governor Wallace wants to get behind a man for president who'll smash that Eastern lock on Supreme Court nominees."

"Does the governor just want a general commitment, or do you have something more concrete in mind?" Wayne asked.

Charlie reached into his pocket, removed an envelope, and passed it to Wayne. "Inside are the names of two very fine federal circuit judges. Both men are from the South, both are strict constructionists, both are solid and reliable conservatives, and both would bring a much-needed balance to the Supreme Court."

"May I open it? I'd like to see if I recognize the names."

"Of course you may. Under the circumstances, I think we'll all need to trust each other's discretion. But I suggest you not open it until you're back on your plane. I don't know if we've been followed here, or whose prying eyes might be trained on us right now."

"Since we're being candid—and I hope this won't be a problem—but as you know, Earl Warren has already announced he's retiring. The next president's first order of business will be to select a new chief justice. Mr. Nixon has already made a preliminary commitment on that. I assume that Governor Wallace wasn't anticipating picking the chief."

"That sounds fair, but he expects there will be several vacancies over the next four years. He'll want these two men nominated after the chief justice."

"If the governor will accept that once we fill the Warren seat, and if these two judges are acceptable to my boss, then I expect this condition will find a very receptive audience in New York. I can also assure you that the governor will be very pleased with Mr. Nixon's selection of a new chief, assuming we have the opportunity to make the choice. Is there anything else we need to know before we head back to meet with our principal?"

"No—I think the governor will find your representations to be a very satisfactory solution to his concerns."

Charlie and David stood and shook hands with their two guests. "Have a safe flight home, boys," Charlie said. "I know the governor would like Mr. Nixon's answer by Friday."

"I think you'll have it by tomorrow morning."

Within the hour, Jason and Wayne were flying back to relay the proposition to Nixon. Wayne unsealed the envelope, pulled out the single piece of paper inside, and unfolded it. After reading it, he passed it to Jason. "I've never heard of them," Jason said. "Have you?"

"Nope. But I suspect that, before long, everyone in America's going to hear a lot about them—

"—Judge Clement Haynsworth and Judge G. Harrold Carswell."

David and Charlie returned to Farrar Street to brief Wallace on their meeting. When they arrived, Bill Jones pulled David aside. "Is Miss Lil all right?" Bill asked him.

"Why? Is there a problem?"

"She had one of our people deliver a letter to George an hour ago saying she had to go home to Canada—it was an emergency. I'm guessing there's a family issue."

George's voice called from another room. "Bill, we need you in here for a minute."

"Here—I almost forgot," Bill told David. "She left this for you." He handed David an envelope, and then rejoined George in the study. David walked to the nearby guest bedroom before opening it:

Dear David,

When I awoke and found you gone, I felt embarrassed and ashamed over how I acted. I offended you with my behavior. By leaving, you were able to avoid telling me what you think of me—always the Southern gentleman.

By the time you get this, I will be on my way home. I wrote Governor Wallace and thanked him for giving me the privilege of working with him. May I impose on you to make an appropriate excuse as to why I left without saying a proper goodbye to everyone else? I'm afraid that right now I am in no condition to see anyone.

Please do not attempt to contact me. I will not write, nor will I answer or return your calls. It isn't out of anger. It's out of shame.

I will remain forever grateful for all you did for me, and will carry fond memories of you in my heart. I wish I could leave believing you will do the same for me, but I suspect I threw away that chance.

Forgive me.

David sat on the edge of the bed, closed his eyes, and pressed his hand to his forehead. "Oh, no," he whispered, "God, no."

A few minutes later, Charlie saw David heading out the front door. "Hey, you're going the wrong way. We're all in there," he said, motioning his head toward the study.

"I've gotta go find Lil. It's important."

"Are you going to look for her all over Canada?"

"If I have to. You guys have this under control. I've got to get out of here before it's too late."

"Too late for what?"

"Just too late. Never mind for what."

"Buddy, we're on the verge of making history—you can't leave us in the lurch."

"I'll call my dad. He's feeling much better, and I was only here covering for him while he recuperated. He'll enjoy getting back in the saddle for the final act, and he's a much better press secretary than I am."

Charlie laughed. "Well, that ain't saying much! But seriously, if you leave now, you'll miss the biggest political story of the century. You'll regret it forever."

"I won't miss anything—I can read about it in tomorrow's newspaper. What I'll really regret forever is not leaving right now."

"Something tells me there's more to this than a sick aunt or something. When you get back, will you tell me what the hell this was all about?"

"Probably not. See you, Charlie. Tell the governor my dad will be here within the hour."

David stepped outside into the cold night air, started to close the door, and then turned back. "Hey, Charlie," he called to his friend, "do me a favor. When Nixon calls back, have the governor hold out for one more concession."

"What's that?"

"Tell Nixon we have a woman for him who'll make one helluva White House press secretary."

Official license plate issued in Washington, DC, for the 1969 presidential inauguration. These plates were valid in the District of Columbia for the month of January 1969 (Author's collection)

CHAPTER 52

ON DECEMBER 16, 1968, the 538 members of the Electoral College met in the fifty capitals of their respective states and in the District of Columbia.[1] There they cast in secret their ballots for president and vice president of the United States. By law, Congress tabulated the votes three weeks later.

On January 6, 1969—two months after Election Day—before a joint session of Congress, and at the conclusion of the tally, House Speaker John W. McCormack banged his gavel for order:

"Members of the Ninety-First Congress of the United States," he intoned solemnly, "and my fellow Americans, it is now my high honor and privilege to present to you the president of the United States—"

Premature applause drowned out McCormack's complete introduction, forcing him to shout its conclusion into the microphones:

"—*The Honorable Hubert H. Humphrey.*"

The vice president received a hero's welcome as he rose in the House chamber and raised his arms in an attempt to silence the cheers. Even Republican congressmen and senators, who just two months ago engaged in bitter political warfare against him, joined in the thundering five-minute bipartisan ovation. Finally, with order restored, Humphrey offered these brief remarks:

> In my constitutional role as president of the United States Senate, it is now my duty to proclaim that the Honorable Richard M. Nixon and the Honorable Ronald W. Reagan have been elected president and vice president of the United States, each having received 304 of the 538 electoral votes cast for the term of office beginning the twentieth day of January, 1969. I hereby order this proclamation entered in the official journal of the Congress.
>
> May God bless our new president and vice president, and may God bless the United States of America. These proceedings are adjourned.[2]

Masking his personal heartbreak with a smile,[3] Humphrey became the second incumbent vice president—in his capacity as president of the United States Senate, proclaiming himself the loser of a presidential race. Ironically, the first vice president to do so was the man who just vanquished his White House dream—Vice President Nixon, who declared John F. Kennedy the victor over him eight years earlier.[4]

On May 14, 1969, less than four months into the Nixon administration, White House counsel John Ehrlichman stepped inside the West Wing office of Wayne Paugh. "Let's go," Ehrlichman told his deputy.

"Where to, boss?"

"To see the old man."

"Anything wrong?"

"If there is, be ready to take the blame—it's in your job description."[5] A few minutes later, both men joined Nixon in the Oval Office. The smile on Nixon's face eased Wayne's readiness to accept whatever liability might be forthcoming for his nonexistent mistake.

"Abe Fortas called," Nixon told his counselors. "He just delivered his letter of resignation to the clerk of the Supreme Court. The bastard is getting out before the Senate impeaches him."[6]

"This might be a record, Mr. President," Wayne said. "Two Supreme Court vacancies in your first ten weeks."[7]

"You may be right. The Senate's on the verge of confirming my nominee for chief justice, and now we get this unexpected gift."

"*We* get the gift, or George Wallace gets it?" John asked. "He called me a couple of weeks ago to remind me we still owe him those two guys he wants as Supreme Court nominees."

"We get it. I've had John Mitchell* put a few of his deputies in the AG's office and the FBI digging around on those two characters Wallace gave me. They're both pieces of work. Haynsworth is from South Carolina and has an extensive record supporting segregation. He belongs to exclusive clubs that exclude blacks, and he's filthy rich. Besides the race issue, the Dems will raise hell with his stock holdings. It looks like he may have presided over cases where he had a financial conflict of interest. This Carswell is a lulu, too. They found tapes of speeches he made while running for the Georgia legislature—he said that segregation is the only correct way for people to live their lives. They also tell me the guy is a dumbbell."

"Are you going to call Wallace and explain why you can't nominate these two clowns?" Wayne asked.

"Just the opposite. We'll wait a couple of months to go through the motions of searching for a respectable candidate, and then I'll nominate Haynsworth for the Fortas seat. With their Senate majority, the Democrats will hold their hearings before the Senate Judiciary Committee, and they'll go nuts when they see his record. The Senate won't confirm him.[8] After expressing my grave disappointment over the Dems rejecting a fine Southerner, I'll nominate Carswell for the same seat. The press will get the tapes of Carswell's segregation speeches, the Senate will give him the Haynsworth treatment, and then they'll reject

---

*   John N. Mitchell (1913-1988) served as US attorney general under President Richard Nixon from 1969 to 1972.

him, too.[9] That's when I'll rip the congressional Democrats a new ass-hole for their anti-Southern prejudice.[10] It's a perfect two-fer. In one play, we pay off our Wallace debt, and we turn Southern conservative Democrats into Nixon voters in '72. And then, when the dust settles, I'll pick my own Supreme Court nominee."

"Come to think of it," Nixon said as he rubbed his chin, "that's not a twofer. That's a three–fer."

San Francisco Commonwealth Club announcement for Senator Robert Kennedy's campaign speech at the St. Francis Hotel, May 31, 1968. Following his speech, RFK autographed the program, along with Project Mercury astronaut John Glenn, the first American to orbit the earth, who campaigned for Kennedy. Four days after signing this program, Kennedy was shot in Los Angeles (Author's collection)

CHAPTER 53

THE SPRING AND SUMMER MONTHS of 1969 proved a dispiriting time for Robert Kennedy.

The gut-wrenching narrowness of his and Humphrey's election loss to Nixon ate at him—he believed Drew Pearson's late smear was the thumb that tipped the scale to the Republicans. Beyond that, Jacqueline Kennedy's escape to Greece, her impulsive marriage to Aristotle Onassis, and her later decision to remain incommunicado with all the Kennedys left a gnawing emptiness in him. He felt as if Onassis had snatched away part of his soul, and he hated him for it. Adding to the melancholy was

450

his strained relationship with Ethel since the affair revelation. She had long suspected her husband and sister-in-law, and the public outing of it humiliated her like no previous indiscretion. Even when several ex-Kennedy family employees retracted their claims or insisted that Drew Pearson misquoted them, it didn't move Ethel's trust needle into the black. The public may have bought into those recantations, but she knew from previous experience the power of Kennedy-family money to buy silence. Adding to this unhappy brew were the constant migraine headaches that persisted since the shooting—often hitting with such intensity that he needed to lie in a dark room with his eyes covered for hours.

Although his private life remained forlorn, his political star shone brighter than ever. Bobby remained the Democratic Party's most sought-after speaker and fundraiser. Yet even this increased popularity brought little personal satisfaction. After four years in the Senate, the job bored him. He felt the pace too slow, the procedures too archaic, and it provided little more than a place for old men to talk all day long.[1] Sometimes he confided a desire not to seek reelection in 1970. His staff insisted that he must do so to remain viable nationally: a senator from New York enjoys a strong political and fundraising base from which to launch a presidential race in 1972 or 1976. He agreed to it reluctantly, but the prospect of another six years in purgatory added to his gloom.

To help shake Bobby's depression, Senator Ted Kennedy and their cousin, Joe Gargan, planned a reunion for him and the six young women from his presidential campaign who handled his delegate-tracking operation. Their nickname—"The Boiler Room Girls"—came from the hot, stuffy, windowless office from which they worked in the national campaign headquarters. Ted and Joe timed the reunion around the annual sailing regatta at Martha's Vineyard—a thirty-year Kennedy family tradition in which Ted always competed. That Ethel refused to attend added to his inducement to go. It promised to be a weekend free from her cold shoulder and a relaxing few days of drinking, sailing, and partying with people in his inner circle. Any final hesitation Bobby showed evaporated when Joe dangled the additional bait: "MJ's going," he told Bobby, "but only if you'll come."

Twenty-eight, slender, pretty, with bobbed blonde hair, blue eyes, and elegant deportment, MJ joined Bobby's Senate staff soon after his 1964 election, and she shared a Georgetown apartment with the other "Boiler Room" girls. During the 1968 campaign she traveled often with Bobby on his plane as a secretary. Her presence had purposes beyond stenography. At the end of more than one long campaign day he slipped away from a late-night staff meeting to share her bed.[2]

On July 18, 1969, while most Americans sat before television sets awaiting Apollo 11's lunar landing, the partiers—six married men and six single women—gathered on Martha's Vineyard to cheer Teddy's team aboard his sailboat the *Victura*.[3] Although Teddy finished a dismal ninth in the regatta, it did nothing to dampen everyone's spirits.[4] After boarding the winner's boat and celebrating his victory with countless rounds of rum and Coke, in the late afternoon the Kennedy party took the ferry to the small adjacent island, where they swam on a deserted beach.

Later that evening, after returning to their Edgartown hotels to freshen up, they again ferried back to the island where Joe had rented Lawrence Cottage for a cookout and private bash. It was almost 9:30 p.m. before Joe grilled the steaks—everyone lost track of time while drinking and dancing to phonograph records. Only Ted lagged behind; after securing his boat, he took his crew out for a late dinner and drinks as a thank-you for their help in the race. He promised to join the reunion later.

Ted reached the island cottage at 11:45 that night. "Hey," Joe called to him, "You made it—I didn't hear you pull up."

"I left my car at the hotel. I rode the ferry over and walked from the dock. I felt like stretching my legs after sailing all afternoon."

"We wondered if you'd ever get here. I saved a couple of steaks for you."

"Thanks, but I've had dinner. Keep them in the refrigerator for later." Looking around the room, Ted noticed his brother missing. "Where's Bobby?"

"He left with MJ half an hour ago. I heard him say something about showing her the beach at night. They may have gone back to the hotel."

"Has he been drinking?"

"Sure—we all have. What are you going to do—call Aunt Rose and tell on him?"

"It's dark as hell out there."

Joe looked out the window. "My car's gone. He must have taken it. Don't worry. He's all right. He's not a big boozer—not like you!"

"Give me the keys to one of the rentals. If he's been drinking, I want to make sure they got to wherever they were going."

Joe grabbed a set of keys from the kitchen counter. "Here—take the Olds. Why don't you go ask the ferry skipper if he took them back to Edgartown? If not, then check the beach where we swam earlier. Be careful crossing the pond—there're no lights or railing on the bridge."

As Ted started out the door, Joe called out, "Hey, if you see my car parked outside the Shiretown Inn, then you know where they are—and what they're doing. Don't interrupt!" Once again Joe laughed.

"All right, smart ass. I'll be right back."

Ted left the cottage and drove the short distance to the ferry. The skipper told him that he hadn't seen Bobby since earlier that evening when everyone came to the island for the cookout. He hadn't transported anybody since, and he was shutting down for the night and going home. Ted made a U-turn and drove the few hundred yards toward the small wooden bridge that led to the deserted beach. Suddenly, in the darkness he saw a silhouetted figure off the main paved road. The car's high beams illuminated Bobby kneeling on all fours next to the bridge—soaking wet.

Ted pulled over and rushed to his older brother. "Bob, what the hell are you doing? Where's MJ?"

Bobby looked disoriented. He began crying and speaking incoherently. Ted grabbed his shoulders, shouting, "Come on Bob! Where is she—where's MJ?"

Pointing back toward the small wooden bridge crossing Poucha Pond, Bobby gasped, "She's in the car. I couldn't get her out. I don't know what happened. We went off the bridge. I can't find her." The car headlights illuminated enough of the pond to show the slightly protruding tire of an upside-down car submerged in the water. "Oh, my God," Ted shouted as he kicked off his shoes, pants, and shirt. "Come on, help me!" he yelled as he jumped into the water.

"It's no use—I've tried. I kept trying. . . ."

Ted and Bobby swam down seeking an open window or a door they could move. When their air ran out, they came up, took another deep breath, and dove down again. Despite repeated attempts, it was no use. MJ had to be dead—too much time had passed. Ted helped Bobby out of the water, grabbed his clothes, and they both drove away.

Not wanting to attract undue attention, when they reached the outside of the cottage Ted gave his horn a couple of light toots. When Joe stepped out on the porch, Ted called him over to where they parked in the shadows. "Did MJ come back?" Ted asked hopefully.

"No—and what the hell happened to you guys?"

"There's been an accident. Your car's upside down in the pond. MJ's in it. I couldn't get her out. She's gotta be dead—"

"What! Oh, shit," Joe shouted.

"Shut up, goddamn you—keep it together. We need time to figure out how to handle this. Don't tell anyone inside. We don't want them to panic."

"We have to call the police."

"And tell them what? That Bob drunk-drove some young staffer off a fucking bridge? She's dead—there's nothing we can do to bring her back. We've got to sort through this. Listen—if anyone asks, say that Bobby had a headache and I took him back to the hotel. Say that you loaned your car keys to MJ—she was tired and wanted to go to bed. We can say later she was driving and had an accident."[5]

"That won't work—people saw her leave with Bobby."

"Shit—all right—stay by the phone and be ready for anything I need you to do."

"The party's breaking up right now. Everyone's getting ready to catch the last ferry back to Edgartown."

"They're too late—the ferry's closed. They'll have to stay at the cottage tonight. Just tell everyone Bob and MJ went back to the hotel. Get in—I need you to drop us off at the ferry."

"You said it was closed."

"It is. I need to get him back to his hotel room. We'll swim across. It's not far." Ted drove to the dock, turned over the car keys to Joe, and then he and Bobby slipped into the water and swam across the 500-foot channel.[6] Following orders, Joe returned to the party, delivered the news about the premature ferry closing, and told everyone to bed there for the night.

The next morning a ringing telephone jarred Joe's already strained nerves.

"Joe, this is Ted." Joe listened as his cousin spoke in peculiar, measured tones. "Listen carefully to me. I'm calling from the Edgartown police station. I've just given Chief Arena[7] my full statement. I have bad news. Last night, when I got to the cottage, I ran into Bobby and MJ. She wanted a tour of the island at night. Bobby was having one of his migraines, so I offered to take her. I gave him my car to take back to the hotel so he could get some sleep. I took your car to give MJ a tour. I must've made a wrong turn off the road, because the car rolled off the bridge near Chappaquiddick Road. It landed upside down in the pond. Somehow I got out—I don't remember how. I kept diving down trying to get MJ out of the car. I couldn't reach her. I must have been in shock, because I don't remember what happened after that until I awoke in my room this morning. Once I realized what happened, I came over here and made a report. Right now I need you to get over to the Shiretown Inn and explain what happened to Bobby. I haven't told him yet."

"You mean he doesn't know about any of this—about your police report?"

"No. You need to explain it to him—*all of it.*"

"What about the ferry skipper?"

"That's already been handled, okay? Get over to Bobby, explain what happened, and get him off the island—*now*. The press will descend on this place soon, and I don't want him mixed up in any of this. It's all my fault, Joe. I'm counting on you to handle this. *You understand everything I'm telling you?*"

"This is insane. I don't understand why it has to be this way?"

Ted looked back and saw Chief Arena conferring with another officer. Satisfied nobody could overhear, in a low voice he asked his cousin, "Would Bobby have done this for Jack?"

"Are you kidding? Bobby would have taken Oswald's bullet for Jack."

"Then you understand. We'll discuss it later. The chief told me I can leave in an hour when we finish the paperwork. Get a charter plane ready for me at the airport. But right now get Bobby out of here, even if you have to tie him up and drag him off the island. And make sure he knows that if he says anything different, we're both dead."

"Okay, I'm on it. You can depend on me."

When Ted finished his call, Chief Arena asked one of his officers to take down Ted's information for the accident report. They moved to a small table with a typewriter. Sitting across from each other, the cop began filling out the appropriate form. "What's the victim's name?" he asked Ted.

"Everyone called her MJ."

"Do you know her legal name?"

"Yes. It was Mary Jo—

"—Mary Jo Kopechne. . . ."[8]

CODA*

1954 Lyndon Johnson for US Senate pamphlet (Author's collection)

---

*   Other than the references in this section to Ronald Reagan's vice presidency, Congressman Gerald Ford's selection as Richard Nixon's 1972 running mate, and Robert Kennedy's post-June 1968 activities—all of which were fictional elements in our story—these biographical references are historically accurate.

PRESIDENT LYNDON B. JOHNSON

Johnson left the White House in January 1969 and retired to his Texas ranch. In later years, he built his presidential library, wrote a memoir, and spent time with his grandchildren. He died of a heart attack at age sixty-four on January 22, 1973.

1962 Nixon for California governor campaign button (Author's collection)

FORMER VICE PRESIDENT RICHARD NIXON

During his first term as president (1969-1973), Nixon infuriated conservatives by a continued shift leftward. He became the first sitting president to visit China and the Soviet Union, and he toasted their communist dictators while freedom fighters wasted away in their concentration camps and gulags. He created massive new bureaucracies such as the Environmental Protection Agency. He expanded welfare programs, proposed a nationalized health care plan, and implemented affirmative-action quotas. During a recession, he abandoned free-market principles and imposed wage and price controls. Of the four US Supreme Court appointments he made, two of them—Lewis Powell and Harry Blackmun—ended up as key liberal swing votes. When he ran for reelection in 1972, by mutual agreement, Ronald Reagan withdrew from vice presidential consideration for a second term. Nixon traded the conservative Reagan for a moderate, Michigan Congressman Gerald Ford, as his running mate. Running against the ultra-liberal and deeply flawed campaign of Democratic nominee George McGovern, the Nixon-Ford ticket won a forty-nine-state landslide. Within months of the start of his second term, the Watergate scandal engulfed Nixon, who resigned and turned the presidency over to Ford on August 9, 1974. Over the next twenty years, during and after a period of public rehabilitation, Nixon wrote books and articles, gave speeches and interviews, and counseled his successors—both Democrat and Republican. He suffered a stroke and died at age eighty-one on April 22, 1994.

1940 badge from Quaker Puffed Wheat and Rice movie premium set: RONALD REAGAN, A WARNER BROS. STAR (Author's collection)

GOVERNOR RONALD REAGAN

After leaving the vice presidency, Reagan returned to California and began broadcasting a series of weekly radio commentaries on political issues. Unhappy with the Nixon-Ford abandonment of conservative principles, he challenged President Ford for the 1976 GOP presidential nomination. Ford beat Reagan in a close race and then went on to lose the presidency that November to former Georgia Governor Jimmy Carter. Four years later, Reagan won the Republican presidential nomination and swamped Carter in the general election, winning 489 electoral votes to Carter's forty-nine. After winning a landslide reelection in 1984, Reagan left the White House in 1989. In 1994 he announced that he suffered from Alzheimer's disease and withdrew from public appearances gradually. He died of complications from the disease at age ninety-four on June 5, 2004.

1948 Hubert Humphrey for US Senate campaign button (Author's collection)

VICE PRESIDENT HUBERT HUMPHREY

When Eugene McCarthy declined to seek reelection to the Senate in 1970, Humphrey, now the former vice president, jumped into the race and won the seat. Returning to Washington, and itching for a rematch against the man who beat him narrowly in 1968, HHH ran for the 1972 Democratic presidential nomination but lost it to Senator George McGovern. Reelected to the Senate in 1976, doctors diagnosed him late that year with terminal cancer. He fought the disease bravely while maintaining his Senate duties until death claimed him at age sixty-six on January 13, 1978.

1958 Nelson Rockefeller for New York governor campaign button (Author's collection)

GOVERNOR NELSON ROCKEFELLER

Upon assuming the presidency in 1974, Gerald Ford named Rockefeller as his vice president. Declining to seek the 1976 GOP vice presidential nomination for a full term, he retired from public life in 1977 and returned to his philanthropic and business interests. He died of a heart attack at age seventy on January 26, 1979.

1970 George Wallace for Alabama governor campaign button (Author's collection)

GOVERNOR GEORGE WALLACE

After recapturing the Alabama governorship in 1971, Wallace ran unsuccessfully for the 1972 Democratic presidential nomination. During that campaign, on May 15, an unemployed janitor, Arthur Bremer, shot him five times at a Maryland campaign rally. Although Wallace survived the assassination attempt, the shooting left him paralyzed from the waist down and in excruciating pain for the rest of his life. Wallace ran once more for the Democratic presidential nomination in 1976, but his day had passed, so he returned to his duties at the statehouse. In all, he served four terms as Alabama governor (1963-1967, 1971-1975, 1975-1979, and 1983-1987) before retiring from political life in 1987. He died at age seventy-seven on September 13, 1998.

1948 Eugene McCarthy for Congress campaign button (Author's collection)

SENATOR EUGENE MCCARTHY

In October 1968, McCarthy announced that he would not seek reelection to the Senate in 1970. He ran unsuccessfully for the presidency four more times: in 1972, 1976, 1988, and 1992. Although in 1968 he had played a major role in the presidential campaign, his later presidential efforts went largely unnoticed by the press and public. When he sought to reclaim his Senate seat in a 1982 comeback attempt, he received a mere 24 percent of the Democratic primary vote. A prolific author and speaker, he died of complications from Parkinson's disease at age eighty-nine on December 10, 2005.

1962 George Romney for Michigan governor campaign button (Author's collection)

GOVERNOR GEORGE ROMNEY

After winning the White House in 1968, President Nixon named Romney to the Cabinet as secretary of Housing and Urban Development. He served in that post for four years, and then retired to private life, charitable and church work. Stricken by a heart attack while doing his morning treadmill exercise, he died at age eighty-eight on July 26, 1995.

1968 sticker promoting Senator Edward Kennedy for president; distributed by supporters (following RFK's death) at the 1968 Democratic National Convention (Author's collection)

SENATOR EDWARD KENNEDY

In 1969, following an official investigation into the death of Mary Jo Kopechne, Kennedy pleaded guilty to leaving the scene of an accident and received a suspended two-month jail sentence. The following year he won reelection to the Senate. In 1980 he ran for the Democratic presidential nomination, but the unforgiving specter of Chappaquiddick upended his effort; he lost the nomination to President Jimmy Carter. Kennedy returned to the Senate, where he served for almost forty-seven years before his death from brain cancer on August 25, 2009.

1964 Robert Kennedy for US Senate campaign button (Author's collection)

SENATOR ROBERT KENNEDY

Following the Chappaquiddick tragedy, RFK reconciled with his wife Ethel. In 1970 he announced his candidacy for reelection to the United States Senate.

In the midst of that campaign—on June 5, 1970—the second anniversary of the assassination attempt, Bobby boarded a cross-country flight from New York to Portland to headline the Democratic Party's state convention there. Halfway through the flight, feeling heavy-lidded and drowsy, he put down his book, finished a beer, reclined his seat, and closed his eyes.

The medical examiner later reported that continuous pressure from a bullet fragment lodged against a cranial artery (which accounted for Bobby's recurring migraines) ruptured the blood vessel and triggered a massive cerebral hemorrhage. He was 44 years old.

It fell to Bobby's widow, Ethel, to raise their brood of eleven young children without a father. Fifty years after his death, Ethel (at age 90) lives on.

She never remarried.

• • • • •

In our story, RFK survived the Ambassador Hotel shooting and resumed his 1968 presidential campaign. In fantasy we bent the arc of history, but our obstruction of fate proved temporary. Even with the intervention of the writer's pen, destiny brought the world the same ultimate results—the Humphrey-Nixon-Wallace faceoff that November, Nixon's victory, Chappaquiddick and the end of Edward Kennedy's presidential prospects, Watergate, Nixon's resignation, the presidencies of Gerald Ford, Jimmy Carter, and Ronald Reagan—

—and a world that never saw Robert Francis Kennedy grow old.

We need not be surprised. Scripture tells us that fate's trajectory is fixed and unchangeable. In Ecclesiastes 1:9, King Solomon wrote, "What has been is what will be, and what has been done is what will be done."

Despite the conjectured premise of this book, one final observation requires no speculation: in 1968, nine consequential leaders battled for the presidency of the United States. Their clash changed the political dynamic of America, and that impact endures. They etched their names on the history, law, and culture of their time—and of ours.

That's what happens when titans take the stage.

APPENDICES

APPENDIX A

BIOGRAPHICAL SKETCHES OF THE CANDIDATES (AS OF 1968)

1. THE DEMOCRATS

LYNDON B. JOHNSON: president of the United States. First elected to Congress in 1937, Johnson later served as US Senate majority leader and vice president under John F. Kennedy. He succeeded to the presidency upon Kennedy's assassination in 1963. The following year, LBJ won a landslide election by beating his conservative Republican opponent Barry Goldwater in a forty-four-state rout. Soon thereafter, Johnson ordered US combat forces into Vietnam in an effort to halt the spread of Soviet and Red Chinese-backed communists. By 1968, over 20,000 US troops died fighting there, and with no end in sight. As the war's unpopularity grew, finding a satisfactory resolution bedeviled the incumbent president as he prepared for his 1968 reelection race.

HUBERT H. HUMPHREY: vice president of the United States. A former mayor of Minneapolis, Humphrey won election to the US Senate in 1948. One of the leading liberals in Congress throughout the 1950s and 1960s, he sponsored landmark legislation such as Medicare, the 1964 Civil Rights Act, the Peace Corps, and nuclear disarmament. When President Kennedy signed the 1963 Nuclear Test Ban Treaty, he gave Humphrey the pen as a souvenir and told him, "Hubert, this is your treaty—it had better work." Chosen by Johnson as his 1964 running mate, Humphrey remained a loyal vice president, but by 1968 he felt conflicted between private concerns over LBJ's Vietnam policies and personal loyalty to his leader.

ROBERT F. KENNEDY: US senator from New York and younger brother of President John F. Kennedy. RFK served as attorney general in JFK's administration. Despite a lengthy feud with, and a hatred for, Lyndon Johnson, in 1964 Kennedy hoped to maneuver himself onto the ticket as LBJ's running mate. After Johnson scotched that hope, Kennedy resigned from the Cabinet and ran for the US Senate successfully by beating an incumbent Republican (with LBJ's significant help). Although supportive of America's incursion into Vietnam initially, by 1968 RFK adopted increasingly critical views of the war. Appealing to young and minority voters, and inheriting the large remnant of so-called "Camelot" sentimentalists, RFK stood as a potentially formidable challenger to Johnson's 1968 reelection.

EUGENE J. MCCARTHY: US senator from Minnesota. A twenty-year congressional veteran, McCarthy was more at home writing and reading poetry than engaging in the arcane rituals of lawmaking. Like almost every senator, McCarthy supported military action in Vietnam initially, but he soon became a vocal opponent. In late 1967 McCarthy tried to recruit a "peace" challenger to Johnson's expected 1968 Democratic presidential renomination campaign. When none materialized, he took upon himself the longshot effort.

2. THE REPUBLICANS

RICHARD NIXON: former vice president of the United States. Elected to the House of Representatives in 1946, Nixon gained national fame for exposing Alger Hiss, a high-ranking State Department official in the Roosevelt and Truman administrations, as a Soviet agent. Winning a US Senate seat in 1950, two years later Dwight D. Eisenhower tapped him (at age thirty-nine) as his running mate. After eight years as Ike's vice president, he lost the 1960 presidential election to John F. Kennedy by a whisker. Two years later, Nixon ran unsuccessfully for California governor. In a legendary concession speech, he announced the end of his political career and then lashed out at the press, telling the assembled reporters, "You won't have Nixon to kick around anymore, because, gentlemen, this is my last press conference." Leaving California for New York, and joining a white-shoe law firm, he traveled the world, wrote articles, and eased back into political life from his new East Coast base. In 1964, when many Republican leaders avoided campaigning with Barry Goldwater, Nixon stumped the country for the GOP nominee, covering thirty-six states and making more than 150 appearances on behalf of Republican candidates.* After Goldwater's overwhelming defeat, the Republican Party teetered on the verge of permanent minority status. However, during the 1966 midterm election campaign, Nixon became America's most peripatetic campaigner, traveling 127,000 miles, visiting forty states, and delivering over 400 speeches for GOP candidates and Party organizations.** Republicans won stunning gains in November, picking up forty-seven House seats, three US

---

* Steven E. Ambrose, *Nixon (Volume Two): The Triumph of a Politician* 1962-1972 (New York: Simon and Schuster, 1989), 56. See also Patrick J. Buchanan, *The Greatest Comeback: How Richard Nixon Rose from Defeat to Create the New Majority* (New York: Crown Forum, 2014), 18.

** Buchanan, *The Greatest Comeback*, 56, 96; Lewis Chester et al., *An American Melodrama: The Presidential Campaign of 1968* (New York: Viking Press, 1969), 185; Richard Nixon, *RN: The Memoirs of Richard Nixon* (New York: Grosset & Dunlap, 1978), 272; Ambrose, *Nixon (Volume Two): The Triumph of a Politician 1962-1972*, 60.

Senate seats, eight governorships, and 557 state legislative seats. Around the country, scores of winning and losing candidates credited Nixon for helping them when nobody else would. Not surprisingly, a large number of them would be delegates to the next Republican National Convention. As 1968 approached, Nixon's popularity rose greatly with both establishment and rank-and-file Republicans. However, these same Party regulars also worried that he could not shed his loser image to make a comeback.

NELSON A. ROCKEFELLER: three-term governor of New York, heir to one of America's greatest fortunes, and the leader of the GOP's Eastern liberal wing. Rockefeller's public service dated back to the Franklin Roosevelt administration. FDR tried to recruit "Rocky" to the Democratic Party unsuccessfully. In 1960, Rocky aborted his brief challenge to Nixon for the presidential nomination. In 1964, he sought the nomination again and battled Barry Goldwater in a nasty primary fight. After Goldwater defeated Rocky, the bitterness between the rival camps persisted. When Rocky tried to address the 1964 GOP convention, he suffered sixteen minutes of booing. In the general election, Rocky endorsed "the entire Republican ticket," but he refused to endorse Goldwater specifically. LBJ massacred Goldwater, furious conservative activists blamed Rockefeller for the stinging defeat, and they never forgave him. However, by late 1967, many rank-and-file Republicans started giving Rocky a second look. After the Democrats trounced the 1964 GOP ticket, Republicans wanted a winner next time. With nagging concerns that Nixon was a perpetual loser, and polls showing Rocky beating LBJ in head-to-head matchups, 1968 looked like it could be his time.

RONALD REAGAN: newly elected governor of California. Although only in office since January 1967, Reagan was no stranger to voters. After a decades-long Hollywood career coupled with political activism—first as an FDR Democrat, and later as a corporate spokesman for General

Electric, Reagan gained political stardom for his 1964 nationally televised speech supporting Barry Goldwater. California Republicans recruited the former actor to challenge Democratic Governor Pat Brown, the man who beat Richard Nixon four years earlier. In 1966, Reagan trounced Brown by a million votes. Almost immediately after taking office in Sacramento, conservatives saw the charismatic Reagan as an electable ideological heir to Goldwater. In 1968, with Rockefeller's Eastern support matching Reagan's phenomenal popularity in the South, Nixon feared a Rocky-Reagan cabal could stop his drive for the nomination. If that happened, it would set the stage for a California-New York convention duel for control of the Republican Party.

GEORGE ROMNEY: Governor of Michigan. Romney embodied the Horatio Alger spirit: a devout Mormon missionary from a poor family who never finished college and, as a young man, took an entry-level job in the automobile industry. Later moving into management, Romney worked his way up the corporate ladder and became chairman of American Motors. In 1962, he won the first of three two-year terms as Michigan governor and was the only Republican statewide candidate that year to win in the heavily Democratic state. His overwhelming reelection victory in 1966 made him the early frontrunner for the GOP presidential nomination in 1968. Enjoying strong support with civil rights groups and union leaders, the moderate Romney had crossover appeal with independents and blue-collar Democrats.

3. THE WILD CARD

GEORGE C. WALLACE: former governor of Alabama. The poor, wiry farm boy from Clio, Alabama, won two state boxing titles while in high school. After working his way through college and law school, he entered the Army Air Corps and saw combat in World War II before returning home and becoming a prosecutor, a state legislator, and a circuit court judge. During an unsuccessful run for governor in 1958, Wallace's comparatively moderate views earned him the endorsement of the NAACP, while the Ku Klux Klan supported his opponent. Four years later, with federal court decisions ordering desegregation in the Deep South, Wallace ran again and challenged the US Supreme Court's legal right to force its unelected will upon the states. Wallace campaigned in 1962 on a platform of preserving racial segregation and destroying the bloated and increasingly intrusive Washington bureaucracy. A *Saturday Evening Post* story related that Wallace "campaigned like a one-man army at war with the federal government."[1] Winning 96 percent of the vote (no Republican filed against him), Wallace proclaimed in his inaugural address, "I draw the line in the dust and toss the gauntlet before the feet of tyranny, and I say segregation now, segregation tomorrow, segregation forever." Early in his term, Wallace made his point defiantly: when Robert Kennedy's Justice Department sought to integrate the University of Alabama with federal troops, Wallace stood in front of the college's door and confronted Kennedy's deputy as cameras recorded the temporary standoff.[2] In 1964, Wallace entered three Democratic presidential primaries to test his populist message outside the South. Hammering away on states' rights, a strong national defense, and law and order to combat violent racial and campus protests, Wallace showed surprising strength. Primary voters in Indiana, Wisconsin, and Maryland gave him 34 percent, 30 percent, and 43 percent, respectively. As 1968 approached, Wallace prepared another presidential run, this time as a third-party candidate leading his newly formed American Independent Party. The specter of an independent Wallace campaign worried both Republican and Democratic leaders. The GOP feared Wallace would siphon votes from the conservative South, while Democrats feared a hemorrhage of union and blue-collar voters—from *all* regions—to "Alabama's Fightin' Governor."

APPENDIX B

CHRONOLOGY

1960	John F. Kennedy defeats Richard Nixon for the presidency.
1962	Nixon loses his race for California governor. He quits politics in a bitter farewell press conference.
1963	Lee Harvey Oswald assassinates Kennedy; Vice President Lyndon Johnson becomes president.
1964 JULY 15	Conservative US Senator Barry Goldwater defeats liberal New York Governor Nelson Rockefeller for the Republican presidential nomination. Rockefeller refuses to endorse Goldwater publicly in the general election.

AUGUST 2   North Vietnamese gunboats fire on the *USS Maddox* in the Gulf of Tonkin. Two days later, the *Maddox* and the *USS Turner Joy* report coming under fire. Six days later, Congress passes the Tonkin Gulf Resolution, giving President Johnson authority to order an armed response to protect American forces in Vietnam. The Senate passes the resolution eighty-eight to two; the House passes it unanimously.

NOVEMBER 3   Johnson trounces Goldwater in the general election. Conservative Republicans blame Rockefeller for Goldwater's loss.

1965   Johnson begins escalating American military involvement in Vietnam, citing the Tonkin Gulf Resolution as his authority. He enjoys widespread public support.

1966   During a tough campaign for a third term as New York governor, Rockefeller promises the voters that he will not run for president in 1968. He wins reelection in November.

Nixon stumps tirelessly for Republican candidates in the national midterm elections. When the GOP win significant gains on Election Day, Nixon gets much credit for the victory.

1967
NOVEMBER 18   Michigan Governor George Romney announces his candidacy for the Republican presidential nomination; Nelson Rockefeller endorses Romney and becomes his de facto campaign director.

NOVEMBER 30   Senator Eugene McCarthy announces he will enter the Democratic primaries and challenge President Johnson for the nomination.

1968

JANUARY 31   "The Tet Offensive": North Vietnam violates the Vietnamese New Year ("Tet") cease-fire and launches 70,000 troops against over 100 South Vietnamese cities, including the US Embassy in Saigon. Although the offensive is repelled with relative ease, it takes several weeks to push back the enemy. Because of Tet, American public support for continued US intervention in Vietnam begins to slide. Polls show an increasing disbelief in Pentagon and White House assurances that half-a-million US troops routed the weakened communists. Two weeks after Tet, the Gallup Poll reports that 50 percent now disapprove of Johnson's handling of the war.

    On that same day, at an off-the-record breakfast at the National Press Club in Washington, Senator Robert F. Kennedy says there are no "conceivable circumstances" under which he would challenge President Johnson for renomination. At the frantic urging of his press secretary, Kennedy changes the word "conceivable" to "foreseeable" before releasing the statement officially.

FEBRUARY 1   Richard Nixon announces his candidacy for the Republican presidential nomination and enters the New Hampshire primary.

FEBRUARY 8   Former Alabama Governor George Wallace announces his presidential candidacy under his newly created American Independent Party.

FEBRUARY 24   After endorsing Romney, Rockefeller mentions casually to a reporter he would accept a convention draft. The comment angers Romney, whose support continues to evaporate as his gaffe-plagued campaign limps along.

MARCH 9   Faced with collapsing poll numbers, Romney withdraws from the presidential campaign three days before the New Hampshire primary.

MARCH 10   Rockefeller (reconsidering his decision not to run for president) meets privately with key leaders and advisers.

MARCH 12   The New Hampshire primary: thanks to thousands of college students invading the state as part of a grassroots effort, McCarthy stuns the political world by nearly defeating Johnson (LBJ was not on the ballot, but he won with write-in votes). Johnson's humiliating showing signals that his reelection effort may be jeopardized.

In the New Hampshire Republican primary, with Romney's withdrawal three days earlier, Nixon won almost 78 percent of the GOP vote there.

MARCH 13   The day after McCarthy's unexpectedly strong performance in New Hampshire, Robert Kennedy announces he is "reassessing" his decision not to run for president.

MARCH 16	Kennedy announces his candidacy for the Democratic presidential nomination. His late entry infuriates McCarthy's antiwar supporters. They view Kennedy as an opportunist, a nakedly ambitious politician exploiting McCarthy's efforts, and one whose selfishness threatens to split the Democratic "peace vote."
MARCH 21	Despite widespread speculation he would enter the campaign, Rockefeller again announces he will not seek the Republican presidential nomination.
MARCH 31	In a nationwide address, Johnson astonishes the nation by announcing he will not seek reelection. This opens the way for Vice President Hubert Humphrey's entry into the race.
APRIL 2	The Wisconsin primary: McCarthy sweeps the state with 56 percent of the Democratic vote.
APRIL 4	James Earl Ray assassinates Dr. Martin Luther King Jr. in Memphis; riots break out in over 100 cities. Police arrest tens of thousands of rioters and looters, and scores of people die in the violence.
APRIL 27	Humphrey announces his candidacy for the Democratic presidential nomination. His entry is too late to file for any primaries.
APRIL 30	Changing his mind again, Rockefeller announces he will seek the Republican presidential nomination. His entry is too late to file for any primaries.

MAY 1

The day after he announces his candidacy (and without appearing on the ballot), Rockefeller wins all thirty-four convention delegates in the Massachusetts primary; Nixon and Massachusetts Governor John Volpe (running as a favorite son) receive zero delegates.

MAY 3

United States and North Vietnam agree to peace discussions in Paris beginning May 10.

MAY 14

Kennedy defeats McCarthy in the Nebraska primary; Nixon wins the GOP primary, beating both Ronald Reagan (whose name appeared on the ballot, although he had not declared his candidacy) and a Rockefeller write-in effort.

MAY 28

McCarthy beats Kennedy in the Oregon primary, making RFK the first Kennedy ever to lose an election. Kennedy tells friends he will withdraw from the race if he does not beat McCarthy in the upcoming California primary. Nixon wins the Oregon primary easily.

JUNE 1

Seeking to shore up Southern delegates (and block any right-flank assault by a potential Reagan candidacy), Nixon meets with Senator Strom Thurmond of South Carolina, who endorses Nixon after the meeting. This support will have tremendous influence on Southern delegates to the GOP convention, as well as with Southern voters in the general election.

JUNE 4-5   The California primary: shortly after midnight, Kennedy addresses supporters at the Ambassador Hotel in Los Angeles and claims victory over McCarthy. After his speech, Kennedy exits the stage; moments later, Sirhan Sirhan shoots him.

JUNE 6   Kennedy dies.

AUGUST 5   The Republican National Convention opens in Miami. On that same day, Reagan announces he will seek the presidential nomination.

AUGUST 7   Nixon wins the Republican presidential nomination over rivals Rockefeller and Reagan; his margin of victory is a mere twenty-five votes. Nixon selects Maryland Governor Spiro Agnew as his running mate.

AUGUST 20   After several months of the Czechoslovakian "Prague Spring" and its growing democratic movement, the Soviet Union invades Czechoslovakia with over 200,000 Warsaw Pact troops and crushes the revolt.

AUGUST 26   The Democratic National Convention opens in Chicago. During the week, bloody riots and antiwar protests erupt. America watches on live television as the Chicago police put down the riots with night-sticks and tear gas. The violent confrontations shock America and cast a pall over the proceedings.

AUGUST 28   Humphrey wins the presidential nomination on the first ballot and selects Senator Edmund Muskie as his running mate.

SEPTEMBER 30   After months of lagging poll numbers, Humphrey breaks with Johnson on Vietnam. In a speech at Salt Lake City, Humphrey announces that if elected, he will halt bombing North Vietnam to aid the peace process. Following this speech, many previously disaffected RFK and McCarthy voters return to the fold and support Humphrey.

OCTOBER 3   George Wallace selects retired Air Force General Curtis LeMay as his running mate.

OCTOBER 20   Former First Lady Jacqueline Kennedy (age thirty-nine), the widow of the slain president, shocks the world by marrying sixty-two-year-old Aristotle Onassis, a Greek shipping magnate. She and her children move to Greece amid negative public opinion surrounding her remarriage.

OCTOBER 31   As the presidential race between Nixon and Humphrey tightens, and with only five days until the election, President Johnson delivers a nationwide address and announces a bombing halt in North Vietnam, coupled with a major peace overture, which signals a possible end of the Vietnam War. After the speech, Humphrey pulls ahead of Nixon in the polls for the first time.

NOVEMBER 1   A few hours after Johnson's speech, South Vietnam announces it will not participate in the peace talks. This halts Humphrey's momentum amid confusion as to whether a peace settlement is imminent. LBJ privately blames Nixon and his campaign for interceding secretly with the South Vietnamese government to get them to boycott the peace negotiations.

NOVEMBER 5   In one of America's closest elections, Nixon defeats Humphrey by less than 500,000 votes out of 73 million cast. Third-party candidate Wallace wins five states and receives almost 14 million votes.

NOVEMBER 26   South Vietnam announces it will join the peace negotiations.

1969

JANUARY 20   Richard Nixon and Spiro Agnew become president and vice president of the United States.

1972

NOVEMBER 7   Despite a brewing scandal surrounding an attempted burglary in the offices of the Democratic National Committee at Washington, DC's Watergate office complex, Nixon and Agnew win reelection in one of the largest landslides in history. The Republican ticket carries forty-nine states.

1973

OCTOBER 10   Vice President Agnew resigns; facing an indictment for tax fraud, bribery, and other felonies dating back to his years in Maryland politics, he pleads no contest to one count of failing to report income. Pursuant to a plea bargain, Agnew receives probation, a fine, and no jail time.

OCTOBER 12   President Nixon nominates Congressman Gerald Ford as his new vice president. Both houses of Congress confirm Ford, who takes office on December 6.

1974   As a result of the Watergate scandal, and facing almost certain impeachment, Nixon resigns the presidency on August 9; Ford becomes president.

1976   Former California Governor Ronald Reagan challenges Ford for the 1976 GOP presidential nomination. In their convention showdown, Ford beats Reagan narrowly. In November, Ford loses the election in a close race to former Georgia Governor Jimmy Carter.

1980   Reagan wins the 1980 GOP presidential nomination; in November, he beats President Carter in a landslide.

APPENDIX C

BACKGROUND ON US MILITARY INVOLVEMENT IN VIETNAM

ALMOST FIFTY YEARS LATER, most Americans (when asked) believe that Vietnam was a "bad" war, but they don't know why. Tell them the US went in to stop the spread of communism, and to blunt Soviet and Red China's domination in the region, and they blink in confusion. They don't know about the Soviet Union—that totalitarian empire crumbled nearly thirty years ago. "'Red' China? Is that like today's 'red state-blue state' political distinctions?" Try explaining the "Domino Theory" (if South Vietnam fell to the communists, then surrounding countries might fall like a row of dominos) to a generation that never played dominos—or any other game not accessible on a video screen. To the "bad war" crowd, Vietnam was just bad—period—and everyone knows it. What's your next question?

This simplistic approach is unsatisfactory, because to understand the 1968 election and its continuing impact, a few paragraphs explaining why America fought in Vietnam will help, since the battle for the presidency that year was in many ways a battle over Vietnam policy.

After a century of occupation by various countries, and following the end of World War II, a peace agreement divided Vietnam into two states—the communist North and the democratic South. Later, the North attacked the South to force reunification under communist domination. The Soviet Union and Red China (so called in those days to distinguish it from the non-communist Republic of China, which the communists drove onto the island of Taiwan during their civil war in 1949) supported their fellow communists in the North. Since the South was ill-equipped to defend itself against this troika, America faced two choices: let South Vietnam fall to the communists and risk the spread of totalitarianism in the region, or help.

America chose to help, but our mission was probably doomed from the start. As Hubert Humphrey later noted, "We went into Vietnam… and found military allies who were poorly trained, poorly equipped, and without much stomach for battle. As we trained and equipped, the battle somehow became ours."*

Originally, in the 1950s, President Eisenhower sent advisers; President Kennedy sent military personnel in the guise of more advisers. Combat operations began in 1964 under President Lyndon Johnson, with congressional approval, in retaliation of Northern communist guerillas reportedly firing on two US ships in the Gulf of Tonkin. Congress voted for the Tonkin Gulf Resolution thinking it authorized a limited armed response to aggression. During the next four years, Johnson treated it as a de facto declaration of war. From 1965 until the end of his presidency, Johnson ordered his generals to attack the North, but to do so without provoking the Red Chinese to intervene militarily (as they did in Korea in 1950). Johnson's policy was to squeeze the North into seeking peace, not to destroy them. Vice President Humphrey recalled the night in 1966 when Johnson told neutralist Burmese President Ne Win that he was doing everything he could for peace, and then asked

---

* Hubert H. Humphrey, *The Education of a Public Man: My Life and Politics* (New York: Doubleday & Co. Inc., 1976), 341.

him why that goal eluded him. Ne Win replied, "What you are doing wrong is asking for peace. The North Vietnamese view that as a sign of weakness." Johnson insisted that, as president, he must do everything possible for peace. Ne Win told LBJ, "The North Vietnamese do not hear your peace overtures as an honest, legitimate desire for peace, but as weakness. You must make them believe there will be no peace until they are defeated. When they understand you are going to destroy them, then there will be peace."

Johnson shook his head: "I can't do that," he replied. Thus, Lyndon Johnson's war of attrition doomed America's prospect for military success in the region.

Throughout most of his presidency, Johnson continued his Vietnam military policies with solid bipartisan congressional support. The first Democratic intraparty fissure occurred in the US Senate on March 1, 1966, when Wayne Morse (D-OR) offered an amendment to repeal the Gulf of Tonkin Resolution. The Senate defeated the Morse amendment 92-5. Eugene McCarthy supported the amendment; voting to continue the war was Robert F. Kennedy.** Even into late 1967, with Johnson expanding the war, the antiwar forces mustered a meager five votes in the Senate to end American involvement. It was then that Eugene McCarthy challenged Johnson for the presidency on the platform of ending US military action in Vietnam. When the Minnesota senator announced his candidacy, he trod a lonely road.

And then came 1968. . . .

**   Eugene McCarthy, *Up 'Til Now* (New York: Harcourt Brace Jovanovich, 1987), 184.

ACKNOWLEDGMENTS

The author's original notes outlining his concept for *On to Chicago*, August 19, 2015

OVER MY LUNCH HOUR on August 19, 2015, I sat alone at a small window-table at the Stadium Tavern (now Fullerton Brew Co.) in Fullerton, California, and ordered my burger. I looked forward to my upcoming vacation, during which I planned to write the sequel to my third book, *And Then I Met...Stories of Growing Up, Meeting Famous People, and Annoying the Hell Out of Them.* Somewhere between the delivery of the food and my first bite, and from out of nowhere, came the inspiration for this book. While my food grew cold, I sketched the entire outline for this story on four note cards. Over the next sixteen months, researching and writing *On to Chicago* became my mistress. For those of you waiting for the sequel to *And Then I Met,* thank you for your patience—I'll get to it one of these days.

• • • • •

Along with the nine main protagonists in the story, scores of other people mentioned in the book were actual participants in the 1968 campaign. To help move along the narrative, at times I created fictional characters to present the factual history in a more condensed fashion.

Making guest appearances in *On to Chicago* were the following players (in order of appearance):

CHRIS EVANS (ROBERT KENNEDY'S CALIFORNIA POLLSTER)

Unlike our doomed character in the book, Chris Evans remains very much alive. In real life, Chris is not a pollster; he is a former homicide prosecutor with the Orange County District Attorney's Office and a retired commissioner of the Superior Court of California. If RFK were alive today and running for president, I have no doubt that Chris would be one of his key "three-figure" donors. If you want to know how he met his "widow," Nikki Boncè Evans, you'll have to ask him.

JEFF SOLSBY (ROBERT KENNEDY'S DEPUTY PRESS SECRETARY)

Jeff served as my very able congressional press secretary from 1997 to 2001. He is the vice president of communications and membership for the Wine and Spirits Wholesalers of America, Washington, DC.

CLINT BOLICK (ROBERT KENNEDY'S AIDE WHO INFORMED THE BOSS THAT LBJ WOULD NOT SEEK REELECTION IN 1968)

My buddy since our eighth grade Advanced Government class at Ben Franklin Junior High School, Clint went on to become one of America's premiere lawyers defending liberty, choice in education, and free enterprise. He serves as an associate justice of the Arizona Supreme Court.

ACKNOWLEDGMENTS

JON FISH (EUGENE MCCARTHY'S SMART-ALECK CONSERVATIVE REPUBLICAN STAFFER)

A former gang homicide prosecutor with the Orange County District Attorney's office, Jon serves as a judge of the Superior Court of California.

ROGER MAHAN AND DAN SWANSON (ROBERT KENNEDY'S ADVANCE MEN AT THE AMBASSADOR HOTEL)

Like Clint Bolick, Dan and Roger are lifelong friends since our days together in junior high school. Roger is a senior policy adviser to the majority leader of the US House of Representatives, and Dan is a lawyer and a partner at Gibson, Dunn & Crutcher.

JEREMY BURKS AND DEAN ALLEVATO (THE TWO CAMPAIGN-BUTTON MANUFACTURERS WHO TURNED THE UNCUT KENNEDY BADGES INTO WALLACE BADGES AFTER RFK'S SHOOTING)

Both Jeremy and Dean are deputies with the Orange County Sheriff's Department. Jeremy was, and Dean is, my courtroom bailiff. Both are great husbands and fathers, and tremendous public servants.

ALEX DOURBETAS (THE NEUROSURGEON HUBERT HUMPHREY ORDERED FLOWN TO CALIFORNIA ON AN AIR FORCE JET AFTER RFK'S SHOOTING)

Alex is the young son of my friend and colleague, the Honorable Nico Dourbetas, judge of the Superior Court of California. Alex already shows great promise as a political historian and collector of presidential campaign memorabilia. He and his sister Christina are the future of America.

THOMAS BARKER, M.D. (ROBERT KENNEDY'S SURGEON AT GOOD SAMARITAN HOSPITAL)

Tom is a medical doctor in Orange County, California, and has been

488

my physician for years. While writing this book, I often interrupted my annual examination (sometimes at moments quite awkward for both of us) with medical questions as to how doctors in the 1960s would have handled brain injuries, bullet wounds, and related surgeries and treatments.

WALT LEWIS (THE DETECTIVE WHO INTERVIEWED ROBERT KENNEDY IN THE HOSPITAL AFTER THE SHOOTING)

Walt served as a prosecutor in the Los Angeles County District Attorney's office for thirty-two years. When I joined the office as a rookie Grade I deputy DA in 1985, Walt was my first boss. Since retiring from the law, he authored the widely acclaimed book on the criminal court system, *The Criminal Justice Club.*

TRUDY KRUSE, R.N. (ROBERT KENNEDY'S REPUBLICAN NURSE AT GOOD SAMARITAN HOSPITAL)

Trudy is, in reality, my beloved mother-in-law. The no-nonsense approach she took with her celebrity patient mirrors how she handles her son-in-law.

TERRY GREEN (RETIRED MINNESOTA JUDGE AND HUBERT HUMPHREY'S LIFELONG FRIEND)

Terry is a former prosecutor in the Los Angeles County District Attorney's office and was my immediate supervisor at the Pasadena courthouse during my time as a rookie DA. Terry is a judge of the Superior Court of California.

JON H. JACOBS (THE PENNSYLVANIA DELEGATION CHAIRMAN WHOSE VOTE PUT HUBERT HUMPHREY OVER THE TOP AT THE 1968 DEMOCRATIC NATIONAL CONVENTION)

My oldest friend—we've known each other since fifth grade—when we were both ardent supporters of HHH during his 1968 campaign against Nixon. Jon remains a loyal Democrat and HHH admirer, and his keen editing eye caught many typographical errors in this book that my other volunteer readers overlooked. He is a retired database analyst/developer in the San Diego area.

JASON ROE (NELSON ROCKEFELLER'S POLITICAL DIRECTOR WHO TIPPED OFF THE NIXON CAMPAIGN ABOUT GOVERNOR AGNEW'S SCANDAL)

When I served in Congress, Jason was my political director, and he later became my chief of staff at the Commerce Department during President George W. Bush's administration. A longtime Washington and California political veteran, Jason served as senior adviser to Marco Rubio's 2016 presidential run, deputy campaign manager for Mitt Romney's presidential campaign in 2007, and chief of staff to Congressman Tom Feeney. He has managed many state, local, and national campaigns, and is the principal at Roe Strategic, a political consulting firm in San Diego. I am the proud godfather of Jason and Patty's son, Jackson.

GABRIELA CERVANTES (NELSON ROCKEFELLER'S LUSCIOUS SECRETARY)

With my previous three books, my longtime courtroom clerk Gloria Cervantes complained that I never put her in any of them. When I began this book, she insisted that I correct this oversight. I told her I had an open role for a woman to play Nelson Rockefeller's beautiful secretary/tart. Her response was Classic Gloria: "I'll take it, but make him give me a clothing allowance—and health insurance!" For the story, she preferred a more glamorized version of her first name, so "Gabriela Cervantes" was born. I modeled Gabriela's positive attributes after Gloria. As for the rest—well—that's the trade-off for the clothing allowance.

WAYNE PAUGH (THE YOUNG ATTORNEY IN NIXON'S LAW OFFICE AND LATER NIXON CAMPAIGN AIDE)

Wayne succeeded Jason Roe as my chief of staff when I served at the US Commerce Department. Wayne is a prosecutor for the Department of Homeland Security at the federal courthouse in Denver. He is the father of two beautiful twins, Reagan and Rogan (one of my greatest honors came when Wayne and Camille named their son after me). When Wayne read this manuscript, he didn't feel I captured sufficiently his old boss Jason Roe's "asshole-ness." With his help, I tried to present the reader with the Essential Jason that Wayne and I know and love.

DANA ALICE (THE NEW HAMPSHIRE DESK CLERK WHO MISTOOK RICHARD NIXON FOR JACK WEBB AND GOT HIS AUTOGRAPH FOR HERSELF AND HER TWIN SISTER, CLAIRE)

Dana and Claire are my adorable twin daughters, and the great delights of their parents' lives. As an aside, having now authored four books, I write under the immense disability of being about a four-finger typist who must look at the keys to proceed. That makes typing quotations a special problem for me: I memorize a few words, look away to type, and then try to find my place in the source so I can pick up where I left off. Dana helped solve that problem. When I needed to type a quotation, she put down whatever electronic gaming device happened to occupy her attention and read it to me slowly, which allowed me to watch the keys as I typed. Dana provided this service for free, and she did it until I discovered the wonders of speech-recognition software. Her sister Claire, however, is a natural-born capitalist. Claire let me use her laptop to write the manuscript (the one I bought her, incidentally)—but she rented it to me—for twenty dollars a month! Thank you, Twin A and Twin B. Your mom and I love you both very much.

"MR. POOCHIGIAN AND MR. PRINGLE" (THE TWO MAJOR DONORS WHO STOOD UP JASON ROE AT THE COSMOS CLUB AFTER GOVERNOR ROMNEY DROPPED OUT OF THE 1968 PRESIDENTIAL CAMPAIGN)

When I served as majority leader in the California State Assembly, my two roommates and beloved friends were my colleagues Chuck Poochigian (chairman of the Assembly Appropriations Committee) and Curt Pringle (speaker of the Assembly). Chuck serves as a justice on the California Court of Appeal. After serving two terms as mayor of Anaheim, California, Curt founded his own consulting firm, Curt Pringle and Associates.

MICHAEL ACOSTA (FIRST BASEMAN FOR THE BREA WILDCATS INJURED BY A WILD PITCH AND THE SON OF GABRIELA CERVANTES)

Michael actually was his high school's first baseman and team captain for the Brea (California) Wildcats, and he really is Gloria's (aka Gabriella's) son. Michael works for FedEx; he is a fine young man and an outstanding credit to his wonderful mother.

FRANK AMBROSE (MICHAEL ACOSTA'S DOCTOR AT ST. JUDE HOSPITAL)
Frank is another lifelong friend since the end of junior high. A Navy veteran, Frank is retired and living in Los Angeles.

CURTIS IAUKEA (ADMINISTRATIVE ASSISTANT TO MARYLAND GOVERNOR SPIRO AGNEW)

Like Frank Ambrose, Curtis ("Rocky" to his friends) has been my lifelong pal since before high school. My exploits with Frank and Rocky are memorialized in my first book, *Rough Edges*. Rocky is a retired professional wrestler and a retired skipper of his own tourist-boat concession in Honolulu.

THE AGNEW PRESS CONFERENCE REPORTERS:

- **BOB WYATT (BALTIMORE SUN)**
- **BRET MUNCY (FREDERICK, MARYLAND POST)**
- **ANDRE MANSSOURIAN (STATION WBAL)**

Bob, Bret, and I worked making pizzas at Straw Hat in Livermore, California, when we were students. Bob and I moved to Los Angeles together after college in 1979, and I am the proud godfather of his son, Joseph Wyatt. Bob is retired from state and federal government service; Bret is a retired sergeant for the San Jose Police Department, and Andre is a judge of the Superior Court of California.

PAT AND JOHN ROGAN (NELSON ROCKEFELLER'S *BALTIMORE BOYS*)

How can I write a book and not stiff in the names of my baby brothers? Pat is director of engineering operations for the San Francisco 49ers at Levi's Stadium in Santa Clara, California. John is the senior chief engineer for Wells Fargo Bank's San Francisco headquarters.

ALLEN BRANDSTATER (RONALD REAGAN'S DEPUTY PRESS SECRETARY)

A respected conservative columnist and GOP activist, Allen actually did work for Reagan—but not in 1968. He served as Reagan's 1976 deputy campaign manager (under Lyn Nofziger) in the Western states. At the 1968 Republican National Convention, Allen, along with Shawn Steel and Pat Nolan (see below) were in Miami as young warriors working hard for Reagan's nomination over Nixon.

PAT NOLAN (YOUTH FOR REAGAN COORDINATOR AT THE 1968 GOP CONVENTION)

As a teen, Pat was active in Youth for Reagan at the 1968 GOP Convention. He went on to become a successful lawyer, California State Assembly minority leader, and in later years headed Charles Colson's ministry Justice Fellowship. Pat was my predecessor in the California State Assembly, and his story of courage and fortitude is chronicled in my book *Rough Edges*.

"MONTY" (THE CHAIRMAN OF JASON ROE'S "LITTLE THINGS COMMITTEE")

During my 2000 congressional campaign, whenever my political director, Jason Roe, needed something handled, shall we say "delicately," he called on Monty Floyd. I once asked Jason what was Monty's official role in the campaign. He replied, "Let's just say he's chairman of 'The Little Things Committee.'" When I asked him what that meant, Jason turned and walked out of the room without answering. I guess some things are better left unknown. Monty is a writer who lives in Germany.

SHAWN STEEL (THE 1968 REPUBLICAN CONVENTION PAGE ASSIGNED TO TRACK DOWN SENATOR BARRY GOLDWATER)

Like Allen Brandstater and Pat Nolan, Shawn attended the 1968 Republican Convention as a Reagan campaign volunteer. A successful attorney in Southern California, he is the former state chairman of the California Republican Party and a member of the Republican National Committee.

DAVID AZBELL (GEORGE WALLACE'S PRESS SECRETARY)

It was David's father, Joe Azbell (1927-1995), the Alabama reporter who first broke the story of the Montgomery bus boycott in 1955, who worked as a press aide on George Wallace's 1968 campaign. Joe served as director of communications for Wallace's 1972 and 1976 presidential races, as well as his 1970 and 1974 gubernatorial reelection campaigns. Just as in our story, David later took over his father's duties, serving as Wallace's spokesman and personal aide from 1995 to 1997, when the former governor was retired from office but still active publicly. David now runs Azbell Communications, a political consulting firm in Montgomery, Alabama.

LILITH JAMES (GEORGE WALLACE'S BEAUTIFUL DEPUTY PRESS SECRETARY)

"Miss Lil"—elegant, beautiful, smart, fun, seductive, perfect. Our paths crossed once, but only in fantasy… where she remains. Special thanks to Elisabeth Babarci for helping me breathe life into Lil, whose gentle grace mirrors her own.

THE NEWS MEDIA:

- JEFF FERGUSON (CHRISTIAN SCIENCE MONITOR)
- ALICIA DUBOIS (COPLEY NEWS SERVICE)
- MICHAEL LEVERSEN (GANNETT NEWS SERVICE)
- SCOTT STEINER (PITTSBURGH POST-GAZETTE)
- JACKI BROWN (KXTV NEWS PRODUCER DURING THE REAGAN-KENNEDY DEBATE)

Alicia is my wonderful courtroom reporter; Jeff, Mike, Scott, and Jacki are judges and my colleagues on the Superior Court of California.

JOHN VARGO (THE ANTI-HUMPHREY ACTIVIST WHO CHANGED HIS MIND AND TRADED HIS "STOP HUMPHREY" BUTTON FOR A "HUMPHREY-KENNEDY" BADGE)

John is a longtime congressional staffer who, as a young man, worked as a "gofer" in HHH's vice presidential office. In 1968 his friend at the Democratic National Committee gave John a DEMOCRACY DEMANDS—STOP HUMPHREY campaign button. The friend said that an anti-Humphrey activist sent a letter to the Committee saying that he didn't need it anymore after Humphrey broke with LBJ over Vietnam. John shared that story with me; when I included it in the book, I made him the author of that 1968 letter.

HELEN KLEUPFER AND DELLA GLOVER (THE ELDERLY SISTERS DISCUSSING THE RFK-JACQUELINE KENNEDY AFFAIR REVELATION)

My grandmother, Helen Kleupfer, and her sister (my great-aunt), Della Glover, both raised me as a young boy. Grandma died in 1966, and Aunt Della died in 1971. They were Irish-Catholic Democrats—and all the Drew Pearson smear columns combined would not have diminished their affection for the Kennedys.

CHARLES SNIDER (WALLACE CAMPAIGN AIDE)

As a young man, Charlie really was one of Wallace's campaign aides in 1968. Later he became the national director of Wallace's 1972 and 1976 presidential campaigns. He and his wife Nancy live in Montgomery, Alabama.

• • • • •

During the year and a half it took me to complete a draft of *On to Chicago,* I imposed on a number of people for various favors, including reviewing parts of the manuscript and helping me with my innumerable questions. Many thanks to: Ann Anooshian Esq.; David Azbell; Elisabeth Babarci; Thomas Barker, M.D.; The Honorable Jacki Brown; Jameson Campaigne; Barbara Cline (archivist, The Lyndon B. Johnson Library); Dr. Monica Crowley; The Honorable Christopher J. Evans; The Honorable Jon Fish; Michael Fleming; Cheryll Fong (assistant curator, Eugene J. McCarthy Papers, Special Collections and Rare Books at the University of Minnesota Libraries); The Honorable Newt Gingrich; The Honorable Beatriz M. G. Gordon; Peggy Grande; Jon H. Jacobs; Nancy Finley King; Sandi Lee (technical service manager, Concord, New Hampshire Public Library); Terrence Lisbeth (reference assistant, The Library of Congress); Kathy Lubbers (The Lubbers Agency); Jillian Manus; Tal Nadan (reference archivist, New York Public Library); The Honorable Patrick J. Nolan; Wayne Paugh Esq.; Laura Poochigian; Jason Roe; Christine Rogan; Claire Rogan; Dana Rogan; Robert Schlesinger; Charles Snider; Jeff Solsby; The Honorable

Scott Steiner; Ted Van Dyk; John Vargo; Frank Weimann (Folio Literary Management); and Anthony Ziccardi.

Because the literary agent representing me on my first three books had retired, once I finished the manuscript for *On to Chicago* I was in need of a new one. I spent a couple of months trolling the relevant Internet websites and sending out scores of "query" letters to agents asking them to consider representing me. One of the few who got back to me was Sealy Yates, the founder of Yates and Yates. He told me that he read the manuscript I had sent him and that he loved it. However, he said that his specialty was representing authors within the Christian publishing community; he had never represented an author on a work of political historic fiction. Since he did not feel he could do the best job for me, he turned me down. During our later discussions, Sealy and I became friends, and his great professionalism and work ethic cemented my belief that he was the only person I wanted representing me. When I told him so, he again protested that he had never handled a book like this. I replied that we were even—I had never written a book like this. Besides, I told him not to worry about whether he got me the best publishing deal. Considering that my previous books never became blockbusters, the "deal" bar was very low. Thus, America's premier Christian literary agent ended up representing a sometimes-backsliding Christian author whose new book has enough F-bombs in it to qualify as a drill instructor's boot camp training manual (for which Sealy bears no responsibility—and for which I blame Lyndon Johnson!). I'm grateful that the Lord allowed me to write this book if, for no other reason, than to bring Sealy and his wonderful family into my life.

This is my fourth book for WND Books and Joseph Farah, editor-in-chief, chairman, and founder. Joseph seems determined to keep publishing my works until the literary world discovers them! Once again, Joseph, I am honored to have your hand overseeing this project.

Blessings to you and your dear wife Elizabeth, the chief marketing officer and cofounder of WND Books.

With this book I am blessed to be reunited with a group of tremendous WND artists. On this project, as with our previous ones, my deepest thanks to editorial director Geoff Stone (who came up with an infinitely better subtitle for this book than the one I submitted); creative director Mark Karis (who once again devised a brilliant and eye-catching book cover design), and layout guru Ashley Karis. To my two new friends Art Moore (copy editor) and Shana Bell (proofreader), thanks for undertaking the daunting task of checking the writing style of a lawyer (a profession whose members are noted for composing dull and cumbersome language).

Love and hugs to my wife Christine, who tolerates my writing clutter each time I embark on a new book project. Thanks for your unending patience. I remain *forever yors* (the inscription on my wedding ring thanks to an illiterate Nordstrom jewelry engraver).

Lastly, my thanks to you. With your imagination, and after a half century wait, Robert F. Kennedy has completed his journey.

ORANGE COUNTY, CALIFORNIA, JUNE 5, 2018
THE 50TH ANNIVERSARY OF RFK'S ASSASSINATION

SENATOR ROBERT F. KENNEDY

Photograph signed during the 1968 California presidential primary

Author's collection

PRESIDENT AND MRS. LYNDON B. JOHNSON, 1968

Photograph signed for the author

1969

VICE PRESIDENT HUBERT H. HUMPHREY

Photograph signed for the author

February 19, 1971

SENATOR EUGENE J. MCCARTHY

Photograph signed for the author

June 27, 1970

FORMER VICE PRESIDENT RICHARD M. NIXON

Photograph signed for the author

April 13, 1978

GOVERNOR RONALD REAGAN

Photograph signed for the author

July 30, 1970

GOVERNOR NELSON A. ROCKEFELLER

Photograph signed for the author

December 20, 1971

GOVERNOR GEORGE ROMNEY

Photograph signed for the author

December 22, 1972

GOVERNOR GEORGE WALLACE

Photograph signed for the author

January 3, 1972

BIBLIOGRAPHY

1968 Republican National Convention Telephone Directory and Guide. Miami: Systems Programing Services, Inc., 1968.

Agnew, Spiro T. *Go Quietly ... or Else.* New York: William Morrow and Co., 1980.

Alsop, Stewart. "Hubert Horatio Humphrey." *The Saturday Evening Post*, August 24, 1968.

Ambrose, Stephen E. *Eisenhower: Soldier and President.* New York: Simon and Schuster Paperbacks, 1990.

Ambrose, Stephen E. *Nixon (Volume Two): The Triumph of a Politician 1962-1972.* New York: Simon and Schuster, 1989.

American Presidency Project, Papers of Lyndon B. Johnson. "Remarks at a Dinner of the Veterans of Foreign Wars." March 12, 1968. http://www.presidency.ucsb.edu/lyndon_johnson.php.

American Presidency Project, Papers of Lyndon B. Johnson. "Remarks at the Astrodome at a Democratic Party Rally." November 3, 1968. http://www.presidency.ucsb.edu/ws/?pid=29221.

Associated Press. "California Delegation's Resolution Forced His Hand, Reagan Claims." *Santa Cruz Sentinel*, Santa Cruz, California, August 6, 1968.

Associated Press. "Clark to Head McCarthy Bid for President." Fitchburg, Mass., *Sentinel*, December 13, 1967.

Associated Press. "Disappointed Md. Gov. Agnew to Review Draft Rocky Drive." *The Cumberland News*, Cumberland, Maryland, March 22, 1968.

Associated Press. "Election Results Hint at Realignment." North Adams, Massachusetts, *Transcript*, May 2, 1968.

Associated Press. "Like a Space Shot, Pat [Nixon] Says." *Florence Morning News*, Florence, South Carolina, August 8, 1968.

Associated Press. "M'Carthy Urges LBJ to Campaign." *Bridgeport Post*, Bridgeport, Connecticut, March 13, 1968.

Associated Press. "Nixon Calls it 'Smashing Win.'" *Bridgeport Post*, Bridgeport, Connecticut, March 13, 1968.

Associated Press. "Nixon Holding Lead as Balloting Begins: Tabulation Shows Top Commitment." *Florence Morning News*, Florence, South Carolina, August 8, 1968.

Associated Press. "Reagan Will Run: Candidacy is Official." *The Lincoln Star*, Lincoln, Nebraska, August 6, 1968.

Associated Press. "Rockefeller Won't Seek Nomination: N.Y. Governor Leaves Door Open to Draft." *The Cumberland News*, Cumberland, Maryland, March 22, 1968.

Associated Press. "Rocky Entry Sparks GOP Enthusiasm." *The Salt Lake Tribune*, May 1, 1968.

Associated Press. "Rocky Still Backs Romney." *Independent*, Long Beach, California, February 2, 1968.

Associated Press. "Senator Gets 42% of Vote; President 48%." *Bridgeport Post*, Bridgeport, Connecticut, March 13, 1968.

Associated Press. "What They Said." *Post Crescent*, Appleton, Wisconsin, March 13, 1968.

Axelrod, Alan. *Patton: A Biography*. New York: St. Martin's Press, 2009.

Azbell, David. Facebook post, American Political Items Collectors page, July 18, 2014. https://www.facebook.com/groups/apicusa/search/?query=azbell%20wallace%20cigar.

Bass, Jack, and Marilyn W. Thompson. *Strom: The Complicated Personal and Political Life of Strom Thurmond*. New York: PublicAffairs, 2005.

Bell, Jack, Associated Press. "LBJ Can Expect Rise in Fury of Criticism." *Bridgeport Post*, Bridgeport, Connecticut, March 13, 1968.

Bennett, Jim. "I Covered George Wallace's Presidential Races in the 60s." Alabama Media Group, March 16, 2016. http://www.al.com/opinion/index.ssf/2016/03/i_covered_george_wallaces_pres.html.

Billington, James H. *Respectfully Quoted: A Dictionary of Quotations*. Mineola, New York: Dover Publications, 2010.

Buchanan, Patrick J. *Nixon's White House Wars*. New York: Crown Forum, 2017.

Buchanan, Patrick J. *The Greatest Comeback: How Richard Nixon Rose from Defeat to Create the New Majority*. New York: Crown Forum, 2014.

Buckley, William F. Jr. *The Reagan I Knew*. New York: Basic Books, 2008.

Burka, Paul. "Presidential Hopefuls Juggle Appealing to the Common Man While Benefiting from Their Sizable Bank Accounts." *Los Angeles Times*, July 25, 2004.

Burke, Cathy. "Bobby Kennedy Was Ronald Reagan's 'Supreme Villain.'" *Newsmax*, October 7, 2015. http://www.newsmax.com/Politics/Robert-Kennedy-Ronald-Reagan/2014/12/05/id/611395/.

Busby, Horace. *The Thirty-First of March: An Intimate Portrait of Lyndon Johnson's Final Days in Office*. New York: Farrar, Straus and Giroux, 2005.

Boyd, Joseph H. Jr., and Charles R. Holcomb. *Oreos & Dubonnet: Remembering Governor Nelson A. Rockefeller*. Albany: Excelsior Editions, 2012.

Cannon, Lou. "Actor, Governor, President, Icon." *Washington Post*, June 6, 2004. http://www.washingtonpost.com/wp-dyn/articles/A18329-2004Jun5.html.

Cannon, Lou. *Governor Reagan: His Rise to Power*. New York: Public Affairs, 2003.

Cannon, Lou. *Ronnie & Jesse: A Political Odyssey*. Garden City: Doubleday & Company,, 1969.

Caro, Robert A. *The Years of Lyndon Johnson: The Passage of Power*. New York: Alfred A. Knopf, 2012.

Chafets, Zev. *Roger Ailes Off Camera*. New York: Sentinel, 2013.

Chester, Lewis, Godfrey Hodgson, and Bruce Page. *An American Melodrama: The Presidential Campaign of 1968*. New York: Viking Press, 1969.

Chicago Tribune, "A Diary of Convention's Triumphs and Tragedies." September 8, 1968.

Chris's Hot Dog Stand. Facebook. https://www.facebook.com/ChrisHotDogs/about/.

Clifford, Clark. *Counsel to the President: A Memoir*. New York: Random House, 1991.

Cohodas, Nadine. *Strom Thurmond & The Politics of Southern Change*. New York: Simon & Schuster, 1993.

Conklin, Ellis. "Hospital Where Robert Kennedy Died Rich in Other History." UPI Archives, May 29, 1985. http://www.upi.com/Archives/1985/05/29/Hospital-where-Robert-Kennedy-died-rich-in-other-history/4136486187200/.

Connally, John B., with Mickey Herskowitz. *In History's Shadow: An American Odyssey*. New York: Hyperion, 1993.

Cross, Brigadier General James U. *Around the World with LBJ: My Wild Ride as Air Force One Pilot, White House Aide, and Personal Confidant*. Austin: University of Texas Press, 2009.

Crowley, Monica. *Nixon Off the Record: His Candid Commentaries on People and Politics*. New York: Random House, 1996.

Dallek, Robert. *Flawed Giant: Lyndon Johnson and His Times 1961-1973*. New York: Oxford University Press, 1998.

David, Mark. "Rock It Like a Rockefeller." *Variety*, February 27, 2008. http://variety.com/2008/more/real-estalker/rock-it-like-a-rockefeller-1201227746/.

Deaver, Michael K. *A Different Drummer: My Thirty Years with Ronald Reagan*. New York: HarperCollins, 2001.

DeFrank, Thomas M. *Write It When I'm Gone: Remarkable Off-the-Record Conversations with Gerald R. Ford*. New York: The Berkley Publishing Co., 2007.

de Toledano, Ralph. *R.F.K. The Man Who Would Be President*. New York: G.P. Putnam's Sons, 1967.

Dorley, Edward, United Press International. "Nixon Begins His Presidency Fight," *The Times*, San Mateo, California, February 2, 1968.

Duncan, David Douglas, *Self-Portrait U.S.A.* New York: Harry N. Abrams, Inc., 1969.

Dunlap, David W. "New York Says Farewell to American Bible Society, and Its Building." *New York Times*, October 21, 2015. http://www.nytimes.com/2015/10/22/nyregion/new-york-says-farewell-to-american-bible-society-and-its-building.html.

Ehrlichman, John. *Witness to Power: The Nixon Years*. New York: Simon and Schuster, 1982.

Eleazer, Frank, United Press International. "Possibly Last Electoral College Meets to Formally Elect Nixon." *The Technician*, North Carolina State University at Raleigh, December 16, 1968.

Elmer, John, and William Fulton. "Rockefeller Begins Campaign in Miami." *Chicago Tribune*, August 4, 1968.

Encyclopedia of Television, "Kennedy-Nixon Presidential Debates, 1960." http://www.museum.tv/eotv/kennedy-nixon.htm.

Eskew, Glenn T. "Lurleen B. Wallace (1967-1968)." *Encyclopedia of Alabama*, updated September 30, 2014. http://www.encyclopediaofalabama.org/article/h-1662.

Feldstein, Mark. *Poisoning the Press: Richard Nixon, Jack Anderson, and the Rise of Washington's Scandal Culture*. New York: Picador, 2010.

Frank, Jeffrey. *Ike and Dick: Portrait of a Strange Political Marriage*. New York: Simon and Schuster Paperbacks, 2013.

Freeburg, Russell. "Bartlett Withdraws, Indorses Nixon." *Chicago Tribune*, August 4, 1968. [Author's note: in its 1968 storyline, the Chicago Tribune editor used the "indorse" variant of "endorse"]

Freeburg, Russell. "Rocky's Halt Nixon Plan—Secret Hot Line to Reagan Camp Set Up at Parley: Staff Ordered to Shadow Leading GOP Figures." *Chicago Tribune*, August 4, 1968.

Garment, Leonard, *Crazy Rhythm: My Journey from Brooklyn, Jazz, and Wall Street to Nixon's White House, Watergate, and Beyond....* New York: Time Books, 1997.

Gentry, Curt. *J. Edgar Hoover: The Man and the Secrets*. New York: W.W. Norton & Company, 1991.

Goodwin, Richard N. *Remembering America: A Voice from the Sixties*. Boston: Little Brown and Company, 1988.

Griffin, Thomas. "The Nixon Era Begins: What the Election Wasn't About." *Life* magazine, November 15, 1968.

Guthman, Edwin O., and Jeffrey Shulman, eds. *Robert Kennedy in His Own Words: The Unpublished Recollections of the Kennedy Years*. New York: Bantam Press, 1988.

Halberstam, David. *The Unfinished Odyssey of Robert Kennedy*. New York: Random House, 1969.

Healy, Patrick. "An Exclusive Club Gets Included." *New York Times*, July 27, 2008. http://www.nytimes.com/2008/07/27/weekinreview/27healy.html.

Herman, Arthur. *Joseph McCarthy: Re-Examining the Life and Legacy of America's Most Hated Senator*. New York: The Free Press, 2000.

Hersh, Burton. *Bobby and J. Edgar: The Historic Face-Off Between the Kennedys and J. Edgar Hoover That Transformed America*. New York: Carroll & Graf Publishers, 2007.

Herzog, Arthur. *McCarthy for President*. New York: Viking Press, 1969.

Hewitt, Hugh. *A Mormon in the White House? 10 Things Every American Should Know About Mitt Romney*. Washington: Regnery Publishing, Inc., 2007.

Heymann, C. David. *Bobby and Jackie: A Love Story*. New York: Atria Paperback, 2009.

Heymann, C. David. *RFK: A Candid Biography of Robert F. Kennedy*. New York: Dutton, 1998.

Hoeh, David C. *1968 • McCarthy • New Hampshire: "I Hear America Singing."* Rochester: Lone Oak Press, 1994.

Humphrey, Hubert H. *The Education of a Public Man: My Life and Politics*. New York: Doubleday & Co., Inc., 1976.

Janis, Ronald H. "Stop the Bombing Says Humphrey." *Harvard Crimson*, October 1, 1968. http://www.thecrimson.com/article/1968/10/1/stop-the-bombing-says-humphrey-pvice-president. Only in Our State. "These 8 Amazing Alabama Restaurants are Loaded with Local History." http://www.onlyinyourstate.com/alabama/historical-restaurants-al/.

Johnson, Lyndon B. *The Vantage Point: Perspectives of the Presidency 1963-1969*. New York: Holt, Rinehart and Winston, 1971.

Johnson, Sam Houston. *My Brother Lyndon*. New York: Cowles Book Company, 1970.

Jordan, Winthrop. *The Americans*. Boston: McDougal Littel, 1996.

Kampelman, Max M. *Entering New Worlds*. Norwalk: The Easton Press, 1991.

Kearns Goodwin, Doris. *Lyndon Johnson and the American Dream*. New York: Harper & Row, 1976.

Kengor, Paul. "The Great Forgotten Debate." National Review, May 22, 2007.

Kennedy, Edward M. *True Compass: A Memoir*. New York: Twelve/Hatchette Book Group, 2009.

Kennedy, John F. "America's Stakes in Vietnam." Speech to the American Friends of Vietnam, June 1956. https://en.wikipedia.org/wiki/Vietnam_War#cite_note-133.

Kilgore, Ed. "The Ghost of Curtis LeMay." *Washington Monthly*, December 4, 2013. http://washingtonmonthly.com/2013/12/04/the-ghost-of-curtis-lemay/.

King, Martin Luther, Jr. *The Autobiography of Martin Luther King, Jr.* (Chapter 15, Stanford University Libraries) https://swap.stanford.edu/20141218230019/http://mlk-kpp01.stanford.edu/kingweb/publications/autobiography/chp_15.htm.

Kopelson, Gene. *Reagan's 1968 Dress Rehearsal: Ike, RFK, and Reagan's Emergence as a World Statesman*, Los Angeles: Figueroa Press, 2016.

Langer, Emily. "Robert L. Hardesty, Speechwriter for President Lyndon B. Johnson, Dies at 82." *Washington Post*, July 9, 2013. https://www.washingtonpost.com/national/robert-l-hardesty-speechwriter-for-president-lyndon-b-johnson-dies-at-82/2013/07/09/907f1834-e8b8-11e2-8f22-de4bd2a2bd39_story.html.

Lardner, George Jr. "Chappaquiddick, 1989." *Washington Post*, July 16, 1989. https://www. washingtonpost.com/archive/opinions/1989/07/16/chappaquiddick-1989/28d50758-314b-49e1-90bd-78eb8fddf64f/.

Larner, Jeremy. "Nobody Knows: Reflections on the McCarthy Campaign of 1968." New York: Macmillan, 1970.

Lawrence Berkeley National Laboratories Image Library, Collection: Berkeley-Lab/Seaborg-Archive. "Breakfast at Owls Nest Camp, Bohemian Grove, July 23, 1967." http://imglib.lbl.gov/ImgLib/COLLECTIONS/BERKELEY-LAB/SEABORG-ARCHIVE/index/96B05411.html.

LeMay, Curtis. Interview with the *Washington Post*, October 4, 1968.

Lesher, Stephen. *George Wallace: American Populist*. New York: Addison-Wesley Publishing Co., 1994.

Lewis, Joseph. *What Makes Reagan Run?* New York: McGraw-Hill 1968.

Life magazine, "The Bomb Halt Decision." November 15, 1968

Mailer, Norman. *Miami and the Siege of Chicago*, New York: Random House, 1968 (2016 trade paperback edition).

Mankiewicz, Frank. "Nofziger: A Friend With Whom It Was A Pleasure To Disagree." *Washington Post*, March 29, 2006. http://www.washingtonpost.com/wp-dyn/content/article/2006/03/28/AR2006032802142.html.

Marlin, George J. "Is Trump Repeating George Wallace's '68 Disaster?" *Newsmax*, November 7, 2016. http://www.newsmax.com/George-J-Marlin/george-marlin-george-wallace-1968-cautionary-tale/2016/06/11/id/733409/.

McCarthy, Eugene J. *The Year of the People*. Garden City: Doubleday and Company, Inc., 1969.

McCarthy, Eugene J. *Up 'Til Now*. New York: Harcourt Brace Jovanovich, 1987.

McGowan, Tom. *The 1968 Democratic Convention*. New York: Children's Press, 2003.

Mears, Walter R., Associated Press."McCarthy 4,000 Votes Behind Johnson." *Post Crescent*, Appleton, Wisconsin, March 13, 1968.

Mecham, E.L., letter to the author, July 3, 1991.

Meese, Edwin III. *With Reagan: The Inside Story*. Washington: Regnery Gateway, 1992.

Moldea, Dan E. *The Killing of Robert F. Kennedy: An Investigation of Motive, Means, and Opportunity*. New York: W.W. Norton & Company, 1995.

Mondale, Walter F. *The Good Fight: A Life in Liberal Politics*. New York: Scribner, 2010.

Montgomery, Gayle B., and James W. Johnson. *One Step from the White House: The Rise and Fall of Senator William F. Knowland*. Los Angeles: University of California Press, 1998.

Morin, Relman, Associated Press. "Rocky Reverses—'In Race to Win.'" *Salt Lake Tribune*, May 1, 1968.

Morris, Edmund. *Dutch: A Memoir of Ronald Reagan*. New York: Random House, 1999.

Muskie, Edmund S. *Journeys*. New York: Doubleday & Co., 1972.

Narvaez, Alfonso. "Gen. Curtis LeMay, an Architect Of Strategic Air Power, Dies at 83." *New York Times*, October 2, 1990. http://www.nytimes.com/1990/10/02/obituaries/gen-curtis-lemay-an-architect-of-strategic-air-power-dies-at-83.html.

New Hampshire Union Leader. "1968: McCarthy Stuns the President." May 3, 2011. http://www.unionleader.com/apps/pbcs.dll/article?AID=/99999999/NEWS0605/110509966.

Newsweek. "Ted Kennedy Car Accident in Chappaquiddick," August 3, 1969. http://www.newsweek.com/ted-kennedy-car-accident-chappaquiddick-207070.

Newsweek, "The Ronnie-Bobby Show." May 29, 1967.

Nixon, Richard. *RN: The Memoirs of Richard Nixon*. New York: Grosset & Dunlap, 1978.

Nixon, Richard,. *RN: The Memoirs of Richard Nixon*. New York: Simon & Schuster, 1990.

Noah, Timothy. "The Legend of Strom's Remorse." *Slate*, December 16, 2002. http://www.slate.com/articles/news_and_politics/chatterbox/2002/12/the_legend_of_stroms_remorse.html.

Nofziger, Lyn, *Nofziger*. Washington: Regnery Gateway, 1992.

O'Brien, Lawrence F. *No Final Victories: A Life in Politics from John F. Kennedy to Watergate*. New York: Doubleday & Company, Inc., 1974.

O'Donnell, Kenneth P., and David F. Powers (with Joe McCarthy). *Johnny, We Hardly Knew Ye* Boston: Little, Brown and Co., 1972.

Official Program, The Twenty-Ninth Republican National Convention. New York: Wickersham Press, Inc., 1968.

Official Report of the Proceedings of the Twenty-Ninth Republican National Convention Held in Miami Beach, Florida. Republican National Committee, 1968.

O'Neill, Tip, and William Novak. *Man of the House*. New York: Random House, 1987.

Pearson, Drew, and Tyler Abell, ed., *Diaries 1949-1959*. New York: Holt, Rinehart and Winston, 1974.

Pearson, Drew, and Peter Hannaford, ed. *Washington Merry-Go-Round: The Drew Pearson Diaries, 1960-1969*. Lincoln: Potomac Books, 2015.

Persico, Joseph E. *The Imperial Rockefeller: A Biography of Nelson A. Rockefeller*. New York: Simon & Schuster, 1982.

Price, Raymond. *With Nixon*. New York: The Viking Press, 1977.

Public Broadcasting Service (PBS). "The American Experience: George Wallace—Settin' the Woods on Fire," Program Transcript. http://www.pbs.org/wgbh/amex/wallace/filmmore/transcript/transcript1.html.

Public Broadcasting Service (PBS). "The American Experience: The 1964 Republican Campaign." http://www.pbs.org/wgbh/americanexperience/features/general-article/rockefellers-campaign/.

Roberts, Sam. "Curtis Gans, 77, is Dead; Worked to Defeat President Johnson." *New York Times*, March 16, 2015. http://www.nytimes.com/2015/03/17/us/curtis-gans-77-is-dead-worked-to-depose-president-johnson.html.

Rogan, James E. "And Then I Met...Stories of Growing Up, Meeting Famous People, and Annoying the Hell Out of Them." Washington: WND Books, 2014.

Rosenberg, Jonathan, and Zachary Karabell. *Kennedy, Johnson, and the Quest for Justice: The Civil Rights Tapes*. New York: WW Norton & Co., 2003.

Salinger, Pierre. *P.S. A Memoir*. New York: St. Martin's Press, 1995.

Schlesinger, Arthur M. Jr. *Journals 1952-2000*. New York: Penguin Books, 2007.

Schlesinger, Arthur M. Jr. *Robert Kennedy and His Times*. Boston: Houghton Mifflin Co., 1978.

Sherman, Norman. *From Nowhere to Somewhere—My Political Journey: A Memoir of Sorts*. Minneapolis: First Avenue Editions, 2016.

Shesol, Jeff. *Mutual Contempt: Lyndon Johnson, Robert Kennedy, and the Feud that Defined a Decade*. New York: W.W. Norton & Company, 1997.

Smith, Richard Norton. *On His Own Terms: A Life of Nelson Rockefeller*. New York: Random House, 2014.

Smith, Stephen, and Kate Ellis, "Campaign '68: Timeline of the 1968 Campaign." American Radio Works, American Public Media. http://americanradioworks.publicradio.org/features/campaign68/timeline.html.

Sorensen, Theodore C. *Counselor: A Life at the Edge of History*. New York: HarperCollins, 2008.

Sorensen, Theodore C. *The Kennedy Legacy*. New York: Macmillan, 1969.

Spectator. "Duty of a Prime Minister." February 19, 1942.

Stavis, Ben. *We Were the Campaign: New Hampshire to Chicago for McCarthy*. Boston: Beacon Press, 1969.

Steel, Ronald. *In Love with the Night: The American Romance with Robert Kennedy*. New York: Simon and Schuster, 2000.

Stepman, Jarrett. "Why We Use Electoral College, Not Popular Vote." *The Daily Signal*, November 7, 2016. http://dailysignal.com/2016/11/07/why-the-founders-created-the-electoral-college/.

Stone, Roger. *Nixon's Secrets*. New York: Skyhorse Publishing, 2014.

Sullivan, William C., and Bill Brown. *The Bureau: My Thirty Years in Hoover's FBI*. New York: W.W. Norton & Company, 1979.

Thomas, Evan. *Robert Kennedy: His Life*. New York: Simon & Schuster, 2000.

Thomas, Robert McG. Jr. *John W. King, 79, Governor Who Instituted State Lottery*. New York Times, August 14, 1996.

Time. "Anchors Aweigh," October 20, 1967.

Time. "General Nguyen Ngoc Loan," July 27, 1998.

Time. "In Unpath'd Waters," October 27, 1967.

Time. "Romney Rediyivus," January 26, 1968.

Time. "The Brainwashed Candidate," September 15, 1967.

Time. "The Tenacious Muckraker," September 12, 1969.

Torry, Jack. "Don't Blame Nixon for Scuttled Peace Overture." *Real Clear Politics*, August 9, 2015. http://www.realclearpolitics.com/articles/2015/08/09/dont_blame_nixon_for_scuttled_peace_overture_127667.html.

Town Meeting of the World: "The Image of America and the Youth of the World with Senator Robert F. Kennedy and Governor Ronald Reagan," as broadcast over the CBS television and radio network May 15, 1967, Charles Collingwood, moderator. http://reagan2020.us/speeches/reagan_kennedy_debate.asp.

Tribe, Laurence H., and Thomas M. Rollins, "Deadlock," *Atlantic Monthly*, October 1980, http://www.theatlantic.com/past/docs/issues/80oct/deadlock.htm.

Trohan, Walter. "Final Campaigns are Opened for Nomination," *Chicago Tribune*, August 4, 1968, 1-2.

Turner, Robert L. "Eugene McCarthy Confidently Predicts Victory at Fenway," *Boston Globe*, July 26, 1968.

United Press International. "Decision Hard Blow to Rocky Backers," *The Cumberland News*, Cumberland, Maryland, March 22, 1968.

United Press International. "GOP Convention Opens Amid Fast and Furious Politicking," *Panama City News-Herald*, Panama City, Florida, August 6, 1968.

United Press International. "Kennedy 'Reconsidering' His Role in 1968 Election." *Bridgeport Post*, Bridgeport, Connecticut, March 13, 1968.

United Press International. "Nixon, Aides to Spend 10 Days in San Diego," *Chicago Tribune*, Chicago, Illinois, August 9, 1968.

United Press International. "Wallace Through? Nixon Points Up," *Kingsport Times-News*, Kingsport, Tennessee, June 2, 1968.

United States House of Representatives, Office of Art and Archives, *Electoral College Fast Facts*. http://history.house.gov/Institution/Electoral-College/Electoral-College/.

Updegrove, Mark K. *Indomitable Will: LBJ in the Presidency*. New York: Skyhorse Publishing, 2014)

Valenti, Jack. *A Very Human President*. New York: W.W. Norton & Company, 1975.

Van Dyk, Ted. *Heroes, Hacks & Fools: Memoirs from the Political Inside*. Seattle and London: University of Washington Press, 2007.

Visitor: The Resort Magazine of South Florida, Souvenir Edition, 1968 Republican National Convention. Miami Beach: The Visitor Publishing Company, 1968.

Wainstock, Dennis D. *Election Year 1968: The Turning Point*. Enigma Books, 2012.

Wallace-Wells, Benjamin. *George Romney for President, 1968*. *New York* magazine, May 20, 2012. http://nymag.com/news/features/george-romney-2012-5/.

Washington Merry-Go-Round. "History of the Column." http://washingtonmerrygoround.com/history-of-column/.

Washington-Williams, Essie Mae. *Dear Senator: A Memoir by the Daughter of Strom Thurmond*. New York: HarperCollins, 2005.

Welna, David. "Strom Thurmond at 100: Colorful South Carolinian Set Record as Oldest Living U.S. Senator," National Public Radio, December 5, 2002. http://www.npr.org/templates/story/story.php?storyId=865900.

Whalen, Richard J. *Catch the Falling Flag: A Republican's Challenge to His Party*. Boston: Houghton Mifflin Company, 1972.

White, F. Clifton, and Jerome Tuccille. *Politics as a Noble Calling: The Memoirs of F. Clifton White*. Ottawa: Jameson Books, 1994.

White, F. Clifton, and William J. Gill. *Why Reagan Won: The Conservative Movement 1964-1981*. Chicago: Regnery Gateway, 1981.

White, Theodore H. *The Making of the President 1968*. New York: Atheneum Publishers, 1969.

Wicker, Tom. "Nixon Makes a New Gain as Republicans Convene; Reagan Avows Candidacy; Drops Favorite Son Role," *New York Times*, August 6, 1968. https://partners.nytimes.com/library/politics/camp/680806convention-gop-ra.html.

Wikipedia. "1968 in Television." https://en.wikipedia.org/wiki/1968_in_television.

Wikipedia. "Don Hewitt." https://en.wikipedia.org/wiki/Don_Hewitt/.

Wikipedia. "Federal Bureau of Investigation." https://en.wikipedia.org/wiki/Federal_Bureau_of_Investigation.

Wikipedia. "FBI Television Series." https://en.wikipedia.org/wiki/The_F.B.I._(TV_series).

Wikipedia. "Gridiron Club." https://en.wikipedia.org/wiki/Gridiron_Club.

Wikipedia. "Wentworth by the Sea." https://en.wikipedia.org/wiki/Wentworth_by_the_Sea.

Witcover, Jules. *85 Days: The Last Campaign of Robert Kennedy*. New York: Putnam, 1969.

Witcover, Jules. *Very Strange Bedfellows: The Short and Unhappy Marriage of Richard Nixon and Spiro Agnew*. New York: Public Affairs, 2007.

Wolff, Natasha. "Room Request! Gurney's Montauk Resort & Seawater Spa, DuJour Newsletter." http://dujour.com/lifestyle/room-request-gurneys-montauk-resort-seawater-spa/.

Zelizer, Barbie. *About to Die: How News Images Move the Public*. New York: Oxford University Press, 2010.